16

STAY THE NIGHT

Other Novels of the Darkyn

If Angels Burn
Private Demon
Dark Need
Night Lost
Evermore
Twilight Fall

STAY THE NIGHT

A NOVEL OF THE DARKYN

Lynn Viehl

AN ONYX BOOK

ONYX
Published by New American Library, a division of
Penguin Group (USA) Inc., 375 Hudson Street,
New York, New York 10014, USA
Penguin Group (Canada), 90 Eglinton Avenue East, Suite 700, Toronto,
Ontario M4P 2Y3, Canada (a division of Pearson Penguin Canada Inc.)
Penguin Books Ltd., 80 Strand, London WC2R 0RL, England
Penguin Ireland, 25 St. Stephen's Green, Dublin 2,
Ireland (a division of Penguin Books Ltd.)
Penguin Group (Australia), 250 Camberwell Road, Camberwell, Victoria 3124,
Australia (a division of Pearson Australia Group Pty. Ltd.)
Penguin Books India Pvt. Ltd., 11 Community Centre, Panchsheel Park,
New Delhi - 110 017, India
Penguin Group (NZ), 67 Apollo Drive, Rosedale, North Shore 0632,
New Zealand (a division of Pearson New Zealand Ltd.)
Penguin Books (South Africa) (Pty.) Ltd., 24 Sturdee Avenue,
Rosebank, Johannesburg 2196, South Africa

Penguin Books Ltd., Registered Offices:
80 Strand, London WC2R 0RL, England

First published by Onyx, an imprint of New American Library,
a division of Penguin Group (USA) Inc.

For Edward.
Love endures.

I too pass from the night,
I stay a while away O night, but I return to you again
and love you.

Why should I be afraid to trust myself to you?

—Walt Whitman, "The Sleepers"

April 17, 1408

Only Death is immortal. Everything else, no matter how powerful, inviolate, or deserving, must come to an end. As we set out on our journey, I tried to remember that.

The reports sent to me were not exaggerated; wherever we traveled I witnessed their truth. The cities are being abandoned, ships deserted to rot in dock; whole villages stand empty. The bodies of the mortal dead are left wherever they dropped. We saw them in the roads and doorways and on the steps of churches; we could not escape their stench.

There are too many to bury. They will have to be burned.

I met with the others near dawn at the road leading to the convent. Under the circumstances, I had expected some of them might abstain, but no, they all answered my summons. Tristan brought a petition from her remaining blood Kyn, begging for leniency. Boons were offered; promises were made. I bade him read it aloud to the others.

Of her innocence there is no question. The father blamed himself for her elopement, and pledged to keep her confined. He offered his men, lands, and wealth as restitution if we would but spare her. His pleas were moving, and his appeal to our sense of justice a righteous thing, but none of us were swayed.

The stink of mortal decay had poisoned more than the air.

We marched on the convent. All of the sisters had died or fled; we found her praying in the chapel. She was radiant, lovelier than the statue of the Blessed Mother before whom she knelt. I called her name, and she rose and walked to us. She did not speak or resist. I told her of what had to be done, and why.

She did not weep.

When we left the convent she came willingly, and I had thought her reconciled to my judgment and what her fate had to be. At the glassworks she finally spoke, making her last confession and asking for absolution. Sevarus himself performed the last rites, and Cordoba prayed with her before the furnace.

She looked upon our faces, marking each one as if to commit it to memory. She smiled like an angel. Then she said: "I have saved my last tears for you, my lords."

I bade the others flee as I drew my sword. They remained at my side, their own blades ready. In that moment we knew ourselves to be dead men, but we would not go alone into hell. We dared not.

She retreated to the mouth of the furnace, all the time laughing, the madness glowing like fever on her face. I expected her to change her direction and try to run from us, but as the scarlet tears ran down her cheeks, she turned and cast herself into the fire. Zhang slammed the door shut and barred it. We heard her laughter turn to screams. We heard her fists pounding.

No one approached the door.

We stood vigil at the glassworks for three days and four nights, until the furnace's flames burned away. Then we set fire to the place itself, and waited again until it had been reduced to ashes.

I alone remained behind as the others gathered their men and returned to their lands. I paid for laborers to haul the ashes and the blackened debris by cart to an old Roman mine, where they dumped each cartful into the deepest shaft. I then had the shaft filled with rock and sealed.

Only then did I feel it was done, and we were safe.

It will take time, but the mortal world will recover. I do not know if I can say the same. Her tears are gone from this earth, but God forgive me, I can still hear her laughter.

Richard Tremayne

Subj: (None)
Date: 3/12/2008 7:50:59 a.m. Eastern Daylight Time
From: CRenshaw@chicago.fbi.gov
To: NDL1691@netzero.com

Norman,

I haven't been able to reach you, and your attorney will say only that you're not available. We need to talk. The informant on the Antonelli case has disappeared, as has the case file. If you have it, you'll need to return it. If you'd like, I'll come to pick it up, no questions asked.

Call me at the office tomorrow if that's convenient for you.

Chris

P.S. If you'd rather deal with someone else, I understand.

April 7, 2008

Mr. William Scarlet
Armstrong Building
714 Peachtree Street, Suite #1
Atlanta, Georgia 30303

Dear Will,

It is my pleasure to enclose the documents and information that you requested in regard to his lordship's property. It seems that the item has for some time been in the possession of an Italian-American named Antonelli, currently incarcerated in Illinois while awaiting extradition orders.

I regret to report that my people were unable to retrieve the item before it was processed into evidence and then turned over to the Federal Bureau of Investigation. However, we were able to acquire the pertinent transfer data, and can confirm that it will be delivered by a private courier service to the FBI's security drop in Atlanta on the seventeenth of this month, where it will be stored in the vault until Antonelli is moved to Atlanta to stand trial for murder.

Please contact me at the usual number if you have any questions or require further assistance, and extend my best wishes to his lordship for a successful recovery.

Faithfully,
C.T.B.

Enclosures:
CPD evidence photos and report
Transportation order
Security systems diagrams
Building blueprints
Underground system access map

Chapter 1

At midnight on April seventeenth, Luisa Lopez silently celebrated her twenty-first birthday by looking into the future.

Her visions had begun five years ago, shortly before four men had attacked her as she came home from night school. They had dragged her into her own apartment, where she was beaten, raped, and nearly burned alive. Luisa had foreseen the attack two days earlier, but until it happened she had thought her visions were only nightmares. It wasn't until she woke up in the hospital burn ward that she knew the strange things she saw in her mind were real.

At first Luisa didn't know the people in her visions. The one she saw most often, the beautiful, angry lady doctor, had been taken away to operate on a man with white-streaked hair and no face. The doctor had also helped some of his strange friends: the crazed warrior, the golden-haired killer, the green man, the girl knight, the swan lord, and the smiling thief. Sometimes Luisa caught fleeting glimpses of two others, the feral king and the shadow prince, but their futures were never revealed.

Luisa had been frightened when she began meeting the people from her visions, but they had never harmed her. The lady doctor, Alexandra Keller, had come to the hospital to operate on her face, and had given Luisa's mother the money for her treatment. The swan lord, Valentin Jaus, had brought Luisa to this rehabilitation hospital to continue her medical treatments and to keep her safe.

It had not been easy living with the visions, as well as with what had been done to her. In the first, worst weeks Luisa had wanted to die, and tried several times to kill herself. It wasn't until she began to dream of the shadow prince that she found a reason to live.

As he struggled, Luisa had done the same, holding on to life, enduring what the doctors did to her in order to heal her injuries. Sometimes it seemed worse than the attack. She accepted the visions she had of the secret war between the immortals who called themselves Darkyn, and their enemy, the zealot Brethren, but that wasn't easy either. There were nights she woke up weeping, sometimes screaming.

The most pitiful part of having her gift was that Luisa couldn't warn anyone. Who would believe that a poor, ignorant girl from the projects saw the future? Even if she could convince the immortals who had helped and protected her that her visions were real, as was what she saw coming for them, they would try to change it before it happened. Luisa already knew the events could not be changed; any interference by her or them would bring about the end of the world.

So Luisa remained silent and watchful, and took what comfort she could from her faith. Each night she prayed to the God whom both the Darkyn and the Brethren had abandoned, and asked Him to watch over her and His lost children.

Tonight her vision was of the smiling thief with eyes the color of violets. He stood watching a red-haired woman sitting in a crowded room. In front of the people a man stood talking very fast and gesturing toward an old painting. The vision faded almost as soon as it had begun, but Luisa felt exhausted, as if she had watched it for hours.

She closed her eyes and drifted off to sleep.

Luisa saw the shadow prince walking through a forest, touching nothing, his dark face grim. She trailed after him as she did in every dream, watching and wondering but never trying to intrude on his solitude. She sensed his emotions, and knew that the only time he was at peace was when he was alone.

He stopped walking. *You should be asleep.*

Luisa froze. He had never acknowledged her presence. *I'm not very tired.* Then, very tentatively, she asked, *Are you okay?*

You have surgery tomorrow. He moved closer, his eyes never leaving hers. *It's your birthday.*

She shrugged.

Everyone forgets I still have them, too. He didn't smile, but his expression softened a few degrees. *Happy birthday, Princess.*

She would have laughed, hearing someone else call her that. *Where are you?*

In the mountains. He seemed to lose interest in her as he looked around him and saw a pool of violets growing alongside a fallen, lightning-struck tree.

He wouldn't touch them. Luisa knew from watching him all these months that he was afraid of touching anything. *You won't hurt them. Unless you want to.*

The sky turned as dark as his thoughts. *I hurt everything I touch.*

A blinding light filled Luisa's head. Visions hardly ever came to her when she was dreaming, but this one smashed through her thoughts like a bulldozer speeding out of control.

The shadow prince turned around. *What is that light?*

A vision. She couldn't keep him out of her head; he was

seeing everything through her eyes. He saw the girl throw herself in the furnace, and the other immortals standing guard as she burned. The vision whisked them away from the glassworks and hurled them over the land to an old abandoned building, and through its empty corridors and into a tiny room. A man in dirty clothes and a funny pointed hat was using a blade to saw through the covering of a grass-filled mattress on a bed of ropes.

The man pulled out handfuls of grass until he grinned and grabbed something inside the mattress. He pulled out a bundle of leather and, after glancing at the window, put it under his sweat-stained shirt. He ran out of the room, through the silent halls, and jumped onto the back of a crude-looking cart. An older man driving the cart slapped the reins on the back end of a donkey, which pulled the cart across the grass and onto a dirt road.

The book. Luisa closed her eyes to the images and held her throbbing head between her hands. *They can't find it. Not yet. They're not ready*.

What about this book? the shadow prince asked. *Why is it so important?*

It's been lost for seven hundred years, Luisa whispered, opening her eyes to look at him. Instead she saw her vision blur and change, the countryside becoming a modern city, the cart on the road becoming a police cruiser. It took her past dozens of armed officers and through shattered glass panels into a smoke-filled room. A man emerged from the smoke and dropped his briefcase next to a pool of blood. *But they're going to find it very soon, and she will have to choose*.

The shadow prince watched with her. *Who will find it? Who has to choose? Why are you so afraid of an old book?*

I can't tell you. Luisa backed away from him. *I'm sorry, but there's no more—*

*   *   *

Time.

Norman dropped the briefcase and walked out of the men's room. In the smoke-filled lobby of the bank, two SWAT officers in helmets and body armor grabbed him by the upper arms and hauled him out through the shattered glass of the front entrance. Flashing red and blue light filled Norman's watery, stinging eyes as they dragged him through a labyrinth of barricading patrol cars. They shoved him between a fire rescue truck and an ambulance before trotting back to the bank.

An end. It's time.

The uniformed cops using their vehicles as cover paid no attention to Norman, and kept their weapons and attention trained on the bank entrance. Two EMTs had hunkered down to work on an unconscious woman, one taking her vitals while the other bandaged a bleeding gash on her forehead.

One of the medics glanced up. "Are you hurt, sir?"

"No." Norman held his lacerated hand behind him and waited until the EMT turned his attention back to his patient. He then walked around the ambulance and out of the parking lot.

An end to this.

It took Norman two minutes to return to where he had parked his rental car, and another forty minutes to drive from there to his downtown motel. Before going to his room, he left the keys in the ignition and his rental agreement papers tucked under the window visor.

Put an end to this. An end. It's time.

Once inside his motel room, Norman locked the door and stripped, folding his clothes as he removed them. He stacked them in a neat pile on the end of the bed. He removed his wallet from his trousers pocket, opened it so that his driver's license was visible, and placed it by the telephone.

Blood dripped from the gash on the back of his hand in

big, watery drops, leaving an uneven trail as he went to the tiny desk under the mirror. He used the blank back of his motel bill to write a brief note of explanation, punctuating his sentences with wet, red drips and smears.

Once the note was finished, he folded it and slipped it under his wallet. Finally he took the last thing he needed from his suitcase and carried it into the bathroom.

Put an end to this, then.

Norman saw the ghost of his reflection move across the white tiled walls. Who would believe that he'd never meant to do any of this? No one. He had spent his life upholding the law, but that would count for nothing now.

He still considered the day he'd graduated from the academy as the best day of his life. He hadn't been top of his class like his partner, but he'd done okay. His parents, both high school dropouts from Newark, had been so proud of him.

Norman painted a streak of blood across his forehead as he rubbed it and closed his eyes.

"Empty both drawers," DeLuca said as he tossed the gym bag in front of the teller. The wads of cotton he'd stuffed inside his cheeks altered his voice, just as they had for Brando in *The Godfather*, but he had to speak slowly or risk choking on them. "Put all the money in the bag."

When the wet-eyed brunette dropped one of the hands she had clasped behind her head to reach under the counter, he parked the silencer's muzzle against the sweet little dimple in her chin.

"Don't touch the buttons." There were two, he knew, parked out of sight where she couldn't accidentally bump them. Either one would set off the silent alarm.

The teller glanced up and then, lightning-fast, focused back on DeLuca's black ski mask.

"I'm watching that, too." He eyed the small electrical box

in a corner above the manager's office. Two lights on the outside panel of the box, visible to all the tellers, indicated the current status of the bank's security system. "Keep it green and I know you're being a good girl. It turns blue, I blow your pretty face off."

"Please don't," she whispered. Tear-snot ran, thin and quick, from her right nostril to dribble over her top lip. "I won't do anything. I promise."

DeLuca eased back enough to watch her fill the bag, his satisfaction growing along with the number of stacks she shoved inside. Six weeks ago they'd taken away everything from him: his job, his bennies, and his pension. All that because he'd lost his temper with a suspect. Was it his fault the whiny little weasel had rotten teeth and a glass jaw? Or that his partner had left him alone with the perp with the video running? What about the fifteen years he had put in on the job?

You have to take the deal, DeLuca, his brain-dead lawyer had told him. *They've got it all on tape. It's resign or jail time.*

DeLuca had gotten the foreclosure notice in the mail the day after he'd taken the deal, and that had been the final insult. After the divorce, every penny he'd earned had gone into paying the mortgage on his house. It was all he had left, the last thing he owned, and now they were going to take it away from him? He wouldn't have fallen behind on the payments if his ex, the money-grubbing pig, hadn't garnished his wages for the back alimony he owed her. And what about all the years he'd paid on time? Didn't that count for something?

Even then, he'd tried to do the right thing and talk to them. But banks didn't lend money to people who really needed it. No job, no income, no extensions, no refinancing.

DeLuca had always played by the rules, but they kept changing them to screw him. Then he'd met the Italian, who had listened to his troubles and given him the comfort and sympathy that he deserved. The Italian, who had been short-changed by life just as badly, didn't see him as a leper. Far from it. After one night with his new friend, DeLuca finally understood the truth: that it was his turn—no, his God-given *right*—to get some payback.

Now everything was going perfectly. By this time tomorrow night he'd meet the Italian, who had promised to take good care of him in exchange for this job. DeLuca would have enough money to retire permanently to Miami, where life for a man with serious cash was nonstop beaches, beer, and blondes.

It just didn't get any better than that.

The teller's top drawer, the safe money, held all the bills she'd started her shift with and another two thousand and change from the transactions she'd made that day. DeLuca focused only on her hands when she opened the reserve bottom drawer and began pulling out the neat, paper-banded bundles there.

He had no intention of stealing the teller's money. The real payout for this job made it look like chump change. But he needed the money as a smoke screen so he could get what he'd really come for: the small aluminum case a private government courier had just delivered to the vault manager's office.

The radio on his hip, tuned to scan the outgoing calls from the Atlanta Police Department, continued to put out a static buzz. During a bank heist the real threat was time, not the guards or the security system. DeLuca had worked in Atlanta; he knew the drill. Once the silent alarm tripped it would take two minutes for the monitoring company to notify Atlanta PD. In a big city like Atlanta, metro patrol units needed only two to four minutes at most to get to the branch. The alarm hadn't been tripped—yet—but that four- to six-minute escape window didn't apply to DeLuca.

He didn't have to run out of the bank. He'd arranged a little insurance, and when it was time he was going to walk out of here a free man. The uniforms would even hold the front door open for him.

"Wait." He saw one packet that didn't bend as it should have when the teller tried to stuff it in the bag. As he caught her wrist and pulled it toward him, sweat from her skin slicked the black leather of his glove. "You trying to be cute?"

She looked at the pack she held, sucking in a breath as soon as she recognized the retired bills. "I'm sorry," she told his ski mask. "I didn't know. They never tell us where they are. I swear."

DeLuca turned and pointed his nine at the pale-faced security guard huddled on the floor with the loan officer, five tellers, and half a dozen customers who had still been inside when the manager had locked the front entrance doors. A palm-size flower of blood and tissue decorated the cap of the rent-a-cop's left uniform sleeve. More blood painted his arm and dripped into a pool of the same on the floor under his useless limb.

"You." DeLuca beckoned with the gun. "Get over here."

When the security guard had trouble standing, the thirty-something bank manager scuttled over and took his arm.

"Don't get up, Joe." The sun from the atrium turned the manager's pretty blond wedge cut yellow-orange, and faded out the pink polka-dot jacket of her casual-Friday suit. "He's hurt too bad," she said as she stood. "I'll do it."

As DeLuca adjusted his aim, Joe's eyes widened.

"No, he'll shoot you." The guard grabbed the manager's arm and yanked her down, a little too hard. One pink polka-dotted shoe banana-peeled out from under her and she fell sideways, tripping over some of the others. A sharp crack sounded as the manager's head hit the side of the lobby table. She landed on top of an old lady still clutching her endorsed social security check.

Joe's face turned gray as he clapped a hand over his own wound and crawled over to haul the limp blonde off the shrieking elderly woman. He checked the wide gash on the side of her head and the pulse in her neck before he gave DeLuca a filthy look. "You piece of shit."

"You did that to her, not me." DeLuca tossed the stiff pack of bills so that it landed in the guard's lap. "Pop it." When Joe didn't pick up the pack, he targeted the horrified senior. "I can ruin her makeup, too, if you want."

Joe took the pack and bent it in half. As DeLuca expected, the pressure triggered the tiny canister of CO_2 hidden inside the pack, which exploded with a muffled bang. Purple dye powder showered the guard, the old lady, and three of the tellers clustered around their fallen manager.

As new screams erupted, DeLuca checked his watch. He still had a lot to do: grab the goods from the vault and make the switch. He'd need a few minutes to stow them in the manager's office and jam the door.

"Zip it closed," he told the teller. She didn't move, even when he aimed for her dimple again. "Don't try me now, you stupid bitch."

"I didn't know." Shock had made her into a bug-eyed, lock-jointed robot. "It's not my fault. I didn't know."

"Give me that." DeLuca threaded his free hand through the handles of the gym bag and tried to haul it over the front of her station. The teller refused to let it go, clutching it as if it were her only lifeline. "Take your hands off or I'll shoot you in the face."

"If you do, you'll get her blood all over the money," a deep male voice with a distinct British accent said. "Damnably hard to launder out. Almost as much of a nuisance as that dye powder."

DeLuca turned as something whizzed in front of him and

slashed the back of his glove, knocking the gun out of his hand. Whatever it was kept going and buried itself in the wall on the other side of the lobby. The thin wooden shaft bobbed, wagging its brown-feathered end at DeLuca like a disapproving finger. Even with the flaring burn of pain from beneath the gashed leather over his hand, it took him a moment to register what it was and what had happened, and even then he didn't quite believe it.

Shot me with an arrow?

DeLuca turned to see where it had come from, and saw that two strange men stood there. The shorter of the pair, a stocky bleached blond dressed in a red T-shirt and black cords, held two knives in his broad fists. The dark, polished blades glowed like gold. Beside him, a taller, rangy-looking man in an off-white fisherman's sweater and faded gray jeans drew another arrow from a quiver hanging from his hip. The powerful-looking longbow he held was as tall as he was, at least six feet long, and had strange markings carved into its sweeping wooden curves.

The short one sniffed the air like a curious bulldog. "Two wounded, Rob." His accent sounded different, thicker and harder to understand. "One male, concealed."

The one he called Rob fitted another arrow to his bow and pointed the sharp-looking copper head of it at DeLuca. "Find him, Will."

DeLuca didn't know what to think. Neither one of these guys had been inside the bank when DeLuca had come out of the john; they'd just appeared out of thin air. But that couldn't have happened. As soon as DeLuca had walked in and taken over, he'd forced the manager to dead-bolt the doors and barricade them with the loan officer's massive desk. The doors were bolted, the barricade still in place.

*Why the hell was the dark one using a *bow*?*

He started to tell the one called Will not to move, and then caught his breath as a peculiar odor filtered through his mask. It warmed his lungs and smelled as if he had his face buried in a pricey gift basket of oranges and chocolate. Not perfume, but something just as powerful. The scents seemed to linger in his chest even after he exhaled, sweet and heavy.

"You," the one called Rob said to him, "stay where you are and do nothing." He lowered the bow, replacing the arrow in the quiver hanging from his hip and slinging the weapon over his shoulder and across his torso before he walked over to the cluster of hostages.

DeLuca would have gone after him right then, but for some reason his legs wouldn't move. Or didn't want to move. The longer he stood there, however, the more sense it made. Rob, whoever he was, had it right: He needed to stay where he was and do nothing.

"Is she unconscious?" Rob asked Joe, who nodded. He checked the guard's shoulder, and then gently removed the scarf from the manager's throat and wrapped it like a bandage around her head. "If she rouses, my friend, keep her still and quiet. Help should arrive momentarily."

DeLuca barely heard him. He remained in place and studied the bank's entrance doors. They were still locked, and the heavy oak desk remained in place. How had they gotten inside? Had they been hiding in the back? Then he saw the vault door standing open, and through it could see that some of the safety-deposit boxes had been pulled out. They'd been in the vault, robbing it—that's why he hadn't seen them.

They couldn't be here for the same thing. He'd assured the Italian: No one else but the feds in Chicago knew about moving the goods to Atlanta for the sting operation.

"Hey, you. Rob." DeLuca waited until the pretty purple eyes focused on his face. "You guys looking to score?"

Rob said nothing, but wrapped his hand around one curved end of the wooden bow as if to pull it from his shoulder.

Sweat made the inside of the ski mask cling to DeLuca's

face. The last thing he wanted to do was to make Rob angry or upset. "If you are, maybe we could join forces. Split the take three ways."

"Very generous," Rob said at last, "but I think not. The authorities have this building surrounded."

"Not yet." DeLuca heard a rusty sound come from his own throat, and felt the corners of his mouth stretch around the chuckle. "No one tripped the alarm."

"No one had to." Rob turned his attention to the teller still clutching the gym bag. "Come away from there now, dear girl."

"Sure." The brunette's expression relaxed as she released her grip on the gym bag, smiled, and walked around the corner toward Rob as if greeting a favorite customer. "You know, you have the most beautiful eyes I've ever seen."

"Like amethysts," the old woman on the floor said, and sighed with pleasure as she sat up. Dye transferred from her gnarled hand to her cheek as she pressed it there in the old-fashioned gesture of a dazzled girl. "Paul Newman had eyes like that."

"Nah, Newman's were washed-out blue," Joe said as he propped the unconscious manager on his lap and cradled her bandaged head with his good arm. "His are more like Liz Taylor's." Embarrassment turned the guard's cheeks dark red and his voice gruff. "Ya know. If Liz were a guy."

Rob went over to the front entrance doors and pushed aside the heavy desk as if it were made of cardboard.

"Please don't do that," DeLuca called out, afraid now. "You don't want to let the cops in."

"On the contrary." Rob released the dead bolt. "I phoned them from the vault."

He'd called the cops on him? DeLuca couldn't believe it. "Why would you do that?"

Rob didn't look at him as he studied the parking lot. "Because you've injured the innocent, you fool."

The insult made DeLuca's chest tighten, and tears of self-pity burned his eyes and clogged his nose. Rob didn't like him. Rob, who had risked his life to save all these poor people, thought he was foolish. And he *was*. He'd let Rob stop him, hadn't he? With nothing more than a bow and arrow.

DeLuca wasn't walking out of here with anything. The Italian would never pay him for showing up empty-handed at the rendezvous. No three million dollars. No easy life in Miami. No revenge.

Tears soaked the wool covering DeLuca's nose and mouth, making it harder to breathe but a little easier to think. He'd screwed up, but he could turn things around. He just had to get his head straight, figure out what went wrong. He didn't have to stand here and wait to be arrested . . . so why was he doing that?

What had this snotty English asshole done to him?

DeLuca scanned the faces of the hostages. Two minutes ago he'd put the fear of God into these people; they'd been under his complete control. He'd terrified them into submission. Now they were happy and grinning and chatting as if nothing had happened.

As if DeLuca weren't even there.

The sweet, smothering smell of orange and chocolate had been thinning along with the haze of confusion clouding DeLuca's mind, and he looked down at the floor. The gun the arrow had knocked out of his hand lay only four feet away.

Jesus, he'd forgotten about dropping the gun.

White lights flashing outside the window illuminated the handsome symmetry of Rob's face. "The medics are here now." He went over to help the old lady up.

With some effort, DeLuca shuffled over and picked up his weapon. "Look over here, you rat bastard." When Rob turned toward him, he fired three rounds into the center of the ivory sweater. The silencer muffled the shots, the impact of which knocked Rob flat on his back.

"Now who's the fool?" DeLuca turned and sneered at the brunette teller. "Not so pretty anymore, is he?" She didn't answer. "You deaf?"

"No, I heard you." Her sleepy gaze shifted past his face. "Sir, are you all right?"

"My sweater wants mending." Rob stood there, his head bent. Long, pale fingers, crosshatched with innumerable thin white scars, plucked a distorted slug from the torn wool of his sweater and tossed it away.

DeLuca looked at the man he'd just killed and mechanically raised the nine to fire again, but chocolate wafted in his face, and a broad, muscular hand snatched it away and tossed it to Rob.

"This is why we never gave them the right to bear arms," Will said to Rob, his brawler's face twisting into a scowl of disgust.

DeLuca lunged, but the shorter man seized him by the throat with a hand so hard it felt like a stone vise.

"No need to send him to Morpheus just yet," Rob said as he flipped on the safety and pocketed the nine. "Did you find the other male?"

"Not yet." Will made a casual gesture with his free hand. "He's concealed himself somewhere."

DeLuca groped at the back of his belt until he felt his throwaway piece. He thought about jamming it into the Brit's belly, but the other man moved too fast, and this was the only gun he had left. "Leggo," he wheezed.

"My pleasure." Will shoved DeLuca away.

"How the hell did . . ." DeLuca trailed off as he clearly saw the three holes in Rob's sweater. No blood stained the knit, and through the holes only pale, unmarked flesh showed. His eyes shifted to the other distorted slugs scattered on the lobby floor before he met Rob's gaze. "What the hell are you?"

"Rather more than a rat or a bastard." Rob stepped between DeLuca and the hostages. His eyes began to change, the centers shrinking to thin slivers of black while the purple turned darker and became bright, shiny rings of copper. "Where is your accomplice hiding?"

A small vent dropped from the ceiling and landed on one of the teller's windows with a loud clatter. Something like an unmarked soda can immediately followed and hissed gray-white smoke into the air.

Norman backed away.

"It would seem that SWAT has arrived, my lord," Will said, kicking the grenade into a far corner.

"Apparently they've no interest in negotiating." Rob knelt beside the unconscious bank manager to cover her mouth and nose with a white handkerchief. "Take care of them for me, Will. I'll secure the vault."

Will began to sing what sounded like a lullaby, his voice soft and low, and went from person to person, resting his hand briefly on an arm, shoulder, or neck. As soon as he touched someone, they smiled and closed their eyes.

When he finished his song a minute later, everyone in the lobby had fallen asleep.

The tear gas burned DeLuca's eyes as he kept backing out of the reception area. He didn't know what kind of weird hypnosis the blond guy was using, but neither he nor Rob was paying any attention to him. On the job he'd seen some bizarre things happen, but the way this was going down defied all logic or explanation.

The hell with the Italian and the goods; I've got to get out—now.

DeLuca aimed at Will, pumping three shots into his forehead before swiveling and emptying the rest of the magazine into the back of Rob's skull. He then hurried to the men's room, ducking inside and locking the door behind him.

The businessman he'd jumped earlier still sat where he'd left him, handcuffed to the sink piping. His groggy eyes opened to watch DeLuca strip out of his mask and jumpsuit and straighten the checked blue jacket and white trousers he wore underneath.

"Hey. I've been mugged," the businessman said as soon as DeLuca yanked the duct tape from his mouth. The Rohypnol he'd been forced to swallow made his words slurry. "Mugged in my own bank." He looked down at the jumpsuit DeLuca had dressed him in earlier. "And these aren't my clothes."

"There's been . . ." DeLuca paused to dig the soggy cotton balls out of his mouth, and stuck them in his pocket. "There's been a robbery." He uncuffed the businessman and pulled a clean ski mask over the man's head. "You've got to get out of here."

"That right?" Dilated eyes rolled comically around the holes in the mask. "Why did you put this on me? It cold outside?"

"They shot tear gas inside the bank," DeLuca told him. "It'll protect your face."

He popped open the businessman's briefcase, the contents of which he had dumped into the trash earlier, and transferred the money from the gym bag to it. It wasn't enough, but it would get him out of Atlanta.

DeLuca stuffed his own jumpsuit and mask into the gym bag. "Don't let anyone take this away from you," he told the man as he uncuffed him and helped him stand up. "It's evidence."

The business man gave him a goofy grin. "I've got evidence. I'll be a hero."

"Yeah." DeLuca finished by pressing his empty backup

piece into the man's hand. "You'll need this, too. Watch out for the bank robbers. They're dressed exactly like cops."

The businessman lifted the gun and used one eye to peer into the barrel. "Smells like firecrackers. Should I shoot at them?"

DeLuca picked up the briefcase and straightened his jacket. "No, just point it at them. That'll scare them, and they'll back off."

"Okay." The businessman nodded and lifted his arm, pointing an unsteady finger past DeLuca. "What about that guy?"

DeLuca turned and saw Rob standing against the door.

"No. Can't be. You . . . you're dead."

"Killing me takes more than a few bullets." Rob walked over to the businessman and pulled the ski mask from his head. "Sending this poor fellow out, drugged and dressed as he is, however, would work very well. Are you a murderer as well as a thief?"

The restroom became an unseen grove of perfumed oranges.

"No," DeLuca heard himself murmur.

"It's time to put an end to this, then." Rob unzipped and began removing the jumpsuit from the swaying business-man.

It's time to put an end to this, then.

With Rob's words echoing in his head, as they had been mercilessly for the last twenty minutes, Norman opened his eyes and stepped into the bathtub. As he sat down, he bent his elbows and knees to fit his arms and legs inside. The fiberglass tub felt cold against his back and ass. He turned on the water, adjusting the temperature to lukewarm, but left the drain stopper open.

He'd been a Catholic once, a long time ago. Had gone to confession each Saturday to offer up his pitiful sins to God and dutifully if mechanically make his penance. Life, the job, and the disillusionment inflicted by both had erased most of the prayers from his memory. All he remembered now was the very beginning of confession.

Forgive me, Father.

For his sins, Norman DeLuca put the barrel of his service pistol in his mouth, angled it up against his palate, closed his eyes, and put an end to everything.

Chapter 2

"Hey there, pretty lady."

Chris Renshaw looked into the mirrored wall behind the bar. A florid, fleshy man stood just behind her, his bulk diverting the flow of people walking to and from the hotel elevators. This forced one waitress to quickly jack up her heavily loaded tray before it smashed into the back of his head.

First the auction, now the meat market. Chris had already had her fill of being hit on by desperate middle-aged Viagrathons. *This is turning out to be a great night.*

Once he saw that he had Chris's attention, the big man leaned in, staggering a step and catching himself before fanning her with his rum-and-Coke-scented breath. "You know what? You got the prettiest red hair I've ever seen in my life."

Chris didn't turn around or respond. In his condition he probably would interpret either as an invitation to have sex with her on the bar.

Undiscouraged, the big man hitched up his belt and began moving his hips in a pelvic thrust that almost kept time with the Village People hit pounding out of the bar's overhead speakers.

Chris's rusty sense of humor kicked in as she watched him gyrate in the mirror—*air-humping attack of the macho, macho man*—while her training created a more professional mental snapshot: *White, mid-thirties, six foot one, two thirty, silver-brown hair cut in a crew, close-set light blue eyes, trimmed reddish brown mustache, quarter-inch vertical keloid under left jaw. Ocher off-the-rack suit, pale green shirt, stainless sports watch, tan belt.*

Thanks to her excellent visual memory, Chris could pick him from a lineup or, six months from now, positively identify him in court.

Here's hoping I don't have to. She picked up her drink and took a sip.

"I'm Dave." Without waiting for an invitation, he dragged the nearest empty stool too close to hers and sat. His butt missed most of the dark brown cushion, making him lurch sideways, but he shifted in time to keep from landing on the floor. "Rickety damn things."

Tension knotted in Chris's shoulders and neck, and once more she debated the wisdom of coming to the bar this late at night. Six other men had approached her since she'd arrived, and she doubted Dave would be the last. That, combined with the attention she'd received during the art auction, only made her feel like nothing more than a dangling hunk of bait.

Which, naturally, she was.

Going for a run tonight before coming here might have improved her mood, but she didn't like jogging in a strange city, especially at night. She had access to a state-of-the-art workout room back at the field office; Ray Hutchins mentioned it the day Chris had arrived. An hour or two on a treadmill would have burned off some stress. It would have also given Chris too much time to think, and second-guess, and blame herself.

She'd done enough of that back in Chicago.

She didn't need Dave harassing her while she checked out the place. This was her op; she had to evaluate the setup and decide how to continue the on-site surveillance. But the bar, which Ray had insisted was a regular meeting place and drop point for some of the less reputable local dealers, simply didn't feel right. She couldn't imagine the Magician coming here to broker deals for the art he stole. Interpol estimated that her target was at least in his seventies—far too old to blend in with this forty-and-under crowd.

Chris knew he'd hate the cheesy atmosphere of the place, too. *You wouldn't be caught dead in an out-of-towner sleaze pit like this, would you, Magic Man?*

Although she almost felt Dave's eyes crawling up and down her body, two inchworms racing to measure her assets, Chris felt no inclination to leave. She could handle the Daves of the world better than the hollowness of the tasteful, expensively furnished apartment they'd set up for her cover during the operation. She knew when she went back there she'd spend the rest of the night sitting by one of the arched windows and staring down at the empty streets of Atlanta, alone with the if-onlys.

If only I hadn't left him alone.

If only he'd stayed in Chicago.

If only I'd realized how desperate he was.

If only he hadn't written that note.

"You're not from around here, are you?" Tired of being ignored, Dave brushed shoulders with her and flagged the busy bartender, engulfing her in a cloud of his pungent aftershave.

"No." She faced him, tacking ten more years to his age for using Old Spice and the Jurassic-era pickup line. The broken capillaries around his nostrils and eyes indicated his long-term fondness for rum-and-Cokes, but Chris noted the high color and damp condition of his skin. She also caught a faint, acrid scent that his aftershave didn't quite mask.

Not an antiquities smuggler or an international art thief, but borderline plastered and hitting the meds daily.

"Me either." Dave smiled, showing off expensive porcelain caps framed by food fragments. From the appearance of the detritus, he'd snacked heavily on nacho chips and salsa. "I've got an executive suite all to myself one floor down. So what do you say? Want to join me for"—his eyebrows went up and down precisely three times—"a private drink?"

The cagey eyebrow action decided Chris's next move.

"Not tonight, thank you. Excuse me." Before he could protest, she slid off the bar stool and went around him.

Dave turned and peered after Chris as she made a tactful retreat to a deserted, dark corner. As soon as she sat down she saw him take a step in her direction, as if to join her again and press the issue.

Don't make me throw you to the ground and read you your rights.

Fortunately a sultry brunette in a turquoise blue dress chose that moment to occupy Chris's abandoned bar stool. Dave stopped in midstalk, and once he inspected the brunette's neckline and how it showcased her generous breasts, his expression changed to that of a lover scorned to one who'd just been clubbed over the head by a Playboy Bunny.

Red hair might have its privileges, Chris thought, *but killer cleavage grinds it into the dirt every time.*

"It'll never work," a man's mellow voice said on her left.

Not another one.

She turned her head and for the first time saw the outlines of a tall, lean form sitting in a deeper well of shadows. *Male, dark business suit, British accent*—that was all she could put together on him.

There was no one else sitting in the immediate area around them, so she assumed he had spoken to her. "I'm sorry; what did you say?"

"This stratagem of yours." He sat forward. Soft light

from an overhead spot gilded the straight black hair brushing his shoulders, but only skimmed down the imperial line of his nose to jump to the rim of his wineglass. "It won't work."

Stratagem. Chris couldn't remember ever hearing another person actually use that word in conversation. "I don't know what you mean."

"Using that large, friendly fellow at the bar as an excuse to change seats was utter genius," the stranger told her. "Anyone would think that you moved here simply to escape him."

Chris caught the scent of something like citrus and dark, sweet violets, and guessed it came from the red wine he was drinking. "Anyone but you."

White teeth flashed briefly before he picked up his drink and merged back into the shadows.

Chris watched Nacho Man lead Killer Cleavage out of the bar and toward the nearest elevator. "Am I that obvious?"

"You're a quiet, beautiful woman in a loud, ugly place. An orchid among weeds. You define obvious." He placed his empty wineglass back on the table. "Men have been besieging you since the moment you arrived, yet each time you've politely declined their attentions and sent them on their way. One must draw from that certain conclusions."

Usually Chris picked up right away on other people watching her—an occupational hazard—so she felt mildly annoyed not to have noticed his interest. "What have you concluded?"

"You came here for me."

He was either deadly serious, or simply having fun with her. Even with her ten years of experience evaluating what people said, and why, the elegant accent made it hard to judge.

Chris waited to hear more, but he didn't expand on the outrageous statement. Instead he lifted a narrow, long-fingered hand and with a single, sinuous gesture conjured up a cocktail waitress.

He might have the voice, the class, and the moves to be the Magician, Chris thought, but he was too young. The fact that he was British also didn't fit. They knew the Magician had helped himself to rare art collections and museums in seventeen countries, but he'd never pulled a job or sold his goods in the U.K.

Magic Man didn't seem to like the Brits, so it was a safe bet that he wasn't one himself.

"Yes, sir?" The waitress's grin stretched so wide it distorted the shape of her nostrils. "Would you like another glass of wine?"

He shook his head. "A ginger ale for the lady, if you would, please."

The waitress trotted to the bar, ignoring three other patrons trying to flag her down, and returned in thirty seconds with the soda, which she plopped in front of Chris without a glance in her direction.

"Thank you." Chris waited until the waitress reluctantly withdrew to attend to another table before she asked the stranger, "How did you know what I was drinking?"

He answered with only a deep, velvet-soft laugh. The resonance of it danced across her skin, as intimate and warm as a lover's whispered secrets.

Slightly unnerved by her physical reaction, Chris drew back. *You're here to work,* she reminded herself, *not to flirt with mysterious foreign strangers in the dark.*

Across from the main bar, the three-piece band returned from their dinner break and positioned themselves behind their instruments. After a short sound test and tuning, the eldest member of the trio switched on the microphone overhanging his keyboard.

"How are we all doing tonight?" The Jerry Garcia look-alike waited a beat, but no one replied. "That's great, that's

great. Ladies and gentlemen, we'd like to welcome you all
to the Bar with a View at the St. Carlson Hotel in beautiful
downtown Atlanta. I'm Greg Martin, and these two crazy
guys behind me are Izzie Palerma and Scott Chiznowski,
and we are"—he stopped and played the opening chords to
the first song of the set—"the Eighties Machine."

The houselights dimmed, and a disco ball descended out
of the ceiling over the dance floor, turning slowly to reflect
the multicolored beams directed at it from a circle of flood
lamps. Chris automatically blocked out the band's enthusi-
astic, slightly discordant version of Duran Duran's "Hungry
Like the Wolf" and several other nostalgic megahits while
she finished her soda. She watched the clientele and studied
the furnishings and fixtures, picking out what she thought
were the best spots to plant microphones and recorders.

As Chris made her survey, several waitresses, women,
and a couple of men drifted over to speak to the man in the
shadows. She might have suspected he was dealing drugs,
but she saw no exchanges of money or the sly handoffs that
were usually involved in trafficking in public. She did over-
hear the man refuse from everyone who came to him offers
of drinks, dances, and company for the evening. Yet everyone he turned away left smiling. In Chris's experience the
only people who commanded that degree of deference were
either wealthy, famous, or both: actors, rock stars, tycoons,
and politicians.

No wonder he thought I came over here to hit on him.

Whoever the Brit was would have to remain a mystery;
Chris had to keep focused on the job. And right now the job
had her teetering on the edge of depression and exhaustion.
Realizing it was time to go, she took a five out of her wallet
and tucked it under the edge of her coaster before sliding out
from behind the table.

"Admitting defeat already?"

"Calling it a night." She saw a woman walking to the

ladies' room slow down to stare in his direction. "You shouldn't be lonely for too long. Good-bye."

She hadn't taken two steps away from the table when a cool, strong hand slid around her wrist.

"Don't go yet, love."

The mortal female didn't resist Robin of Locksley's hold. For this he was glad, absorbed as he became in the texture and warmth of her silky skin against his. From the moment he'd first laid eyes on her several hours ago at the auction, she'd enchanted him. He'd recognized her at once as the art dealer pictured in the advertisement for the gallery's medieval art show, but it had not done her justice.

"There's no reason to stay," she said.

Along with her obvious virtues she had a manner as direct as a man's and as pitiless as one of Robin's arrows. That, too, he found captivating; it had been centuries since any mortal female had denied him anything.

Of course, he could not tell her that when she had left the auction, he had followed her here. That would frighten her and spoil the game.

"If you go now," he lied, "we may never see each other again."

She gently eased her wrist from his grip. "I'll try not to let that ruin my life."

Her resistance puzzled him. A small percentage of people were slow to be affected by or were immune to *l'attrait*, the scent his immortal body shed to attract and control humans. But his talent, the ability to charm any mortal he touched, had never failed to sway even the most defiant human.

Perhaps it had more to do with her than him, Robin thought. Everything about her attested to her character, from the dignified set of her shoulders and spine to the clever choice of her garments: a businesswoman, her well-cut dark rose jacket and slim skirt said, one who disdained hiding or apologizing for her sex. The pale pink silk scarf she wore knotted around her slim neck suggested that equally delicate lingerie lay beneath the lace confection of her cream-colored blouse.

Many human men had watched her with avaricious gazes during the auction. So many that Robin had not attempted to approach her there.

Perhaps it was due to her legs, which could only be called superb. Robin imagined easing the thin straps of her heels from her feet and sliding the shimmering stockings from those long, curvy limbs. He might have done so had she succumbed to *l'attrait*. Bespelled by his scent, she would not have been able to leave his presence or resist any request he made.

The woman's obvious intelligence and confidence indicated a very strong will. Perhaps she could not easily be swayed by anything, even his Kyn talent. Which would be a problem indeed, for this human female possessed a prize that had eluded him for half a millennium: *The Maiden's Book of Hours*, a medieval illuminated manuscript that Robin had coveted, chased, and lost for more than five hundred years. Now that he knew exactly where it was, he would not permit it to slip through his fingers again.

"It is getting late," she was saying.

Robin had no intention of allowing her to leave him, not until he further tested her remarkable restraint. "You will never know, then."

"Know what?"

He took her hand again, lifted it, and brushed a kiss across her knuckles. "What *my* stratagem was."

The intimate gesture seemed to amuse rather than impress her. "So tell me before I leave."

Robin wondered how she would react if she knew that he'd deliberately sent the brunette call girl over to distract the last inebriated male who had pestered her at the bar, or that he'd cleared everyone from the tables around him to create an oasis of calm in the noisy club. An oasis intended to bring *her* to him.

"I have endeavored to keep you from discovering"—he turned her hand and touched his lips briefly to the thin blue veins on the inside of her wrist—"that I came here for you."

At last gratifying surprise slightly rounded her cognac-colored eyes, revealing the glints of fawn and gold in her dark irises. A moment later it was gone. "Seeing as we've never met, I doubt that."

"In life, perhaps not." He admired the play of the light cast by the mirrored ball over the strands of fiery hair she'd tamed into a smooth twist at the back of her head. "There are other worlds. Other lives."

She studied him just as closely in return. "I don't believe in quantum theory, past lives, or reincarnation."

"Nor do I." Slipping into the old way of speaking was dangerous, but he didn't care. "It matters not, as long as you will stay."

"I don't know you," she replied, her tone remaining maddeningly reasonable, "and I never pick up strange men in bars."

"I'm Rob." He gave one end of her scarf a playful tug. "Tell me your name and we'll no longer be strangers."

"It's Chris." Her head turned as the music slowed, and the humans gyrating on the dance floor embraced and began swaying together. Without looking at him, she added, "I really can't stay. I have to go into work early tomorrow."

As she made her excuse, Robin could hear a wistful note in her voice, and saw a glimmer of envy in her eyes as she watched the other mortals dancing.

She might not want him, but she wanted to dance.

"Then we shall not waste another moment." He laced his fingers through hers. "Stay for this song, Chris. Stay and dance with me."

She regarded him for the space of ten heartbeats before she turned and led him toward the crowded dance floor.

Robin enjoyed many of the freedoms of this modern era, but none so much as the dances that permitted a man to take into his arms and hold close any woman who gave her consent. During his human lifetime, such scandalous contact would have resulted in the instant ruination of the woman's reputation and an immediate end to her partner's bachelor status, if the woman's father didn't demand other, more lethal forms of satisfaction.

Not that dancing with this mortal was completely safe. As his seneschal so often reminded him, he was Robin of Locksley, immortal Darkyn lord and suzerain of Atlanta. Becoming personally involved with a human and interfering in the business of the mortal world, however superficially or justifiably, endangered him and his *jardin*.

Ever since returning from the Realm, however, Robin had felt restless. He shouldn't have gone to the Kyn's annual tournament, at which the Darkyn gathered to spend a few weeks away from humans in order to live as they had during medieval times. Usually Robin enjoyed the challenges and celebrations that had long ago been their only form of entertainment, but this year too many old tragedies had come back to haunt him. The unhealed wounds of the past had nearly cost him his friendship with Aedan mac Byrne, suzerain of the Realm, as well as Jayr, the woman they both loved.

Entangled with the ugly plots, brutal confrontations, and attempts on the lives of Jayr and Byrne had been the tragedy of Robin's past and his darkest secret. No one but Dr. Alexandra Keller, the *sygkenis* of the American seigneur, Michael Cyprien, had guessed why Robin so loved Jayr, the only child of his long-lost lady, Marian, who had died in childbirth. God willing, no one else ever would discover that Robin was Jayr's father.

Once on the dance floor, Robin guided Chris around to face him, encircling her waist with his free arm while lifting their entwined fingers to hold her hand over his heart. She was tall for a woman; if she moved two steps closer she could tickle his mouth with her curly red eyelashes or kiss the hollow of his throat.

Chris did neither of those things, but stepped back until several inches separated their bodies.

Undaunted, Robin spread his free hand over the gentle curve of the small of her back, where a delicious amount of body heat permeated the thin material of her dress to caress his palm and fingers.

"You feel very warm," he said, bending his head so that his breath stirred the smooth strands of hair coiled above her ear. If he could get her alone with him, he could question her about the manuscript, discover where it was, and learn what sort of security the gallery would be using to guard it. "Are you uncomfortable?"

"I'm fine." Chris did not press herself against him; nor did she strain away as she followed his lead. She maintained that respectable distance between them as she danced. She did not look up at him, however, but kept her eyes on the band's gray-haired singer as he crooned the words to the gentle tune.

"It's pretty, isn't it?" she asked. "I think it was the only hit Spandau Ballet ever had."

"Spandau Ballet." He'd heard of many dance troupes, but never that one. "I cannot say that I am familiar with them."

"Before our time," Chris said. "My mother loved this song." Her eyes shuttered and her voice changed, growing crisp and impersonal again. "How did you know what I was drinking? Did you ask the waitress or the bartender?"

"Neither." She guarded herself more carefully than a Scotsman did his purse, Robin thought, while asking questions better left unanswered. He decided to tell her the truth and see what she would make of it. "I could smell the ginger ale on your breath."

"You couldn't have done that," she told him flatly. "You were sitting at least ten feet away from me."

"Alas, I'm cursed with a sensitive nose." He took in the scent of her on a slow, deep breath. "You also smell of rain, herbs, honey, and"—he bent his head close to her mouth—"maraschino cherries. Did you steal them when the bartender wasn't looking?"

"No, he put two in the first drink he made for me." Her fine cognac eyes grew wary. "That's quite an impressive trick."

He moved his shoulders. "It's nothing."

"I washed my hair with rain-scented shampoo and conditioner today," Chris said, "and I drank a cup of herbal tea with honey."

He grinned. "So I was right."

"I did all that," she continued, "when I got up this morning." She waited a beat. "Seventeen hours ago."

Robin's smile faded as her words invoked an image of her in his bed, her pale skin and auburn hair glowing against the dark sienna of his silk sheets, her arms open and welcoming. The book could wait; having her could not. He would have to lay siege to the fortress she had built around her heart, and quickly, before her suspicions drove her from him.

"If this is a practical joke, it's a good one," Chris continued. "Did Hutchins put you up to it?"

"I don't know anyone named Hutchins." He could barely speak as primal need surged through him, lodging in his groin to distend and harden his cock while demanding he find some manner in which to turn the fantasy into reality. Feeding earlier lent him a certain measure of control he might otherwise have lost in this astonishing rush of desire for her, but suddenly Robin did not trust himself. "I am not joking with you."

"You're not." She sounded uncertain now.

Robin couldn't think, not with the urgency of his hunger pounding inside his head. He could not tolerate another moment of this. He had to have her. Tonight. *Now*. He kept a suite of rooms at the hotel where he frequently used willing females. The only thing that kept him from sweeping her up into his arms and carrying her off to the nearest elevator was the sound of her voice, asking him more questions.

"Do you know a fair-haired man who wears a lot of red?" She nodded toward the other side of the dance floor. "There's one over there staring at you."

Robin glanced over to see his seneschal, Will Scarlet. He made a simple gesture behind Chris's back, and Will scowled but retreated into the crowd.

"Pay no heed to him." He noticed the other couples staring and smiling at him and realized how badly his control had slipped; somehow he'd flooded the entire dance floor with his scent. No wonder Will had come to see what the matter was. Soon every occupant of the bar would fall under his spell.

Except one, it seemed.

Robin peered down at the woman in his arms to see if her pupils had dilated, but the dark color of her eyes made it impossible to tell. "How are you feeling?"

"This is nice." She sighed. "I don't want to go home."

At last, her fortress was crumbling. He didn't know if it was due to his talent or *l'attrait*, and he didn't care. He tugged her closer, fitting her body to his and pressing his aroused flesh against her belly. She did not pull away, and indeed the movements they made caused her abdomen to rub lightly over the ridge of his erection.

Robin gritted his teeth. "What if I ask you for more than a dance, love?"

"You can ask." She emphasized the last word oddly.

Robin knew women, delighted in them. He had spent several lifetimes enjoying their company, learning their ways, and recognizing their wiles. He knew the subtle changes arousal caused in their voices and their bodies, the tantalizing signs that showed their interest in a man.

Although Chris was perhaps the most reserved human female he had ever encountered, and possessed great skill in masking both her true thoughts and emotions, he did not doubt now that she desired him. No mortal he touched had ever resisted his charm for long. Not even this stubborn wench, who had wanted nothing to do with him but five minutes ago.

Fool. Inside Robin's skull, his father's angry voice shouted across seven centuries. *You want her only because you cannot have her.*

The scent of bergamot thinned as Robin's self-disgust grew, and gradually the other couples on the dance floor lost interest in them. When the song ended, he released Chris and stepped away from her, breaking all physical contact. As long as he didn't touch her, his talent could not influence her decisions. As soon as he left, the effects of *l'attrait* would rapidly dissipate.

And he would never know her, because once he took the manuscript from her he would have all that he truly wanted, and that was how it would be. How it would have to be.

Robin bowed to her. "I thank you for the dance."

Chris began to say something, and then hesitated as if choosing her words.

"It's all right, love. This is not your doing." Because he couldn't help himself, he added, "My home in the city is on the penthouse floor of the Armstrong building. It is that unsightly tower of black glass and steel at the end of the street. Do you know it?"

She nodded.

"Good." At least he could offer this much. "Come to me there, whenever you wish."

"Come to you? Rob—"

"Listen to me now." He felt the tips of his *dents acérées* emerge in his mouth, aching for a taste of her flesh. He slid his hand to cup the back of her neck and pressed his cheek to hers, using his talent to enforce his words. "I want you, love, more than I can say. But it must be what you want. When I am gone, when your head clears, then you must choose to do as you wish. Nothing more. Do you understand me?"

"Yes, but—"

Robin pressed his scarred fingers against her lips. "You know where I shall be. I do not sleep until after dawn." He put his mouth to the back of her hand, careful not to let her feel the sharp tips of his fangs. "I hope that we meet again, my lady."

Chapter 3

Chris watched Rob walk out of the club before she retreated to her table and sat down alone. She'd enjoyed the dance, and the rare opportunity to be treated as nothing more than a pretty woman, but something she had said or done had definitely given Rob the wrong impression.

Maybe he'd read her wrong when she'd mentioned how nice it was to dance, and that she didn't want to go home. Somehow those innocent remarks had driven him wild. So much so that he hadn't even bothered to conceal his erection, or the lust that he'd assumed was mutual.

I want you, love, more than I can say.

Chris had worked in a male-dominated field for years, and she knew how fragile men's egos could be. She also avoided being cruel whenever possible. She would have let him down gently; she'd had every intention of doing so as soon as the song was over. But from the moment he'd made it clear that he wanted more than a dance, Rob had hardly let her get a word in edgewise. In fact, he'd behaved as if *she* were the one acting out of control.

It matters not, as long as you will stay.

She'd noticed immediately the odd shift in his speech when he'd become aroused, too. Maybe he was an actor obsessed with Shakespeare or Tolkien or something. He'd certainly been so preoccupied with being noble that in the end he'd done the dirty work for her.

. . . it must be what you want.

Had she sent him some mixed signals? It wouldn't violate Chris's cast-iron principals to admit that Rob *was* one of the most attractive men she'd ever met. Or that being in his arms had brought back to life feelings that she'd thought the job had smothered long ago.

No, that wasn't true. She'd forgotten the job and her responsibilities, and for a few minutes had enjoyed simply being a woman. That could have been what set Rob off. Then he'd had that panic attack or whatever it had been and seemed as if he couldn't get away from her fast enough. She still felt a little guilty for allowing him to leave in such a state. Had he been drunk? She should have seen the signs if he had been.

It's all right, love. This is not your doing.

Chris left the club and took the elevator down to the lobby, where a doorman offered to hail a cab for her. Without thinking she shook her head and glanced down the street.

You know where I shall be.

That she did. She could see the Armstrong building from here. It was exactly as he'd described: an ugly column of dark glass and polished steel girders. All the windows were dark, except for the rows on the very top floor. Those windows glowed with diffused light from within.

I do not sleep until after dawn.

She wouldn't sleep at all tonight either. Not after this.

. . . you must choose to do as you wish.

Without knowing exactly why, Chris began walking down toward the end of the street.

The hollow sound of her heels on the concrete sidewalk kept time with her pulse, slow and then quickening, faltering as her common sense tried to turn her around, speeding up as the low, velvety voice in her head persuaded her to keep going.

. . . it must be what you want. What you want. What you want.

As skeptical and pragmatic as Chris was, she did believe in love at first sight. Her parents had taken one look at each other across a crowded room and, twenty-four hours later, had stood in front of a justice of the peace to make things legal.

"I would have gone sooner," Jack, Chris's dad, often claimed, "but you know how long it takes your mom to get ready for anything."

Upon hearing this Beth, Chris's mom, would always laugh. "I seem to remember someone who wouldn't let me out of bed long enough to get dressed."

Jack and Beth Renshaw had scandalized their families, dumbfounded their friends, and, forty years later, were as much in love and devoted to each other as they had been after that one look back in 1968. The only flaw in their relationship was the fact that they had never been able to have a child together, but they had solved even that problem by adopting Chris.

As much as the story of her parents' speedy romance charmed Chris, she was a realist. She had never felt that kind of passion, and her personal desires rarely played any role in her decisions. Whatever was necessary to meet her goals, solve the situation, and get the job done, she did. Someday there would be time enough for love; until then she allowed neither her emotions nor her needs to run her life.

Yet here she was, standing at the lobby entrance of the Armstrong building, looking up at the top-floor windows and wondering about the man who lived behind them.

Who is he, and how can he afford this?

Chris eyed the doorbell panel. A single neatly typed label

listed what evidently was the building's only occupant: ARCHER ENTERPRISES, INC.

"If you wish to gain entrance," a familiar voice said over the panel's speaker, "you must press one of those buttons to indicate that you are at the door."

She looked into the lens of the closed-circuit security camera above the panel. "But you already know I'm here." She didn't touch the buttons. "Have you been watching for me all this time?"

"No. I've been too busy on my knees praying. Come up." An electronic buzz released the entry lock.

Chris didn't like being rushed. She preferred time to think over what she was doing, analyze her motives, and base her choices on the most prudent course of action. Out of nowhere, a cold draft made her skin shrink and sent a jolt up her spine, as if the warm summer night had turned winter-icy.

The truth was that she didn't know this man; in reality he could be anything from a sexual sadist to a serial killer. Despite her training and confidence, she had no business placing herself alone in an intimate situation with him. And he'd made it very clear what he wanted, so any further voluntary contact on her part would virtually be the same thing as giving her consent.

. . . it must be what you want.

The buzz mocked her, rushed her, demanded she ignore her common sense and go to him. She knew that if she went inside she would be risking a great deal more than her personal safety. Her boundaries of behavior existed for very good reasons. She had come to this city to do an important job, one that would probably make or break her career. She had debts to settle and a reputation to restore. In the wake of the scandal, catching the Magician constituted her only real chance of redemption. She didn't have time for one-night stands.

Then make this one count.

A split second before the buzzer switched off, Chris opened the door and walked inside.

Reds, golds, and browns dominated the color scheme of the interior lobby, which had been cleverly arranged around a massive dark walnut reception desk. Several Michael Tischler prints of the Catskills hung on the walls behind crescent-shaped clusters of red leather chairs and love seats. Large tables were surfaced with mandalas of hubcap-size polished agates seated on wood bases carved to resemble tree stumps. The ebonized floor tiles diffused the amber beams streaming down from a series of enormous, sphere-shaped brass lighting fixtures in the high, coffered ceiling.

Welcome, madam, the lobby said, as if it were a snooty English butler. *If you have to inquire about price, then it is likely that you can't afford it.*

Chris knew interior design and how much it cost to achieve this level of quiet, glowing affluence. If Rob owned Archer Enterprises, he had serious money and wasn't afraid to spend it.

She paused in front of the elevator doors. A small table there held a quintet of ivory tree peonies sprouting from a shallow, crimson glass bowl. She touched the delicate petals, not terribly surprised to discover they were real. They reminded her of the brush of his silky black hair against her cheek as they danced. That had been as much of a jolt as the feel of the hard-toned muscles under his clothes, and the impact of those gorgeous violet eyes watching her. Rob seemed almost too beautiful to be real.

Like this place. Like this night.

Chris knew she had only one advantage left: She could turn around and walk out right now. He couldn't stop her. She'd never meet him again. No harm, no foul.

"Are you coming up," Rob's voice asked, "or should I return to my prayers?"

This time Chris didn't see the speaker or security camera. "You're very impatient."

"If I were," he said, "I would never have survived our first dance." His tone softened. "You've nothing to fear, love. I promise you." The elevator silently slid open, beckoning to her as he did: "Come to me."

She stepped over the threshold. The elevator closed and began to rise, soundlessly rushing past twenty-six floors before a low bell chimed and it came to a smooth stop. She expected to see Rob on the other side of the doors, ready to grab her and go to town, but found only an empty corridor.

He meant it. It has to be what I *want.*

Chris knew what she wanted. She walked past a forest of trompe l'oeil ferns hand-painted on sandstone to the only door, a wide panel of gleaming fruitwood inlaid with dozens of small brown birds. This one didn't open automatically for her, and knocking on it seemed foolish. Before she could find another hundred reasons to turn around and hurry back to the elevator, she let herself in.

If the lobby said, *Welcome, you can't afford this, now get out*, the penthouse merely said, *Hello, there.*

In Chris's experience, penthouse suites were exalted places with sweeping vistas and cold, obvious displays of wealth. Rob's home had the million-dollar views—she could see most of downtown Atlanta through the endless walls of arched windows—but everything else inside murmured more of comfort and atmosphere than grand impression-making and strategic investment.

Sectional furniture, positioned both to exploit and to ignore the spectacular prospects of the city, sat waiting for occupation. Books that had obviously been read and enjoyed marched in uneven rows across long stretches of freestanding shelves. A massive fireplace, definitely an incongruous touch here so far in the South, burned what appeared to be real wood and threw flickering light over a rectangular pit of velvet and satin pillows.

And everywhere she looked, vases, baskets, and pots of lush, green plants and small trees spread their shoots, limbs, and leaves in near-wild abandon.

A rich man's tree house, Chris thought, turning around to appreciate the entire effect. *In the middle of Atlanta.*

"I have no ginger ale to speak of," Rob said, appearing on the other side of the room. He'd shed his jacket and rolled up the sleeves of his shirt, and he was barefoot. His straight black hair hung loose and somewhat disheveled around his unsmiling face. "But there's wine, tea, or water, if you'll have it."

On some level Chris had been convinced that Rob wouldn't be as attractive as he had seemed in the uncertain lighting back at the club. He wasn't. He was magnificent, all sinuous limbs and elegant muscle, a visual feast from the silky jet mane of hair to his long, arched feet.

Beautiful, beautiful man.

"I'm not thirsty." Chris put her purse down, took off her own jacket, and carefully draped it over the back of a love seat. She'd never done anything like this, so she felt awkward handling the preliminaries. *First I put down my stuff, then we sit and talk, and then I lose it completely, drag him to the floor, tear his clothes off, and ride him until he begs for mercy or dawn, whichever comes first.*

Chris wondered if she could skip the sitting-and-talking part. If she did, she'd probably brand herself forever in his memory as a sex-starved slut—if coming to his apartment like this hadn't already done that.

Jesus Christ, just get on with it.

Rather than approach her, Rob moved around the room, his bright eyes intent on her. "Are you hungry? I could order some food. Or some entertainment. Musicians. Acrobats. Fireworks. Whatever you desire."

She shook her head as she began untying the knot in her scarf.

"Talk to me, Christine."

She watched him as she drew the length of her scarf from her throat. "My name isn't Christine." The pink silk slithered through her fingers, but then Rob was there, catching it before it touched the ground. "It's just Chris."

She found out that the intriguing scent she had attributed to his wine back at the nightclub didn't come from his breath; it rose from his skin, too warm and pervasive to be cologne. Chris, who had never cared for strong fragrances, especially on men, found herself breathing him in deeply, as if she had to imprint his scent deep inside herself, where she could recall it at will and never forget this man.

Something already told her that she never would.

"*Just* Chris." He straightened and draped her scarf around his own neck. His amethyst eyes—surely the most stunning eyes she'd ever seen in anyone's face, man or woman—took on a burnished sheen. "Is it a singular name, then, like Madonna, or Jewel?"

"It's . . . easier to remember than the long version." She took his hand and brought it to her face. "Chris. It rhymes with *this*." She brushed her lips, whisper-soft, against the center of his palm.

Rob closed his eyes for a moment, and then bent as if to slide his arm under her knees and lift her off her feet.

"Wait." She touched his shoulder. "Dance with me again."

He slowly straightened. "There's no music."

"I don't care." She stepped closer.

Rob took her in his arms, enfolding her this time as she rested her cheek against his shoulder. Here, alone with him, with no one around them, she could finally do as she pleased for once. This once.

Chris moved with him, slipping her fingers up to unfasten

the buttons on his shirt one by one. She didn't expect to see the thin green lines wrapping around his throat, and ran her finger across an inch of them. They felt hard, almost like calluses. "Someone messed up the tattoo on your neck."

"For which I am eternally grateful." He took in a sharp breath when her fingers trailed down across the bare, smooth skin of his chest. "I see. You've come to continue the torture."

"You're wrong." She guided his hand to the pearl buttons hidden under the lace of her blouse. "I came here for you."

As Rob opened her blouse, Chris pushed his shirt back from his shoulders and drew it down his arms with little trouble. However he worked out, his regimen had left him with layer upon layer of tight, streamlined muscle so tough her fingertips couldn't dent them. The firelight lent a little color to his pale skin, and shadowed a small depression on his chest, just above his left nipple.

She saw no surgical mark to explain the absence of muscle, and idly wondered what sort of injury healed without scarring. As his fingers tugged free the comb holding her hair in place, she tilted her head and kissed the old wound.

Without warning Rob used the hair in his fist to pull her face away from his chest. "I thought you wanted to dance."

Harsh words from a man holding her by the hair and the hip, and sporting an erection that felt like a tire iron wedged between them. He didn't want her kissing his old injury or whatever it was; that much was plain.

She understood. She had her own scars to hide.

"I do." Chris shrugged out of her blouse and took hold of the ends of her scarf around his neck, using it to bring his head down to hers. "But is this"—she punctuated her words with little nips on his jaw, chin, and lower lip—"the only dance you know?"

Rob's mouth curved against hers. "I think not."

She expected him to kiss her, but instead felt his hands

shift and heard the hiss of her skirt's zipper. Cool air whispered against the stretch of skin between the bottom hem of her chemise and the narrow hip band of her garter belt. She stepped out of the puddle of her skirt and moved back enough to watch his expression.

She would never be as beautiful as he was, but she knew how she looked almost naked.

"More splendid than I'd imagined." He traced his fingertips across the slippery shell of her satin lingerie, circling with his thumb her nipple, her navel, and the curve of her hip bone. "What else do you hide from me, my lady?"

Too much.

Chris felt an impossibly strong, wholly uncharacteristic impulse to tell him her life story right then and there. Chris, who had never confided anything to anyone outside her immediate family. Her parents were the same; they let people assume she was their biological daughter so that no one would know the truth about her real mother, and how cruelly she had abandoned Chris.

She should have asked, "What do you want to know?" but the words seemed locked in her throat.

"Look at me, love." Rob cradled her face between his hands. "Look." When she did, he stared into her eyes, muttered something under his breath, and covered her mouth with his to give her a brief, hard kiss. "I would trade all my worldly possessions so that I might not have to say this, but you must leave me."

"Leave you." Chris wasn't sure she'd heard him right. "Leave you *now*?"

"Aye." He turned his back on her, showing her a stretch of muscle that made her mouth water. "I'll have a car brought 'round to take you home."

After a few moments Chris followed him over to where he was dialing a cordless telephone. "Where is your bedroom?"

Rob gestured to the left as he lifted the phone to his ear.

Chris removed the receiver from his hand, switched it off, and placed it back on the charging station. "I'm not going anywhere." She put her hand in his and tugged him toward his bedroom. "Unless you take me."

Gordon Middleton checked through thousands of international air travelers as they streamed through his customs station at Heathrow's terminal two every day. He enjoyed his job as well, in a surly and somewhat grim fashion. Twenty years ago, Pan Am flight 103 had exploded over Lockerbie, Scotland, only thirty-eight minutes after it had left Heathrow. The bomb, probably concealed in a bag that had not been properly checked, had taken a mate of Gordon's and 269 other souls on board and on the ground to a fiery death only four days before Christmas. Ever since that bitter night, Gordon had distrusted every passenger who came through his gate.

His suspicious nature had earned him three special citations of merit as well. He'd personally nabbed a pair of drug mules declaring plaster vases that turned out to be molded from pure cocaine; an HVAC mechanic from the U.S. with a case filled with unclaimed specialty compressor parts worth thousands of pounds; and a sweet-looking grandmother toting eight handguns in her knitting bag.

For twenty years, no one and nothing got past Middleton.

Gordon kept his eye on the three Americans as soon as they'd joined his queue. He didn't get many Yanks through his station; most came through terminal three with the rest of the passengers from U.S. flights. These three had probably come in on a private jet; they had the designer clothes and that particular bloody air of privilege about them.

The two men, one tall and dark, the other broad and scarred, kept a little bit of skirt in heaven-blue silk between them. The bint had a phone to her ear and a frown on her small face; likely she thought it made her look less suspicious. Yanks, Gordon knew, were idiots that way. He pegged them for a full inspection.

"Passports, if you please." Gordon carefully examined all three before looking up at the dark one, who seemed to have an air of authority about him. He also smelled of rose perfume, or maybe it came from the little fancy on the phone. "Have you or your friends anything to declare before you enter the United Kingdom, Mr. Cyprien?"

"Nothing at all, *mon ami*," Cyprien said.

Gordon, who thought Frenchmen were the only thing on earth worse than Yanks, stiffened. "Would you put your cases on the table?" Sensitivity training be damned; he would not say *please* to a sodding frog.

"Of course." Cyprien smiled. "But may I first tell you something very important?"

The bint's rose perfume made Gordon blink several times before he grinned back. "Anything you like, mate." He bent over and, although he hated being touched by passengers, didn't flinch as Cyprien put one long, cool hand to the side of his neck.

Then Gordon listened, and nodded, and agreed with every word that Michael Cyprien told him.

"We have questioned every member of the Methodist church where John was seen attending services on the morning he disappeared," Valentin Jaus, suzerain of the Chicago *jardin*, told Dr. Alexandra Keller. "None of them remember your brother leaving the sanctuary."

Alex moved several paces away from her lover, Michael Cyprien, who was speaking in a low murmur to the customs agent who had stopped them. "And you thoroughly searched the property again?"

"Several times. He cannot be hiding there." Valentin's voice softened with sympathy. "I know you are deeply worried about John, my lady, but you should leave this matter to me and my men now."

She had done just that by accompanying Michael to London, where the six other Kyn seigneurs were gathering along with Richard Tremayne, the Darkyn high lord, to hold an important tribunal that Michael referred to as *le conseil supérieur*. Alex had no reason to feel guilty about abandoning the search for her brother, either. She had spent months walking the streets of Chicago, questioning every hooker, junkie, and homeless wretch she could find. She knew her brother; if he intended to take refuge anywhere, it would be among the lost souls on the street. She'd shown them John's photo over and over, and compelled them with *l'attrait* to tell her the truth. No one had seen him.

All the evidence pointed to two conclusions: Either her brother didn't want to be found, or John was dead.

Alex still couldn't accept either answer. "If there's a sighting, or any new leads—"

"Of course I shall contact you at once. You have my word on it, my lady."

"I appreciate it, Val. Give Liling my best." Alex switched off the mobile phone and handed it to Michael's seneschal, Phillipe. "No luck with the last of the church people."

"Do not worry so, Alexandra." Phillipe pocketed the phone and spoke to her with the same gentle sympathy that Valentin had. "If your brother is still in Chicago, Suzerain Jaus will find him."

"Assuming he's still alive."

Ever since John had vanished, Alex had been having nightmares about standing over her brother's body, sprawled in an alley, and watching rats feed on his gaunt corpse. She knew why she was having the bad dreams, too. At the time of his disappearance, John had been suffering serious complications from a strain of malaria Alex had been unable to identify. John disliked doctors and hospitals, and without treatment his chances of surviving the disease were almost nonexistent.

Alex glanced back at the gate leading to Cyprien's private jet, which would remain on standby until they were ready to return to the States. "How long do I have to stay at this thing?"

"As long as the master does." Phillipe took her arm in his in a familiar, comforting manner. "If you go back alone, it will hurt you both. You know how it will be. The last time was very bad."

The reminder made Alex's throat tighten. She had just recovered from some frightening physical and mental aftereffects of being kidnapped and separated from Michael. The bond she shared with him as his *sygkenis*, or life companion, went much deeper than she had ever suspected. They had a dependency on each other that defied explanation. Being away from Michael had made her vulnerable to other Kyn in ways that still haunted her. If she returned to America by herself, she had no doubt they'd both go through hell again.

"I'm not interested in giving myself Michael withdrawal," she assured Phillipe. "I was just wondering if we could somehow, you know, cut this short."

Phillipe gave her a wry look. "Kyn do not do short." He glanced at Michael, and his expression grew serious. "What happens at the tribunal is important to him, to you, to all of us. He needs you here, Alex."

Michael had told her that the Kyn leaders were holding *le conseil supérieur* in order to decide what action to take against the Brethren, a radical group of religious zealots that had been secretly warring with them for centuries. Recently their ancient enemy had been conducting widespread arson attacks against Kyn *jardins* in France and Italy, and even now were moving into Spain.

Aside from avoiding any more bond-straining issues, Michael also wanted Alex with him to report to Richard on the experiments she had been conducting on Kyn blood. Alex's interviews with some of the early refuges escaping the Brethren persecution in Europe had prompted her to test how Kyn blood reacted to heat. Although the Kyn had long believed that fire was one of the few things that could kill them, Alex had proven otherwise, and that it might be possible for the immortals to heal from even the worst burns.

Alex didn't think she was the only one who had discovered these facts, either. After reviewing many arson reports prepared by the European police, and learning that no Kyn remains had ever been recovered by authorities, she theorized that the Brethren might be using fire not to kill but to capture and disable the Kyn.

Michael agreed that her findings were troubling, but he was more concerned with managing the consequences of the Brethren's latest campaign of terror. He now ruled over most of the survivors of the arson attacks, as nearly all of them had fled to America. He also felt strongly that actions had to be taken to safeguard the refugees and redistribute them in Europe and Asia to create new strongholds rather than concentrating their numbers on one continent.

Then there were the rumors of a growing desire among the Kyn to launch a counterattack against the Brethren and wipe out the order once and for all. Michael had no love for the zealots, but as Alex had often pointed out, to declare war on the Brethren in this day and age might finally expose the existence of the Darkyn to the rest of humanity. If government and military leaders learned of the race of immortals secretly living among them, immortals who could heal spontaneously and whose individual talents rivaled that of comic-book superheroes, the Brethren would be the least of their problems.

Michael joined them. "We have cleared customs."

Alex couldn't help the slightly jaded look she sent his

way. "What you mean is, you used your talent to lift the memories of our coming through here from the guy's mind."

He shrugged. "That is how we go through customs, *chérie*." He studied her face. "Do you wish to rest before we call on Geoffrey?"

Alex knew she could fake exhaustion, avoid meeting Geoffrey, the suzerain of London and host of the gathering, and spend the day in one of the luxurious hotel suites the Kyn kept leased and ready for visitors. Being alone with Michael would definitely soothe her bruised soul. But Geoffrey was expecting them, as was Richard, and this time she had serious business to put on the table.

Alex knew she couldn't keep dodging her responsibilities. Technically speaking she was no longer a human being. After years of research, trial and error, she was beginning to believe that nothing short of a divine miracle would ever reverse her condition. Being infected with the Kyn pathogen didn't change the fact that she was still a physician, sworn to save lives. The Darkyn were her people now, and she had to start taking care of them.

"I'm not that tired," she told Michael. "Let's get this show on the road."

Chapter 4

Chris opened her eyes, saw the plaster sunflower medallion in the center of the ceiling above her, and wondered why she'd expected to see a painting of tree branches making lace out of a blue sky. Then her body reminded her, from the ache between her thighs to the tenderness of her lips, of the other bed in which she'd spent a good part of the night.

With Rob . . . She put her hand over her face. She'd done things with him that weren't even mentioned in the Kama Sutra, but she hadn't bothered to ask him his full name. *Why the hell didn't I just go jogging?*

Three sharp knocks startled her up into a sitting position. "Agent Renshaw?"

That was her new partner's voice, which meant she'd overslept. "Give me a minute, Agent Hutchins."

She shoved sheets away and swung her legs over the side of the bed. She swore softly as she saw that she was still wearing her clothes from last night.

At the academy Chris had learned how to dress and prep in two minutes or less. She changed her jacket and skirt, slid on a new pair of stockings, and pinned up her hair in less time than it took most other women to put on lipstick. A glance in the mirror assured her there were no telltale marks or abrasions on her face and neck from last night's workout. Her mouth appeared slightly redder and fuller, but no more so than that of someone who had used a lip plumper.

Then Chris saw that she still wore her pink scarf, bundled and knotted like a blindfold, around her neck. His voice came back to her, a brush of invisible velvet.

Close your eyes.

Rob?

I have to protect you.

Chris untied the scarf, grabbed another from her drawer, and tied it as she walked out.

She found Special Agent Ray Hutchins in the kitchen, where he stood pouring coffee from a thermos into two cups. His pale gray chauffeur's uniform, which he wore as part of his cover, emphasized the darkness of his skin and eyes. Her new department chief had told Chris that Hutchins had played college ball as a lineman before giving it up to join the bureau, and he still had the broad, heavy build and lightness on his feet that had made quarterbacks quail.

Chris didn't know Ray Hutchins well, but she liked what she knew of him. "Morning."

"Agent Renshaw. I guess I should have mentioned that we all have keys to this place." He offered her a mug. "Did you turn down the AC last night? It feels like a meatpacking plant in here."

She frowned. "No one mentioned where the thermostat is, so it wasn't me."

"Dennis probably fooled with it. He's from South Dakota, and anything over sixty degrees is Death Valley to him." He subjected her to a swift but frank inspection. "You look a little frayed about the edges. Bad night?"

"Trouble sleeping. The bed in there is a little too soft." She sipped from her mug. "This is great."

"Starbucks. You might try out the guest room. Resources put a brand-new Sealy in there." He added a generous amount of creamer and sugar to his cup. "What did you think of the bar? Good place for our boy?"

"It's a pickup palace." And didn't she know it. "I doubt he goes there at all; he's older, and he'd stand out too much among the regulars and the hotel trade. The Magician likes to blend. We've never been able to get a description of him, even from people who should have been eyewitnesses."

"You're the expert." He regarded her for a moment. "How'd you end up pulling this kind of duty?"

"The Chicago office first tagged me to work with Interpol on the Poleteze case," she said. "They set up my identity as a fine-art expert and dealer, and had me infiltrate the counterfeiting ring as a buyer's rep. Luckily my cover was never compromised, so they've used me a couple dozen times since then to run the same sort of game."

"You do look the part."

Chris noted the time—she'd overslept by thirty minutes—and quickly finished the coffee. "A/V are supposed to be finishing wiring the gallery showrooms this morning. They'll need us for voiceprints."

"I'd like a word with you before we go." Hutchins pulled out one of the dainty little chairs encircling her bistro table, carefully lowering his bulk onto it. When Chris sat down across from him, he said, "The doorman keeps a log for us. He said you breezed in here around five thirty a.m."

She waited. Sometimes saying nothing was more effective than offering excuses.

"We all got lives. Chief would say, 'As long as it doesn't interfere with the op, what you do on your time is your business.' " He turned the coffee cup between his massive hands. "I don't agree. You want to bust the Magician because he killed your partner. I get that. But there's more riding on this. Half the cops in the world are counting on us to make this collar." He paused to inspect her face. "I guess what I'm saying is, I'm your partner now. What you do at any time is my business."

"The Magician didn't kill DeLuca." Chris kept her voice bland. "He committed suicide."

"*Something* happened in that bank," Hutchins insisted. "Something that put every hostage to sleep, wiped out their memories, and let the Magician leave the building while it was surrounded by SWAT and every cop in the metro area. An hour later your partner writes you a note, tells you the Magician pulled the job, and then blows his head off. That'd be enough to make me walk the floors all night."

Chris wondered if he'd heard any of the rumors running around the Chicago office. They'd ranged from Chris sleeping with DeLuca to her setting him up because she hated him. All of them blamed her for making him crazy enough to eat his gun. "This isn't my personal crusade, Agent Hutchins—"

"Losing a partner is as personal as it gets," he told her bluntly. "You wouldn't have taken a permanent transfer down here if it wasn't. But you're on point with this, and we need you sharp. If you're tired, you could slip up and blow your cover. Have you thought about that?"

"I know what I'm doing."

"Do you?" Hutchins shook his head as if to answer his own question. "This guy has moved two billion dollars plus in stolen art over the years. He's wanted in twenty-two countries besides this one. We take him down and make it stick, we're going to be legends."

"That's not important to me." She needed closure for DeLuca, and justice for all the victims the Magician had robbed over the years. "What I want is to put him away. For good."

"Then you get yourself some pills, drink some warm milk, or whatever it takes to stop walking the streets until dawn," Hutchins said. "If you don't, you're going to crack up or flame out. Assuming you don't get jumped some night by one of our fine, upstanding young crackheads."

Chris relaxed a little. "All right, partner."

"You don't argue much; I'll give you that." He held out his hand. "My partners call me Hutch."

She took his hand as it was offered, with respect. "Chris."

"Are you a Christine, a Christina, or a Christa?"

Norman hadn't even cared what her name was. "None of the above."

They left the apartment and took the elevator down to the parking level. To preserve Chris's cover as a fine-arts dealer, Hutch played the part of her chauffeur, requiring her to sit in the back of the Mercedes the bureau had leased for her use.

"This is a little ridiculous," Chris grumbled as Hutch opened the door for her. "I'm not Miss Daisy."

"Oh, but you in Jawja now, Miz Renshaw," he said, rounding his shoulders, widening his eyes and exaggerating his drawl. "All the nice rich white ladies 'round here got theyselves a colored driver."

"Colored." Chris sat back on the leather seat. "Do people actually still use that word?"

He chuckled as he climbed in behind the wheel. "If you think Atlanta's bad, you should spend some time at the central Mississippi office. Some of those old boys still display Rebel flag stickers on their personal vehicles."

The downtown art gallery that the FBI had appropriated for the operation had been abandoned by its owner when he had absconded to Australia with a collection of priceless European art on loan from France as well as all of his investors' money. The Australian police had agreed to suppress news of his capture and extradition back to the States, which allowed the bureau the time and means to take over operating the gallery and set up Chris as its new curator/director.

"This informant who contacted you in Chicago and told

you about this shipment of Nazi art," Hutch said as he worked his way through a snarl of downtown traffic. "How did he know that the Magician was the one who smuggled it into the U.S.?"

"He's a private collector," Chris said. "The Magician contacted him to offer him bidding rights. When he found out that the art had been stolen from the original owners by the Nazis during World War Two, he had a crisis of conscience."

He eyed her in the rearview mirror. "And you believed him?"

"Normally I wouldn't," she admitted, "but this collector is a Jew who had grandparents murdered in Auschwitz."

Hutch nodded. "That'll do it."

Heavy damask curtains covered the glassed-in front of the gallery, effectively concealing the hive of activity behind them. Hutch parked in the side lot and ushered Chris inside the building. Once out of sight, he removed his hat and jacket and accompanied her to the manager's office, which was being used as their command center.

"Agent Renshaw, Agent Hutchins." Dennis Engleman, the A/V technician, didn't look up from his laptop but gestured vaguely toward a pair of microphones set up on the cluttered desk. "We'll be ready for you in five or so."

Another agent carrying a small aluminum case stuck his head in the door. "Hutch, you got the keys for this?"

Hutch reached into his pocket, rummaged, and produced a pair of keys, which he tossed to the other agent. "Bring it in here for a minute." He turned to Chris. "You haven't seen the book yet, have you?"

"No, but I'm hoping they did a good job on it." In the past Chris had handled a number of copied artworks produced by the bureau's resource division, and all of them had been good enough to pass visual inspection.

"We're not using a copy," Hutch said, and nodded to the

other agent, who unlocked the case and popped the lid. "This is the actual book."

The sight of the ancient manuscript, carefully packed in a nest of protective foam strips, made Chris's heart skip a beat. Recovered during a raid on a Chicago mob boss's home, *The Maiden's Book of Hours* had somehow survived the ravages of time intact, as perfect as it had been when it was created by Brother Thomas de Crewes. Brother Thomas, who had spent most of his life working as master of the scriptorium in a Benedictine monastery, had been one of the greatest illuminators of the Middle Ages. *The Maiden's Book of Hours*, which he had filled with obscure prayers, fables, and portraits of famous personages of his time, was the only example of his work still in existence.

"I know what you're thinking," Hutch said as he handed her a pair of latex gloves. "Using the real book is risky."

"Using an irreplaceable, priceless artifact that men have been killing one another to possess for the last seven hundred years," Chris said as she pulled on the gloves, "is insanity."

Hutch gloved and removed the manuscript from the case. "A fake won't fool the Magician. He'd take one look and walk on by."

Chris knew her partner had a point. During several jobs the Magician had pulled, he'd left behind at least a dozen paintings assumed to be worth millions. They were all later discovered to be forgeries.

"Hard to believe they had to make all the books back then by hand." Hutch lifted the manuscript out of the case and carefully placed it on the desk. "It weighs a ton."

"Forty-three pounds, eleven and a half ounces," Chris corrected him absently as she lifted an edge of the protective padding to admire the gem-encrusted front cover. "It looks as if it were handmade yesterday, doesn't it? Time, war, and ignorance destroyed almost all of the paintings made during the Middle Ages, but manuscripts like these were usually overlooked or better protected. They're like time capsules of lost art."

"I thought even the most expensive books fell apart after a century," Hutch said.

"Brother Crewes developed some secret recipes to make his inks, paints, and vellum more colorful and, at the same time, more resistant to smearing and tearing. Experts have analyzed samples and identified linen, hair, and bone fibers, all preserved by a blend of five or six unknown organic substances. Whatever he used made the ink and paint permeate the vellum—that's why he glued the back of each page to the front of the next one—and rendered it as sturdy as varnished canvas, but as flexible as wood-pulp paper. Over time, his formulas also prevented mold, fungus, and every other deteriorating agent from attacking the manuscript."

The binding made an odd, slithering sound as Chris opened the cover to gaze at the first page, which had been covered with a layer of solid gold leaf, inlaid with enameled eluminures in the shapes of letters that spelled out the title. The brilliant jewel-tone colors of the lettering appeared as if they had been painted an hour ago.

"Are those rubies?" Hutch asked, peering at the rows of square-cut flat gems forming a rectangle around the words.

"Beryls." Chris had to clench her fingers to keep from touching the surface of the page. "Rubies over three carats are rare, and they're harder to find, so they didn't come into common use until a few centuries later." She took a letter opener from the desk drawer and used it to carefully turn the page. The next illustration, a miniature painting of the Garden of Eden bordered by interlacing colonnades of angels with flaming swords, took her breath away. "You can count the veins on every leaf. I read one book about Crewes that claimed he painted the smallest details with an eyelash he had filed down and glued to his own fingertip."

Hutch's whistle stirred the edge of the page. "He had some steady hands on him—and skinny eyelashes."

"This is an incredibly well-preserved artifact, but it's seven hundred years old. Even our breathing on it could damage the pages." Chris gently closed the manuscript and returned it to the case. "It's wrong to use this. It shouldn't be handled by anyone but a trained conservationist. It should be in the Smithsonian, right next to the Hope Diamond."

"We're putting it in a hermetically sealed glass case," Dennis put in. "Coincidentally, we convinced the Smithsonian to lend us one of their new laser security nets for arming the case. Don't worry, Agent Renshaw. No one will be putting a finger on it."

Chris thought of some of the security systems the Magician had disabled, pulled off her gloves, and stood. "I'd like to personally oversee the installation."

All the wrong Jane Moran had done was shoplift some diet pills that her mother refused to buy her. She could have bought them, but they were expensive, and she was saving her allowance for a new wardrobe. By summer she planned to be in size threes. That was it; that was all.

But the stupid clerk at the stupid drugstore had seen Jane put the pills in her purse, and the manager had called the police, and everyone had totally overreacted. Then the family-court judge had decided to really make her suffer.

She would never have touched so much as a Slim-Fast bar if she'd known about community service. For the next six months she had to spend every Saturday at a church hall with no air-conditioning, standing around for hours feeding homeless people.

It was beyond disgusting.

"You put one sandwich, one bag of chips, and one apple in the box," the shelter manager was saying. "Then you close the lid and hand it to the client."

Jane looked at the long line of dirty, shabby people waiting along one wall. "You call them *clients*?"

"I'd better not hear you call them anything else." The shelter manager handed her a pair of cheap, clear plastic gloves. "You have to wear these while you're handling the food."

Gloves. As if *she* were going to contaminate something. Jane thought about walking out, but her caseworker had warned her that any problem with her community service would get her tossed into juvie. Jane would certainly rather feed these people than have to spend the next six months living with their kids.

She put on the gloves and went to her place on the serving line. Prewrapped sandwiches were piled in one box, chips in another, and a plastic bin of rinsed apples sat on the floor. She took a cardboard box from the stack piled behind the counter and filled it with the food before folding over the top and completing the box lunch.

Definitely not rocket science.

She looked over the counter at the first of her "clients." Despite the heat of the day, the old skinny guy was wearing four jackets and a knit cap under a battered straw cowboy hat. His eyes were swollen, his eyelashes encrusted with some greenish white stuff that looked like dried snot. The amount of dirt on his face made it hard to tell if he was black, white, or other.

"Hi." Jane held out the box. "Happy lunchtime."

"I want three sandwiches." His fetid breath stank of rotten teeth and sour wine.

Jane shook her head and jabbed the box at him.

"Three," he insisted, trying to reach across the counter for the pile of wrapped sandwiches.

Jane screeched and backed into the shelter manager, who pushed her aside and came to the counter in her place.

"Now, you know you can only have one sandwich, Mr.

Patterson," the manager said, her voice sugary-sweet as she pushed the boxed lunch into his trembling hands. "Otherwise we won't have enough food for everyone else."

Patterson muttered, "Frigging nigger," before snatching up the box she offered and moving on to the boxed-drinks server.

"Did you hear what he just called you?" Jane demanded.

"Last week he called me a fucking wop," the shelter manager said. "I think his eye infection is finally clearing up."

Sinking into a sullen, resentful silence, Jane kept working and handing over boxes to the homeless. Some were dirty old men like the foul-mouthed Mr. Patterson; some were bony women with sores around their mouths and running up and down their arms. A few teenagers like Jane came through the line, but they were just as dirty and smelly as the drunks and the junkies.

One good-looking guy did come through the line, and held it up for a while as he stared at her. He smelled great, too, like her favorite candy. Jane pretended not to notice, but the man sat at a table just across from her station and watched her.

She didn't mind older guys, really, and this one had the prettiest eyes.

"Lady." A little black girl looked over the edge of the counter, distracting Jane. "Can I have choklit chip cookies?" she asked, smiling and showing that she'd recently lost her front teeth.

Jane knew the cute guy was watching her, so she put on a sympathetic smile. "I'm sorry, honey, but we don't have any cookies."

"Bitch, don't you be talking to my baby." A big, scowling black woman strode back from the drinks station and scooped up the little girl. "Just gimme her box."

Jane handed her the box, looked over, and saw that the cute guy had left. "Shit."

"What did you say?" the black woman yelled.

"Nothing." Jane cringed. "Sorry."

By the time everyone had been served, Jane had knots in her stomach and a pounding headache. The cute guy never came back. When it was time to go home, she wanted nothing more than to burn her clothes and spend a week in the shower.

"You give this to your caseworker when you report to him," the shelter manager said, handing her a form. "It's proof that you worked a full shift here."

Jane glanced at it. It was her first evaluation, and it wasn't what she expected at all. "You only gave me an average rating."

The shelter manager began stacking the empty food boxes inside one another. "Uh-huh."

Tears filled Jane's eyes. "This is so unfair. I've been standing here handing out boxes for three hours. I did everything you told me to."

"You don't work fast enough, you upset two clients, and your attitude is terrible," the older woman said flatly. "But this was your first time here, so I'm willing to give you another chance."

"I have a great attitude," Jane argued.

"Okay, then you should remember my name, because I introduced myself to you when you reported for your shift." The black woman watched her squirm for a minute. "It's Alice."

"Alice. Right." Jane pouted.

"Boxing lunches is the easiest shift at this shelter, Ms. Moran," Alice continued. "What are you going to do next weekend when I put you on the dinner shift, and you have to serve hot food to these folks? You going to throw it at them?"

"No. I'll do whatever I have to." Furious, Jane yanked off her gloves. "Can I go home now?"

"How are you getting there?"

"I'm taking the bus," Jane said through her teeth. "My mom took away my car for, like, forever."

Alice nodded as if that sounded sensible to her. "If you'll wait a minute, I'll walk you to the bus stop."

"It's only a hundred feet from the front door," Jane snapped. "I think I can make it."

Outside the sun was setting and the people she'd handed boxes to all afternoon were forming a new line for the dinner shift. Jane ignored them and stalked over to the bus stop. Three old black women and their bulging shopping bags occupied the bench, so Jane couldn't even sit down.

"That's the new girl at the church," one of them said, pointing to Jane. "I bet she on parole."

The other old ladies stared at her, and one asked, "What you get arrested for, girl? Smoking crack?"

The three began cackling like happy hens.

Jane turned in a huff and walked away from the bench to stand in the shadows by the church sanctuary. She refused the sandwich that Alice or whatever her name was had offered—as if she'd ever eat anything made for homeless people—and now her stomach growled miserably. She knew she'd binge on cookie-dough ice cream as soon as she got home, and she'd never learned the trick of making herself throw up.

She was never going to get into size threes by summer.

"I hate this." She wrapped her arms around her sunken waist. "It's so unfair."

"So it is," someone whispered behind her.

Jane smelled candy, and her mouth watered as she turned around. It was the cute guy. He must have been waiting out here for her all afternoon.

"Hi." Seeing him made her feel a little dizzy, but the emptiness in her stomach and chest faded, replaced by something warm and wonderful. "I thought you took off for the night."

He held out a black glove.

Jane smiled as the warmth spread out, liquid sunshine through her arms, hips, and legs. He'd waited for her. He wouldn't have done that if he thought she was complete trash like the rest of these people. He wanted to be around her. Maybe he even liked her.

She put her hand in his.

He pulled her into the little space behind the wide square column, where everything smelled like candy.

Sunset painted the city's skyline with wide ombré bands of gold, orange, and red before giving way to the deep blue fringe of the night. As Robin of Locksley came awake, he felt the last of the day's light fading as silently and completely as the woman beside him slept.

The day is gone, and I am not alone.

He didn't reach for her at first, somewhat astonished to know he had slept so long, but brought his hands to his face so he could breathe in her scent. She was, as she had been last night, all over him. She hadn't used perfume, as so many human females did, and he was grateful; her body's natural fragrance delighted him. He couldn't put a name to it, but had the tang of eastern spices and a rich sweetness like that of dark molasses.

As he breathed in, Robin remembered how boldly she had pushed him back on the bed and saddled herself over him.

You have a very nice bedroom. Do you bring all your women here?

Only you. I keep my other women in the harem on the third floor.

Rob had never brought a female, human or Kyn, to the penthouse, but Chris was different. Her presence in his city home seemed to fill a void he had never before noticed, and yet someplace inside he had always felt.

Unable to spend another moment without touching her, he rolled onto his side and extended a hand, feeling for the delicious warmth of her mortal body. Which wasn't there, a fact that startled him into opening his eyes. The pillow next to his still bore the impression of her head, but no one lay beneath the rumpled silk sheets.

The devil? Robin lifted his head to gaze around, but saw no sign of her. "Chris?"

No one answered, but he heard the sound of water running in the sink of the adjoining bathroom, and relaxed. She'd be thirsty, of course, and doubtless hungry as well. He would have food brought, a gourmet dinner, fine wines, strawberries, chocolates. He couldn't share her food, but he could feed her and watch her and kiss the taste of champagne from her lips. He'd tease her into feasting from his own skin. He had a fierce curiosity to discover whether she would be as playful as she was passionate.

Smiling, Robin rolled out of bed, pulled on his trousers, and went to see if he could coax her into the bath with him. Inside the bathroom, however, he found only his seneschal at the sink rinsing two wineglasses.

"Will?" He glanced at the empty shower and tub. "Where is Chris?"

"Do you mean the human female from last night? I cannot say, my lord." Will turned off the taps and dried his hands. "I assume that she returned to her home after she departed."

"She left?" Robin distinctly remembered her falling asleep sprawled over his chest. Her slight weight and radiant warmth had been so soothing he had dropped off a few moments after her. "When? How?"

" 'Twas near dawn; I secured the elevator after she used it. I saw no car, so I presume she went on foot. I sorted through the mail, and it seems you were summoned for jury duty again. We can hide from mankind for near a millennium, but try as I may I cannot seem to purge your name from the county courthouse mailing list." Will faced Robin and frowned. "What is wrong? Did something happen with the female?"

"Yes. No." Robin strode back into his bedchamber and inspected the carpet. No lingerie, no shoes, not a single trace of her. She'd taken everything. He moved on to the front rooms, where she had left her outer garments and purse, which had also vanished.

Robin slowly returned to his bedchamber, unsettled and bewildered. "She is gone."

Will set the glasses aside. "Rob? Why do you look that way? Did she take something?"

Aye, she had taken something. His dignity. Chris had left without waking him, without bidding him farewell, without so much as a by-your-leave. She had walked out as if last night had meant nothing to her.

No mortal had ever done such a thing to Robin.

Perhaps she had been frightened by the many intimacies that they'd shared. Yes, that would make more sense. She had seemed so cautious, so controlled—at least, before she had led him into his bedchamber. There she had become warm and loving and seemingly wholly at ease in his arms.

Robin glanced at the display of longbows he had mounted opposite his bed, interspersed with some of the arrows he had made over the centuries. The weapons represented many memories for him, all he had left of Sherwood, really. To a modern mortal like Chris, they may have seemed more intimidating.

Had she seen them upon waking? Had they caused her to flee?

"How did she appear to you when she left?" he asked his seneschal. "Was she disoriented? Did she seem upset?"

"I watched her through the security monitors only long enough to assure that she left the building," Will said, "but she seemed well."

"How well?"

Will made a vague gesture. "She was tidily dressed and moved with purpose. She did not weep or drag her steps. She did not take anything, and she did not look back." He cocked his head. "Did you not send her down?"

"No." Robin saw something glitter, and went to the bed. From the sheets he retrieved a short, plain gold chain. He had unfastened it from her ankle, he recalled, just before taking off her stockings. He wound the delicate thing through his fingers. "I never bade her to go."

"You . . ." Will's pale eyes rounded. "I do not understand, my lord. You never allow humans to stay the night."

"This one I did. Or should have." Robin touched the creased silk sheets on his bed. They felt as cold to his touch as his heart. "I slept with her, and she left me."

"I'm sure it was for the best. Had she remained, and awoken before you—"

"You do not understand me," Robin said. "I *fell asleep* with her. With her in my arms. I slept with that woman and did not wake, did not dream. I slept as I have not since my human lifetime." He closed his hand over the ankle chain. "How could she go like that?"

"You must have compelled her to leave before dawn," Will said. "She would not have departed herself, not while bespelled."

Robin thought of how she been with him. She had been eager and willing, and had startled him more than once with her boldness, but she had not behaved as if she were spellbound. "I begin to doubt that she was ever under my power."

"Could she be a Brethren operative?" Will sounded grim now. "We have known them to be resistant to *l'attrait*. 'Tis said they are bred that way."

Had Chris behaved differently, Robin might have shared his seneschal's suspicions. "Why would one of those zealots seduce me, much less leave me alone and sleeping in my bed, when she could kill me or have me taken?"

Will's expression turned wry. "True."

Robin saw something wedged beneath the base the lamp beside the bed, and retrieved it. The small square of paper smelled of her, and he unfolded it slowly.

Thank you for the dance. C.

Dark, tight resentment welled up inside him. "She wrote a note."

Will began straightening the bed linens. "You would be wise not to contact her again, my lord. A mortal who cannot be compelled is unpredictable, even dangerous."

"She does not offer me her phone number or contact information," Robin told him. "She thanks me."

Will cleared his throat to cover another sound. "That was very, ah, polite of her."

"Am I *no* one to her, then? Someone she must thank in writing? For what? A mistake she never intends to repeat?" Robin threw the note to the floor. "She used me. A mortal. A mortal used *me*."

"The stone-hearted bitch." Will fluffed the pillows. "Shall I track her back to her lair and offer her a sternly worded rebuke, my lord?"

Robin hardly heard him. "She did not purchase anything at the auction last night, but she did register as a bidder. She would have had to show her identification and give them a credit card. You will go to the auctioneer's office and obtain whatever information they have for her. I particularly want her full name and where she resides." He remembered something she had said at the club. "She told me that she recently transferred here from Chicago. One you have her full name, call Jaus and ask him to run a background check on her."

"Rob." His seneschal came to stand before him. "It was ill-mannered of this mortal to leave in such haste, but her actions are hardly worth so much trouble. Forget this."

"No. I was not finished with her." He went to his closet and jerked out fresh garments, tearing the sleeve from a shirt in the process. He tossed it aside and took out another.

"You know that women of this time are not like Kyn females," Will suggested carefully. "They have much freedom and independence, and they do as they wish. They do not respect men as we expect they should, but that is how things are in this society—"

"When have you known me to sleep the day through, from dawn to dusk?" Robin demanded. "With a mortal in my bed?"

"Never," Will admitted.

"Just so." He thrust his arms into the sleeves of the second shirt. "She did something to me, this female. I shall learn exactly what it was."

"She could not drug you or exhaust you," his seneschal said as he picked up the torn shirt from the floor. "Could it be that she made you happy?"

Robin turned on him. "Do I look happy to you now?"

"Not in least, my lord. Forgive me for suggesting otherwise." Will's radio buzzed, and he pressed the response button and spoke into it. "What is it, Sylas?"

"An Italian lady has arrived to call on our lord," the guard said. "She gives her name as Contessa Salvatora Borgiana."

Robin nodded.

"Escort her to the reception room," Will replied. "Our lord will meet with her shortly." He switched off the radio. "Were you expecting the contessa to call?"

"I did not know she was in America."

The last thing Robin felt like doing was receiving a

suzerain's widow, but Kyn customs gave him no choice. The contessa was obliged to pay her respects upon entering his territory, and it was his duty to welcome her—and find out what she was about.

Then he would deal with Chris.

His seneschal looked thoughtful. "She may have been driven out of Italy by the Brethren. So many have, these last months. Shall I prepare rooms for her and her men?"

"Sylas and Bergen can attend to her needs," Robin said as he buttoned his cuffs. "You have work to do. Go. I want to know everything you can learn about this mortal before dawn."

Chapter 5

On the outskirts of London, Michael Cyprien escorted his *sygkenis*, Alexandra Keller, from their limousine to the couple waiting for them on the front marble steps of the baroque mansion. He knew from her closed expression that she was feeling apprehensive, and kept her hand in his.

"Do you smell apricots?" she whispered.

"Geoffrey has an orchard of them, and keeps great heaping bowls all over the house," Michael murmured back.

"What for?"

He wondered why she had never noticed the baskets of lavender he had instructed Phillipe to keep around their home in New Orleans. "I imagine that their scent pleases him."

"Seigneur, welcome to my territory, our home, and England." Geoffrey, suzerain of London, stepped down and folded his tall, rawboned frame into a bow that would have seemed theatrical, had it been made by any other Kyn.

"Suzerain, I am most happy to be here." Michael returned the bow before offering his hand. "It has been too long, Geoff. Lady Braxtyn." He turned and bowed to the lady beside the suzerain, straightening to admire her artfully draped sarong of blue-green batik and the elegant folds of the sapphire scarf she wore wrapped around her head. "You dazzle me, my lady, as always."

Pleasure glowed in her dark eyes. "It is wonderful to have you here with us, Seigneur."

"You should have come to see us after you laid siege to Dundellan," Geoffrey said, winking shamelessly. "But you have made up for it by bringing to me an angel from heaven."

Michael never tired of watching his lover meet his oldest friends among the Kyn. At first it had secretly amused him to see his *sygkenis* cope with being showered with flowery praises, generally for her grace and beauty. A thoroughly modern woman, Alexandra had never learned how to accept compliments for anything except her medical skills, and to be told she had the tresses of a forest nymph or the eyes of a river sylph often left her speechless. Over time, however, she had grown accustomed to the effusive Kyn manner of greeting, and had learned to respond with an acceptable measure of grace.

After Michael performed the introductions, the suzerain seized Alexandra's hand.

"My dear lady." Geoffrey bowed so low over her knuckles that the tip of his nose bumped into them. "At long last we meet." He straightened, looming over her, and placed his rather ridiculous feathered green hat over the untidy thatch of his carrot-colored hair. "Your praises have been sung to me both near and far, but I see they fail to encompass the paragon of beauty, intelligence, and charm that you are." His wiry orange brows drew together over pale green eyes. "I fear I shall be spending these next weeks at your feet."

"I'll have to wear nicer shoes while I'm here." She returned his smile. "I'm happy to meet you, too, Suzerain . . ."

"Call me Geoffrey, my lady," he insisted. "I avoid at all times my surname, as it could not be humbler, and I dread to be thought of as naught but a shoemaker."

"Well, I'd curtsy, Geoffrey," she said, "but whenever I try I usually stumble or fall over."

"Perfectly all right. May I present another goddess of goodness and light?" He urged forward the quiet, dark-skinned woman standing beside him. "The only meaning in my life, Braxtyn of Canterbury, my beloved wife."

"My lady," Braxtyn said in her melodic voice, "you are most welcome to our home. I confess, I do not curtsy well either, and it gives me the headache to attempt to make po-etry of my sentences. The latter remains an exclusive and annoying practice of my husband's, which he will cease doing." She eyed her spouse. "At once."

"I live but to please you, my darling." Geoffrey held up hands mottled with faint ink stains in a gesture of surrender. "And the only manner in which to continue would be to compare Lady Alexandra to a starling. Beautiful they may be, but a damned nuisance in the garden."

Alex gave Michael an amused look. "Sounds about right." She clasped hands with the suzerain's wife, hesitating again as she looked down at the contrast between their skins.

Braxtyn's full cheeks dimpled. "If you are wondering how a woman of the islands came to be Darkyn, Geoffrey's father purchased me from a slaver as a girl. He put me to work in his kitchens, and eventually I became cook. Fortunately for me, Geoffrey loved food almost as much as he does writing."

"All of this is Braxtyn's fault," the suzerain said, gestur-ing around them. "I became a Templar only because we fell in love but could not marry. I released her from servitude be-fore I took my vows, you know, but the damn woman didn't want her freedom. Then I returned from the Holy Lands, cursed by God, a damned blood-drinking monster, and here she was, waiting for me with open arms."

"Someone had to look after you," his wife chided. To Alex she said, "He became a Templar so he could glean more stories from Holy Land pilgrims, although he always dreadfully distorted everything they told him. There was talk in Greenwich of having him hanged for the lies and immorality he published with his tales."

"That was all the doing of Arundel," Geoffrey said, and glanced at Alex. "He was the archbishop of Canterbury. He despised attacks on the clergy, and reformists like me who made them highly amusing. He tried twice in one day to have me killed in Greenwich."

"Really." Alex frowned, and Michael took pity, leaned forward, and murmured the French version of Geoffrey's surname. As soon as he did, her expression cleared. "Oh, so you're *that* Geoffrey." She put her hands on her hips. "They made me read your book in high school."

"Who said Americans had no taste?" The suzerain adjusted the frill at the end of his sleeve. "My published work remains the greatest example of classic English literature ever written."

"Sure, if you can read that Middle English stuff," Alex said. "I couldn't have understood half the words without the modern translation on the facing page."

Geoffrey sniffed. "'Tis tragic how our noble language has deteriorated over the centuries."

The suzerain finished the formal introductions between his men and Michael's while Alexandra answered Braxtyn's questions about their journey and her first impressions of London.

"I daresay Thirty St. Mary Avenue was that building you describe as a striped rocket ship—we call it 'the Gherkin'—but I cannot recall a structure that resembles a miniature of your American house of Congress with a blue rooftop," Braxtyn said.

"I think Lady Alexandra means the Imperial War Museum," Geoffrey put in. "Before it stored the weapons of empire building, it housed much more violent occupants. In those days it was called the Bethlehem Royal Hospital for the Insane."

Alex's eyebrows rose. "It was a mental hospital?"

"An asylum—the most notorious in our country's history, I fear," Braxtyn admitted. "You would know it as Bedlam." She offered Alex her arm. "Come. Let me take you to your rooms and help you settle in before Geoffrey begins describing the delights of Madame Tussauds."

"Nonsense, everyone loves the waxworks," Geoffrey called after them. "They have actors put on executions by guillotine in the Chamber Live now. There's a wonderful exhibit on Vlad the Impaler, who may or may not have been Kyn. And who can resist watching Guy Fawkes being hung, drawn, and quartered a hundred times a day?"

"That is precisely why," Michael heard Braxtyn say, "I never permit him to take our visitors sightseeing."

Michael watched as the two women walked up the wide, winding staircase leading to the upper floors. "You are blessed by your *sygkenis, mon ami*."

"I had heard that you were cursed with yours, but she seems most polite for a female of this time. I'm slightly disappointed." Geoffrey gestured toward his study. "You must tell me how you curb her tongue, although I hope beatings are not involved. Unless Braxtyn should administer them to me."

Michael chuckled and followed him into the large room, which was crowded with stacks of books, magazines and newspapers. The oddly designed chairs by the fire drew his attention. "You have redecorated. Again."

"I am shamelessly addicted to IKEA," Geoffrey said. "Braxtyn shudders over it—over the centuries she has become a dreadful furniture snob—but I adore the ingenuity of the Swedes. Besides, no one faints in horror if I dribble a bit of ink or wine on the cushions. You can't do that with

Renaissance antiques—or, at least, I recommend you do not."

Michael nodded. "Has Richard arrived?"

"He journeyed from Ireland yesterday but spent the night in the city with that French *tresora* of his. I expect he will grace us with his presence before midnight." Geoffrey poured two glasses of bloodwine and offered one to Michael. "I propose a toast: to our appalling treatment of excellent wine, our love for our beautiful and saucy women, and our devotion to our always noble if sometimes misguided Kyn brothers. May our Heavenly Father forgive us for the first, bless us for the second, and help us keep the last from wavering too much over the next fortnight."

"Amen." Michael raised his glass and drank before going to stand by the fire. He could not bring himself to sit down in a chair that resembled a warped chest protector made of straw. "How have you managed to live all this time so happily with Braxtyn?"

"Aside from this mewling, pathetic love I've felt for her since I was an idiot human boy? Probably because she has allowed me to. Sit down, man; the furnishings won't bite. I'm infatuated with these Gungholt rockers." Geoffrey demonstrated by dropping his long frame into one of the odd-shaped chairs.

Michael gingerly followed suit. "I do not mean to pry."

"Yes, you do." The suzerain grinned. "I've never seen you look at a woman as you do your Alexandra. Has the lady any idea of who you are? Or, more precisely, were, before you became her mewling, pathetic lover?"

"No, thank God." He set aside the wineglass and hunched over his folded hands. "I should tell you that Alexandra is not like other Kyn females. She has not fully accepted our ways, and she refuses to feed from mortals. She still seeks a cure that will turn us back to humans."

Geoffrey made a hideous face. "Good God. Cannot you convince her to take up needlepoint instead?"

"She is a doctor, and that is what they do—cure things." Michael felt a surge of bitterness. "I think someday she will come to accept what we are. I hope. She can be as unpredictable as she is difficult."

"Difficult women have defined this nation. Boudicca. Eleanor of Aquitane. Elizabeth the First, long-lived toothy-quimmed Grendel that she was." Geoffrey flung a long arm across the back of his chair and gestured with his wineglass at the portrait over the fireplace of a young, plump Queen Victoria. "And, lest I ever forget, our beloved Vicki. She certainly forgot us."

"You were wise to summon me," Michael pointed out. "If I had not removed her memories of the attack you thwarted, she would have told her advisers about you and the Kyn. You know how humans were in that time. They would have blamed you for the murders and hung your head from the gates of Windsor."

"At least we stopped Jack, may he still be busily sizzling in hell." Geoffrey leaned over to spit into the fire to seal the curse. "I had an interesting chat with Halkirk some weeks back. Among other interesting tidbits, he mentioned a rumor that Jaus had turned a human female. While crashing planes and being assaulted by a Brethren hunter, no less. He knew none of the details, but I wager that you do."

Michael made a mental note to have a talk with his lords paramount about their penchant for transatlantic gossip. "We are still investigating the matter."

"You know how Halkirk is; teenage girls have more discretion." The suzerain's expression turned shrewd. "Jaus's *sygkenis* would make the fifth mortal to be turned since your much-needed face-lift. Five in the last five years. And none could be turned for the previous five hundred years."

Michael inclined his head, acknowledging the veiled

warning. "There may be others hiding from us, as Nicola Jefferson did. She made the change alone after she was attacked."

"You mean, after Elizabeth killed her parents, tore out Nick's throat, and buried her in the ground with mum and dad, or so Gabriel told Croft." Geoffrey shook his head. "Ghastly business, that."

Croft Pickard, Geoffrey's *tresora*, slipped into the study. "Forgive the intrusion, Suzerain, Seigneur." He bowed respectfully to Michael before addressing his master. "My lord, Caen has called from town. He reports that the Irish contingent has left the Savoy and should be arriving within the hour."

"Thank you, Croft. Alert the guard and advise Lady Braxtyn that the cat is out of the bag." When the *tresora* bowed and departed, Geoffrey said, "My lady will keep yours occupied while we greet the high lord, if you like."

Richard Tremayne, high lord of the Darkyn, had abducted Alexandra from America and held her hostage in Ireland in hopes of forcing her to give him a method of changing other mortals to Kyn. Alexandra had instead found a treatment for Richard's changeling condition and thwarted a plot by Richard's own wife to assassinate the high lord.

Michael still had not forgiven Richard for taking Alexandra from him, but extenuating circumstances forced him to accept that the high lord was not responsible for all of his actions during that time.

"That is not necessary. Alexandra does not hold a grudge, and she wishes to examine Richard to see what progress he has made with the changeling treatment." Michael recalled how angry she had been with Richard's seneschal, who had tried to bond with Alex while she was being held hostage. "I think I will have a word with Korvel before she sees him."

*   *   *

"This is beautiful," Alex said, looking around at the gold and green splendor of the suite, and the breathtaking view of the gardens, the hedges and flowers of which had been arranged and trimmed into symmetrical perfection. "Michael will love it."

"He favors these rooms, so I reserve them for him whenever I know he is to visit us. Now, there is bloodwine in the lounge cabinet over there, and a supply of plasma in the dressing room's minifridge. If you need more syringes, you have but to ask." Braxtyn finished lighting the candles and blew out the taper's flame before she saw Alex's face. "I had thought you might want some privacy for your injections."

Alex felt a little embarrassed. "I see someone called ahead about my quirks."

"In truth it was Lord Tremayne who advised me on the supplies you might need, my lady. I only wished you to feel comfortable in our home." She offered a gentle smile. "Your lord did tell mine that you have never before visited London. I would be happy to show you our city."

"I'm not much of a tourist, but I would like to have a look around while I'm here," Alex said.

"If you enjoy art, there is the National Gallery. Van Gogh's *Sunflowers* and Turner's *Temeraire* are but two of the treasures in its collections. If you prefer to shop, there is Church Street for antiques, Kings Road for boutiques, Knightsbridge for Harrods, or Covent Garden for fanciful things."

"Michael is kind of the shopper in this relationship." The thought of browsing through stores made Alex's hands itch for her medical case. "I'm much happier in a lab or a treatment room."

"Then I shall have to take you to the Florence Nightingale Museum." Braxtyn gave her a shrewd look. "You remind me so much of her."

Alex grinned. "You knew Flo?"

"We met on several occasions when Geoff and I were involved in the war effort," Braxtyn said. "Lady Florence inspired me to no end. She did not care for what was appropriate, only for what was right and just. That spirit and determination created a marvelous aura around her; one you could almost feel when in her presence. After she returned from serving in Crimea, even the queen did not dare to cross her."

Alex frowned. "I don't think I strike fear into anyone's heart. I'm too short. Annoyance, now *that* I have totally covered."

"You needn't worry, my lady," Braxtyn said. "The high lord and his entourage will be staying on the opposite side of the mansion."

Alex sat down on the sumptuous master bed. "Do you think anyone would notice if I stay in here for the next two weeks?"

"I would." Braxtyn came to sit beside her. "Richard's *tresora* does not care for me, or any woman, for that matter. The other seigneurs' ladies do not attend *le conseil supérieur*, but stay in town to shop and amuse themselves. If you do not come out, I shall be left to debate floral arrangements with Navarre and hide the inkwells and quills from my lord."

"Phillipe really likes to garden," Alex said. "I'd put him to work outside, weeding." She sighed. "I thought I was ready for this tribunal thing, but I can already feel my feet icing up."

"It shall not be as trying as you imagine." Braxtyn patted her hand. "The seigneurs argue, Richard listens, he takes a vote, and then things are decided and everyone returns to their homelands." She stood. "Come. I wish to show you the rest of our home and ask you a great many bothersome questions about yourself and America. I particularly adore your science-fiction shows. Do you happen to follow *Battlestar Galactica* on the telly?"

Alex was so busy filling in Braxtyn on the latest season of Capricans versus Cylons that she didn't pick up on the distinctive scent of cherry tobacco until she almost walked into the cloaked figure in the hall.

"Jesus Christ."

"Not a personage for whom I am generally mistaken." The voice that came out of the deep hood sounded deeply amused. "We meet again, Dr. Keller."

Alex felt like swatting him with her case, but forced a smile. "How's it going, Richard?" She heard Braxtyn take in a quick breath behind her. "Don't worry, Lady Brax. His high lordness is used to my mouth. He had to listen to it for a couple of months after he kidnapped me and locked me up in his castle."

"An experience the delights of which have yet to fade from my memory." Richard touched her cheek with the back of one gloved hand. "As it happens, I *have* missed you, you impertinent wench."

"Right. Like Kevin misses Britney." Alex grabbed his hand before he drew it away and turned it over. Instead of the modified mitten he once wore to conceal the fact that his hand had mutated into a paw, he now wore a human-shaped glove with five fingers. "At least the treatments seem to be moving things right along." She reached for the edge of his hood to push it back.

"They are." Richard caught her fingers. "My modesty, however, insists that you conduct your examination later, perhaps in my chambers."

"You, modest? Oh, you mean like I'm diplomatic." She peered at the shadow of his hood. "Are you all right in there?"

"I have not felt better in two centuries, my dear." He bent

over her hand, and Alex felt the brush of almost human lips against her knuckles. "You will come to see me soon."

As long as I don't have to see your seneschal.

"Sure." She tugged her hand free. "Just ring a bell or something."

As Robin of Locksley performed introductions between his men and hers, Contessa Salvatora Borgiana indulged in one of her personal vices and imagined him naked. She had seduced many Kyn lords in her time, but Sherwood's prodigal son had always eluded her. Perhaps, like her, he preferred to be the one in control in the bedroom.

One wolf, her dear, departed husband Arno had always said, *cannot be a mystery to another.*

She mourned the many missed opportunities just the same. Locksley, she felt certain, would have been a skillful lover. He had a penchant for women that seemed insatiable, and the athletic build of his long, princely body guaranteed a woman vigorous sport. Salva personally preferred larger, more muscular men in her bed—bringing such brutes to their knees gave her great personal satisfaction—but she had no doubt that, had she tried, she could have enslaved Locksley just as easily.

A pity circumstances as they were made that impossible now.

Robin sent his men out of the room, and with a nod to her *tresora* Salva did the same. Once they were alone, she occupied a chaise lounge and refused Robin's offer of bloodwine.

"I apologize for calling upon you like this without proper notice," she said as he sat down across from her. "I have not traveled for many years, not since the time of the *jardin* wars. Losing poor Arno in the final battle broke my heart, and I have struggled to keep together our *jardin*, elude the Brethren, and find some peace for myself these last centuries. I fear my labors and concerns have turned me something of a recluse."

Robin's expression softened. "I know what you have endured, Contessa. You need never apologize for it."

"Thank you, my lord." She folded her hands in her lap and prepared herself to grovel. "I come to you in some distress. It seems that your seigneur has taken himself off to London, and I am not acquainted with any of his lords except you. In my heart, I have counted you as a friend since you brought my husband's body home to me. I confess, I could think of no one else to whom I might come and beg assistance."

"I am gratified that you did." Robin studied her for a moment. "What happened to make you leave Italy?"

"The Brethren. They found my villa in the country and came in the middle of the day to set fire to everything. Most of my human servants were murdered, and the *jardin* forced to scatter into the hills and hide for days. Had I not been in town at the time with my personal guard . . ." To hide her emotion, Salva looked away from him. "We had heard of attacks in other regions, but I never thought it could happen to us. We have been so careful, so discreet."

"Were you able to salvage anything?"

"Once we gathered our people and tried to make arrangements to leave Italy, I discovered that all of our bank accounts had been emptied, our properties sold, and our assets stripped. We were obliged to persuade a caravan of tourists to hide us and transport us over the border." She looked down at the chic dress she had purchased in Paris on the journey from Venice. "My *tresora* insisted that we stop in Paris to rest and acquire money, papers, and new clothing before crossing the Atlantic. I dislike using my talent to persuade humans to give me such things, when a week before I might have purchased them with my own coin, but I discovered that one becomes quite avaricious when one is fleeing for one's life."

"The Brethren will be made to pay for what they have done." His expression darkened. "I promise you."

"I have great hope that the high lord and the seigneurs will feel the same. Too many of our kind have been taken from us." Salva drew a cigarette from the case in her bag and leaned forward to permit Locksley to light the tip. She blew out a stream of smoke before settling back. "So there you have it, *caro.* I have come seeking asylum, but my immediate task is to secure the *jardin.* There are seventy-four of us."

"Cyprien has been allocating new territories for all of the Kyn being driven out by the zealots," Robin said. "When he returns, he will help you. Until then you are welcome here, my lady."

"Your generosity overwhelms me," she said, pleased by the offer. "I would gladly accept, but most of the men and women of my *jardin* have family serving one of your lords to the north. You are acquainted with Suzerain Jaus?"

Robin nodded. "Valentin is an old ally of mine."

"I am happy to hear it. You see, because of their connections, my people would feel safer if we were to settle in his territory," Salva said. "I have never met Jaus, however, and I am reluctant to approach him without someone he knows well to vouch for me and mine. I would not trespass any further on your kindness, my lord, but would you consider assuming that responsibility and performing the appropriate introductions between myself and Suzerain Jaus?"

"I cannot guarantee that Valentin will grant you permission to settle in his territory," Robin warned her. "But I shall do my level best to persuade him."

Salva began to thank him, but was interrupted by a knock on the door and the appearance of Locksley's seneschal.

"I beg your pardon, my lord, my lady." Will Scarlet bowed to them both. "I would not intrude, my lord, but an urgent matter has arisen in regard to last night's business with the mortal female that I must relate to you at once." He glanced at Salva.

"The contessa is an old and trusted friend," Locksley said. "You may speak in front of her."

"I went to the auction office as you directed, and obtained the information you desired," Scarlet said. "The female listed a Chicago address that I verified with our friends in the north. If it existed—which it does not—it would occupy the middle of Lake Michigan."

Locksley shrugged. "Someone must have noted it wrong."

"I had thought so as well at first," Scarlet agreed, "but the driver's license she provided was not registered with the Chicago department of transportation. Also, her credit card was issued by a government-managed credit union in Washington, D.C., but one week ago."

That got Locksley's attention. "What else?"

"I felt I should go to the gallery to question her employer," Scarlet said. "It is closed until the night of the show, but I intercepted one of the humans exiting from the back door—a man named Dennis. Under my influence, he admitted that he did not work for the gallery or any art dealer. He is an electronics expert who specializes in covert monitoring devices. He said that he, the woman, and everyone associated with this show are special agents of the Federal Bureau of Investigation."

Oh, dear. Salva suppressed a smile. *Someone hasn't been telling the truth.*

"She is an FBI agent." Locksley appeared stunned.

"Aye, my lord, and that is not all that the man told me," Scarlet said. "Agent Renshaw came to Atlanta to work undercover as an art dealer and set up what they refer to as a 'sting operation.' The FBI wishes to identify and arrest those

responsible for transporting to the States the stolen art recovered by the Kyn in France."

Robin said nothing for several moments. "I am the one
responsible for that."

"Yes, my lord." Scarlet shuffled his feet. "According to
the man Dennis, the FBI has been interested in your, ah, activities in the art world for some time. The agents have not
yet identified you by name or appearance, and they have no
witnesses, but they know a great many details about your
most, ah, daring exploits. They call you 'the Magician.' "

Salva chuckled. "Most appropriate, my lord, given your
skills at making things disappear."

"I do not believe that the female knows that you and the
Magician are one and the same," the seneschal continued.
"If she did, she surely would have tried to arrest you last
night. But she and her cohorts are staging the gallery show
specifically as a trap for you. *The Maiden's Book of Hours*
is being used as the bait."

"How could she know that I wanted that manuscript?"
Locksley demanded. "For that matter, how did they know I
live here, in Atlanta?"

Scarlet shrugged. "I cannot say, my lord, but their information is very good."

"Too good." Robin began pacing up and down the length
of the room. "You are certain that she does not know who
I am?"

"My lord, given that your activities date back several
decades, the FBI believes you to be an elderly mortal,"
Scarlet replied. "Even if Agent Renshaw did suspect, you
appear too young and affluent to fit what Dennis called their
'profile.' "

"I cannot believe it." Robin shook his head slowly. "First
this mortal treats me like a discarded garment, and now she
means to entrap and imprison me."

Salva finally understood Locksley's anger, and the odd

smell of human female lingering about him. *He has been with her, while she deceived him about her identity.*

"If I may be so bold as to make a suggestion, my lord?" When Robin turned to her, she continued: "As I have told you, my talent is persuasion. I could attend this gallery show with you, and easily convince this mortal female to surrender the manuscript to you voluntarily. Would that not be fitting revenge for what she has taken from you?"

Locksley made a curt gesture. "She took nothing from me."

She saw that he was tempted. "Perhaps nothing material, my lord. But your trust has obviously been violated, and by a woman who would gladly do much more harm to you. You are a suzerain; she is but a mortal. If word of this were to spread among our kind . . ." Delicately she trailed off.

"No one need know anything about this," his seneschal said, frowning at Salva. "I'm sure such an *old* and *trusted* friend as you, my lady, will keep my lord's confidence."

"You can depend on me to be as silent as a mute," Salva said. "But what will you do about this mortal who dares to hunt you, my lord?"

"I will teach her a lesson," Robin said. "One she will not soon forget."

Chapter 6

Chris adjusted the small gold brooch the A/V tech had pinned to her jacket lapel. The cluster of crystals covering the ornate pin disguised a tiny camera lens, which would transmit everything she saw in the gallery.

"How's the picture on your end, Dennis?" she asked.

"Great," he said over her earpiece. "The mikes around the gallery are picking up every sound you make, so you don't need to wear the wire. Video transmission's good, too. At this moment I can see every pore on your partner's big, ugly black nose."

"If you're talking about my nose again, Dennis, I'm going to come back there and kick your tiny white ass." Hutch checked his watch. "We've got thirty minutes to go. Let's walk through it one more time."

As they went through the gallery, Chris examined everything with a critical eye. The carpets had been professionally cleaned, the furnishings polished, the paintings—all excellent forgeries that Chris had brought with her from the Chicago art and antiquities task force's collection—properly hung and lighted, and the display cases wiped down. What didn't glitter, gleamed.

"Childers and Barclay are covering the entrance," Hutch

said. "Alpert and I will have both ends of the alley, and Wardell and Anderson are on the roof."

Despite the many precautions they'd taken, Chris still felt uneasy. "Is there any other way in or out of the building?"

"All the windows have been wired, so Dennis will sound the alarm if he tries to climb his way in." He stopped in front of the case containing the illuminated manuscript. "Don't mother-hen it, but watch this thing. If one of the guests bumps it the right way, it'll set off the net. I still think we should have used agents to play the attendees."

"Then we couldn't have advertised it, and how many guys in the bureau do you know who would look like patrons of a gallery?" Chris asked, amused. "If the Magician is familiar with the local fine-arts scene, which we have to assume he is, he's not going to be fooled by a bunch of feds in off-the-rack suits pretending to be fascinated by medieval treasures."

"Yeah, well, if things get hairy, you pull the plug and protect the citizens." He inspected her. "You should wear your hair down more often. You look good."

"Thank you." Chris never wore her hair down if she could help it; it made her look too young and frivolous. "It covers my earpiece."

"You should know that Hutch's wife is a six-foot-two ex-hurdle jumper who looks like she could stomp John Cena into dust," Dennis said over her earpiece. "Just in case you're feeling a little partner love there, Agent Renshaw."

"I appreciate the advice, Dennis," Chris said smoothly. "I'll pass it along to Agent Hutchins. I'm sure he'll remember it the next time we need someone to search an overflowing Dumpster."

"Okay, okay," Dennis said. "Geez."

Chris straightened her jacket carefully to avoid jogging the brooch. She was more accustomed to wearing a wire underneath her clothes, but Dennis had assured her that they'd planted so many bugs around the gallery that no one would even hiccup without him getting it on tape.

"Did I tell you we got the report today from forensics on that weird slug from the bank job? Turns out it wasn't a slug at all. They identified it as a copper arrowhead."

"An arrowhead? From someone's pendant?"

"From a real live arrow. The found some splinters of wood from the shaft embedded in the metal." Hutch bent to pick up a piece of snipped electrical wire caught in the carpet pile. "All handmade, so it couldn't be traced to a manufacturer."

During her years in the bureau, Chris had heard plenty of stories about the strange weapons some bank robbers employed. They ranged from open jars of hydrochloric acid to homemade flamethrowers. But this? "Hutch, they're not seriously suggesting that the Magician held up the bank with a bow and arrow? The guards would have shot him."

"Yeah, once they stopped laughing," Dennis put in.

Hutch shrugged. "They found traces of blood and black leather on it."

Chris remembered the odd cut the medical examiner found on the back of DeLuca's hand, and the blood he'd dripped all over the hotel room before shooting himself. "Have they run the blood?"

"Yeah. It was DeLuca's."

Chris saw a well-dressed couple standing outside the locked entrance, and set aside the ten thousand other questions she had. "Here we go."

Helen Moran usually didn't like the boys her daughter, Jane, brought home, but for once she'd found herself a nice, quiet boyfriend. He wore the most unusual cologne—it reminded Helen of the pomfrey cakes her aunt used to send her from England—and it seemed to fill the air whenever he came near her. Jane explained that she'd met him at the shelter where she'd been working off her community-service sentence.

He was so thin and tired he could speak only in a whisper, and Helen felt so bad about his being homeless that she had immediately offered to let him stay as long as he liked in their spare room.

Later she'd seen Jane go into the spare room, but Helen didn't mind. Her daughter was almost an adult, and certainly mature enough to have an intimate relationship with a man. She'd listened outside the door, but the sounds of pleasure Janey made reassured her. Her new boyfriend was obviously a very skillful lover: something every girl should have at least once in her life.

Helen had been a little startled when he'd come into her bedroom late that night, but then he'd whispered what he needed into her ear, and she'd moved over to make room for him. That he wanted to have sex with her didn't bother Helen at all. Janey was very young, of course, and she didn't have the experience her mother did with men. That and Helen hadn't been to bed with any man since her ex-husband had left her for a twenty-two-year-old bookkeeper's assistant at his accounting firm.

The sex she had with Jane's new boyfriend had blown Helen's mind. She'd done things with him that she'd never imagined, much less tried. She was still a little sore from the long hours he'd used her.

If only they had time to do it again before they left.

Jane did look a little pale as they got ready to go out, but Helen put that down to her daughter's endless obsession with dieting. She was so happy that was all over. From now on things were going to be so good for her and Jane. Her new boyfriend would take care of them. He'd take care of everything.

"You remember where he wants you to park the car?"

Helen asked. She would be busy watching the side door for him, and she worried that Jane might forget his instructions.

"Sure, Mom. Right next to the emergency exit." Jane's smile widened as he came into Helen's bedroom. "Did you sleep okay?"

He nodded.

"That suit never looked that good on my ex-husband." Helen wanted to hug him, but settled for a touch on his arm. "Can I get you anything before we go?"

He curled his hand around her neck and drew her closer. Helen's eyes closed as he kissed her neck, and she moaned when she felt his teeth pierce her skin. It was over too soon for her, and she clutched at him until he removed her hands and reached for Jane.

Once he had been satisfied, Helen drove them all to the boutique downtown where she worked. She closed the shop at five, but as the manager, she had the alarm codes and the master keys to the building, so there was no problem getting back in through the service entrance. The old basement door had been painted over, but he was so strong it opened for him the first time he pushed on it. Once he had walked through the old underground passage that ran the length of the street, he came back up into the shop.

"Move the car to the side of the building," he whispered to Jane. "Keep the engine running."

After her daughter left, Helen went to stand with him by the windows and watched the people going into the gallery next to the boutique. "Are you sure you don't want me to go with you?"

"You will wait here." As he spoke, the sweet smell of pomfrey cakes intensified. "When Jane returns from the airport, you will forget everything that has happened be-tween us."

"Wait. Jane. Forget." Helen's eyes teared as part of her,

the part that loved him, fought the need to obey. "But can't Janey and I come with you?"

"No, madam." He looked through the window. "I leave your country tonight."

As all of the seigneurs had not yet arrived for *le conseil supérieur*, Geoffrey invited Michael and Alex to join him that evening for an informal get-together with the ones who had.

"Gilanden will wish to play billiards, and Tristan will mope until someone plays a song on the pianoforte that he can sing to. Which would be none of those that have been written since music was invented." Geoff laughed at his own joke and turned to Alex. "Are you musical, my lady?"

"Sorry, I can't even whistle in tune." Alex glanced through the window and spotted Braxtyn out in the gardens. "If you boys don't mind, I think I'll go hang out with Brax. She promised to show me how not to get lost." When Michael gave her a puzzled look, she added, "Walking through Geoff's labyrinth."

Michael kissed her brow. "Enjoy yourself."

Braxtyn and several of her maids were gathering flowers in baskets, but as soon as she saw Alex coming toward her she handed hers to one of the women. "Good evening, my lady. I see you successfully evaded the men."

"They're going to shoot pool and gossip," she told her. "And someone named Tristan is probably going to sing."

"Perhaps we should call it a most fortunate escape." She winked. "I had intended to come in search of you. Geoff and I were hoping we could persuade you to look in on some of our patients in the hospital."

Alex perked up. "You have a hospital? Here?"

Braxtyn nodded. "'Twas necessary to convert the basement level into a ward for the burn victims. Lord Gabriel and Lady Nicola have been bringing survivors of Brethren attacks to us from France, Spain, and Italy for some months now."

"Michael told me," she said. "Are you having any problems with the patients?"

"To be frank, yes." Braxtyn's smile faded. "Many come to us with wounds that do not heal. Geoffrey told me today that you were once a surgeon who specialized in repairing humans with such wounds. I do not know if you can do anything for our patients, but I would be grateful if you would examine them."

Alex agreed, stopping only to retrieve her medical case and one of her white lab coats to wear over her dress. She didn't need the coat but felt it gave her an appearance of authority—something she always needed when dealing with injured Kyn. She found a clip in one of her coat pockets and put the end of it in her mouth as she began dragging back her curls and twisting them with both hands.

"How many have you got down there?" she asked around the clip.

Braxtyn thought for a moment. "Twenty at present, I believe. Lord Gabriel and his lady are tracking a cell in Portugal that is attacking Kyn strongholds there, so I expect at least a dozen more will be brought to us before the end of *le conseil supérieur.*"

Alex secured the bundle she'd made of her curls with the slide, and picked up her case. "Who's been treating the patients who are here now?"

"Geoff and I do what we can." Braxtyn spread her hands out. "Under the circumstances, bringing human physicians here is dangerous, and we have no doctors among the Kyn, my lady. At least, not until you came to us."

Alex nodded. Because of their unique physiologies, the Kyn couldn't go to hospitals or have any sort of conventional medical treatment. "How serious are their injuries?"

"Very grave, but it is their mental state that concerns me." The other woman's expression grew sad. "Two lost limbs during the attacks on their strongholds, and chose to end their lives. Another, Lady Blanche, was so badly burned that she is permanently disfigured. I fear she is on the brink of suicide."

"We'll just see about that." Alex headed for the door.

Two of Geoffrey's men stood guard on either side of a wide elevator in an unoccupied section of the house. They bowed to the women but remained silent and alert.

Once they were inside and the doors closed, Alex saw multiple lights on the control panel. "How far down is this basement?"

"Geoff had Sir Robert put in four lower levels, and about a dozen escape tunnels," Braxtyn said. "He's never trusted the stability of the human government, not since Cromwell banned Christmas. That, and he never forgot what happened to the families who were left behind during the *jardin* wars."

"That was a long time ago," Alex said. "Do you really need to post guards *inside* the house?"

Braxtyn nodded. "In these times, with the way the Brethren have been attacking us . . . I think you will understand better when you see what the zealots have done to our people. It is why our seigneurs are prepared to take drastic measures."

"How drastic?"

"Most of the Kyn are in favor of war," Braxtyn said. "Geoff and I do not support counterattacks on the Brethren, as they would surely expose our kind to the world. But so many have died, and their blood kin are very angry."

"Michael and I are on your side." Alex wondered what the other woman would say if she knew that Alex's brother had once been a Catholic priest, used by the order to get to her and Michael. "We'll do what we can to keep the peace."

The "hospital" was more like a barracks, if a luxury hotelier had designed and furnished it. Crystal chandeliers cast sparkling light over two rows of large antique beds. Fine lace draperies cascading down from carved posts and canopies gave the beds' occupants a measure of privacy. Bowls of pretty potpourri occupied three-legged tea tables between each bed. Dozens of Persian rugs covered the floor, making an expensive patchwork under Alex's feet. At the end of the makeshift ward, classical music played soft and low from an elaborate, high-tech stereo system.

Nowhere did Alex see nurses, orderlies, medical supplies, or anything useful in treating patients. Then she breathed in and realized why Braxtyn had set so many bowls of potpourri next to the beds.

"Are you keeping any dead bodies down here?" Alex asked as she went to the first bed.

Braxtyn was breathing through her mouth. "Not unless someone has died since this morning."

Alex drew back the edge of the bed drape. "Hello," she said to the man inside. "I'm Dr. Alex Keller."

"Cyprien's lady," he said, his voice rasping. "I have heard tales of you."

"Don't believe the ones that say I have horns and a pointy tale," Alex said. "I only grow those during a full moon." There didn't seem to be anything wrong with the man, other than that he'd been buried under a huge pile of bedclothes, but the stench of decomposing flesh radiating from him almost gagged her. "I'm going to take a look at you, okay?"

He nodded and closed his eyes.

She drew back the top coverlet and exposed a blood-soaked mound of linen someone had layered over his abdomen. She lifted one side of it, looked at the gaping horror that had once been his torso, and gently put it back in place.

She turned to Braxtyn. "How long has he been like this?"

"Three weeks," the man answered her. "It will not close, my lady, no matter how much I feed."

"What he says is true." Braxtyn sighed. "The wound remains as it was when he first came to us."

Alex could smell something else, something that tainted

the ghastly smell of the wound. "How much blood does he take every night?"

"He is too weak to feed from a human, so we give him bagged blood." Braxtyn thought for a moment. "He uses three, sometimes four bags."

"He's bleeding out about that much, too, isn't he?" Alex put her hand on the patient's forehead, which burned against her skin. To the warrior, she said, "I'll be back to see you later."

"It is good of you to look after us, my lady," he murmured, drifting off.

Alex went to the next bed, which was occupied by a woman with second- and third-degree burns covering her legs, hips, and hands. She remained unconscious, even when Alex carefully rolled her onto her side. The gunshot wound to her back was large and still open and bleeding.

"Is it the same thing with this one?"

"She takes less blood, but we must change her mattress several times a week," Braxtyn said.

Alex made rounds of the entire ward, and found nearly all of the patients with open wounds and terrible burns. She couldn't rouse a third of them, and the rest responded to her with varying degrees of weakness and apathy.

She asked Braxtyn only the most necessary questions, and after seeing the last patient she walked out of the ward and into an adjoining room. She looked around at the stacks of linens, pillows, and towels being stored there and tried to get a grip on her temper.

"My lady?" Braxtyn hovered in the open doorway. "Do you think you can help them?"

"Come in here and shut that, please." Alex waited until she did. "I need a room set up as a surgical suite. This one will work. I'll write a list of the medical equipment, supplies, nurses, and chemicals—"

Her eyes widened. "Chemicals?"

"—to make Darkyn anesthetic," Alex continued. "I don't operate on patients when they're awake, and some of them are too far gone to do the autohypnosis thing. You have to get all of this here as quickly as possible. Can you do that, or do I need to talk to someone else?"

"I can, but . . . I do not understand," Braxtyn said, glancing back over her shoulder and then back at Alex. "Are you quite certain that you must operate on them? Surely with time and care they will eventually heal."

"Care? What care?" Alex shouted. "You've been wrapping them in bedsheets and letting them bleed out and rot away."

Geoffrey's wife stared at her slippers. "This is all that we could do for them."

"Jesus." Alex pressed the heels of her hands against her eyes before she let them drop. "I don't know how things work in England, but in my country we don't care for people like this. We call what you're doing depraved indifference. Right before we throw your ass in prison."

Braxtyn's eyes flared. "For your information, my lady, I have cut open my own arms and poured my blood onto their wounds countless times, trying to heal them. It has always worked on other wounded Kyn in the past, but for them it does nothing."

"Can't you smell it?" she demanded. "Don't you know why they're not healing?"

"No, I do not." Braxtyn made an angry gesture toward the ward. "Why do you think I asked you to come down here and attend them? We Kyn have no doctors. We *always* heal."

Alex felt like slapping her. "Not from wounds still contaminated with copper, you don't."

Braxtyn looked stricken. "But I checked their wounds when they were brought in. I found no bullets in them."

"It's not copper from bullets. I can't even see where it's coming from, but I'd know that smell anywhere." Realizing that she'd been unfair to the other woman, Alex took a deep breath. "I'm sorry. You're right; you couldn't have known. I shouldn't have yelled at you. This isn't your fault."

"Lady Alex, you may shout at me all night long, as often as you wish," Braxtyn assured her. "Only please, help them. I will obtain whatever you need. You have but to say it and it will be yours."

Alex checked her watch. "If you can get what I need delivered in the next three hours, I'll start operating tonight."

Chapter 7

"I'd be more interested in making an offer if I could see the actual contents of the manuscript," Mortimer Cuzman said, fogging the glass top of the display case with his choppy breath as he peered at the gem-encrusted cover. "Brother de Crewes's work is described in all the appraisal books. I could tell right away if it is a forgery."

"As I said, the book is too fragile to be handled, but we've had it authenticated by six different experts on illuminated artworks." Chris's cheeks felt numb from the effort it took to maintain an interested smile. "I could arrange a private showing for you tomorrow, perhaps. Do you live in Atlanta, Mr. Cuzman?"

"New Jersey. I flew in from Newark this afternoon for the Renaissance exhibit at the arts center downtown." The old man licked his dry lips while he plunged one liver-spotted hand into his trousers pocket.

Chris stepped back and reached inside her jacket.

The elderly collector produced a somewhat creased business card, which he dropped on top of the display case. "You can reach me at the number on the back. I won't pay a penny over one hundred thousand, and I have to see the entire book and have my own experts authenticate it."

Chris slipped her hand out of her jacket. "Thank you, Mr. Cuzman. I'll pass your offer along to the owner. May I show you anything else?"

"However clever they are, forgeries don't appeal to me, young woman. Good evening." With a jab of his cane into the carpet, Cuzman pivoted and hobbled off to the entrance.

"He knew the paintings were fake, and he's certainly old enough," Dennis said over her earpiece. "Should I have one of the mobile units tail him?"

Chris nodded to a pair of women who went around the manuscript case to admire a triptych mounted on the wall behind it. "The Magician would never consult an appraisal book, or offer a hundred grand for a manuscript conservatively worth five million."

"So that's a no-go on the tail?"

"Yes, Dennis. That's a negative." When no one else approached the case, Chris decided to stop hovering and work her way around the gallery one more time.

Circulating allowed her to size up the guests, but she had already made the rounds four times, and no one but Cuzman had seemed promising. Now she was beginning to wonder if the Magician was deliberately waiting until after they closed the show to make his move.

"Ms. Renshaw." One of the local journalists, a reedy young woman with hot-pink spiked hair and a cool blue minidress, tapped her green fingernails against Chris's arm to get her attention. "Great show. I've never seen so much old church stuff in one place."

"I'm glad you're enjoying yourself." Chris couldn't remember the name the reporter had mumbled the first time they had spoken. "I apologize again for not allowing your photographer to take pictures of the displays."

"No problem. Most galleries don't unless they're hurting for patrons. I was more interested in who came tonight; my editor likes me to drop a lot of names in my column.

Speaking of which . . ." She made a discreet gesture toward the front of the gallery. "Can you please tell me who that gorgeous couple is?"

Chris stepped to one side to get a better look, and stopped breathing when she saw whom the reporter meant.

"I don't know the woman," she heard herself say, "but I believe the man's first name is Rob."

"Rob. Thanks." Pink spikes bobbed as the young woman hurried off toward the couple.

"Who's Rob?" Dennis asked over her earpiece. "One of ours?"

"Not now, Dennis." Chris stayed where she was and watched the couple's progress as they walked around the exhibits.

Rob wasn't wearing a jacket or tie, and he'd unbuttoned the collar and rolled up the sleeves of his khaki-colored shirt. His trousers, in a darker shade of coffee, appeared to be made of leather rather than cloth. The thin, uneven green line of his neck tattoo looked from a distance as if he'd wrapped a piece of barbed wire around his throat.

Chris's gaze shifted back to Rob's companion, who hung on his arm as if she were glued there.

Raven-haired and sloe-eyed, Rob's dark goddess had the sort of body that men wanted to see in a magazine foldout. She filled out every dart of her scarlet and silver lamé dress, which fit her so well it couldn't be anything but a tailored original. It was semitransparent, too; Chris saw the shadow of black lace move under the thin material as the woman turned to say something to Rob.

Whoever she was, she had money. Emeralds and topazes, some the size of quarters, hung from her ears and wrists and studded a complicated-looking belt made of gold around her narrow waist.

He couldn't even go one night without a woman?

Even as she thought that, Chris guessed the dark goddess

wasn't a one-night companion Rob had picked up somewhere. Judging from her appearance, she probably didn't
even know what the inside of a bar looked like. Rob had
probably gone to her mansion and begged for an audience.

Neither one of them had noticed Chris yet.

Walking over and greeting them would be impolite, Chris
decided. It would also be worth it, just to see the look on
Rob's face when he tried to explain to his high-maintenance
lady friend how he knew Chris—if he didn't pretend she was
a complete stranger right off the bat. But she didn't want to
meet his smoldering Mediterranean beauty—not now, not
ever. She could happily go the rest of her life without ever
knowing the woman's name.

*What if he's in a relationship with her? What if they're
engaged, or married?*

Chris knew that a man who wanted sex more than a pure
conscience would have no difficulty lying through his teeth
to get it. Rob's penthouse apartment might be his little love
nest away from home. But if he was regularly cheating on
that woman, he was out of his mind.

Chris saw Rob's head turning in her direction, and spun
on her heel. Wildfire anger burned through her, scalding her
from the inside out. This situation made it impossible to
think or work rationally. She needed to take a few minutes
and pull herself together before Rob brought over his beauty
and tried to have another cozy chitchat with her.

*Did you use the same lines on her when you two met? Did
you go to whatever snobby country club she belongs to and
ask her to dance? Did you tell her that you wanted her more
than you could say?*

This was unacceptable. She had a job to do; she couldn't
let irrational, jealous rage distract her like this. She'd gone
to bed with Rob an hour after she'd met him—what the guys
in the Chicago office called pulling a four-one-niner. That
gave her exactly zero right to be treated as anything else.

"Dennis," she murmured, knowing her voice would be picked up by the microphone hidden behind the frame of the painting in front of her.

"Yes, ma'am."

She pretended to wipe off some nonexistent dust from one scroll of the frame. "I've got to grab some aspirin. Let the others know I'm taking five."

"No problem."

Chris made her way to the manager's office, slipping inside and locking the door behind her. The state she was in shocked her. Her hands shook, her heart pounded, and she still couldn't catch her breath. Fortunately she wasn't wearing a sound transmitter, and Dennis hadn't bugged the manager's office, so he wouldn't hear her hyperventilating.

She took off her jacket, hanging it on the back of the door, and sat on the edge of one of the client chairs. She had five minutes to pull herself together, and she was going to need every second of it.

Robin had watched Chris Renshaw pretending to be an art dealer for some time before she noticed him and the contessa from the other side of the gallery.

Special Agent Chris Renshaw, he corrected himself as she retreated to a room at the back of the place. *An undercover agent with America's version of Scotland Yard. Agent* sounded especially ridiculous, as if she were a spy. She wouldn't be called a constable or an inspector. No, in this country they called their investigators detectives or cops.

That was a particular thorn in his side: He'd slept with a cop. He, Robin of Locksley, the greatest thief of all time, had rested in the arms of the enemy.

I might as well have taken a Brethren to bed.

"That scowl on your face makes me think the woman with the titian locks is your Agent Renshaw," the contessa said. "She was staring at you just before she scurried off to hide."

"So she was." Robin guided his companion around a persistent young woman with an appalling head of pink hair and led her to the case containing *The Maiden's Book of Hours*. One glance told him it was the book Brother Crewes had presented to the king just before the greedy bastard had sold Marian to Guisbourne.

Robin was more interested in the door to the office where Chris had disappeared. It remained closed.

"It is such a beautiful thing," Salva murmured, examining the manuscript through the glass. "I can see why you have coveted it all these years." She gave him a quizzical look. "But, *caro*, why have you not taken it before now?"

"It was stolen from me and given to my cousin during my human lifetime, and then pilfered from his household and taken out of the country," Robin said, watching the office door. He didn't care for the fact that Chris had come to Atlanta only to catch him, and had baited the trap with the one prize that had always eluded him over the years. Still, it made no difference. No one had ever captured him, not once since he had turned to the outlaw life seven hundred years ago; she would fail just as thoroughly as all the others.

What he could not accept, what he would not tolerate another moment, was her hiding from him. She couldn't ignore him like this, though, as if nothing ever happened between them. He had allowed her into his home. He had been her lover. He had slept in her *arms*.

The contessa was speaking to him, and Robin frowned. "What did you say?"

"I asked if you tried to recover it from the original thief who took it from England," Salva said.

Robin forced himself to answer her in a civil fashion. "At the time it was stolen from my cousin, I had to flee the country for my own reasons. It was fifty years before I had the means and time to track the thief. He sold it to a convent in Rome, but it was again stolen from there and resold to the Vatican. It disappeared from their secret archives, then was taken and sold in France, and then Spain, and then Germany." His hands curled into fists. "Each time it surfaced in the centuries after, some bloody mortal always got to it before I could."

"How greedy and inconvenient humans can be." The contessa trailed her scarlet-nailed fingertips over the glass. "I am happy that it will be yours at last, my lord. Shall I go and have the female give it to you after the show, or would you prefer she personally deliver it to your stronghold? Perhaps I could persuade her to crawl on her knees on her way to you there."

Robin couldn't believe Chris had not yet come out. Not another second would he wait for this faithless mortal to acknowledge his presence.

"I shall see to her," he told Salva. "Wait here."

Robin strode to the office, but found the door locked when he tried it. A simple twist of his hand using his Kyn strength broke the locking mechanism and allowed him to enter the room.

Chris Renshaw straightened as soon as he closed the door behind him. He twisted the knob again to jam it shut. "You can't come in here."

"Yet I have." He regarded her steadily as he deliberately shed his scent, surrounding her with it. "I had expected you would come and greet me when I arrived. Unless perhaps you have gone blind since last night?"

"I can see fine." Her eyes remained clear, her pupils normal as she offered him a brief, polite smile. "I apologize for not saying hello. I didn't notice you coming in."

That proved beyond a doubt to him that she could resist *l'attrait*. "You are a better liar than that, madam."

"I don't know what you're talking about, Rob. I have to

get back to the show." She stepped toward him and glanced up when he didn't move out of her way. "Excuse me."

"No, I do not excuse you," he said, enjoying the way his tone startled her. "I know you saw me. Why did you not come to me?"

Chris backed away from him. "All right, I did catch a glimpse of you and your companion when one of the press asked me about you. I didn't come over because I felt awkward about approaching you."

"Awkward."

"I didn't want to say anything that might embarrass you in front of your date." She had to force her next words out. "I didn't mean to be rude. Again, I apologize."

"You were protecting me. I see." Robin advanced on her. "Tell me, what did you think would embarrass me most? That you might slip up and mention that you used me for sex? Or perhaps that you never told me your full name? Or that you left my bed this morning without bothering to wake me or say farewell?"

"I wrote you a note—"

"Oh, God, yes, how could I forget? The effusive, affectionate, one-line note of thanks." He had her pinned against the desk now, and leaned down until their faces were only a breath apart. "I've not earned such an unstinting amount of gratitude since the last time I held a door open for an elderly woman using a cane."

"Rob."

"Robin. *That* is my name. Say it. Say all of it."

"Robin." Her lashes came down, hiding her eyes from him. "Listen, I've never done anything like that, and I really didn't know what to do except leave. I told you, I don't pick up guys in bars. I don't have one-night stands."

"There, now, *that* has a ring of truth to it." He used a finger to trace the edge of her blouse's front placket. "But technically speaking, I wasn't a one-night stand, was I? You didn't stay the night." He wove his fingertip in and out of the row of buttons. "By my calculations, love, you owe me two more hours. I'd like to collect."

"I can't—" She stopped as he brought his hand up and used his thumb to pop off the first button at the top of her blouse, and her throat worked as she swallowed. "Don't do this, Robin."

"Why not?" He circled the second button, watching the frantic throb of her pulse hammer in the hollow between her collarbones. "You liked it well enough last night. You put my hands on you. You wanted me to do it." The second button fell on the desk.

"That was then. This is my job."

"Your job." He moved his fingers down to the third button. "You didn't tell me what that was, either."

"Someone is going to come looking for me any minute," she warned.

"Let them try."

"Robin." She put her hand over his, trapping his fingers between her cold palm and her warm body. "Please stop."

Her indifference had shocked him; her lies had enraged him; but the manner in which her voice quavered over the *please* struck him like a burning mace to the side of the head.

He looked into her eyes, as wounded by her fear as her deception. "Did it truly mean nothing to you?"

"Maybe it started out that way," she said slowly, "but when I woke up and saw you sleeping next to me, and remembered . . . I didn't know I would feel like that." Her shoulders rounded, and she stared at the floor. "I didn't even think about you, not really. I got dressed as fast as I could, and I ran."

"You can't regret being with me," he said, shaken. He ran a piece of her hair through his fingers and looked all over her face. "Not how we were together." When she didn't reply, he put his arm around her waist and pulled her against him. *"Chris."*

"No. No, I don't." She spoke as if she were ashamed of that fact. Then her expression cleared, and she touched his cheek. "You were better than any fantasy I've ever had."

Robin's confusion doubled. "If that is true, why did you run away?"

"Haven't you ever done something amazing and dangerous and exciting," she asked, "that you later wished you'd never done at all? Because you know it could change everything you have, everything you are?"

"So you ran away because you wanted more." Bitter memories made him laugh. "Yes, actually, I have done that myself." Robin urged her closer, folding her against him, and rested his chin against the top of her head. "I believe this is where my severely bruised pride takes a tumble."

"It's not you. It's me. My life. My choices." Chris tilted her head back and kissed his cheek. "I am glad you understand. I'll never forget you, or the night we spent together."

Now she thought he was being understanding. Accepting. Happy to slink off into the night and leave her to her sting operations and undercover work. But at least he had the comfort of knowing that she would never forget having sex with him.

If he left this room without throttling her, Robin thought, it would be a miracle.

"Before you send me on my way," he said carefully, "and go back to living your life as it was, there is something else I want you to remember." He put his hands around her waist, lifted her off her feet, and brought her mouth to his.

Chris tried to push him off for all of five seconds before her hands shifted and wound around his neck and her lips parted for his tongue.

Robin groaned. She might look like a posh barrister, his Chris, but she kissed like a Persian courtesan. As she had last night, she met his hunger by offering her own. Her soft, silky mouth tugged and caressed; her tongue stroked and tasted.

His anger had not vanished, and Chris's generous response added resentment to the ire he felt. He knew how to use finesse with a female, but she had brought forth the brute in him, and he took it out on her mouth. She didn't go passive, however. She met his fury with an affectionate indulgence, catching his lip between the edge of her teeth or stroking his face with her fingers, petting him, as if she meant to dare him to do more, take more.

After centuries of embracing softly yielding human females willing to meet his every need, the erotic challenge of kissing this one drove Robin wild. No one had ever made him feel this, and he would not let it end. To hell with the manuscript, the FBI, humanity, the Kyn, and the rest of the bloody world. She would not dismiss him from her life. He would find a way to win her heart.

"Wait." She gasped the word between ferocious kisses. "Fire."

He found he had to literally wrench his mouth from hers in order to hear her over the miserable clanging sound in his brain. "What?"

"Alarm." She tore free of his hands and heaved in a breath, staggering a little as she went around him. *Fire alarm.*

Chapter 8

Chris couldn't get out of the office, not until Robin reached past her and jerked the door open. As soon as he did, she heard men shouting and women screaming beneath the earsplitting screech of the fire alarm. A crackling sound drowned out the hiss of water spraying from the ceiling, but she saw no flames or smoke in the air.

As she came around the corner she had to swerve to avoid a huge cage of jagged glass. Inside, three people huddled on the floor, their clothes covered with what looked like white flour. Their teeth chattered as they held on to each other and called for help. All around the gallery the guests were caught in a dozen other identical cages.

"Hold on. We'll get you out." Chris grabbed the bars, and the cold, slick bars stung her palms. She pulled her hands away and stared at the water on them.

The cages weren't made of glass, but ice.

Robin looked up. "It's the water from the fire sprinkler system," he told her, his mouth tight. "The spray has been frozen."

Chris saw a thick column of ice at the top of each cage attached to the metal heads of the sprinklers in the ceiling. The frozen carpet crunched as she walked around it, and she saw a thick layer of ice crystals covering almost everything else in the gallery.

"How could it freeze inside like this?" Disbelief made her spin back and forth as she looked for a rational explanation. The air felt so cold that breathing in made her teeth ache. "Atlanta doesn't have blizzards. This is crazy. It's *April*."

Ice shattered as a short, stocky blond man dressed in red leathers broke out of one of the cages and trotted over. Chris recognized him as the same man who had tried to get Rob's attention at the club. As soon as he stopped before them, the smell of spicy hot chocolate stung her cold nose.

"My lord," the blond said in a low, rough British accent, " 'twas done by Kyn."

"By one Kyn," Robin agreed, his accent suddenly much thicker. "This is Guisbourne's work."

"What are you talking about?" Chris's gaze bounced between the men's angry expressions. "Who's Guisbourne?"

The blond ignored her. "I did not see his face. He set off the water system somehow, and used his talent to freeze the streams. Once the mortals and I were trapped, he smashed the case and helped himself to the book."

Chris turned toward the display case containing the manuscript, now an empty, shattered box. The frozen gallery had sent her reeling, but this shut down everything inside her. Five million dollars' worth, gone like that.

On her watch, no less. She wouldn't be bounced out of the bureau. She'd be tarred and feathered and hung from the nearest flagpole.

You win, Magic Man.

"Cyprien banished him at the winter tournament," she heard the blond saying to Robin. "To defy the seigneur's order of exile would be signing his own death warrant."

The bizarre references Robin's friend made finally dented the roaring in Chris's head. She'd just lost a priceless, irreplaceable part of history to the best thief in the world, and he was babbling as if he'd just stepped out of a role-playing game.

"He has nothing left to go to, Will," Robin replied. "His seneschal is dead, his Saracens deserted him, and his *jardin* was burned out. All he has left is his vengeance."

Chris put her hands against her ears to try to block out his voice. This didn't feel like a drug-induced hallucination should, but what else could it be?

"Why would he do this instead of challenging you directly?" the blond named Will asked.

"He knows I would kill him." Robin walked over to the broken case and touched the empty velvet-covered pedestal inside. "This is more personal than a duel. He could not have her in life, so he would keep from me the only likeness of her that exists." All the emotion left Robin's voice. "Track him. Now."

Chris shook off the paralyzing shock as she remembered her own people. She went back to the storeroom and found Dennis and the other techs trapped in cages of white ice. A thick layer of frozen foam covered all of the monitoring equipment.

"Agent Renshaw." Dennis looked relieved. "Something triggered the chem units we set up over the computers, and dumped foam all over everything. Then things got really weird and it froze. You okay?"

"Things got weird out there, too. But yeah, I think I am." Chris gave him the once-over to assure herself he wasn't wounded. "Have you seen Agent Hutchins?" Maybe Hutch would know what the hell had caused all this.

"As soon as the alarm sounded he ran in here with Agent Alpert, but then the foam started pouring down and freezing." Dennis rubbed the sides of his arms with his hands. "Alpert went out to the gallery, but two guys came in, grabbed Hutch, and dragged him out of here." He poked the frozen foam separating them. "You didn't happen to see a hacksaw anywhere, did you?"

"I'll get some help." All the phones in the storeroom were frozen, so Chris went back out into the gallery, where Robin was breaking loose the ice bars of one cage. Chris tried to do the same to the ice closest to her, but discovered she couldn't budge the thick, frozen column. The people inside the cages were starting to shiver and pale, Chris saw, and she ran back to the office, the only room in the gallery that hadn't been frozen over, to get to the phone.

Robin had smashed out the bars of five cages of ice by the time Will returned.

"Guisbourne's scent disappeared in the street outside," his seneschal told him. "He must have used a car to escape."

"Did you disable the telephone lines?" When Will nodded, Robin felt a little better. "Contact the *jardin*. We will need a dozen men here while we clean up this mess and attend to the humans. Alert our friends at the police department as well."

Marigold suffused the air. "I regret to say that your men cannot come to your aid, my lord."

Robin faced the contessa, who stood flanked by four armed Kyn warriors. The sly smile on her lips confirmed his suspicions, but he gave her a chance to deny them. "You were a part of this?"

"I intended only to take the manuscript from you," Salva said. "Unfortunately, it seems that Nottingham had a better plan than I."

Robin had never hit a woman in his life, something he now regretted deeply. "Why do you want the book?"

"My family bought it from Nottingham when he came to settle in Italy. My father made a gift of it to my younger sister, Beatrice, when she took her vows. 'Twas the only earthly possession she ever treasured, and upon her death it was supposed to come to me." Something ugly moved in the contessa's dark eyes. "I have waited seven hundred years for this night."

Robin held on to his temper. "Obviously, my lady, you will have to wait a little longer. Now, if you will permit me—"

"I have just sent word to all of my warriors to capture your men and take control of your stronghold," Salva told him, as if he hadn't spoken. "I have also secured your mortal female's partner as another hostage. You will find Nottingham, retrieve the manuscript, and bring it back to me."

"You do not command me, madam." Robin eyed her guards. "If you wish to hunt down my cousin, send your own men after him."

"My men have other responsibilities." Salva made a quick gesture, and suddenly four copper swords appeared in the hands of her guards. "It should be no trouble for you to retrieve the book. But if you need more reason to pursue Nottingham, consider the lives of all the Kyn and humans under your rule. One call from me, and my men will begin executing them, twenty at a time."

Robin knew the contessa well enough to assume she was not making an idle threat. "I thought you named me your friend, Salvatora."

"A woman can have no friends in this world, my lord. Not if she wishes to survive." She gestured at Will. "You may have your seneschal verify that I speak the truth, if you like."

Robin nodded to Will, who took out his mobile phone and dialed a number. He spoke for a few moments, then ended the call.

"They permitted Sylas to speak to me, my lord," Will said, his voice strained. "It is as she says. Her men have captured the *jardin*, and are holding all of our people in the underground tunnels."

Chris gave up on the phone in the manager's office after finding no dial tone and checking the connections. The line had been cut or was dead. She remembered the two agents watching the front of the building; they might not have been affected by the bizarre freeze-over inside the gallery. She headed for the entrance, only to stop when she saw four men armed with swords surrounding Robin and his girlfriend.

"You will call me at your stronghold as soon as you have secured the book," the woman was saying. "We will arrange an exchange point, and then my men and I shall leave your territory peacefully and never trouble you again. You have my word, my lord."

Robin's violet eyes had somehow changed color; now they were the color of new pennies. "Your word means nothing to me anymore, Contessa."

Contessa. My lord. They spoke to each other as if they were acting out parts for some sort of live-action Dungeons & Dragons game, Chris thought, and seriously considered drawing her weapon and placing them all under arrest. But the long-bladed swords the men around the "contessa" held appeared to be razor-sharp, and if they were real, the last thing she wanted to do was provoke them into using them on her or the people in the gallery.

Maybe it's some kind of new gang scenario for delusional adults.

Before Chris could decide on an alternative course of action, the contessa said something in what sounded like Italian, and left the gallery. Chris followed them, stopping only when Robin called her.

"Where is she going?" she asked him. "Who's Nottingham? Is he working with this guy Guisbourne?"

"I shall explain everything, but you must come with me now."

"I can't leave these people like this. I have to call the police." Chris heard the sound of a siren approaching, and relaxed a little. "Looks like someone else did. We still have to stay to help them get these people out and give statements."

"The police." He swore softly, using a language Chris didn't recognize, and then called out for Will. The blond nodded to him and walked out through the front entrance. Robin then turned to her, his eyes still a bright, almost glowing copper color, and his pupils constricted so tightly they appeared like slits.

"What kind of drugs are you on?" she demanded.

"None." He rubbed his eyes, and when he took his fingers away his pupils were round and dark again, although a shiny copper ring still encircled his amethyst irises. "Chris, I know you are an agent of the FBI."

She stopped worrying about the effects the drugs he'd taken were having on his eyes. So much for her cover. "Could you say that a little louder? I don't think everyone in the gallery heard you."

"There is more I must tell you."

"There always is." She rubbed her eyes. "How involved in this robbery are you? Is it part of this weird role-playing game or gang thing you're running? Who told you I was an agent?"

"I had you investigated."

Chris took a moment to absorb that statement. "What are you on, meth? Crack?"

"I wished to know who you were. I learned that, and why you came to Atlanta to set up this show. I know why you brought *The Maiden's Book of Hours* here." He paused to look at the front entrance again. "I know because I am the Magician."

"*You're* the Magician." She watched him nod. "The master thief who has stolen hundreds of artworks from collectors and museums all over the world."

"Aye. 'Twas my doing. All of it."

She surveyed him. It might not be drugs. He might be under some sort of massive delusion. "I'd really love to know the name of your personal trainer and your plastic surgeon. Or your dealer."

"I am being honest with you," Robin insisted. "I came here tonight to steal the manuscript."

A laugh escaped her before she controlled it. "Sure you did. I suppose you also tripped the fire alarm and froze the sprinkler water while we were necking in the manager's office. Okay, so did you do it psychically, or were there some sort of remote-control ice machines involved?"

"I am not jesting with you." He put his hands on her shoulders. "I am the one you came for. The one you wish to imprison."

"Is this part of the game you've got going with your girlfriend and that guy Will? Did you roll the thief?" Before he could answer, Chris gave up the fight, clutching her sides as laughter spilled out of her.

"I know why you do not believe me," Robin said over the sound of her helpless mirth. "You seek an elderly man. I am too young."

She shook her head and held up her hand, hoping he would stop before he had her rolling on the floor.

"When I stole the Botticelli altarpiece from the cathedral in Naples," he told her, "I wrapped it in a red velvet curtain that I took from one of the confessionals. The Gauguin I took from Geneva had been framed with plaster covered in lead paint, so I removed it from the frame first. I replaced the van Gogh owned by that very famous actress with a forgery, so as not to upset her. She had just had another surgery on her back. I believe despite advice from experts that she still insists hers is the authentic painting."

Chris stopped laughing at his description of the Gauguin theft. "How could you . . . No one knows about the van Gogh, not outside the bureau."

He inclined his head. "So you will believe what I tell you now."

"Maybe you got into some confidential files, and I'd really like to know how, but you can't be the Magician." Absently she wiped at the tears of laughter clinging to her lashes. "He's been active since the nineteen forties. That would make you seventy years old, minimum."

He stepped closer. "What if I were to tell you that my father was the original Magician? That he trained me, and I took over his work after his death? That you and your colleagues have been looking for a dead man?"

She reached into her jacket. "I don't want you to say anything else to me." When he frowned, she took out her handcuffs. "Turn around and listen carefully." As she cuffed him, she continued, "Robin, I am arresting you on charges of grand theft, larceny, fraud, breaking and entering, transporting stolen property over state lines, and possession of stolen property. You have the right to remain silent." She finished informing him of his rights, and then asked, "Do you understand what I've told you?"

"Aye." As the first of the uniformed cops entered the gallery, his mouth flattened. "Now can we go?"

Will would see to the humans; of that Robin was sure. He had once used his talent to put to sleep an entire mob of vengeful mortals intent on burning Sherwood Forest to the ground. A small gallery would prove no challenge.

That left to Robin to handle Chris and the police officer she had drafted to escort them downtown.

"Seven Charlie one," their driver said over his radio. "Transporting suspect and federal agent from Peachtree Street art gallery to central booking."

Like any common criminal, Robin had been made to sit in the rear of the patrol car. The dim interior allowed him to assess what weapons were within Chris's grasp. He was thankful the patrolman wore his service pistol on his left hip, out of her reach.

He had to accomplish this without any blood being shed, especially hers.

Robin breathed in, taking in the sweet-sharp fragrance of Chris's body, and the salty tang of the cop's sweat. The two helped him shed his own scent, which slowly filled the interior of the car.

"Officer, what is your name?" Robin asked, leaning toward the mesh divider.

"Larry Kent," the cop answered slowly, looking at him in the rearview mirror.

Chris turned to look through the divider. "Keep quiet, Rob."

"I fear I feel very sick," he lied. In a more authoritative voice, he said, "Officer Kent, please pull this vehicle to the side of the road and stop there."

The patrolman nodded and left the road, braking on the shoulder until the unit came to a stop.

Rob broke in half the handcuffs binding his wrist, tore the mesh divider out of its frame, and seized Chris's arms from behind, holding her in place.

"Agent Renshaw is carrying a gun in a holster under her right arm," he told the cop. "Take it away from her and place it under your seat."

Kent reached into Chris's jacket, removed the nine millimeter, and stowed it beneath him.

"Thank you." Robin released his hold on Chris, who immediately went for the door handle and jumped out of the car.

She had crossed two hundred yards of uneven ground by

the time Robin caught up and seized her from behind. He lifted her kicking and clawing into his arms.

"Please stop," he said as he subdued her. "I know you are frightened, but you must listen to me." She went still, and he continued. "Everyone I care for, as well as your partner, will die unless I can get the manuscript to the contessa by morning." He shifted his hands to her shoulders and caressed them, hoping his touch would reassure her. "I need your help to do this. You were given information that I must have."

"Go to hell." Chris spun around and tried to run again.

Robin tackled her to the ground and pinned her there, blocking out the smells of damp grass, soil, and car exhaust with his own scent. "Someone must have told you that I would try to steal the manuscript, or you would not have brought it to Atlanta. What name did he use?"

She stared at his mouth before she averted her face. "I'm not telling you a damn thing. Get off me."

She'd seen his *dents acérées*. "I shall not hurt you. Give me his name, Chris."

She remained silent, and after several attempts to persuade her to speak Robin lifted his weight from her and pulled her to her feet.

Officer Kent walked over to them, his eyes still darkened by the effects of *l'attrait*. "Do you need some help with her, sir?"

"This man is an international fugitive," Chris said to Kent, almost shrieking the words. "He is kidnapping me. *Do something*."

"Do not believe what she says," Robin told the officer. He saw a long black car slowing and pulling up behind the patrol car. "Return to your vehicle and your regular duties. You will forget me, this woman, and everything that has happened since you arrived at the gallery."

The patrolman nodded and wandered back to his car.

"How did you make him do that?" Chris demanded.

"I promise you, I shall explain everything when this is over." He turned to Will as his seneschal walked up to them. "Were you able to deal with all of them?"

He nodded. "I sent the police back on patrol; they were most obliging. Our friends in the department will see to any records. The guests are locked inside the building. They will sleep until dawn, and have no memory of the attack. The ice should be melted by then, and then our friends will go 'round and finish tidying up." He made a casual gesture toward Chris. "She is the only one left."

"You're not drugging me." Newly outraged, Chris struggled to break Robin's hold.

"Tell me his name," Robin said, "and I shall release you."

"Let me have her, my lord," Will said, unsheathing a dagger. "She will tell me what you wish to know."

Chris's eyes shifted to the blade in Will's hand and then to Robin's face. "His name was Paul Sherwood. Now let go of me."

"I said I would release you," Robin told her. "I did not say I would do it now." As she began fighting him again, he held on to her and turned to Will. "Be aware that *l'attrait* has no affect on her whatsoever. I am none too sure that our talent does, either."

"I could kill her," his seneschal offered. "That would solve the problem."

Robin felt Chris stiffen against him. "He is only joking." He could do nothing more with her here, out in the open. "Take us back to the penthouse."

Chris fell silent once more, but did not struggle or try to escape again. Robin could almost hear the intensity of her thoughts as Will drove them back to the Armstrong building.

Along the way his seneschal made use of his mobile phone to place several calls.

"She told the truth. A Paul Sherwood left Hartsfield-Jackson International on a chartered flight for Rome," Will said after he ended the final call. "The charter was paid for by a Helen Moran. Our people at the airport are examining their security tapes to see if this Sherwood matches Guisbourne's description."

"He will," Chris said unexpectedly, her voice dull. "Helen Moran manages the clothing shop next to the gallery."

"Thank you," Robin said.

"If he's left the country, there's nothing you can do," she said, her tone changing to urgent, almost wheedling. "Let me go, and I'll alert Interpol. They'll arrest him as soon as he steps off the plane in Rome." When he didn't reply, she added, "Robin, that book is priceless."

He had once thought the same, until the contessa had made her hideous threat. Now all he could think of were the men and women who had served him so well, and how much more they were worth to him.

Once Will parked at the building, Chris made one more abortive attempt to run. Weary of her tricks, Robin swept her off her feet and carried her inside.

In the elevator, Robin deposited Chris back on her feet before he pried the remnants of her handcuffs from his wrists and handed them to Will.

"Were there any of our Kyn who were not at the stronghold when Salva's men took over?" he asked his seneschal.

"Fazio, Mason, and Sullivan were on guard duty here. Sylas said to give his love to Rebecca, so I think his wife must have gotten some of the humans and the other women out before they could secure them."

Robin nodded. Since the *jardin* wars, when the families of the warriors left behind were attacked and slain, the women of the Kyn had been trained to protect themselves and the humans who served them during any conflict.

"Rebecca will bring them to our friends in Marietta before she attempts to contact us." She would have much to say about the contessa's betrayal as well. "As soon as she reports in, I shall speak to her."

"Should we not call on our allies for assistance, my lord?" Will asked as he pocketed the twisted steel remnants of the cuffs. "Suzeraina Jayr could have her garrison here in a matter of hours."

Jayr. The legacy of his love and shame.

"No. I do not wish the suzeraina involved in this." The doors opened and he stepped out into the hall, frowning when Chris did not. "You cannot stay in the elevator all night, love. There is no place to sit but the floor."

She didn't move. "You took those cuffs off like they were made of plastic. You can make cops—anyone—do anything. You've got *fangs*." She looked from him to Will. "What *are* you people?"

Will glanced at Robin. "I shall prepare some tea."

"Make it strong and sweet. Everything will be all right, Chris. Come." Robin stepped back into the elevator and gently guided her out of it. Once he had her inside the apartment, he brought her to the settee by the windows and sat down with her. "I am sorry. We take care to be completely discreet when we are among humans, but there has been no time for the usual precautions tonight."

"Humans." She seemed bemused. "You belong to another species? Is that just a human suit you're wearing?"

"We were human once, long ago." He looked out at the city lights. "Will and I and others like us were soldiers. We fought in wars for many years. 'Tis said that God cursed us for the atrocities we committed in His name, for when we returned to our homelands we fell ill and died. Three days later we dug our way out of the ground, alive but vastly changed. We were much stronger and a great deal harder to kill. Very little could harm us, and any wounds that could be inflicted on us healed instantly."

Her face had gone completely white. "So you're . . . a zombie."

"Ah, no." Now he would have to tell her the rest of it. "We are much like you, except in how we feed. Once changed, we could no longer eat or drink ordinary fare. We needed the blood of humans to survive."

"How do you need it?"

"We feed on it."

Her eyebrows arched. "So you think you're vampires."

"We do not . . . We are not vampires as you know them from your books and movies." Robin tried to think of how to explain the Darkyn to her. "We do not kill humans for their blood. We are not evil. Sunlight, garlic, crosses, and wooden stakes cannot harm us. Sunlight irritates our eyes and makes us weary, but it does not burn us or reduce us to ash. We live in the night."

"Like zombies."

He shook his head. "We are not dead. The Greeks called us *vrykolakas*, the undead. We call ourselves Darkyn."

"But you heal instantly, you have fangs, and you drink human blood," she said, and when he nodded, her mouth thinned. "Is this part of this game you're playing? Did you switch my handcuffs and put those fangs on to make me believe it's real?"

"This is not a game. It is real. *I* am real." She didn't look convinced. "Let me show you." He allowed his *dents acérées* to emerge, and opened his mouth.

Chris didn't scream, run away, or faint. She looked at him, her expression solemn, her eyes burning in her pale face. "I can't help you with this, Robin, but I know there are good doctors out there who can. I'd like to take you to see one of them. He's treated other people who think that they're special beings like you. Will you let me do that?"

She didn't believe him. She thought he was inventing the entire tale.

"I shall demonstrate how we heal." Robin drew out his dagger and handed it to her and began rolling up his sleeve.

"This is real," she said, turning the blade over in her hands. "It's beautifully made."

"Our flesh is resilient. Usually copper is the only metal that can pierce it." He extended his forearm. "Cut me." When she didn't move, he smiled. "Please do leave my hand attached. I'm rather fond of it."

Chris lunged, knocking him to the floor and holding the dagger to his throat. "What if I cut you here?" she asked, pressing the edge in. "Is *that* going to heal instantly, Dracula?"

"I have not fed, so it will take a few moments." He felt the burn of the blade against his skin, and the coolness of his blood oozing from beneath it. "If you mean to kill me, you must stab me in the heart or cut off my head." When she didn't move, he added, "All the way through, love. Half measures don't work on my kind."

"I am through playing this game, Robin."

"So am I." And her wrath aroused him in a perverse way, Robin realized. He had not thought she would try to attack him with the blade. He had no idea what she would do next, and it excited him. Even with a dagger at his throat.

Somewhere near them metal hit the floor, and porcelain shattered. "Bloody hell."

"Stay where you are, Will. Whatever she does to me, you will not touch her." Robin kept his eyes on Chris's flushed face. "Kill me and it will be over. My seneschal will not harm you. But the contessa will see to it that hundreds will die—humans and Kyn, my entire *jardin*. One of them will be your partner."

She shook her head slowly. "I don't believe you. I don't believe any of this."

"If I give you proof, will you help me get the book?"

Chris straightened and drew the dagger away from his neck. He felt the wound on his neck close and disappear as she watched. Her eyes took on a glassy look, and she didn't protest when Will came over and carefully removed the dagger from her hand.

"It can't be real." She pushed herself off him and stood, her body swaying. "You can't be." She reached for a handhold, and then her eyes rolled up.

Will caught her before she hit the floor. "I'll make more tea."

Robin wanted to take her to bed, lie with her, and hold her until she awoke, but he had to strike a new bargain with the contessa. "Put her in my bedchamber," he told Will as he stood. "And bolt the door."

Chapter 9

Robin didn't waste another moment on impossible schemes, but called the contact number the contessa had given him at the gallery. She greeted him as if the events of the night had never happened, and listened without comment as he related what Will had discovered.

"Nottingham will be landing in Italy in a few hours," Robin said. "He is beyond my reach now. I cannot retrieve the manuscript for you."

Salva made an amused sound. "But of course you can, my lord. I am not an unreasonable woman, and it is perhaps better that we finish this where it began. I shall allow you more time for your journey."

"My journey."

"You will travel to Rome at once," she said smoothly. "Nottingham will think he has succeeded, so he should not be difficult for you to find. You and I will meet at my palazzo outside the city in forty-eight hours. You will deliver the manuscript to me, or I shall give the order for my men to execute all the hostages."

Images of defiant men being forced to their knees in front of a hooded executioner filled Robin's head. "Permit me to contact the high lord. He has people—"

"You will tell no one, my lord," Salva said, her voice sharp and cold. "Not if you wish your people to survive the night. When you journey to Rome, you will also take that mortal female, the FBI agent, with you."

Why would she wish him to take Chris to Italy? "We need not involve humans in our business."

"She is already involved," she replied. "Permit her to escape you and all she will do is alert the authorities here or in Italy. No one is to know about the manuscript or Nottingham. You will take very good care to keep her at your side."

"She will be a hindrance to me." Robin looked at Will. "I shall leave her here with my seneschal. He will keep her sequestered until my return."

"You do not think I shall act on my promises, my lord?" There was a pause, and then the contessa said, "Watch the screen on your phone."

The video she sent began to play on the view screen. It showed two of the contessa's warriors holding a large, wounded black man between them, and a third Kyn beating him. Blood dripped from the human's nose and mouth as he reeled under the blows.

"I've seen enough," Robin said. "Stop before you kill him."

The contessa's beautiful face appeared. "I shall see you and your human lover in Rome in two days. Be sure you have the manuscript, my lord. If you do not, her partner dies, and you will revisit every one of the happy memories you have of the *jardin* war trials."

The screen on the phone went blank.

"She would do not this thing unless she felt sure she could get away with it," Will said slowly. "Once she has the manuscript, she will kill you and Agent Renshaw. Then she can blame your deaths on Nottingham, or make up any story she likes."

Robin opened the weapons cabinet and took out his bow case. "Contact Jayr and Lucan, and tell them only that I am in Europe, and in my absence refugee Kyn have captured my stronghold. Ask them to send as many warriors as they can spare. Surround the keep, but do nothing for two days. If I do not call you by the end of the second, you must lead them in and save as many as you can."

Will's pale eyes narrowed. "While you die alone in Rome."

"I have lived more than seven lifetimes, old friend, and I am certain that death is ready for me. My task is to do whatever I must to protect Chris." Robin put a hand on his seneschal's shoulder. "You helped me build the stronghold; no one knows it as well as you. That gives you an advantage over the contessa's men. Use it. Remember how we routed the king's men in Sherwood. I know you will prevail."

"I shall earn your faith in me," Will promised. "But that bitch will not get away with this. As soon as our people are secure, I shall call the high lord and make him aware of her treachery. Then I shall hunt her down and take her head."

"You will be too busy for that." Robin checked his bow and adjusted the protective pads around it. "If I am slain, you are to take my place as suzerain."

He scoffed. "That is as likely as my assuming the throne of England."

"I have already advised Cyprien," Robin said as he closed the case. "He agreed with my choice. There will be no opposition."

"You are not jesting." Will's jaw sagged, and then he closed it with a snap. "My lord, if you have forgotten, my father was a smith and my mother a laundress. The only noble blood in my veins came from the mortal gentry I fed on whenever I could lure one of them into the woods. If not for you, I should have ended dangling from a rope at a crossroads. Pledging myself to you, taking vows, fighting in the

Holy Land, surviving death, being made Kyn—it surely saved me, but it did not make me another man. I was an outlaw. A thief."

"So was I." Robin handed him the case. "I am not dead yet, Will. There is still hope." He heard the door to his bedchamber rattle. "It seems my special agent has awoken. Call the airport and have a plane standing by."

Chris was looking for something she could use to pick the dead-bolt lock when Robin walked in.

"We are leaving now. We must go to Rome."

He was a raving lunatic, or a real live vampire. Which made him a raving lunatic, because Chris would commit herself to a mental hospital before she believed the latter.

Right now she had to get as far away from him as she could. "We're going after Paul Sherwood?"

"Nottingham." He said the name as if it were an incurable venereal disease. "I convinced the contessa to give us more time. We have two days to find him and retrieve the book before she executes the hostages."

He sounded rational, and Chris hadn't tried reasoning with him. He might be in a better emotional state to listen to her now.

"What if the contessa doesn't actually have any hostages?" she asked carefully. "Maybe she only told you that because she knew you'd believe her. Sometimes if you spend a lot of time playing fantasy games, they can seem very real."

He gave her an impatient look. "What must I do to convince you?"

"Robin, real crimes have been committed," she assured him. "Someone stole the manuscript. You're incredibly strong, and fast, and you can somehow control people. I saw the cut on your neck heal in a few seconds. Or maybe you made me think I did; I don't know."

"I cannot influence you," he said very calmly. "If I could, you would not be wasting my time arguing with me."

"Right." She didn't want to piss him off again. "Whoever you are, whatever you're involved in with these other people, I can't be a part of it. I'm a federal agent. My job is to arrest you. I don't think I can, not by myself, but it's my duty to try—and to keep trying. I can't help you commit more crimes. I can't go to Rome with you."

"I would leave you here if I could," he said, walking toward her. He stopped when she backed away. In a harsher voice, he added, "The contessa will have your partner killed if you do not accompany me to Rome."

"You're just saying that to make me come with you." When he said nothing, she threw up her hands. "Hutch is probably downtown right now, wondering where the hell I am. Robin, I can't just disappear in the middle of an operation like this. When I don't report in, they're going to assume that I've been abducted or killed. If the news gets wind of it, which they usually do, my face will be all over the television."

He took a mobile phone out of his pocket and tossed it on the bed. "I received a video from the contessa fifteen minutes ago. Watch it."

Chris didn't want to pander to his delusions, but she reached for the phone, flipped it open, and replayed the video sent with the last call. Bile surged in her throat as she watched her partner being beaten, and then the recording of the contessa's final message.

"Be sure you have the manuscript, my lord. If you do not, her partner dies . . . ."

She closed the phone. "He has a wife and two kids. Does she know that?"

"She cares for nothing but the book," he told her. "Chris—"

"It's all right." She slowly placed the phone back on the bed. "I'll go with you."

"We will see to it that Agent Hutchins is returned to his family," Robin said. "You have my word."

"I'll do whatever you want," she said. "But when this is over and Ray is safe, I'll see to it that you and the contessa go to jail for the rest of your lives."

He gave her an odd look. "You cannot imprison a prisoner, love."

Robin escorted her downstairs, where Will was waiting with the car. He refused to let her use the car phone to call her parents or anyone else. Although Chris had no intention of endangering Hutch's life by doing something stupid, she thought she might try to somehow tip off the bureau as to their situation. There were important protocols that were followed whenever agents were taken hostage, and while there were no guarantees, Chris knew their best chance of survival was with the bureau's hostage negotiators handling the contessa.

Robin never let her out of his sight, however, holding her hand as they walked into the airport and putting his arm around her when they checked in at the gate. It wasn't until he whisked her onto the private jet that she realized she wasn't going to be able to pass a message to another passenger.

There *were* no other passengers.

"I don't have a passport," she said, feeling a little desperate as he guided her down the aisle and to a pair of seats in the center of the jet. "They won't let me through customs without it."

"We don't need passports, love." As the jet taxied down the runway, he buckled her seat belt over her. "You look exhausted. You should try to sleep. We will need to move quickly once we reach Rome."

Once the jet was airborne, a man dressed in a flight attendant's uniform came back, and Robin left her and went to speak with him for a few moments.

She stared through the window, watching the lights of Atlanta shrink, thousands of embers dying in the darkness. She was really doing this, really leaving the country with a man who thought he was a vampire. Or something like a vampire.

What did he call himself? *Vrykolakas*. Darkyn. She had never heard of an RPG by either name, but new ones were always coming onto the market. She wondered what her department chief would have to say when she finally filed her report. That full-grown adults could delude themselves into playing a real-life version of some game seemed far-fetched to her, and she was now being made to play her own part in it.

When Robin came and sat down beside her, she asked, "Do you own this plane, or did you charter it?"

"I own this and two others."

If he had that much money, they probably didn't need passports, Chris thought, her heart sinking. "I need my purse and my badge, just in case we don't make it past customs."

He put his hand over hers. "We will, love."

Chris watched his fingers rest against the spaces between hers. She wanted to slap him; she wanted to hang onto him and never let go. Whoever he was—whatever he was—he made her feel too much. Somehow she had to get him out of her head and her heart before he took them over completely.

He can't make me do what he wants. Whatever he's using on other people, it doesn't work on me. If it did, I would do whatever he wants, just like them. But if Rob couldn't affect her, then why couldn't she move her hand out from under his?

The male attendant returned with a tray of drinks. Robin took the glass of dark red wine from the tray and tried to hand her the one filled with amber soda.

Chris shook her head. "I don't want anything, thank you."

"It is only ginger ale." When she still wouldn't take it from him, he drank a sip, grimacing a little. "You see? No poison."

Although she didn't want anything from him or his people, she *was* thirsty, and letting herself get dehydrated on top of everything else would be idiotic. Reluctantly she took the glass and drank. The cold soft drink felt good going down her dry throat, and gave her something to do besides avoiding his beautiful eyes. It wasn't until she'd finished the soda that she felt her eyelids grow heavy and her hands go numb.

She turned her head and saw him watching her.

He took the glass from her limp grip. "Sweet dreams, my lady."

Alex finished the last of the sutures and sponged the blood from what had been a gaping abdominal wound riddled with copper fragments. She waited to see the edges begin to pull together—too slowly, but better than not at all—before she draped the Kyn warrior's lower body.

"Before you take him into recovery, swap out that unit of blood for plasma," she told Geoffrey's stable master, whom she had drafted yesterday to assist her in surgery. "And I want him kept on plasma drip only for the next forty-eight hours."

The big man frowned. "My lady, he needs blood."

"Oh, he had blood. Someone"—she gave him a pointed look—"already gave him four units of it this morning without checking his chart or asking me."

"'Twas to make him stronger for the surgery," he insisted.

"Well, it didn't, not with all the crap lodged in the wound. It just saturated his tissues, diluted the toxins, spread them around, made him weaker, and made my job a lot harder."

Alex pulled down her mask. "He's pumped full of euphoriant now, so he won't need another tranq shot."

"But he will need more blood to heal."

"Plasma, nothing else." She saw his expression and reined in her temper. "Listen, pal. I have the M.D. after my name for a reason. You give him any more whole blood before this batch wears off? He'll go into thrall."

"Go alone into the dreamlands?" The stable master sounded horrified. "He would never wake again."

She smiled brightly. "Which is why we're keeping him on plasma."

Michael was waiting outside her makeshift surgery, but she walked past him to strip out of her gloves and gown at the disposal bin. She'd told him she would be working down in the hospital, but she'd spared him the details. He must have been busy with Richard and the other seigneurs upstairs, as this was the first time he had personally checked on her.

"Were you able to help him?" he asked, coming to stand beside her.

"I dug out about a pound of copper shrapnel that's been sitting in his belly and slowly poisoning him for a couple weeks." She untied the strings around her neck and dropped the blood-spattered mask they held on top of her crumpled gown. "His tox levels were through the roof, and my ninny of scrub nurse pumped him full of whole blood before the operation, but the pathogen started healing the edges of the wound as soon as I closed." She glanced at him. "That means yes, I was able to help him."

Michael looked as if he were still trying to process all the information she'd just thrown at him. "I know his family will be most grateful, *chérie*."

"I wouldn't count on it," she told him, brushing past him to go to the sink to wash. "His younger brother died on my table yesterday."

Alex knew she was taking out her temper on Michael, and she didn't care. He and everyone else upstairs were talking and playing billiards and generally partying while she was down here cutting and patching up the Brethren's victims. The only help she had were Kyn nurses, most of whom thought doctors still treated wounds with leeches and cow urine. She'd lost two patients already to copper poisoning, and when Gabriel and Nick brought in the next group, she was fairly certain that she was going to lose more.

Michael continued to hover. "What can I do?"

"Besides get out of my hair? Not a thing." She dried off her hands and stalked out of the prep room into the ward.

Braxtyn and Geoff had tried to make the refugees as comfortable as possible, but silk sheets and elegant canopied beds didn't change the fact that most were in very bad shape. Alex had cleaned and treated dozens of third-degree burns, some so severe that the body parts involved were little more than charcoal.

She had not performed any amputations yet, but unless she found some way to restore the circulation to charred, rotting appendages, those were coming, too.

Knowing Michael was shadowing her, Alex stopped at the first bed and pulled aside the lace curtain. Bandages hid the fact that woman sleeping inside looked as if someone had dipped the upper half of her body in sulfuric acid. And she was one of the lucky ones, Alex thought as she checked her dressings. She hadn't gotten shot with the Brethren's fun new ammunition, so all she needed was extensive reconstructive work.

Eyelids distorted by blisters and scar tissue opened to show slivers of beautiful blue-green eyes. "Good evening, my lady." Bandages muffled the patient's soft, French-accented voice.

At least this one will make it, Alex thought. "How are you feeling, Blanche?"

"Much improved." She glanced past Alex and tried to push herself up into a sitting position. "Seigneur Cyprien, it is an honor."

"It's not that big an honor; stay where you are." Alex pulled a tray over to the side of the bed and opened a packet of gauze. "I've got a couple more backs and bellies to clean out and stitch up, and then you and I are going to start spending some quality time together in surgery."

Blanche lifted one of her bandaged hands to touch the thick mask of gauze covering her entire head. "I am grateful for your ministrations, my lady, but my face cannot be fixed. It healed this way the day after the fire."

"I'll have you know that the Brethren beat my boyfriend's head with copper pipes for a couple of weeks," Alex told her, jerking a thumb at Michael. "He actually had no face until I gave him that one."

"It is true, Lady Blanche," Michael said. "My *sygkenis* can make you as you were before the attack."

"Yeah, I'm a miracle worker." Alex glared at him before she carefully snipped the dressings from Blanche's right hand and examined the scar tissue. "This looks very good. A few more dermal abrasions, a bit more cutting and patchwork, and you won't have to wear gloves unless your hands are cold."

The blue-green eyes glittered. "You are a godsend, my lady."

Alex forced a smile and went to work on replacing Blanche's dressings.

Michael followed her around for the next hour, watching her work and offering encouraging words to her patients. Alex finished rounds, left instructions with the ward nurses to watch the most critical patients, and went upstairs with Michael in tow.

He didn't bug her until they were in their suite. "I know you are upset, Alexandra, but I cannot fathom why. You are doing tremendous things to help our people. You cannot blame yourself for those too far gone to save."

"Who said that I did?" She breezed past him and went into the bathroom, where she turned on the shower and began to strip. As often as she bathed, she couldn't seem to get the smell of scorched, decomposing flesh out of her hair, and the stink of it was driving her crazy.

She was still scrubbing at her scalp when Michael, naked and frowning, stepped into the shower with her. "*Chérie*, talk to me."

"I'm really not in the mood to share," she said, ducking her head under the spray to rinse out the shampoo. "Why don't you go hang with Richard and drink wine and talk about the good old days, when all they did was burn you at the stake?" When she emerged and wiped her eyes clear, Michael was still there. "Christ. Will you get out of here, Seigneur?"

"I am not your seigneur," he told her. "I am your lover. I am here for you."

Rather than snipe at him some more, Alex turned her back on him, worked some instant conditioner through the thick, sodden mass of her curls, and rinsed that away. Still she could smell it, very faintly, and reached for the shampoo bottle again.

Michael took it away from her. "Your hair is clean. Tell me what has made you so angry."

"Other than the piles of scalded, twisted charcoal that used to be people down in the basement? Some of whom I'm going to have to chop arms and legs off of later on this week, if they don't compel my human nurses to kill them first? And the twenty new ones Gabriel and Nick are dragging across Europe, who should be here, like, any minute?" She watched her fist fly past his face into the tile wall, which imploded into a small crater lined with jagged ceramic shards. The skin over her knuckles split and then closed. "Nothing comes to mind."

Michael followed her out of the shower and wrapped a big dark blue towel around her.

"Come here."

She didn't want to be hugged or stroked or soothed, but to save the rest of the bathroom walls and his face, she let him hold her. Being close to him always made her regret the hair trigger of her temper, and how often she aimed it at him.

He doesn't deserve this, any more than the people downstairs merited being torched and tortured.

Against his chest she muttered, "Sorry."

Michael scooped her up and carried her out of the bathroom, lowering her onto the bed and stretching out beside her. He pillowed his head on one arm and began smoothing back the wet curls stuck to her face.

"The first time I rode into battle, I saw hundreds of my brothers fall and die in front of me," he said quietly. "Some lost heads, arms, legs; others were hacked into so many pieces they fell apart. As the tide of battle turned, we chased the Saracens fleeing into the hills. I did not realize until I heard screaming beneath my horse that some of those who had fallen were still alive. In our eagerness to pursue the enemy, we trampled our own wounded."

"If you're trying to make me feel better," Alex said as she rolled away from him, "you need to move on to another anecdote. Fast."

"I only wish you to know that I am not indifferent to what you are feeling." He pulled her back against him. "How it is to hear them cry out. The smell of their wounds. Knowing with a glance who will live and who will die. I have waded my way through a river of dead bodies, breathing in the stench of death, looking for a chest that moved, or eyes that blinked."

"You went back for them?"

He didn't answer her until she turned around and faced him. "Before each battle, the temple master made us all draw lots. Those who lost did not ride against the enemy that day, but waited in camp. When word came that the fighting had ended, those of us who had remained behind put on our vestments and rode to the battlefield. We dismounted and formed a line. We prayed together, and then drew our swords and walked the field."

It took her a second to work out what he was saying. "You *killed* the wounded."

That seemed to stir him out of his reverie. "We had no doctors or medicines with us in the Holy Land, Alexandra. We barely knew how to bind minor wounds, much less keep them clean and heal them. A quick and merciful death was better than one that took weeks of suffering in agony." He watched her face, his eyes so clear and blue that it hurt for her to look into them. "That is why the worst of the wounded will try to kill themselves, or ask another Kyn to dispatch them. It is not because you have failed them, *chérie*. It has always been our way."

Whenever Michael had made such statements in the past, Alex had the feeling that nothing would ever knock down the invisible, impenetrable wall between the Kyn's medieval attitudes and her own modern point of view. Now she only felt tired of slamming headfirst into the wall.

She also had an obligation to tell him what she had discovered while working on the patients in the basement hospital.

"There's something you should know," she said. "About two-thirds of the patients I've seen were shot as well as burned. It's why most of their wounds haven't been healing."

"We have had reports that the Brethren hunters shot at those who fled the fires, but once the slugs are removed, they should heal."

"Not this time," she said. "The hunters used explosive rounds, a kind I've never seen before now. The rounds fragment inside the body, scattering splinter-size shrapnel inside the wound."

"That is new." He frowned. "A sliver of copper lodged in the heart can kill us as quickly as a slug. Perhaps the zealots are using these rounds to be more efficient."

She shook her head. "None of the survivors who were brought here were shot in the chest. They were hit in the back, the belly, the head, or the extremities. Now, maybe a couple of the Brethren have lousy aim, but the patients' wounds are too similar to be mistakes. I think the hunters were trying *not* to kill them."

Chapter 10

"Not kill them?" Michael lifted his head and looked down at her. "If this is so, why shoot them at all?"

"To wound them in a way that wouldn't kill them immediately. To slow them down. Or to make sure they suffered before they died. But why not just shoot them in the head and get it over with?" She had told him this much; she might as well get out the rest. "Based on what I'm seeing down there, I know the Brethren hunters weren't trying to shoot to kill. It could be that they're trying to capture the Kyn they shoot to bring them back alive."

"I must talk to Richard about this." He sat up. "He will wish to discuss the patients with you as well."

"I'll put it on my calendar," Alex said listlessly. "Would you mind if we go to sleep now? I don't think I can work up the energy for the usual kiss-and-make-up sexathon."

Michael left her there and returned with a syringe and a vial of plasma from her case. She watched him fill the syringe, and didn't complain or resist when he injected her.

He ran his thumb over the small hole the syringe left in her arm, which didn't close immediately. "How long has it been since your last needle?"

"I don't know. I got so busy downstairs I forgot." Alex

watched him set aside the syringe. "I'm sorry I've been such a bitch. I'll try to do more of the seigneur's-lady stuff in between patients tomorrow."

Michael eased down next to her. "You do not have to do anything, *chérie*. We can rest, and tomorrow we can make arrangements to go home. You have but to say."

"I can't exactly walk out on my patients." She suspected he was trying to placate her. "You don't want to leave, either. It'll make you look bad in front of all the other seigneurs."

"I can ask Geoffrey to find human doctors who will help the patients. You have but to write up instructions on what they are to do." He gave her a crooked smile. "As for me, how do you put it? I will live."

Plasma didn't light up her insides the way whole blood did, but Alex felt relaxing warmth spreading through her. The never-ending nightmare downstairs, Michael's patience, and her own miserable guilt swamped her. Although becoming Kyn had taken nearly all of her humanity, she could still cry.

"Alexandra." He lifted her onto his lap and pressed her head against his chest. "Shhhh."

"I can't leave," she said through the tears. "Look at Blanche. Braxtyn told me how beautiful she was; from the way she described her she must have been like the Marilyn Monroe of the Kyn."

He nodded. "Knights would fight one another for the chance to win her favor and wear her colors on their sleeves."

"Blanche's face is gone. There's nothing left but scar tissue. There aren't any photos of her, so I don't know what she looked like."

"I will draw a sketch of her for you," Michael promised.

"Then there's Gideon, the warrior who pulled Blanche out of the flames. If he survives the copper poisoning from getting shot in the back, he's going to need a double amputation.

He's so out of it he doesn't know. Blanche asks about him every night." She caught a sob and forced it back down her throat. "I was kind of hoping he'd die so I wouldn't have to tell her that he burned his hands off saving her."

He rubbed his cheek against her hair. "If I could take away your burdens, I would. I would take them all, *chérie*."

Sitting naked on Michael's lap and sobbing into his shoulder was all Alex could manage for a time. When she had gotten most of the immediate misery out of her system, she lifted her face and kissed him. Any other night he would have turned her around and jumped on top of her, but he remained uncharacteristically passive, giving her only what she wanted.

Alex shifted, wrapping her legs around him, and reached down. His long, thick penis slid against her palm, hard and ready for her, as it always was whenever she touched him. The warmth inside her flared into life, driving out the shadows in her heart. Suddenly she needed to feel him stroking the emptiness inside her. She rose up, guiding him into place, and sank down, taking him in, filling the ache, bringing them together in the most basic way of man and woman.

The pupils of his eyes contracted to vertical slits, while the thin band of amber on the outside of the irises expanded, swallowing up the brilliant turquoise. A muscle along the side of his jaw twitched, but Michael didn't move. Not when she placed her hands on his shoulders for leverage, and not when she lifted up, caressing the length of his cock an inch at a time. His scent burned all around them, unseen roses set ablaze, and his arms locked as he dug his hands into the coverlet.

Alex bent her knees, pushing him on his back as she impaled herself on him again, working the rigid shaft deeper. She hunched over, pressing her breasts against his chest, moving subtly from side to side so she could feel his skin abrade the stiff tips. She kept his cock inside her and squeezed the length of it with steady, rhythmic contractions of her vagina, something that usually drove him insane with lust.

Michael muttered something in French, and the coverlet under them tore, but he still didn't touch her.

"The only time I feel safe," Alex told him, "is when you're inside me. All the way in, like this." She rocked a little, rubbing the folds of her sex against the base of his penis. "I could keep you right here forever."

He uttered a tight laugh. "You have seriously over-estimated my endurance, my lady. At most I may last an-other minute."

"A minute, huh?" She bent down to kiss his chin as she clamped down on him. "Then what are you going to do? Take it out? Come all over me?"

His fangs stretched to full length, long and white and sharp. "You know what I want."

"That I do." Alex pushed her hair away from her neck. "You want a taste of me before I make you come. Here?" She traced a slow, winding path with her fingers down to her left breast. "Or maybe here. No," she added when he reached for her. "You're a big, strong, immortal guy. You can hold on another minute, can't you?"

"With you, like this? Ten seconds." He watched her laugh, his eyes slits. "Five."

"Michael." Absurdly touched, she caressed his cheek. "Three."

Alex covered his body with hers. "I love you."

"Enough."

The room flipped around them as he toppled her over onto the floor. Alex didn't have time to brace herself, and the slam of his hips into hers as he shoved himself into her pushed her over the edge. As she shuddered through the orgasm, she felt him bite into her throat and fasten his mouth on her. She held on, riding the furious speed of his powerful, hammering penetration, but it was the exquisite suction of his mouth that held her suspended in the pleasure, ensnared by the climax until she thought it would never end.

His white-streaked black hair dragged over her breast as he moved and sucked at her there, while his big body tensed, coiling above her as he worked his cock in and out of her. He moved back, pulling out of her and grabbing her hand to wrap her fingers around the slick skin covering the swollen shaft.

"Finish it," he told her, bracing his arms on either side of her.

Alex pressed him to the top of her sex, cradling him with her labia and moving her hips so that her hand and her clit stroked him on either side. She felt the trembling first and then the stiffening just before he began to ejaculate, and she pumped him harder, working him mercilessly through his own pleasure and coming herself again as his semen spilled across her belly.

Michael looked down at their bodies and put one hand over hers.

"You are everything to me." He guided her to touch the creamy white rivulets of his ejaculate. "My heart, my soul, all that I am is yours. And you are mine." He used her palm and fingers to rub it in a wide circle around her navel. "There will never be another woman for me, Alexandra. You are my eternity."

Robin found himself alone in the dark with a woman in his arms. On one level he knew he was on the plane, and that he had fallen into the strange sleep of his kind.

This place did not exist, but belonged to the strange realm of the place the Kyn called the dreamlands. He could see nothing, but he didn't have to. The taste of her soft, silky mouth, the clean, simple smell of her skin, and the feel of her half-naked body pressed to his were enough for him.

She branded his chest with her mouth, scattering kisses across his skin. *You didn't want me to leave.*

No. He buried his hands in her hair and wove his fingers through the bright, red-gold silk of it. *I lied to you.*

She lifted her head. *Why?*

If you stay, he said, pausing to kiss her mouth, *I might never let you go.*

The darkness lightened, becoming a blurry place of rosy light and magenta shadows. He knew the woman he held and kissed. She would not tell him her name, but she smelled of gingerbread and tasted of cherries. He had brought her here, intending to take his pleasure of her before he sent her away as he had all the others. That no longer seemed possible. He would not let this end so swiftly, not for slumber or sunrise or even sanity. He needed more than a meaningless interlude. He needed to understand what she was to him.

Robin needed her here, in his arms, in his bed. He thought she might be amenable to the idea. *When do you go to this work of yours?*

Her mouth curved. *Sunrise.*

Today you shall be late. He gathered her in. *Very, very late.*

She sighed her pleasure. *They can dock my pay.*

With agile eagerness she twined herself around him, hands inching up his back, one long leg wrapping around his. She rubbed her nose and mouth against his neck, marking him with a small love bite.

Light curved and melted and folded in on itself, darkening to a dusky rose and then deepening to violet. Armies of trees, some with trunks as wide as a shepherd's cottage, some as slender as a crook, shot up all around them. Silently they formed a forest enclosure, walls of rough brown bark, a dappled emerald roof.

Robin had to have her mouth again, and clamped his

arms around her, lifting her to get at it. She poured so much heat into the kiss that he kept her there, holding her against his chest and cradling the back of her head with his hand to keep it from ending.

He wanted her in his bed, but surely now that lay on the other side of forever. He brought her down, dropping to his knees with her, adjusting her legs as he went down so that she straddled him. Beneath them the ground came alive, spreading a carpet of moss, decorating it with paisleys of brown leaves and bits of broken twigs.

She saddled herself over him and surveyed his features with an enigmatic expression. *Where are we?*

Sherwood. Here, at least, he could speak that name without a thousand demons howling in his head. *My land. My home.*

A shaft of light streamed down, gilding her eyes, brandy set alight. *I know that name.*

Good. He ran his palm down the length of her thigh. *Then perhaps you will tell me the rest of yours.*

She laughed, and the sound tore at him. His self-restraint, which had never been in question around a human woman, was slipping badly. He could almost hear the groan of invisible chains forged long ago, as if the links of pain were stretching and thinning. The slumbering immortal demon they held bound and tethered, the thing he refused to ever let loose again, began to stir.

Robin reached up for the rope he knew would be there and wrapped it around his arm, securing her against him with the other. They soared up, ten feet, twenty, thirty, forty, until the mottled floor of moss and leaves vanished. He turned and with the ease of centuries of practice swung them over onto the sturdy platform he had built between three ancient black oaks.

He had never had much in the way of possessions, not after being stripped of his title and lands. Years of serving as a warrior priest had made him accustomed to having no more to call his own but his sword, his bow, and his mount. Yet here, high above the rest of the world, he had fashioned a place for himself. A bed of willow branches, a ewer of water, a basket of bread, and the birds to sing him to sleep.

She belonged here, with him. She had been the only thing missing, the one he had longed for during the endless decades of running and hiding and taking and giving.

What is your name? he urged, wanting it as much as he wanted her. *Tell me.*

Chris. She brushed her lips against the scar over his heart. *It rhymes with* this.

There is more. He gripped her hips between his hands.

She undulated against him. *There always is.*

Before Robin knew it he had rolled with her, putting her under him, his weight pinning her to the bed that had never been in this place, a place where he had lain alone, night after night, unable to sleep, afraid to dream.

She made a low sound and went still, gazing up at him with the wide-eyed trust of an innocent. *Why are you looking at me like that?*

I do not want to hurt you. He hated that she was mortal and he would never be again. In that moment he felt the full weight of the curse God had flung upon his head.

You can't. She rocked under him. *I came here for you.*

All around them, below them, above them, small animals woke from their sleep and crept out into the dark, calling to one another. They hunted and were chased; they fought and played. They lived in the moment, in that moment, with Robin. With her.

Robin was as much a creature of the shadows as they, but he remembered the pleasures and desires of his human life. He wanted to plant himself inside her and fill her with his seed over and over, so he could watch her belly grow round and heavy. *I wish I could give you a child.*

She reached up, touching his mouth with her fingers. *Maybe you'll have one someday.*

He thought of the daughter he had tried to save, the innocent he had corrupted, the woman he could never tell the truth. All of it lost to him forever now. *It can never happen.*

She nodded, understanding him in this as in everything else. *Then give me what you can.*

The demon awoke, ravenous with the old hunger. Robin's *dents acérées* slammed into his mouth, full-length, as hard and greedy for her as his cock. His scent poured from his skin and wrapped like a shroud around both of them. She could not possibly resist him in full shed, Robin knew. Now she would be his, all his, and he could drink from her and take her and fuck her until dawn.

Wet scarlet streams began trickling down the branches and trunks around them, as if the trees themselves were weeping blood.

There, in that surreal realm, blood thrall would hold her willing and eager while he fell into rapture over her. The rapture that would compel him to love her and feed on her until he drained the last pulse of life from her heart.

Concern replaced the anticipation in her smoky eyes. *Are you all right?*

Give me a moment, love. He ducked his head so that she wouldn't see his fangs. *I'm admiring you.*

No, he wasn't. He'd already spread her legs with his knees and held a handful of her chemise in his fist. Slowly he forced his fingers to uncurl and smooth the wrinkled satin. He needed blood, now, to assuage the beast, but only she was here. Only she could give it to him.

He couldn't drink from her, not here. Even if she was slipping into rapture and wouldn't care, he would not take her life. But he would, unless . . .

He reached for the whispery pink scarf she'd draped around his neck and twisted the ends around his fingers.

Close your eyes. When she did, he used the scarf as a blindfold over them.

As soon as he had knotted the ends, she pushed the edge up over one eye to peek at him. *Do you call out Marco Polo now until I find you?*

No, you stay right where you are. He pulled the scarf back into place. *I won't be a moment, love*.

He left her there, went to the old owl's nest that served as his cache, and reached inside for the bags of blood he knew would be there. He tore open and emptied the first in four swallows, watching her as he reached for a second, and then a third. Only after draining a fourth did he feel the hunger dwindle and the demon subside. He would have emptied a fifth, but by that time she was propping herself on her elbow and turning her head as if trying to hear what he was doing.

Feeding so quickly, even on the chilly stuff, caused heat and pleasure to spread like fever throughout him. He drank from a bottle of heavy red wine to wash the taste of blood from his mouth before returning to her.

Her slim, cool hands wandered over him. *You feel so hot.*

You burn in my blood, Christyn.

My name isn't Christyn.

Robin tugged the blindfold from her eyes. *Why the devil won't you tell me your name?*

Her fingers stilled. *I don't have one.*

You are called Chris for some reason.

My biological mother never named me. She was probably a prostitute or a junkie. Chris traced the old bow scars crisscrossing his fingers. *No one even knows when she gave birth to me, but it was probably sometime in the winter of 1976. She kept me for a couple of years, but she didn't take very good care of me. Maybe she couldn't afford to, or she didn't care. One summer she left me in a playpen with a sheet of plywood over the top to keep me from climbing out, and never came back.*

Robin brushed the hair back from her eyes. *But they found you and took you away from there.*

The manager of the flophouse where she'd been staying came up two days later to collect the rent. He found me. Chris drew her hand away. *It isn't important. It's ancient history anyway.*

Rob kissed her forehead. *It matters to me.*

Keep that up and I just might do something really stupid, like fall in love with you. She pulled him on top of her. *Then think of how much trouble you'd be in.*

Indeed. I'd have to spend a few months in bed, ravishing you. He hooked his thumbs in the soft satin of her panties and pushed them down to bare her to his fingers. He stroked the soft down of her red curls, the narrow cleft they covered, and tested the silkiness waiting for him. *Are you ready for me, love?*

She thrashed under him. *Lord.*

My lord.

"My lord."

Robin opened his eyes, squinting against the glare of the interior cabin lights. He lay reclined in the wide seat with Chris on his lap. She had her arms looped around his neck, and he had his hand between her thighs.

Carefully he shifted his hand and pulled her skirt back into place. "What is it?"

"We are preparing to land, my lord." The attendant nodded toward Chris. "And the lady is beginning to wake."

Chapter 11

Chris didn't like waking up in Robin's lap, or being hustled off the jet before she could get her bearings. She'd slept too hard; her head felt like an overstuffed flotation device.

The erotic dream of the night they had spent together came rushing back over her, but it had been different this time. She'd told him things that she had never mentioned that night, like how she had been abandoned by her mother, and how easily she knew she could fall for him.

Her, in love. With a thief.

He and his friends had wrecked a federal investigation and put Ray Hutchins in terrible danger. And if he was the Magician, as he'd claimed, that meant that he was also responsible for what had happened to DeLuca. When this was over it was her job—her sworn duty—to make sure that Robin went to prison for the crimes he had committed.

Chris pressed the heel of her hand to the dull pain throbbing behind her left eye. *I am not falling in love with the international art thief who made Norman commit suicide.*

As they walked through the gate and approached customs, she saw a kiosk selling canned soft drinks. She felt thirsty, but the aftertaste of the ginger ale she'd drunk on the plane still lingered in her mouth, as bitter as if she'd chewed an aspirin.

She skidded to a halt as she realized why. "You bastard. You drugged me."

"Yes, I did." Robin smiled and kept hold of her arm, marching her toward the uniformed Italian agent. "You needed the rest. We will talk about it later."

"We'll talk about it now," she insisted, trying to stop him and shaken to find she couldn't. "You lied to me. You told me the drink wasn't drugged."

"I told you it wasn't poisonous." He lifted the long, oddly shaped case he carried onto the table between them and the customs agent. "The tranquilizer was harmless."

Chris turned her hand, gripping his as hard as she could. "What did I tell you?"

"Nothing."

"I don't believe you. It wasn't a tranquilizer; it was Rohypnol or something, wasn't it? Did you question me while I was under?"

"Now, now, love," he chided, glancing at the frowning customs agent. "I gave you a Valium so that you could sleep through the long flight from America. Which you did. Please stop trying to make this official think otherwise."

So what she had said about her mother and falling in love had been just a dream. "That's right. I forgot." She smiled at the agent, and said under her breath, "Don't you *ever* do that to me again."

"I won't." He leaned over to kiss her cheek and murmured, "I want you awake for everything else I'm going to do to you."

"Aside from helping me recover the manuscript, that will be absolutely nothing," she assured him.

Rob smiled a little as he brushed his knuckles against the place on her cheek where he'd pressed his mouth. "We will see about that."

Chris expected Robin to produce a pair of phony passports to hand over to the agent, but he did the same thing to him that he had to the patrol officer in Atlanta. She watched closely, determined to know how he performed the bizarre hypnosis. His voice remained steady and friendly, and he didn't spray the agent with any sort of drugged powder or mist. Although he was speaking in Italian, she didn't hear anything that sounded like a threat. Nor did he attempt to pass the agent any bribe money. The agent nodded, smiled, and waved them through.

What Chris did notice was that Robin's smell—that lovely scent of violets and oranges—had intensified as he spoke to the agent. In response, the agent seemed to breathe slowly and deeply while his eyes darkened as if the pupils were dilating.

No matter how pretty it was, no body odor on earth could make a customs agent forget to check for passports.

As they walked through the airport, Chris tried to make sense of what she had just witnessed. If Robin had sprayed himself with a drug, it should have affected everyone who came near him. Chris felt nothing, and she'd woken up in his lap.

I know it doesn't work on me. It would explain why he had acted the way he had at the club, and some of the strange things he'd said to her. He'd expected her to be affected by it, too—later, at the penthouse, he had even checked her eyes before kissing her and telling her to leave. *Did he tell me to leave because he thought I was hypnotized, or because he knew I wasn't?*

The sex had been her idea. That much she knew. She'd certainly gone over the sequence of events from that night often enough. Every time he touched her, some random moment from the hours they'd spent together popped into her head.

She was not going to think about the sex.

Chris stopped as Robin did, in front of a tall brunette dressed in a smart black suit checking the terminals displaying the gate numbers for the departing flights. Long ropes of large matched pearls ran from her neck to her waist, and two more glowed inside the diamond settings in her ears. She had the body of a toned goddess and the face of a dark angel.

"Bellisima." Robin helped himself to the brunette's beringed hand and kissed the back of it.

"I speak English," the brunette said, her surprise changing into pleasure. "You are very handsome, *caro*. Do I know you?"

"In your heart you do," he said, making the outrageous statement with a perfectly straight face. He glanced at the ticket in her hand. "You are on your way to Milan?"

She nodded. "I am visiting my sister for a week. We go shopping for new shoes."

Robin put his hand to her cheek. "Then you will not mind if we stay in your home while you are away."

Chris started to object, but fell silent as the brunette took a set of keys out of her purse and rattled off what sounded like directions in Italian. Chris couldn't help the startled sound she made when the brunette also handed Robin two credit cards and a roll of Italian currency.

"You are so generous. We will take very good care of everything while you are in Milan," Robin promised, bending slightly to kiss both of her cheeks. "You will remember us only as good friends who looked after your flat for you. Hurry now, or you will miss your flight."

"That was easy." Chris watched as the brunette strolled away. "Why didn't you ask if you could borrow her car while you were at it?"

"I did. It's an off-white Mercedes convertible. She said that she left it in long-term parking." Robin twirled the key ring around one finger before pocketing it and taking her hand again. "Come along, love."

She was in Rome with a man who stole things as casually as other people used hand towels in a restroom. What he needed or wanted, he took. He added insult to injury by somehow coercing it from people who probably had no idea they were giving him anything.

No wonder he'd become a thief. The world must have seemed like a free toy store to him.

Chris knew why it bothered her. As a foster kid, she'd never had anything but the clothes on her back and whatever her caregivers bothered to feed her. She might have grown up to be a thief herself, if not for the Renshaws. By adopting her they had saved her from the indifference of the system and the inevitable down-spiraling mess it made out of the lives of unwanted kids left to its mercies. What her mother had done to her might have turned her into a junkie or a whore, if not for her mom and dad.

That she had to go along with Robin's crimes in order to save Hutch made Chris feel disgusted—more with herself than him. But what was really getting to her, what was going to make her explode any minute, was the way Robin kept rubbing his thumb against the back of her hand and smiling at her and acting as if they were on their honeymoon.

Or the fact that in a small, wistful corner of her heart, she wished that they were.

Robin found the Mercedes and unlocked the passenger door for her as naturally as if the car belonged to him. He treated her the same way: as if her coming along with him meant she'd go along with whatever he did.

"Do you want the top down? It's a lovely night." When she didn't get in, he gave her hand a tug. "We only have two days, Christal. Get in."

"My name isn't Christal. This car doesn't belong to you. Neither do I." Chris twisted her hand, but he kept hold of her. If he didn't let go of her right now she was going to make a fool out of herself. To remind herself of who he was, she said, "You can't steal or bully out of people whatever you want, Robin. No matter how good you are with your magic, whatever it is, eventually you're going to get caught."

His dark brows rose. "I don't use magic, and what does this have to do with getting into the car?"

He didn't care. He genuinely didn't care that they were, in effect, stealing this woman's car. "How do you sleep at night?" she demanded.

"I sleep during the day."

"You know exactly what I mean." She was sick of this vampire fantasy role he insisted on playing, too. "Doesn't it bother you knowing everything you have you stole from someone else?"

"I have not stolen *everything*," he told her. "When I bought the Armstrong building, for example, I paid cash for it."

He'd bought a high-rise building in downtown Atlanta for cash. Of course he had; he was the son of the Magician. He could probably buy *Atlanta*.

"Where did you get the money?" Chris asked. "How many priceless paintings did you have to steal to cover the down payment?"

"None. I invest in the stock exchange. Google did very well for me that year." He watched a security guard stroll past them. "A gentleman does not discuss his financial empire in public. Now we have to go."

Chris didn't budge. "What *does* happen to the art you steal? Are you warehousing it? Do you sell it to private collectors?" Maybe if she could convince him to turn himself in and work with the bureau on recovering and returning the artworks he had stolen, it might reduce the time he would have to serve in prison.

Am I trying to work out a plea agreement? For the Magician's son?

Chris backed up a step. "I can't do this. I can't go through with this."

"Yes, you can."

She looked at him, suddenly and inexplicably angrier than she ever had been in her life. "I won't."

"Get in the car, love," he said through his teeth, "or I shall pick you up and stow you in the boot."

Chris opened her mouth, closed it when he rattled the keys, and mutely climbed into the car.

Robin drove through Rome the same way he did everything: with style, enthusiasm, and a lot of nerve. On the way to their "borrowed" accommodations, Chris said nothing. She ran through different self-defense scenarios in her head, trying to use her training to settle her internal agitation and cool down the flames of outrage burning into her brain.

It didn't work very well, but it was better than talking to him.

Robin parked in front of an ancient-looking edifice and came around to open the door for her.

Chris was out of the car before he got there. "Nice. Looks about a thousand years old."

"Four hundred, I'd say." He put her arm through his. As a young Italian couple passed them, he murmured, "Stop scowling like that. You resemble a tourist."

There was no elevator; they walked up an old but beautifully preserved marble staircase to the apartment on the top floor. Robin unlocked the door and paused to input a code on the alarm system keypad inside.

That upset Chris more than the Mercedes. "You made her give you her security codes?"

"How else were we to get in the place?" he countered. "Besides, it will provide a measure of protection for us during the day. Unless you wish to guard the door and windows personally?"

"Never mind." Chris looked blindly at the chic decor and

warm colors of the apartment. There were several paintings on the walls, but none of them were museum quality.

Robin's mobile phone rang, making Chris jump.

"Excuse me." He walked away from her as he answered it, stopping and tensing as he listened to the caller. "I'll be there," was all he said before he shut off the phone and pocketed it.

"Who was that?" Chris asked.

He glanced at her and then shook his head. "No one important." He went to the windows and opened the curtains, looking down at the street.

"You're lucky this lady is single." She took off her jacket. "Her husband might have thought we were burglars breaking in and come after us with a gun."

"If someone shoots at you, use me as a shield," Robin said, walking around the apartment and opening the rest of the curtains.

She followed him. "You're wearing a bulletproof vest?"

"No." He paused to pick up an expensive column of multicolored blown glass and admire it. "Bullets cannot harm me."

She took the vase out of his hand and replaced it on the shelf. "I'll remember to have that engraved on your headstone. Right over 'beloved son of international art thief.' "

"I may not be anyone's beloved," he said, "but I am rather hard to kill."

"So you're planning on dying of old age? With your lifestyle?" She made a contemptuous sound. "Maybe if you get consecutive sentences."

"I do not age." He gave her a narrow look. "My kind are immortal."

Here we go again. "Right, I forgot. Vampires live forever. But wait, you said that you're not a vampire." She was too close to him, too angry to move away. "Does that make you a god, or a half god, or an elf, or what?"

He didn't like that. "I have explained this to you. Very patiently, I might add."

"Yet I'm still confused," she said sweetly. "Maybe you should buy me a deck of the cards or the rule book, so I can keep all the characters straight."

He moved closer to her. "I have trusted you with the truth of what I am."

"What are you?" Chris spread her hands. "Maybe you need to reread the rule book, though, because your special talents are all mixed-up. You drink blood, but you're not a vampire. You rose from the grave, but you're not a zombie. Bullets can't hurt you, but you're not Superman. By the way, is the contessa also immortal?" She folded her arms. "Or did she get another superpower when she rolled the special-abilities dice?"

"I brought a full bottle of Valium from the plane." He gestured to the case he'd brought in. "Perhaps you should take one and lie down."

"What happens if I don't? Are you going to knock me out, or lock me in the bedroom again?" She shoved him, or tried to. He didn't move an inch. "I know—why don't you make *me* an immortal? I'd like to have bullets to bounce off me, and I'd be very happy to spend the rest of eternity hunting down your thieving ass."

"You have no idea what you are saying." His gaze burned into hers. "What it has been like for me and my kind. The centuries of being tormented. Hiding among you, trying to make a place for ourselves. Being treated like animals."

"You're right; I don't. But then, I'm the sane one in the room." Tired of sniping at him, she turned away. She was in a beautiful flat with a handsome man whom she was probably going to fall in love with right before he stole another priceless treasure, this time out from under her nose, and it was the last place on earth she wanted to be. "God, what am I doing here with you?"

He turned her around to face him. "Given a choice, I assure you, madam, I would have left you in Atlanta. I have no time for your human tantrums."

"You're immortal," she goaded him. "All you've got is time."

"You should watch your tongue." Copper heat glittered in his eyes. "Or put it to better use. Is that it?" He cocked his head. "Do you need my direction again?"

Chris felt something inside her snap, and she drew back her arm and punched him in the face.

Phillipe of Navarre had served as seneschal to Michael Cyprien since their human lives, when his master had taken him from the fields to serve in his household. At first Phillipe had been reluctant to trade his scythe for a sword—he was a villein born and bred, trained from the time he could walk to work the land—but his family had been overjoyed. No more would they go hungry during the lean years; Phillipe's position would provide for them. And so he had, even after he took his vows with his master and went to fight with the Templars in the Holy Land.

He had never forgiven himself for the final gift he had brought back for his family from the Crusades. The sickness that had put him into the ground had taken his parents and sister first. Unlike him, they never rose to live as Darkyn.

Centuries had passed since he had held his futile vigil at their graves, waiting for them to join him. It had been Cyprien who had coaxed him away, Cyprien who had kept him from going mad with grief. Stronger than even the curse on their souls, Michael's kindness and understanding had sealed the bond between them. Phillipe pledged to spend the rest of his long life in his master's service.

So he had maintained that bond until five years ago, when after centuries of walking the night alone, Michael

Cyprien had found Alexandra Keller, a mortal physician who had become his *sygkenis*, his life companion.

Once Phillipe realized how serious the bond between his master and the doctor had grown, he had tried not to resent Alexandra. She had not been very fond of him, either, but in time they had become reluctant allies, and then friends.

In truth, Alexandra reminded him a great deal of his older sister, Maeve, another petite, strong-headed woman. That Alexandra loved Cyprien as much as Phillipe did he had no doubt. The doctor had given up nearly everything from her human life to be with Michael.

She had not made peace with her choice, however, and at times he feared that she never would.

Phillipe spent most of his time at *le conseil supérieur* with the other seigneurs' seneschals, discussing household matters and trading tales of intrigue. As the newcomer, Phillipe was pressed for many details about Cyprien and life in America, as well as his opinions on some of the more con-troversial decisions his master had made.

"My lord Sevarus had a choking fit when I gave him the news about the woman seneschal Seigneur Cyprien made suzerain of the Realm," Connor, a cheeky Irishman, told Phillipe. "He proceeded to lecture for me for more than an hour on how I must not get ideas above my station."

Derek, a burly Norwegian who served Gilanden, grunted. "That did not sit well with my master, either. He has one use for females, human or Kyn, and it does not involve rule."

" 'Tis said she is a mannish woman, Navarre," Helmut, Solange's seneschal, added. "Does she swive females, or only dress the part?"

"Suzeraina Jayr took Lord Byrne as her seneschal and her *sygkenis*," Phillipe said, enjoying the stunned reactions on the faces around the table. "I wager she has no time to trifle with anyone else."

"At least your master's leech is content to nurse the sick,

as women should," Poldar, who served Tristan, observed. "I shudder to think of a female at the tribunal, deciding our fate."

Garza, Cordoba's man, snorted. " 'Twas better when we owned them, like villeins and land. Then they could not wear our garments and take up sport and curse like the lowest of sailors. Why, some of our females have petitioned my lord, asking if they may take classes on these wretched computers and learn more of the mortal world."

"That is why my master had our humans ban access to the Internet in our homeland," Shalan, Zhang's seneschal, put in. "It put too many ideas in their heads." He glanced at Phillipe. "What about your female? Does she talk of such things?"

"I keep no woman of my own," Phillipe admitted, catching a trace of the other man's scent, like that of an ocean breeze.

"I thought not." Shalan drank from his goblet, but didn't explain his assumption.

After they had shared another half dozen bottles of bloodwine, the coming dawn sent Phillipe to retire for the day. His room, which adjoined Cyprien's chambers, was small but comfortable, and after he bathed he stretched out on the bed. That was when he smelled the blend of rose and lavender seeping into his room from the crack under the door, discovered how thin the walls between their rooms were.

At most I may last another minute.

A minute, huh? Then what are you going to do? Take it out? Come all over me?

You know what I want.

Phillipe pulled a pillow over his face to muffle his groan. He tried never to listen to the pillow talk between his master and his *sygkenis*, but they were active, passionate lovers, and in certain situations it could not be avoided.

You want a taste of me before I make you come.

Alexandra's voice always went low and smoky when she was pleasuring the master, and she often said such blatant, sexual things during the act that Phillipe's ears sometimes burned. But it was Cyprien's voice that he tried hardest not to hear, for when aroused his master's silky tenor changed to a hard, demanding rasp.

A rasp that made Phillipe go hard every time he heard it.

Closing his eyes, Phillipe listened to his master's voice and reached down. He should have felt shame when he wrapped his straining cock in his fist, but he didn't. Knowing Cyprien preferred women, he had never revealed his secret desires to his master, but instead endured them in silence. The solitary relief he occasionally sought kept his desires in check, and helped him accept what could never change.

Tonight, however, playing voyeur was not enough. He was weary of feeding off the desires of the two people he loved most in the world.

He rolled out of bed, pulled on his trousers, and left his room, making his way through the gardens until he found a small, white marble gazebo tucked away in a remote corner. Although the suzerain and his lady kept their grounds meticulously maintained, for some reason ivy and other trailing vines had been permitted to grow around the elegant structure, very nearly concealing it altogether.

A private trysting spot, Phillipe thought as he parted the vines and stepped inside. Here the air was thick with the smell of greenery and the ever-present, lingering perfume coming from the flowering trees in the orchard. He noted the wide benches lined with soft cushions, and a heavy silk shawl that had been left where it had fallen on the inlaid marble floor. He bent to pick it up and brought it to his nose.

"It belongs to Lady Braxtyn, I believe."

Phillipe turned, the scent of warm apricots fading as he

smelled the wind from the sea and spotted the smaller Kyn male sitting in a shadowed corner. "Forgive me, Shalan. I did not see you here. I do not mean to intrude."

"You assume your presence is an intrusion, when it is quite the reverse. I followed you here." The Asian man tilted his head, allowing his long black hair to fall over one bare, broad shoulder. Like Phillipe, he wore only a pair of trousers. "Do you have to listen to them every night?"

"It is late." Phillipe moved to leave, and looked down as Shalan appeared before him and put a hand to his chest, his smooth, narrow palm oddly warm against Phillipe's cool flesh. *He must have just fed.* "I do not discuss my master's habits with others."

"Then will you confirm two rumors I have heard about you, Navarre?" Slowly Shalan let his hand drift down until it traveled over the front of Phillipe's trousers. Calmly he turned his palm, adjusting his touch to allow for the bulge now growing beneath the fasteners. "They said that you wield an impressive sword. It seems they do not exaggerate."

Phillipe regarded the other seneschal's dark eyes carefully. "You inquired after my . . . weapon?"

"Not directly. Like you, I understand the need for discretion." Shalan curled his fingers, cupping Phillipe easily as he lightly rubbed. "But even Kyn who are not like us talk openly of men they admire. You, Navarre, are greatly envied."

Kyn who are not like us. Phillipe slid his hand under the dark fall of Shalan's long hair, caressing the strong neck beneath it before tugging him closer. "What else do they say about me?"

Shalan moved his hand aside, pressing his hips forward until his own confined erection nestled against the length of Phillipe's shaft. He licked the pad of his thumb, caressing it with the curl of his tongue before using it to dampen

Phillipe's lower lip. "That you do not cross swords with just anyone who comes along."

"Also true." When Shalan tried to put his mouth where his thumb was, Phillipe held him away. He guided him over to one of the benches and sat on it, still holding Shalan before him. "It has been a long time. I cannot promise that I will be especially gentle. Are you certain you wish to match your blade against mine?"

"God in heaven, yes." Shalan's voice dropped to a low, shaking whisper. "I have been thinking about you, about this, since I first saw you."

Without another word he knelt down between Phillipe's thighs, his fingers swiftly releasing the front of his trousers. He flipped his hair back with his hands, but it fell forward again as he bent his head to envelop the straining penis head with his mouth.

Wet heat and erotic suction made Phillipe stiffen and curse softly as he caught Shalan's hair with his hand and held it back. His eyes burned at the sight of his shaft stretching and disappearing between the other man's lips, while his ears drank in the soft sounds of suckling and muffled groans. Shalan worked him with the greed of a hungry youth and the skill of an old lover, sucking Phillipe's cock steadily with deep, slow pulls of his mouth.

Blood roared in Phillipe's head, and distantly he heard Alexandra's voice. *You're a big, strong, immortal guy. You can hold on another minute, can't you?*

He could not. He seized Shalan's hair, dragging his mouth from his cock and bringing it up to his. He pulled him onto his lap as he kissed him, thrusting his tongue into his mouth as deeply as he had his penis, taking what he needed and giving as much as the other seneschal would take.

Shalan broke the kiss first. "Now I begin to understand." He curled up and rubbed himself against Phillipe like a lonely cat, eager and purring. "It is too bad that there is an entire planet between our territories."

Phillipe cupped his hand between the smaller man's legs, cradling the weight there. "There will be nothing between us tonight."

He rose, putting Shalan on his back on the bench so he could strip him out of his trousers, regaining some of his self-control as he leisurely put his mouth to what he uncovered. Shalan tasted as piquant as his sea-wind scent, and his hard, smooth skin proved unusually sensitive for a Kyn male. His cock, a thick, fist-long spike that begged to be stroked and kissed, was covered with an intact, velvety foreskin that slowly reddened and peeled back from the slick head as Phillipe toyed with it. When Shalan cursed he took him into his mouth and soothed his weeping cock head with his tongue, but as soon as Shalan groaned with pleasure Phillipe drew away and returned to his love play.

"Do you mean to deprive me of my wits?" Shalan croaked at last.

"No." But Phillipe liked having the seneschal naked, straining and quivering under his hands. "Well, perhaps a little. I want you to remember this night."

"Trust me, Navarre." The other man laughed helplessly. "I shall."

Phillipe straightened, pausing for a moment to run a hand down the sinewy leanness of the seneschal's thigh.

"You will have me on my knees again," Shalan muttered before he turned his head and pressed his mouth against Phillipe's thigh, sinking his fangs into his flesh. He took only a mouthful of blood before pulling away. "Give me your sword now, Navarre. Give it to me as hard as you can."

Phillipe flipped him over onto his belly, taking Shalan's narrow, angular hips between his big hands and pulling him up into the position to be penetrated. The head of his cock, still slick from Shalan's talented mouth, oozed the clear, silky fluid of his arousal. Phillipe rubbed it up and down the crinkled ruck between Shalan's tight buttocks, moving slowly, teasing him with brief moments of pressure.

"I will scream," Shalan warned, moving his hips back and wriggling against him. "And then everyone will know what we have been doing with our blades."

Phillipe leaned down, kissing him slowly and deliberately before he murmured, "I do not care if they do."

The other man turned his head until their gazes met. Dark eyes gleamed with lust, regret, and something else. "I know you cannot give me your heart, Navarre. Do not make me want to steal it away, along with you."

"Let me give you what we both want." Phillipe gripped his waist, steadying him as he breached the clutching opening and pressed in.

Phillipe sank into the tight, hot channel faster than he wished, but the sounds Shalan made were not of pain. He reached under the smaller man and gripped his short, wide shaft, tugging on it as he slid the last inches of his own past the tightening ring of muscle.

Shalan began muttering words in his native language as he hung, skewered and writhing, squeezing Phillipe from root to tip.

"I have never felt . . ." Shalan lost the rest on a gasp as Phillipe pushed deep, bumping the tender head of his penis against the sweet mound hidden inside Shalan's body, the secret center of a man's pleasure.

Phillipe braced one hand against the back of the bench as he drew out and thrust back in, prodding the same spot, dragging the flared ridge of his tip over it as he withdrew. Shalan made a strangled sound. "There. There you are."

He rode Shalan hard, not sparing him an inch as he used his strokes to bring deep grunts and cries of delight from his partner's throat. His balls tightened as he heard Shalan chant his name, and he felt him pulse under his fingers as he jetted his seed. But it was only when Shalan went limp under him that Phillipe closed his eyes and pumped his semen into the seneschal's tight, trembling ass.

He lifted him, keeping him firmly impaled as he maneuvered them both into a reclining position, and held him until Shalan disengaged their bodies and turned to put his mouth to Phillipe's for a long, fervent kiss of gratitude.

"I would stay and match blades with you again, but my master rises early." He rose and moved with gratifying reluctance to pick up his clothes and dress. "You know where our rooms are, should you wish a rematch." He smiled before he slipped out through the curtain of ivy.

Phillipe lay staring at the vines that had grown across the gazebo's ceiling, enjoying the lingering pleasure but unsettled by the encounter. He had never thought to take a Kyn lover; the old stigmas made it unwise to advertise his preferences, and there were more than enough mortal men who enjoyed other men in bed to keep Phillipe physically satisfied. He did not deceive himself into contemplating a relationship with Shalan; as the seneschal himself had pointed out, they served masters on opposite sides of the world. Even with their lords' blessing, the logistics involved would have made it impossible.

Still, the thought of having a Kyn lover waiting in his bed each dawn made Phillipe feel a little wistful. His jealousy of Alexandra had been due in part to the fiery passion she and Cyprien shared, as well as the loving bond they formed that had since endured so much. Who could not look upon Alex and Michael when they were together and not feel a little lonelier?

Phillipe pulled on his trousers, made his way back to his room, and collapsed on his bed. He had nearly fallen asleep when he heard the door to Cyprien's chamber open and close, and smelled his master's scent. Concerned, he rose, dressed, and followed it. He found Cyprien in the suzerain's library, sitting before the fire and smoking a cigarette.

"Master, I had thought you had retired for the day." Phillipe saw his expression and bowed. "Forgive me. I will leave you."

"*Non, mon ami*. Sit with me."

Phillipe eased down into one of the suzerain's oddly shaped chairs and waited, but Cyprien said nothing.

"All is well, master?" he ventured at last.

"I am faced with some uncomfortable truths." Cyprien told him what Alexandra had learned from treating the refugees, then took a final drag from his cigarette and pitched it into the fire. "This, at a time when the Kyn do nothing but talk of war."

"There is always talk of war. We have managed to avoid it these five hundred years." Phillipe leaned forward. "You do not believe that we can this time?"

"When I meet with Richard and the others and tell them of what Alexandra has discovered? I think not." Cyprien met his gaze. "I went to war to show my father that I was a man of faith and conviction. I made you go with me; I dragged you into that horror, and I have never apologized to you for that. I am sorry, old friend."

"I was not made to accompany you, master," Phillipe pointed out. "I chose my place at your side. I have never regretted it."

"Your loyalty—no, your friendship—has been a great blessing in my life." He sighed. "I fear I will be the only seigneur opposing a war. Now Alexandra has brought me this knowledge that may very well hurl us all into that hell again."

Phillipe sat back, almost tipping over the chair before he made it steady. "This furniture is the devil."

Cyprien smiled a little. "Geoffrey loves to unsettle everyone." He took an envelope from his jacket. "Should I fail to sway the others, you will need this when you return to America with Alexandra. It names you as commander over all of the suzerains. You will need to send copies to all of our *jardins*."

Phillipe didn't touch the envelope. "My place is still at your side, master."

"Not this time, *mon ami*. If war is declared, Richard will name me as his successor and have me serve as his general. I will not be returning for some time, if at all."

At last Phillipe understood the crushing weight on Cyprien's shoulders. "Alexandra will not go back without you. The last time you were separated it almost destroyed your minds."

"That should serve me well when I lead our warriors against the Brethren," Cyprien said. "I am not convinced we can prevail over them, not with the weapons and tactics they will employ. Should I fall in battle, Alex will be left alone."

They had spoken of this once before, Phillipe remembered, when Richard had taken Alexandra. Michael had come to England to fight to the death over her. His master had asked him, if he failed, to free his *sygkenis*, take back to her homeland, and replace the bond she shared with Cyprien. Fearing that his master would be killed by the high lord, Phillipe had agreed.

"Phillipe?"

He looked at Cyprien, and the irony of the situation made him speak without thinking. "You are ever trying to give me your woman, master."

"You are like a brother to me," Cyprien said simply. "I could not bear the thought of her being with anyone else." He hesitated, and then added, "I had never considered how difficult that might prove for you until tonight, when I went to look for you, and . . ." He glanced toward the garden.

Phillipe thought of what he had said and done in the

gazebo, and recalled the sounds Shalan had made, and rubbed his hand over his face. *"Mon Dieu."*

"Your private life is your own," Cyprien said. "Only now I realize how much I have asked of you, without ever once considering your feelings."

"Master, it is not as you think. I have been with women, and I have enjoyed them. I love Alexandra like a sister. It is only . . ." He trailed off, unsure of the words. "At least now you know why I cannot be what you are to her."

"That is why I struggle with this," Cyprien said. "You should be free to choose your own life companion, even if the rest of the Kyn do not recognize another man as such. But Alex loves you, and more important, she trusts you. Should the worst happen, I beg you to take her and bond her to you as your *sygkenis*. For my sake, and for hers."

Phillipe loved them both, so there was only one answer he could give. "I will do whatever I can, master. I promise you."

Chapter 12

Robin was tired and worried. He knew that if he couldn't find Nottingham and the manuscript, the contessa would carry out her threats. Forcing Chris to come with him to Italy made him feel as manipulative and scheming as Salva, but he knew that if the contessa killed her partner, Chris would never forgive herself.

He had been kind and patient. He had explained as much as he could, and had seen to her comfort. She refused to stop fighting him, but she was a stubborn wench. She didn't know about his past, how he kidnapped Marian to take her to Scotland and prevent her marriage to Nottingham.

Chris, like Marian, was completely devoted to her duty, and made it all too obvious that she cared nothing for him. He found it deeply ironic that the first time he met a woman who might make him forget about his long-lost love, she wanted no part of him or his life.

As with Marian, he had accepted it and silently promised himself that he would not force himself on her. Knowing Chris was ready to drop from exhaustion but too upset to rest, he had even assured that she would sleep through the nineteen-hour flight from Atlanta to Rome.

He had not expected her to like the situation, or to give

him any significant amount of assistance. But her refusal to believe what he had told her, coupled with her endless derision, had set him on edge. Even so, he made allowance for that. Chris was an intelligent, resilient woman. She would adjust and come to accept what had to be.

Or so he had thought until she hit him.

Robin's head snapped back as her fist struck his jaw. She could not hurt him, not with her mortal strength, but he saw pain fill her eyes as she cradled her bleeding hand.

That she would injure herself trying to hurt him infuriated him as much as the scent of her blood aroused other feelings inside him.

"You did better with my dagger." He seized her by the arms. "Shall I retrieve that for you while you still have one hand working well enough to hold it?"

Chris swept her foot behind his legs, using it to unbalance him. He held her as he went down, landing on his back with her on top of him. She flipped away from him, kicking him in the side, and he tore off her shoe trying to catch her foot.

"Are you through?" he shouted.

"Why?" she yelled back. "Is it time for the directions?"

"What are you prattling about, woman?"

"You know *exactly* what I mean." She turned and looked at him through the hair hanging over her face. "Is this when you make me kill myself, the way you did Norman?"

"What? Who?"

"Norman DeLuca, my partner in Chicago." She scrambled to her feet, picked up his bow case, and heaved it at him. "Don't you remember? He was in that downtown bank you tried to rob."

Robin caught the case and set it aside. "I've never robbed a bank in Atlanta." He started after her.

"Don't you lie to me," she snapped as she retreated. "We found one of your arrowheads imbedded in a wall. I've seen what you can make people do. I know what you did to Norman."

"I don't bloody know any Norman DeLuca, you silly twit." He snatched at her when she dodged around him, ripping her jacket.

Chris shoved a sofa between them as she told him the date of the robbery and the address of the bank. "Now do you remember him?"

Robin stopped chasing her as the details finally rang a bell. "I didn't rob that bank. I used the old underground tunnels to break into the vault so I could retrieve the manuscript—"

"Oh, more borrowing?"

"—but that was my only reason for being there." He met her angry gaze. "The man who was robbing it escaped."

"Yeah." She braced her arms against the back of the sofa. "That would be *you*."

"No, it was the other man. Describe this Norman to me." He listened as she snapped out the details. "Wait. *He* was the sod who held them up. I stopped him from killing the hostages, but when the authorities stormed the building he vanished." He glared at her. "He was also alive when he nicked out of there. I didn't touch him."

"He was dead an hour later." She turned her back on him and walked to the windows. "He blew his head off. Because you told him to while he was hypnotized. You controlled him. The same way you did that customs agent and that cop back in Atlanta. The way you've been trying to with me."

"I never commanded him to do anything to harm himself. I only said . . ." Robin paused and dragged his hand through his hair. "Wait. It may have been the last thing I said to him. He was still under my influence."

She whirled around. "What did you say to him? 'Go blow your head off'?"

"I told him it was time to put an end to this." Robin

moved to the window before she could react and caught her by the waist. "I meant the violence and the robbery, Chris. Not his life. It's not as if he wore a sign around his neck saying that he was suicidal."

"You bastard." She tore away from his hands, reaching for the vase he had admired. He lunged, knocking her to the carpet, but she rolled out from beneath him before he could pin her. He grabbed the back of her skirt, using it to drag her back, whipping his head to one side as she smashed the vase against his skull.

Robin shook the glass shards from his face and hair before he gave her a grim smile. "Stop breaking the signorina's pretty things. I promised her we would take good care of them."

She gave an outraged cry as she threw herself at him, pummeling him with both hands, striking him in the face and chest, pelting him with tiny drops of her blood.

Robin stayed on his back but wrapped his arm around her, tightening it until she could not wriggle free. He felt her jerking at the front of his trousers, and with his free hand he ripped off the remains of her skirt. As she freed his cock, he tore at her panties until she was naked from the waist down.

Robin slid into Chris at the same instant she impaled herself on him. The rough joining caused their hip bones to collide, and the jolt rocked through both of them, spurring them on. She clawed his shirt open to get at his chest, and he dug his fingers into her bottom, twisting her atop him so that he felt every soft, wet inch of her caressing him.

Robin swore as he felt her teeth on his flat nipple and her nails raking over his ribs. He grabbed her hair and forced her head up.

"You waste your time and energy, my lady. My flesh cannot be pierced by the teeth of a mortal." He allowed her to see his fangs. "You need these to tear into it."

"That's it." She lifted herself until their sexes separated, and would have gotten to her feet if he hadn't held on to her. "I'm done with this. I am *done* with you. So take your fake little plastic fangs and shove them."

"These are my *dents acérées*," he snarled. "They are quite real, I assure you."

"All right, then. Do it." She extended her arm. "Go on. Bite me, suck my blood, whatever. Prove to me that you're a vampire right now." When he didn't move, she sneered, "Go ahead. You might actually draw some blood. I've had an HIV test. I'm clean."

Robin kept his eyes locked with hers as he seized her wrist and brought her forearm to his face. He breathed in her scent and traced the veins running beneath her skin with the tip of his tongue. When he felt her shudder, he lifted his mouth an inch above her flesh and then buried his fangs in her.

Chris inhaled sharply.

He drank from her, swallowing once, twice, and then lifted his mouth from the puncture wounds his fangs had made. "There. It is done."

Chris had not cried out or said anything while he had fed on her, and now she stared at him, her eyes wide. "They are real." She touched his lips. "Unless . . . are they implants?"

"After I feed they retract. See for yourself." He guided her fingers to the sharp tips so she could feel them retreat into the twin recesses in the roof of his mouth. "Implants cannot do that."

She stroked her fingertips gently over the open apertures before she took her hand away. "No, they can't."

He didn't have to ask her if she believed him. He could see it in her eyes, her innocence gone, crushed by the truth. He thought he saw pain as well, and realized only then that he had taken her without any preparation. "Forgive me for hurting you. It seems you are immune to my scent, so I could not bespell you first."

"It didn't hurt that much." She turned her arm from right to left. "Everything else you said is true, isn't it? About being a vampire or whatever you are. About Norman and the bank."

He nodded.

"He left his suicide note for me. He told me that he'd let the Magician get away, and that he was too tired and sad to start over." She dragged in a deep breath. "He told me not to grieve for him. Because of that note, all the guys in the Chicago office thought we were sleeping together."

"But you weren't."

"No, the only guy I've slept with in the last couple of years is you. So what does that make me?" Her gaze moved from her wounds to his face. "Food. Food that you have sex with. Oh, Jesus." She put her hand over her eyes. "That's why you blindfolded me that night. Why I tasted blood when you came back and I kissed you." She stiffened. "You didn't get it from me. Who did you bite? One of the girls in your harem?"

"I do not have a sodding harem. I took what I needed from my stores. Bagged blood, Chris. The same as you'd get in a hospital." Robin brought her down against him and held her until some of the stiffness left her body. "You are not food to me. We do not think of humans in that manner. We need only a little blood to sustain us. We do not kill for it."

"Then what do you need me for?"

There was a terrible bleakness in her eyes. The despair of someone who had seen too much truth and known too little tenderness.

"It rhymes with Chris." He brought her up, sliding her over him until he could reach her lips. She hesitated, and then groaned and opened her mouth for his.

Before, they had gone at each other like animals; now Robin wanted only to take her back to the night when she had come to him, willing and curious and oh, so passionate. He lifted her and carried her to the back of the apartment, into the signorina's bedroom, where he placed her like a jewel on the thick red and gold velvet duvet covering the bed.

"Pretty." She stroked the material. "We shouldn't use her bed."

"She does not need it, and I am not making love to you on a floor covered with broken glass." He pulled off his clothes and bent to remove the rest of hers.

"Making love." Her expression turned bemused. "Is that what we're doing?"

He smiled down at her. "Move over and see."

She rolled onto her side as he joined her, and stroked his arm with her hand. "I'm human; you're not. I'm a federal agent; you're an international art thief. I'm going to grow old and die; you're going to stay young and live forever. You have a harem, probably three or four, and I have . . . This is never going to work."

"I do not have a harem." His hair tickled her cheek as he kissed the edge of her jaw. "What do you have?"

"Nothing. No one. I've never been in love." Her cognac eyes darkened before she looked away. "I don't know how. I don't think I can."

"Then I will show you. I am a man; you are a woman." He pressed her back against the pillows. "I am hard; you are soft." He shifted his hips, settling between her thighs. "I am the blade; you are the sheath. Watch how we fit together. This is us. This is the love we make."

He rubbed the swollen head of his shaft against her, parting her as he pressed in. Their violent joining earlier must have left her tender,for as he worked his penis into her she made soft sounds in her throat and lifted her hips, adjusting herself around his girth.

"Are you hurting?" Robin asked once he had penetrated her completely.

"Not anymore." She arched her back, rubbing her breasts against him as she tried to smile. "What about you?"

"Some of my parts are aching." He slid out of her several inches before carefully easing back in. "This one particularly, Christiana."

"I don't know any Christiana, but I could give it a massage." Her hand moved down and curled around the base of him. As he came out of her, she tightened her fingers. "Hmmmm. You must be in a lot of pain. I can feel it throbbing."

"That it is." He clenched his teeth as she held him. "Let me in, love, before it bursts."

She released him only to cradle the delicate sac beneath as he pushed in. His balls tightened against her palm, ready even now to pump her full of his seed.

"You need to come," she said.

"Not yet," he begged, stroking faster, pressing higher. "I want you with me."

"I don't think . . ." She closed her eyes as he used his fingers to open the folds over her clitoris so that every thrust dragged his shaft across it. "Yes, there. Oh, God. Right there."

Robin fucked his cock into her body over and over, working her into her pleasure until he felt her muscles clasp him and the ripples inside her spreading. She came around him with a thin cry, and he buried himself in the center of the storm, shaking and groaning as she pulled at him, filling herself with the furious streams of his semen. He collapsed on his side, shifting her before their bodies separated so that he could feel his penis soften inside her.

"So good." She buried her face in his chest, her breasts heaving, her hands still clutching.

When this was over, Robin thought, stroking her shoulder slowly, he would not give her up. She belonged to him now, and for all that had been taken from him, he deserved her. He would move heaven and earth if need be, but he would have her, and be the love that she had never had, for the rest of their lives.

I'm human; you're not.

Luisa watched the nurse change the bandages covering her left hand and felt bemused. In one of her visions, she had seen Alexandra Keller do the same thing for a Frenchwoman who had been badly burned, right before she held her hand and told her something that made her cry.

Bad news, she'd thought, and had deliberately shut down the vision.

Some things were never meant to be shared. She had never told the doctor or anyone that the men who had attacked her were Brethren. Like the lost book, and the painful choices that would have to be made because of it, that truth was not for Alex Keller or the Darkyn to know before the proper time.

Luisa.

The connection she shared with the shadow prince allowed him to call to her, too, but she had to wait until the nurse left her room before she could answer him.

I'm here. She closed her eyes so that anyone who might walk into her room while she was in the waking dream wouldn't see her eyes change. *What's wrong?*

She saw that almost immediately. Her prince stood over the small, unmoving body of a baby deer. It lay on the grass next to a highway, and although it was still breathing, the twisted condition of its legs and the blood soaking the ground under it told her it wouldn't be for much longer.

Will it die?

Yes. She felt his despair match her own. *Unless you can help it.*

For the first time since he had come into his talent, he

wanted to try. He began taking off the glove covering his right hand. Only his fear of failure made him stop. *I can't.*

Then do nothing. She hardened her heart. *It's only roadkill.*

The shadow prince picked up the fawn and carried it into the woods, away from the road. He laid it gently on a bed of leaves and took his gloved hands away.

Luisa watched and held on to hope, thin as it was. However much she wanted the fawn to live and the prince's wounds to heal, she couldn't choose for either of them. She could only pray that the baby deer would cling to its life, and the prince would overcome his fear of death before the poor creature bled to death.

Why won't you help me?

He wanted her to push him to do it, Luisa thought, a little startled to learn that he thought she had that much influence over him. *I can only see, and dream.*

I'll trade you.

That hurt. *You aren't the only one who never asked for this to happen to them. Don't you think I would give it back if I could?*

But you wouldn't give it to anyone else.

No. Luisa felt her own bitterness twist in her breast. *Not even to the men who hurt me.*

The shadow prince bowed his head for a moment before he stripped off his gloves and placed his big hands over the fawn's neck and back. He murmured something she couldn't hear—a prayer?—and then closed his eyes.

His sun had set an hour ago, but light began to stream down through the thick boughs overhead, pale and silvery, the memories of moonbeams. They settled around the shadow prince, setting him aglow, and danced over his dark face before gliding down his arms and pooling in his hands. The fawn twitched, and then it lifted its head and looked at the shadow prince with its large, soft eyes.

As he took his hands away and the light faded, the tiny creature struggled, thrashing its hooves before it scrambled upright. It stood on straight, strong legs, spellbound and trembling, but it did not run.

The shadow prince held out his hand and stroked the animal's small head before he, too, rose and stepped away.

The fawn found its legs and dashed off.

Luisa let out the breath she hadn't realized she'd been holding. *You did it. That wasn't so bad, was it?*

He looked up through the trees at the grinning moon and shook his head. *You expect too much from me, Princess.*

Despite his success, Luisa knew he wasn't ready to accept what he was. She wanted to see him come out of the darkness into the light so much that she thought she might scream, but the wisdom that had come with the sight made her understand.

Like her, he needed more time. At least they both had plenty of that.

Luisa felt a vision rising, one of another dark prince. *I have to go now.*

He reached out to her one last time, showing her a rare glimpse of his own longing and loneliness. *Come to me in my dreams.*

I will.

Luisa pulled back into herself, taking the vision with her, and opened herself to see. The other man's lust filled her as she looked through his eyes, and she felt his anger and envy as he watched the lovers.

The man in the building directly across the street from Signorina Lorena DeGrazzi's apartment lowered the binoculars he had been using to watch the couple having sex and released the bulge straining at the front of his trousers.

As he pumped himself with his own hand, he imagined the red-haired mortal straining under him as he plowed into her, her dark eyes on his face. Only when her face changed into that of another did he jerk with hollow pleasure as he came alone in the empty room.

He washed his hands before he picked up the phone to place the call.

She answered with, "Well?"

"I tracked them from the airport to an apartment in the city," he told her in the ruined, whispering rasp that she thought was all that remained of his voice. That his voice was slowly coming back and growing stronger by the day was something he had to conceal until he had his revenge. Then he would use it to tell the truth and right the wrongs committed against him by his cousin and the Americans. "They appear to be staying in for the night. Your call worked."

"You sound jealous of Locksley, my lord," she said. "Perhaps when you are finished with him and his little mortal, you will come and stay at my villa for a few weeks."

He would rather perform the oral arts on a diseased-riddled whore on the steps of the Vatican, but saw no reason to tell her that. "Perhaps."

She laughed. "Such enthusiasm. But I know you are eager to collect your reward. Everything is prepared. You have but to stay out of sight until sunset tomorrow."

"What about the woman?"

"You will need to keep up your strength, yes?" she purred. "I believe that he also cares for her, so whatever you might do to her in front of him might prove most amusing." Her voice grew crisp. "All you must do is bring the manuscript to me, and you will have your revenge. Until tomorrow, my lord."

He put down the phone and returned to his seat by the window. Idly he touched the ring of scar tissue around his neck. Most nights he did not regret the miracle that Alexandra Keller had performed on him. She had told him that he would never speak again, but that part of his throat had somehow grown back in the months since the operation she had performed on him. But tonight he felt the weight of the world and all it had taken from him, and almost wished the pretty little doctor had finished the butchery he had been subjected to instead of repairing it.

If I am to live in purgatory, then I will see him in hell first.

Guy of Guisbourne, Lord Nottingham, lifted the binoculars to his eyes again.

Chapter 13

"Good evening, my lords," Richard Tremayne, high lord of the Darkyn, said as he looked down the long table at the men seated around it. "Thank you for making the journey here."

As Geoffrey's footmen filled their glasses with blood-wine, Michael surveyed the other six seigneurs who had traveled from the four corners of the earth for *le conseil supérieur*. As the first seigneur of North America, Cyprien had never before attended such a gathering, but years of discussing Kyn policies and decisions had given him an idea of what to expect.

Like him, these seigneurs ruled over hundreds of *jardins* all over the world. As leaders, they were directly responsible for ensuring the safety and prosperity of their kind.

Michael knew Sevarus, the seigneur over the European continent, best; they had both served as Richard's commanders during the *jardin* wars. Sevarus had been a temple master during the rule of Philip the Fair in France and, when the Templar order had been disbanded and its warrior-priests arrested by the pope, had smuggled many of their kind to safety in England. During his final trip, he had been ambushed at the docks by the king's men and had lost his right hand and left eye in the ugly battle. No one who looked into the scarred eye socket or saw the emptiness at the end of his sleeve could ever doubt his loyalty to the Kyn.

Beside him Gilanden, seigneur of the Scandinavian countries, looked restless and out of place. The big Swede, a ship's captain who had circled the globe more times than even he remembered, had transformed the raiding Kyn under his rule into fleet of shrewd maritime traders. He lived on his own ship, which he sailed through the icy seas of his territory, and was never happy on land.

Cordoba of South America and Tristan of the Mediterranean, also old allies, appeared to be complete opposites. Cordoba, a Spaniard of an old and respected family, was as dark and earthy as Tristan, the son of a Norman baron, was fair and angelic-looking. The two had fostered together as boys, taken their vows, and fought in the Holy Land, always at each other's side. Michael had known twin brothers who had not been as close as the Spaniard and the Norman.

Zhang, the seigneur of Asia, had in his human lifetime been the result of a love affair between a shipwrecked English duke and the Chinese woman who had dragged him out of the sea. Upon his return to England, his father had sent him to the Templars, mostly so that he would not have to explain the blond-haired, black-eyed boy to his aristocratic family.

The voice of Zhang's seneschal crying out Phillipe's name still buzzed in Michael's ears. He had not meant to eavesdrop on their tryst, but the grunts and groans had at first made him think the two were having a different sort of battle. He had not lied when he had spoken of it later to his seneschal; Phillipe's personal life was none of his business, and knowing his seneschal had sex with men did not change Michael's regard or respect for him. He only wished things could be different for both of them.

Michael had never met Solange from Africa, but knew he and his lords had fled from Eastern Europe to the Dark Continent to escape the Nazis during the Second World War. Like Zhang, he had little contact with the Kyn of other countries, but accepted Richard's rule and maintained friendly ties to the other seigneurs.

Geoff's footmen finished serving and bowed before retreating from the reception room. Only then did the high lord begin the business of *le conseil supérieur*.

"I have brought you together so that we may address the growing threat against the Kyn," Richard said. "The Brethren have moved on and disbanded *jardins* in Italy and France, and it appears now they are continuing their attacks against our brothers in Spain. From the reports I have received from you and your suzerains, I conclude that it can be nothing less than an orchestrated campaign."

"This new Lightkeeper, Cardinal D'Orio, has instigated it," Tristan said. "From the time he replaced Stoss as the new head of the order, he has been rallying and goading the zealots."

"He does more than that." Sevarus leaned forward to glare at Richard through his good eye. "He has been systematically identifying and tracking my lords and their holdings through their financial dealings with humans. Somehow he has convinced the banks to aid him, for our accounts are being frozen and emptied, our properties seized and sold off, and the humans loyal to us bankrupted or arrested."

"Loss of our wealth does not concern me as much as these atrocious attacks on our strongholds," Cordoba put in. "They have burned Tristan's lords out of Italy and Sevarus's from France; as we speak Spain is under siege. Hundreds have come to my suzerains seeking refuge."

"You and Cyprien have accepted the tide of the refugees without complaint." Richard toyed with the stem of his glass. "Do you wish to them to seek sanctuary elsewhere?"

"No, my lord. I have more than enough territory, and I shall keep it open to all who accept my rule and yours." As he said that, Cordoba glanced at Tristan, who shook his head slightly.

"Are we to guess what you and your foster brother have obviously already discussed?" Richard asked.

"I have mapped the attacks and found a pattern," Tristan admitted. "They are moving in a chaotic fashion, but always to the west, burning every stronghold in their path as they go. They are shooting those who flee." He eyed Cyprien. "If the order continues the campaign at this pace, the hunters will reach the Atlantic by summer. From there they will have to turn around, or cross the sea and invade South America or the United States."

"They may turn to the north to attack my lords and their strongholds," Gilanden added sullenly.

Solange nodded. "Or move to the south to cross over to Morocco and move against mine."

Sevarus's shaggy head turned right and then left. "We have tolerated these zealots too long, my lord. The Brethren have vowed to destroy our kind, and we know they will never permit us to dwell in peace among humans. The time has come to settle this thing."

"I agree," Zhang said. The quietest of the Kyn rulers, the Asian seigneur rarely spoke, as his talent infused his voice with an enchanting, musical quality that he could use to hold humans and Kyn in a state of enchantment. "The order will never rest until we fill their torture chambers or cover the earth with our ashes. My suzerains and their warriors are ready to fight."

The other seigneurs added their agreements.

"Before we declare war on humans," Michael said sharply, silencing the other men around the table, "I would propose another course for consideration. We can expose the Brethren to the rest of humanity."

Richard's hood turned toward Cyprien. "And how will this protect us?"

"The Brethren are as secretive as we are. For centuries they have guarded their members and practices as carefully as we have our *jardins*," Michael said. "They breed new members for the order to keep outsiders from discovering their mission and the lengths to which they go to carry out their campaign against us. They have been quite successful as well. No human of this era would believe that immortal blood drinkers live among them, or that the Brethren hunt and slay us."

Richard made an impatient gesture. "Go on."

"If we were to make available to the media evidence of the order's membership, methods, practices, and propaganda, they would immediately exploit it." Michael saw the doubtful expressions around the table. "The scandal it would create would be enormous, especially when it was revealed how the order uses the positions they have assumed in the hierarchy of the Catholic Church to shield their identities and activities."

"Michael, if you expose the Brethren," Solange said, "you will expose us."

"Think on it, my lord," Michael replied. "The people of this era are not ignorant, superstitious peasants, cringing before the shadow of the cross. Modern humans wear the armor of disbelief and science, and little can penetrate it. Certainly CNN will run special reports for weeks on the topic, as will FOX and truTV. Secret vampire hunters will become all the rage among human adolescents. Shops in the malls will carry official Brethren T-shirts. Blessed wooden stakes and wreaths of garlic will be sold on eBay."

"It makes me yearn for the days when all we had to fear were the inquisitors and the stake." Gilanden squinted at Michael. "You make a good argument, Cyprien, but it is too much of a risk. The Brethren must have ample proof of our existence."

"Any proof they have, we can easily discredit," Michael assured him. "We have many high-placed friends among our *tresori* and the humans loyal to us."

"I disagree," Tristan said, abandoning his languid air. "Lord Gabriel and his *sygkenis* have rescued dozens of injured Kyn imprisoned by Brethren cells, so we must assume there are more in captivity. All they need produce is one prisoner and the humans will know we exist, and will believe anything they are told about us. If the Brethren feel they have nothing to lose, what is to stop them from doing just that?"

"They could be planning to expose us first," Sevarus said. "Done right, 'twould gain much sympathy for their cause."

Michael thought of the grotesque effects of the new, explosive copper ammunition the Brethren had employed against the Kyn. He had intended to relate Alexandra's theory of why they were using it, but tempers around the table were running too hot. "We cannot fight the order openly, not in this time."

"Battle is reserved for honorable opponents," Gilanden said. "For this work, we need to use assassins."

"What happened to that golden-haired viper who served you, Lord Tremayne?" Cordoba asked. "He seemed most efficient."

"No," Michael said before Richard could answer. "Lucan serves me now, and he is retired."

"Lucan serves the Kyn. He will do as he is told." Richard rose. "We will take the night to consider the matter, and meet again on the morrow to decide our course. Only remember this." He pulled back his hood, exposing his distorted countenance, which looked much more human than it had for the last two centuries, and regarded his seigneurs through his cat-shaped eyes. "Once a course is changed, deliberately or not, one may not return easily to what was in the beginning."

As the seigneurs began filing out of the room, Michael wondered if he should talk privately with the high lord. The rest of the seigneurs seemed hell-bent on going to war with the Brethren, and perhaps were somewhat justified in their attitudes, given the losses they had suffered during the attacks. Still, more violence was not the answer. Richard had averted many such conflicts during their history; he might listen to reason.

"Cyprien," Richard said, taking the decision out of his hands. "Stay for a moment, if you would."

When they were alone, Richard refilled his glass and Michael's with bloodwine. Performing the task of a servant was beneath him, but it was something he had not been able to do physically in more than two hundred years. The reversal of his changeling condition often bedeviled him—it seemed it would take forever, some nights—but such small things as being able to hold the neck of a wine bottle or the stem of a goblet gave him a great deal of secret pleasure.

"You appear much improved, my lord," Cyprien said as he took the glass Richard had filled. "When Alexandra sees the progress you have made, she will be pleased."

"We had a brief interlude in the hall yesterday, your *sygkenis* and I. *Pleased* is not the term I would use to describe her reception of me." Richard drank a little from his glass. After two lifetimes of being forced to live on almost nothing but cat's blood, the blend still tasted odd to him. "You were rather quick to condemn defending ourselves against these Brethren attacks."

"I would welcome a proposal for an intelligent defense, my lord," Cyprien said. "As I will, as soon as I hear one."

Richard had long regarded Michael Cyprien as the son he would never have. He knew that he indulged the other man's temper and independence too often. Sometimes, as today, the fleece of Michael's diplomacy did not always conceal the wolf beneath it.

"You should remember the purpose of this gathering is to come to a unified decision," he chided. "Six for and one against does not make a consensus. But perhaps you have lived too long in a democracy."

Cyprien put down his glass. "I cannot agree to blindly endorse the opinions of the majority. However inconvenient my opinions are, they should be at least regarded as equal in value to those of the others."

Richard sat down. "I forget how little time you actually spent in my courts. Politics are not about what is fair or just or even logical. They are the tools of those who wish to acquire influence, power, and control. Someday you will be made high lord after me. How will you rule over all the Kyn if you are obsessed with making things equal and honest and forthright?"

"I have no desire for your throne, my lord," Cyprien said stiffly. "I am content with my rule, such as it is."

Richard was amused. "That saucy wench has done more than stolen your heart. She has swept away all of your grand ambitions as well. Whatever you may say, I intend to formally name you as my heir. I cannot do that if you have turned against all of my other seigneurs."

Cyprien inclined his head. "Then I think you must choose another successor, my lord."

"You have ruled over your lords paramount in America with skill and imagination. You have not hesitated to take up the sword and lead your warriors to battle when peaceful measures have failed. You did it in New Orleans against Stoss, and again in South Florida when Farel went mad and Lucan attempted to carry out my orders and assassinate me." Richard stretched his mouth in an approximation of a human smile. "You have the spine for it, Michael."

Someone chuckled. "But not the belly."

Richard turned to see that two Kyn had entered the room. One, a green-eyed hunter dressed in leathers and carrying a motorcycle helmet, smiled at them. His companion, a fresh-faced girl with a head full of silvery white curls, eyed them with more reserve.

"Gabriel, Nicola." Michael went to them, embracing his old childhood friend before turning and bowing to his *sygkenis*. "Braxtyn told us to expect you in a few days."

"We had to get our cargo out of Spain," Nick said, turning to meet Richard's gaze. "You're looking better, Vampire King."

"Thank you, my dear." Since Richard's wife had butchered Nicola Jefferson's parents as well as changed the young human to Darkyn, he did not object to her informal address. "How many were you able to recover?"

"Fourteen," Gabriel said. "One died during the crossing. Another three may not survive the night."

"They're all in pretty bad shape." Nick tucked her hands in her black leather jacket. "They were burned out in France, but couldn't make it any farther than the north of Spain. They weren't there three days before the brothers caught up with them and did it again."

"The Brethren tracked them to the stronghold in Cádiz where they were taking refuge," Gabriel explained.

"How did they find them so quickly?" Cyprien asked.

"I think they're using Kyn trackers," Nick said before Gabriel could answer. She glanced at him. "Baby, I know you want us all to be one big, happy, loyal family, but it's the only explanation. How else could they find them that fast?"

Gabriel sighed. "As much as I dislike it, I must agree with Nicola. These hunters are now moving as quickly as we do. They go from one stronghold to another without deviation."

That the Brethren could hunt as swiftly as his two best trackers disturbed Richard deeply. He knew the order imprisoned and tortured Kyn; he and Gabriel had personally suffered that horrendous ordeal. They had also used torture and blackmail to pervert a few Kyn into voluntarily collaborating with them, and even killing for them, as they had Thierry Durand's wife, Angelica.

"We will speak with the survivors," Cyprien said. "If the zealots are using our own kind to hunt us, some of them may have been recognized."

"There's something else you should hear," Nick said. "We grabbed one of the brothers from the cell in Madrid to find out if there were any plans to move on other strongholds in Spain or Portugal. He wasn't able to hold out under the influence like most of them can. He told Gabriel some interesting stuff."

"After I bespelled him, he gave us the locations he knew were targeted for attack, and then he began raving. He spoke of a plot to bring down our leaders," Gabriel said. "When I asked him who they planned to kill, he named you, my lord. You and every one of your seigneurs."

Chris hadn't expected to sleep through the day, or to wake up alone, but when she turned her head she saw twilight through the windows and the other half of the bed empty. Her head told her she hadn't been drugged, but the duvet and the bedsheets were gone, and someone had taken down the curtains and left the windows bare.

He wouldn't leave me here, not if I could just get dressed and . . .

The missing bedsheets and curtains suggested that he'd not only left her, he'd made sure she couldn't follow him.

Chris got up and went from room to room, just to be sure. Her torn clothes, along with every curtain, towel, sheet, and piece of clothing the signorina owned, had vanished from the apartment.

Still naked, Chris walked back into the bedroom to check

the closet. That was when she spotted a folded piece of paper tucked under the base of the bedside lamp.

"He wouldn't." She pulled it out and unfolded it.

I'll be back with the manuscript by midnight, love.
Save the next dance for me. R.

Chris tore up the note and flung the pieces on the bare mattress.

Robin had done more than leave her naked and alone, she discovered as she went to the phone and found it dead, the connector wires gone. He'd also rearmed the security system—the one to which only he had the codes—and taken the cases he'd brought from the airport with him.

He'd been so confident that she wouldn't get out of the apartment that he'd left the signorina's laptop computer there. She immediately tried to access the Internet, but found he'd removed those connection cords as well.

"You think of everything, don't you, smart guy." Chris pulled up the log-in file and saw that that he hadn't erased the Web pages he'd accessed while using it. "Or maybe you didn't." Chris pulled up directions to a costume shop, directions on traveling by car from Rome to Venice, and a map of the latter city, with a red-starred address that appeared to be a private home. She printed out each page on the signorina's smart little ink-jet.

"Why do you need a costume to go to Venice?" She tossed aside the pages and rested her throbbing head against her palms. "And why would you leave me here in Rome?"

It had to be the phone call he'd taken last night before they'd gotten into their wrestling match. Someone had made arrangements to meet him—maybe in costume, maybe at this house in Venice.

Chris went into the kitchen to splash her hot face with some water. Robin had left on the signorina's graceful bistro table a plate of sliced semolina bread, a slice of softened Brie, and plump red grapes next to a bottle of superb Italian wine and a cut-crystal glass. As a final, rather romantic touch, he'd placed a silver bud vase with a single pink rose in it beside the plate.

Chris stood and stared at the food without seeing it, and then plucked the rose from the bud vase and twirled it between her fingers before she brought it to her nose. "You may think you're slick, Magic Man, but you're not a woman, and you never spent a year at Quantico."

From the log-off annotation on the computer, Robin had a half-hour head start on her, which didn't give her a lot of time. Chris showered first, sluicing off with her hands the excess water from her body before using the signorina's handheld hair dryer on her skin as well as her head. She then marched into the kitchen and grimly enjoyed the light meal he'd left for her.

When she finished eating, she scouted through the apartment again, searching expertly to be sure he had removed all of the clothing before returning to the closet. The signorina's expensive leather purses caught her eye, but none of them were large enough to take apart and make into any sort of garment without a sewing machine, and there was none to be found in this place.

Do you sew, Clarice?

She didn't sew, but she loved fashion design, and had watched every episode of *Project Runway* for the last four seasons. As a result Chris knew a dozen ways to make clothing out of the unlikeliest materials.

The signorina had been wearing a silk scarf over her hair; Chris was betting that it was a regular habit of hers to protect her 'do whenever she went out in her convertible. Just as Chris's mom had.

Just as some women wouldn't leave home without

makeup in their purse, Beth Renshaw had always carried a scarf with her, no matter where she went.

Chris began opening the designer purses, grinning as she found a neatly folded scarf inside each one. All of the scarves were in the signorina's favorite colors of white, gold, yellow, and orange and complimented one another.

She shook out each one, studying the dimensions. The thirteen scarves she had found were all made of thin, almost transparent silk, but they were long and wide—almost twice as large as the ones Chris liked to wear.

Chris's mother had often let her play dress-up with all the scarves she had collected over the years. One scarf did not a dress make, but thirteen of them . . .

Slowly a smile stretched her mouth. "I think I just won immunity from the next challenge."

Chris gathered them together and went over to the full-length mirror. She knotted two of the white scarves together behind her neck, drew the ends over her shoulders, and crossed them over her breasts to fashion a halter top. She used eight more to wrap and tie in alternating layers around her hips, beginning with the darkest colors and ending with the lightest, most transparent scarf.

The two smallest scarves she wound around her feet, and crisscrossed and tied the ends around her ankles like toe-shoe ribbons. She studied the results in the bathroom mirror; the outfit looked young, daring, and distinctly designer.

The other purses also yielded a makeup kit, mini spray bottles of Italian perfume, some gold earrings, necklaces, and bracelets, and a nice pile of currency.

Chris put on enough makeup and jewelry to make her look as chic as her impromptu ensemble and then went to deal with the security system.

The signorina had a relatively uncomplicated alarm system with electromagnetic sensors, the sort that would be triggered by anyone opening the door or windows. This

Lynn Viehl

might have defeated Chris but for two bits of luck. Due to the age of the building, the technician who had installed it had gotten creative with the wiring, running it in nooks and crannies around the door and windows to avoid drilling into the apartment's old masonry and plasterwork. That gave her easy access to what ordinarily might not be exposed.

Chris also had the advantage of having spent years studying different techniques used by burglars and thieves to bypass the exact same type of security system, used extensively in Europe by churches and modest-size museums. Because brownouts were common in most cities, she knew the system had a thirty-second signal delay programmed into it to allow for temporary power disruption.

Half a minute was all she needed to bypass the circuit.

She retrieved a sharp paring knife from the kitchen, some metal hair clips from the bathroom, and went to work. It took her ten minutes to strip the wiring she needed from two lamp cords and jury-rig a bypass circuit for the door. She then found the signorina's breaker box and killed the power to the front rooms, running to hook up the circuit before running back and switching the breakers back on.

She tested the results. Her bypass allowed her to open the door and close it without tripping the alarm.

Chris went to retrieve one of the signorina's purses, put two sharp, thin fillet knives from the kitchen inside it, and walked out into the hall. On the stairs she had to pass two tenants as she made her way down, but other than a sniff from the older woman and a grinning lecherous stare from her husband, they didn't speak to her or try to stop her.

Chris didn't see any taxis, but she remembered several that had been parked in front of a busy hotel that she and Robin had passed on their drive through the city from the airport. She walked three blocks down to it, but had to stop halfway to remove the scarves wrapping her feet, as they began to fray and come apart. Barefoot now, she adjusted the folds of silk over her breasts, exposing a little more cleavage before she walked up to the hotel entrance.

The porters, busy unloading suitcases from three different taxis, ignored her. That allowed her to pick up a man's trench coat that had been tossed on top of the suitcases on one of the carts before she climbed into the back of an unoccupied cab.

"Do you speak English?" Chris asked the driver. When he nodded, she said, "Take me to the American embassy, please."

Chapter 14

At a public mooring in Venice, Robin docked the boat he had appropriated a short distance from the home of Pietro and Lucia Mariana, and went below to put on the garments he had borrowed from the costume shop. The brown suede tunic and trousers were well made, although he chuckled at the design of the clothing.

Modern mortals had no idea how much they romanticized the dress from his human lifetime. If he had run about Sherwood in such fine clothing he would have been arrested on sight.

From the pier Robin walked to the manor and went around to the back, pausing only to conceal his face behind a half mask of black and brown feathers before mounting the steps to the delivery entrance. The kitchen, filled with caterers and waiters, was such a hive of frantic activity that no one gave him a second look.

The theme of the party was Carnivale, and the Marianas had invited every young, rich Venetian to celebrate their fifth wedding anniversary. A small orchestra played in a balcony above the ballroom, which was decorated in green, gold, and sapphire. Several hundred guests danced, drank, and wandered down the extensive buffet.

The happy couple were holding court at one end of the room, but Robin was more interested in the lone wolves prowling the room.

When Salva had called and told him that Nottingham would be in Venice tonight to bring the manuscript to his buyer, Robin knew she lied, and that the two of them had set a trap for him. He didn't know why the contessa had sold him out to his old enemy, but he imagined it was to secure the manuscript. In one sense it was a relief; he could leave Chris safely in Rome while stealing the manuscript out from under Nottingham's nose. Once he had it, Robin knew the contessa would do whatever he wanted.

Robin picked up a trace of dark, hot licorice in the air, and began tracking it through the room. It led him out of the ball and to a cloakroom, where a dazed, smiling maid was hanging up a man's trench coat.

Nottingham's scent pooled here, indicating that he had recently used *l'attrait* in this spot for some purpose, but it was another, lighter, mortal fragrance clinging to the coat that made Robin's gut twist.

She couldn't have gotten out. She would have had to walk naked down the streets of Rome. She had no money or means to travel here.

"Did a young lady with red hair give you that coat?" he asked the maid.

"Ah, *si*, Salome." She nodded and smiled.

"Salome?"

"She wear beautiful dress made out of veils." The maid waved her hand up and down. "All veils."

Somehow Chris had found something to wear and *had* gotten out of the apartment, left Rome, and followed him to Venice—or someone had dressed her and taken her from it. Robin clenched his hand against the doorjamb, causing the wood to crack and splinter. "Was she with a man with black hair and eyes?"

"No, Signor, she came alone." The maid gave him a dreamy look, her pupils widely dilated. "The lady, she had no mask, but a man gave me a very pretty ruby mask to take to her." She frowned a little. "That man have black hair, black eyes."

Robin turned and ran back to the ballroom.

Chris blessed the fact that the FBI had offices around the world, and that as an undercover agent she needed only a security pass code to use the resources of the branch office at the American embassy. She had been tempted to relate the truth of her situation to the agent in charge and let him and his staff take over, but the end result would be that the contessa would have Hutch killed. Also, she didn't think anyone would believe her story. Instead she settled for identification, money, a pair of shoes, maps, and a car, and drove down to Venice.

Now that Chris had finally found the private home where Robin had been heading, and searched the faces around her, her frustration mounted. How could she find a thief at a party where everyone was wearing masks?

At least he wouldn't recognize her, not wearing a dress made of scarves, and the black stiletto heels she had borrowed from the embassy secretary were two sizes too large, but they made her three inches taller. The elaborate mask the cloakroom attendant had brought to her covered her entire face from chin to hairline, and sparkled with hundreds of tiny faux rubies and garnets. She caught a glimpse of her reflection in one of the mirrored wall panels and flinched a little. From a distance the mask made her look as if her head were on fire.

Cool fingers skimmed over her shoulder. "May I have this dance, Signorina?" a rasping male voice whispered near her ear.

She turned to face a tall jester dressed in black, white,

and silver. For a split second she thought it was Robin, but the hot eyes looking at her through the alabaster mask were black, not amethyst.

"No, thank you." She smelled licorice-flavored liquor and hoped he hadn't drunk enough to become a pest. "I'm looking for a friend I'm supposed to meet here."

"Wait." He took her hand as she turned away. "We could amuse each other until this friend of yours arrives."

Chris knew she'd look out of place if she kept refusing to dance, so she forced a smile. "Maybe we'll run into him out on the dance floor."

"Of that I have no doubt." He put an arm around her waist and guided her out through the whirling couples to the center of the room.

Chris mainly concentrated on not tripping in the loose stilettos, but she became distracted by her partner a few times. He moved as if the music had been composed for him, but at the same time she got the distinct impression that he was no more involved in the dance than she was. He didn't try to grope her, even when their bodies brushed, which also seemed at odds with the way he stared down at her. Then there were his hands. Although he wore black leather gloves, everywhere he touched her Chris felt her skin tighten, and more than once the sensation made her shiver.

"Are you a friend or a relative of our hosts?" she asked him.

"An old acquaintance of the family." As a man nearby laughed, he turned his head toward the sound, pulling at the collar of his costume.

Chris saw a horizontal scar running across his throat and had to hide a wince. He must have had surgery on his throat; that would explain why his voice rasped the way it did.

Chris absently followed the jester's lead, moving automatically to the final movements of the boisterous Viennese waltz the musicians were playing overhead. She studied the shoulders, hair, and skin color of every man who passed by her. It wasn't until her partner twirled her around and tugged her up against his body that she realized the waltz had ended and everyone had slowed down to the throbbing, sensual strains of a bolero.

"I'd better go," she said reluctantly. "I don't think my friend will be showing up."

"I could perhaps serve as his substitute?"

Chris gave him a rueful smile. "My friends are not as nice as you, Mr. . . . ?"

"Guy." He slid around her, hands encircling her waist, before he took her hands and raised her arms, bringing her face close to his. "You should take the opportunity to make new friends, Signorina."

Chris saw a man dressed like a medieval huntsman moving toward them. From the width of the shoulders and the silken fall of his black hair, it was Robin. The set of his jaw under the feathered mask he wore indicated that he was not happy.

"Perhaps I should." She smiled up into his black eyes before she spun away, tugging at his hand as she wove her way through the dancing couples.

Guy followed, occasionally catching her to bring her close or drop her in a brief dip before allowing her to lead. Chris kept an eye on the huntsman, who was now dancing with a giggling blond Aphrodite in a ridiculously short toga, and stayed out of his reach.

The bolero ended with Chris bent back over the jester's arm, her hands curled over his shoulders for balance. He brought her up slowly, bending at the same time until she turned her head and his mouth skimmed over her cheek.

Guy brought her upright, his gloved hand curling around her neck. "You are an excellent dancer, Signorina."

"So are you." Chris didn't expect him to pull her into a

clinch, but he did, and she stiffened. "I think I'm finished dancing for the night."

"Are you?" He pulled off her mask, caught her face between his big, black-gloved hands, and kissed her. Chris recoiled, but his lips slanted over hers and he tasted her thoroughly before he set her away from him. "Until we meet again, Agent Renshaw."

The next thing she knew he disappeared into the crowd of couples on the dance floor.

Ungentle hands jerked her around to face the huntsman with the brown feathered mask. "What are you doing here?"

"I could ask you the same question." She tried to go after Guy, but Robin's grip brought her up short and, thanks to the borrowed shoes, she stumbled, off balance. When she righted herself, she said, "That man I was dancing with knew my name. He called himself 'Guy.'" She watched his face. "He's Paul Sherwood, or Nottingham, or whatever you call him, isn't he?"

"He is." Robin put an arm around her.

"The contessa called you last night and told you to come to Venice," Chris pointed out, "and he was waiting for you. If you haven't noticed yet, Robin, you're being set up."

"I know," he said, pushing her through the crowd, pausing to take a deep breath before changing direction and walking her toward the terrace. "You were supposed to stay in Rome. I don't want you caught in the middle between us. This is Kyn business."

"What are you talking about? You *put* me in the middle of this." She tapped his sternum with her finger. "You've illegally entered this country and stolen a Mercedes, an apartment, that costume you're wearing, and God only knows what else. You've caused a priceless work of art to be stolen and compromised a federal investigation, not to mention my job. But that doesn't matter, not if Hutch and the other hostages are killed over this thing. We're going to get the book and take it to the contessa and get Hutch freed. That's all I care about."

Out on the terrace he stopped and put one hand on her throat. He didn't choke her, but he looked as if he wanted to. "Your *partner* is all that matters to you? Did we settle nothing between us last night?"

She gripped his wrist. "You left me locked up, naked, and helpless in a city where I don't even speak the language. How do you think that made me feel?"

"I wrote you a note," he said, his upper lip curling a degree short of a sneer. "Was that not a sufficient measure to reassure you?"

Chris ducked her head. "Okay. Maybe I deserved that. But I didn't leave you alone and afraid in a strange place."

"Didn't you? That night I woke up and reached for you, and you were gone." He made it sound as if she'd set fire to the bed. "Do you wish to know how many years it has been since I slept through a day? I cannot remember; that is how long. Yet when I am with you—twice now—I have slept without waking."

"I'm not a sleeping pill," she snapped.

"No, you're mine. My *kyara*, my lover, my heart." He turned away from her and strode the length of the balcony before walking back. "It's right in front of you and you still don't see it? I'm falling in love with you."

She shook her head. "You just like having sex with me."

"You've never been in love, so how would you bloody well know?" He laughed as she flinched. "You're brilliant to hold on to your heart the way you do. Me, I fall in love with a mortal. A mortal who wishes to imprison me. This should end very well."

She lifted her face and saw the bitterness in his beautiful eyes. "It doesn't happen like this. Not this fast. I've only known you for a couple of days. We have nothing in com-

mon. You kidnapped me. I'm supposed to arrest you."
Suddenly she realized she wasn't trying to talk him out of
it. She was talking to herself. "You don't know anything
about me."

"I know you don't want me," he snapped. "That seems to
be the only sort of woman I can fall in love with."

Chris looked out at the water. She wanted him, all right.
More than her career, her self-respect, her dignity, even her
humanity. She was in love with an angry, handsome, om-
nipotent immortal who could have any woman just by
sweating around her.

"Chris," Robin said. "You've just gone completely
white."

"Yeah." The balcony began to whirl a little. "I need to sit
down."

He brought her to one of the stone benches, sat down
with her, and pulled her into the circle of his arm. They both
watched the lights scatter on the gently rippling surface of
the canal.

"Is this because of me?" she heard him ask. She shook
her head. "You didn't know how I felt. I shouldn't have said
anything. I frightened you."

"Sometimes you do. The fangs, the drinking blood, the
way you drive. I should have had three heart attacks and a
stroke already." She glanced sideways at him, and what
she saw in his eyes decided everything for her. "You are
wrong about one thing, and so was I. I've never been in
love before . . . until now."

Robin stared at her for a long time. "God." He pressed
her face into his shoulder.

"How scared are you?" Chris asked, her voice muffled
by his tunic.

"You broke out of the apartment. You tracked me here.
You are wearing a dress made out of silk scarves." He set

her at arm's length and gave her a crooked smile. "You ter-
rify me. So what will we do now?"

"We're in this together, Robin," she said. "I don't have
any superpowers, but I am a trained investigator. From now
on, I watch your back and you watch mine. When we recover the manuscript, when we save my partner and your
friends, then we'll deal with the rest of it."

"This practicality of yours is a superpower, as well as a
damned nuisance," he said, tucking her head under his chin.
"We'll find a way to make it work, Chris. I swear to you."

She blinked back stinging tears and cleared her throat
before she drew back. "How do we find Nottingham now?"

"By his scent. My kind can track one another by following it." He looked out into the night and breathed in. "He's
moving east, toward the old part of the city."

"There's just one more thing." She straightened her legs
to show him the too-large stilettos. "I need some new
shoes."

After convincing one of the human females at the ball
with the same-size foot as Chris to give him her slippers,
Robin took her with him, following Nottingham's scent
through a labyrinth of ancient streets, pausing here and
there to be sure he had not doubled back or left a false trail
by using a human upon whom he had fed to scatter his
scent.

Chris kept pace with him, her eyes alert and her movements as economical as his. He knew from making love to
her that she kept her body in superb condition, but now he
saw how beautifully she had honed her senses as well.
Twice she tugged him back just as he heard approaching
footsteps; for a mortal she had almost Kyn-like instincts.

Together they tracked Nottingham's path until his scent
led Robin to a twenty-foot-high brick wall with a narrow
gated arch. Through the bars of the gate he saw an empty,

boarded-up palazzo surrounded on all sides by other smaller, abandoned outbuildings. Mold marks and the crumbling condition of the outer walls suggested that the former tenants had been driven out by flooding, a problem that regularly plagued Venice.

"This looks new." Robin reached for the padlock on the gate, then hissed and pulled back his burned fingers. "It's made of copper."

"Wait." Chris looked all around the entrance until she spotted a disconnected pipe sticking up out of the ground near the gate. "That looks like it's made of steel; do you think you can break off a piece?"

Robin snapped the pipe off at the ground level and handed it to her.

"Thanks." She ignored the padlock and went to the side of the gate. There she used the end of the pipe like a chisel, not on the gate but on the decaying brick to which it had been attached. Small chunks of the brick began flying away from the wall, loosening the bolts that had been driven into it.

"If I may?" Robin held out his hand.

She scowled a little but handed him the pipe. Robin used it in the same way she had, but put his Kyn strength behind each jab. Within seconds he had freed the gate bolts and hinges from their moldering frame on one side. Chris pulled it out until the gap was wide enough for them to pass through.

"No security cameras, vehicles, or signs of occupation," she murmured after a few moments.

Robin turned his head right, then left. "He's been all over the grounds, but the scent is strongest there." He nodded toward the palazzo's main building. "You should stay here while I search."

"I should have stayed at the apartment, too."

She followed him through the shadows as they approached

the side of the main house. Robin saw one door that hadn't been boarded over, and started toward it.

"Hey. Let's not walk directly into another trap," Chris suggested, and glanced up. "I see another way in. Can you give me a boost up to that second-story window?"

"I can toss you through it," he said, eyeing the boards covering it. "But I fear your head isn't *that* hard."

"Just lift me onto your shoulders," she said, removing one of the scarves tied around her hips and wrapping it around her right hand. "I'll do the rest."

Robin lifted her to sit on his shoulders, and then walked over to stand directly under the window before holding her hands so she could plant her feet. Chris didn't try to open the window, but tossed the scarf up, threading the end over the bottom rung of an old fire-escape ladder and catching it to create a loop.

She held on to the scarf, looked at him, and said, "Let me down easy."

The corroded metal groaned and rained rust down on both of them as Robin eased her to her feet, but the old iron ladder came down intact.

"The windows on the upper floors aren't boarded up, and the floodwater never got that high, so they're probably not warped shut," she said after she tested the steadiness of the ladder. "We just have to climb up there and see."

Afraid the old ladder might collapse, Robin stayed right behind Chris as they climbed it to the fourth floor. As she predicted, the window nearest the ladder remained accessible, and opened after Robin forced the lock.

The empty interior of the room they stepped into magnified every sound they made. The lack of light made Chris blind, but Robin's night-adapted vision allowed him to find the door leading out at once. He stood beside it first, breathed in, and listened.

"He's below us," he said. "I can smell only him, no one

else." Robin pulled his tunic off and draped it around her. When she frowned, he added, "It will help mask your scent."

She regarded his bare chest. "Who is he more likely to smell first, you or me?"

"You." Robin looked down at her. "But he would not expect me to bring a human with me while I am tracking, and may believe that whatever he smells of you comes from me."

She frowned. "Why would you smell like me?"

"You leave your scent on me every time you touch me," he said, bringing her hand to his face and kissing her palm. "After we make love I can smell you on my skin for hours."

Her expression turned wry. "I seem to have the same problem."

"It is why infidelity is not common among my kind. Stop looking at me that way or I shall collect more of your scent." He opened the door a mere crack and peered through it. "The way is clear. I shall go down and draw him out of the palazzo. While I keep him occupied, you must find the manuscript."

She nodded, and then reached up and gave him a soft, lingering kiss. "Be careful."

"The same goes for you, love." He held her for a moment, and then opened the door and slipped out.

Robin was surprised by how much effort had been put into restoring the ruined building. The inside walls and flooring had been replaced, and new furnishings brought in to replace the old. Nottingham could not have done it in a few days; this place must have belonged to him before he'd fled Italy.

If he'd had to flee at all. Robin would not be surprised if his old enemy had struck a bargain with the Brethren to regain his territory. None of the Guisbournes had ever been particularly concerned with honor.

Robin tracked Nottingham's scent down three floors to a

staircase that descended down a dimly lit stone shaft. Another, fresher track led from it toward the back of the palazzo.

"There it is," Chris whispered, moving away from him.

Robin saw the manuscript sitting out in the open, atop a pedestal placed in the center of an octagonal recess in the floor. The recess looked damnably familiar, but he couldn't quite place it. He looked up and saw what looked like a series of pulleys hanging over it, and then peered at the floor again.

It was exactly the same size as the trapdoor to an oubliette.

"Wait, love. Don't touch it."

Chris had already stepped down into the recess and was reaching for the book. Metal shrieked, and the false foundation beneath the pedestal collapsed. Chris screamed as she and the book fell out of sight.

Robin ran to the edge and saw Chris lying at the bottom of the shaft. She appeared to be in some sort of cell. "Chris? Chr—"

A strong, cold hand shoved Robin over the edge.

Alexandra had never thought she'd be happy to see so many burn patients, but her initial assessment of the refugees that Gabriel and Nicola had delivered from Spain revealed that none of them had been shot by their attackers.

"Lady Alexandra," the footman said. "The high lord requests that you attend him in his chambers."

Alex saw a thin blond woman waiting outside the high lord's chambers, and stopped in front of her. They'd never been friends, she and Éliane Selvais. Among other things, the Frenchwoman had set off the chain of events that led to Alex becoming Kyn, but over time the initial vicious animosity between them had gradually altered into a semi-antagonistic form of mutual respect.

She'd never completely trust Richard's *tresora*, Alex decided, but she didn't want to see her dead anymore. "What's going on, Éliane?"

"Lord Tremayne wishes to know how the wounded are faring." The Frenchwoman sounded worried, and looked as if she hadn't slept in days. In a lower voice she added, "Please try to keep this brief. He's very tired."

"I guess all that talking has him worn out." Alex gave her the once-over and noted the slightly wrinkled condition of her suit, and a ladder running up the side of her stocking. She also radiated the smell of burning cherry tobacco. "You look like you could use a few dozen naps. Has Richard been behaving himself?"

"Of course. My lord is much improved, as you will see." Éliane looked as if she wanted to say more, but fell silent.

"All right." Alex went inside.

The scent of cherry tobacco stung the air, but it took her a moment to adjust to the candlelight Richard preferred to electricity. The high lord sat near one of the windows, his body concealed by a full-length black cloak.

"We meet again, Doctor."

Said the medieval spider to the smart-ass fly. Alex kept her expression and tone impersonal. "You needed to talk to me about something?"

"I do." Richard rose from his chair and came around it toward her. His walk, formerly a dragging lurch, now seemed easier and more natural. "What progress have you made with your research on the Darkyn curse?"

"There is no curse. The pathogen infecting us is composed of three separate viral organisms. Two appear to be evolved versions of anthrax and bubonic plague. I haven't identified the third virus yet." She watched him move to a cart with a bottle of wine and glasses. "You want me to get that for you?"

"I've forgotten that you've not seen my progress."

Richard removed one of his gloves and displayed his hand for her. "Once again I have fingers and joints."

Alex walked over and took hold of the hand, turning it over to study the changes. Before, Richard's feet and hands had been little more than oversize cat's paws. Now they looked more humanoid, although a thin layer of black-and-silver hair still covered his skin. "Well, it looks a little better."

"I still possess a great many inhuman characteristics." He contracted his fingers as he drew his hand back, and talon-shaped claws sprang out of the tips. "Shaking hands with me remains somewhat of a risk."

"Richard, it took the Brethren fifty years of feeding you cat's blood in a dungeon to force your DNA to mutate from humanoid to feline," she reminded him. "I warned you in Ireland that the treatments aren't going to switch you back overnight."

"I know, my dear. I am not complaining, merely cautioning you." He carefully poured a glass of bloodwine and glanced at her. "Will you join me?"

"I shot up earlier, thanks." Alex made a show of checking her watch. "If the kidnapping reunion's over, I have patients I need to see."

"Michael has been keeping information from me," Richard said, as if she hadn't spoken. "Such as why he accessed over three hundred reports from human authorities related to the Brethren attacks on our strongholds in France and Italy."

"Well, that's easy. I asked him to pull those," Alex said. "I wanted to see if they found out anything we'd need to deal with, that's all."

"How vigilant of you." Richard lifted his glass to salute her. "Now I suppose you will tell me this has nothing to do with your experiments on our blood."

"I think you should talk to Michael about this stuff. He's

the one in charge. I just sleep with him." Alex headed for the door, only to come up short when Richard stepped in front of her. "Still as fast as the average house cat."

"You will tell me what I wish to know." Richard's voice changed as he poured his talent into it. "Everything, now."

Alex's ears screeched with pain, but the ice-pick effect of the high lord's tone wore off almost immediately. "Talent doesn't work on me the way it used to, Richard."

"You are immune now."

She shrugged. "Maybe I've finally made the full transition."

"No human or Kyn can resist my voice. What does that make you?"

"To be honest?" She folded her arms. "Pretty happy."

"Indeed. I often wonder." He pulled back his hood, revealing a half-human, half-feline head. "You may dislike it, Alexandra, but you are Kyn, and you belong to me. I am your liege lord, and I would know what you have learned. Do not force me to resort to less civilized methods of obtaining what I want."

Alex didn't want to tell him anything. Michael had related how angry the other seigneurs were, and how hell-bent they were on going to war. At the same time, she knew from her experiments that heat did not kill the Darkyn. The Brethren could have recovered hundreds of burned bodies from the arson sites and even now be torturing them.

Richard's threats weighed in as well. She knew how ruthless and unpredictable he could be.

"Come on." She went over to the seats by the window, sat down with him, and began telling him what she had discovered while in Chicago. How her experiments on Michael's blood had revealed that intense heat didn't destroy the pathogen, but merely rendered it dormant—even in Kyn blood heated to five hundred degrees Fahrenheit.

"My test results were conclusive," she finished. "Burning may not kill the Kyn. It may simply put them in a state of suspended animation."

"I have read the same police reports," Richard said. "No bodies of Kyn have been recovered from the fallen strongholds."

She nodded. "I think the Brethren are taking them. I think they're setting these fires expressly for that purpose."

"What of the unusual ammunition they are using on those who are able to escape? Is that being employed for the same reason?" At her startled look, his thin lips bared still-pointed teeth. "One hears a great deal while walking in the gardens."

"Did you eavesdrop the last time I talked about what a nosy bastard you are?" She let her shoulders slump. "All right. I think the explosive copper rounds are supposed to slow them down, make them easier to catch. It's the only thing that makes sense. Otherwise they'd shoot to kill, not to maim."

"I have had an accounting made for all those thought lost in the fires." Richard finished his wine and studied the empty goblet. "If your theory is correct, then I must assume that the Brethren have captured four hundred thirty-one of our kind."

"That many." Alex got out of her chair and walked blindly around the room. "God only knows what they'll do to them."

"God, me, Michael, and Gabriel," Richard said. "There is another matter we will have to resolve before we attempt to recover them."

"Put your matter on hold and call your best trackers." She didn't have time for more of his head games. "Our priority has to be to find them and get them out."

"If they are still alive, we shall," the high lord said. "The question is how. My trackers can follow scent trails if they are fresh. We will need someone who can find Kyn being held captive in secret, well-hidden locations. There is only one among us with that sort of talent, and she, my dear, *is* our unresolved matter."

As Alex realized what he meant, she closed her eyes. "Oh, hell."

Chapter 15

Chris regained consciousness on a stone floor inside what looked like an ancient prison cell. She moved her arms and legs carefully to assure herself nothing was broken before she pushed herself up and looked around.

Nottingham stood at one side of her cell, his back to her. The contessa and five men were gathered on the other side. A sixth man was dragging Robin, who appeared unconscious, into another cell directly across from Chris's. He tossed Robin inside and slammed the door shut.

"There, it is done," the contessa said to Nottingham. A rat ran across the floor, and she stomped on it, making it squeal as she crushed its skull. "The accommodations are not ideal, but I trust you are satisfied, my lord."

Nottingham approached Robin's cage, stopping an inch from the bars. He never took his eyes off him. "Release the girl now."

Salva gestured toward the door to Chris's cell. "Open it."

Chris backed away as one of the contessa's men entered the cell and grabbed her by the hair. She didn't struggle, aware that the man's strength was superhuman, like Robin's and the contessa's. He could probably snap her neck with one flick of his wrist.

"She is prettier than I remember," Salva said, coming into the cell to circle around Chris. She paused to finger the edge of the silk covering Chris's right breast. "You can feed from her for quite a long time, if you pace yourself. She looks fit enough to last weeks. Perhaps even a month."

"No, my lady." Nottingham finally turned around to face her. His whispery rasp echoed around Chris like the voice of a ghost. "She was never part of our bargain."

"Ah, yes. I only promised you Locksley." The contessa picked up the manuscript from where it had fallen before backing out of the cell. "At last." She walked out, clutching the book in her arms as if it were an infant.

Chris heard a groan and saw Robin was out cold. Quickly putting together a bluff, she said, "Contessa, I went to the American embassy in Rome and arranged a surveillance team to follow me here to Venice. In a few minutes they'll have this place surrounded. Let us go, and I'll use my authority to arrange safe passage for you and your men back to the States."

"Safe passage." Salva chuckled, handing the manuscript to one of her men in exchange for a gun. "No one has followed you but us, my dear, and we are going to England directly." She pointed the weapon at Chris's face.

Aware that she could do nothing more, Chris faced her death with her eyes open.

At the last moment the contessa changed her aim and fired. Nottingham reeled back, dropping a dagger in his hand, and then drew another from his belt as he lurched toward Salva. She shot him a second time in the leg, and he went down and didn't move again.

Red blood seeped out from under his body.

"Give me the book." The contessa took it from her guard and opened it, pulling at the top of the binding. She snarled something obscene in Italian, and then threw the book away from her.

It landed open next to Chris's cell, and she saw that the pages were blank.

"You dare give me a forgery?" Salva went over and kicked Nottingham's wounded leg, rousing him to groaning consciousness. "Where is the book?"

Nottingham lifted his head and managed a faint sneer. "Not here, my lady."

"I should have expected this. Once a traitor, always a traitor. Get him on his feet." Salva paced back and forth with jerky movements as her guards hauled Nottingham up from the floor. "I have been patient with you and your demands, my lord. That time is over. Tell me where it is. *Tell me now*."

Nottingham said nothing, and his head snapped back as one of the guards punched him.

"I will skin you alive," the contessa promised.

"Kill me," he rasped, "and you will never find it again."

"Wait," Salva said as the guard prepared to hit him again. "Bring the girl out here."

The guard holding Chris shoved her out with the contessa and Nottingham.

"You desire this female, don't you?" Salva said, moving to stand behind Chris.

Nottingham looked away. "She is a mortal. She is nothing to me."

"But you danced so divinely together." The contessa put her arms around Chris's waist and rested her chin on Chris's shoulder. "I was watching you at the ball. I saw you kiss her. You can have her, my lord, and do whatever you like with her. When he wakes, Locksley will have no choice but to watch. Only give me the book."

Nottingham said nothing.

"Very well."

Chris gasped as she felt the contessa's fangs sink into her shoulder. The pain lasted only a moment before she was pushed away.

"She reeks of Locksley," Salva complained, wiping the blood from her lips with a grimace. "It is like drinking that foul Earl Grey tea."

Chris tried to make a run for the stairs, but one of the guards caught her and threw her to the ground, her face only inches from the crushed rat. He kicked her over onto her back, and she covered her head with her arms, trying to protect her face.

Bars clanged, men shouted, and Chris was plucked up and held, feet dangling, while the guard who had kicked her used his fist on her ribs and chest. She twisted, trying to escape the blows, but then she felt the cold burn of a dagger slice across her upper arm.

"I do not have to feed on her," the contessa said. "I can simply cut bits of her away and watch her bleed." She poised the tip of her dagger against Chris's left breast. "Shall I start here?"

"Stop," Nottingham said. "The book is hidden in the nursery on the third floor."

"Lock him in with the mortal," the contessa said as she and one of the guards mounted the stairs.

Chris was thrown back in the cell with Nottingham, who tried to overpower the guard. The others rushed in, and Chris huddled against the bars as the men beat Nottingham unconscious.

The contessa returned, her guard carrying the real manuscript, and walked over to peer at Nottingham. "You did not kill him, I hope."

"No, my lady."

Robin rolled over and groaned.

"You have what you want now," Chris said quickly. "Take it and go."

"You are eager to bid me farewell." Salva walked over to Robin's cell. She covered her hand with a linen handkerchief as she tested the door lock, and glanced over her shoulder at the guard with the book. "You are certain that the old bars will hold, Caesar?"

"We tested them, as you directed, my lady. Just as in the days of your husband, not even the strongest of us could bear to hold them more than a few moments." The guard nodded toward two of the men. "Dominic and Giancarlo will remain at their posts until we return."

"You are not to give them blood," the contessa said. "Nottingham has the girl for that, and I want to know Locksley died starving."

"Salva." Robin hunched over, rising slowly. "What are you doing here?" He saw Chris, and Nottingham's body, and grabbed the bars of his cell. Wisps of smoke rose from his hands, and he pulled them away. "What the hell is this?"

She pretended surprise. "Why, vengeance, my lord. Not, perhaps, as my lord Nottingham originally envisioned it, but I think he will be satisfied with the alternative I have provided."

"You, allying yourself with Nottingham?"

"He did promise to bring the manuscript to me— something you would never have done." The contessa glanced at Nottingham. "I have been waiting a very long time to find it. Now I may go to England and obtain justice for my sister."

"Your sister."

"You never met Beatrice, did you? Of course not. You are still breathing." Salva's eyes took on a strange cast. "For all the sins heaped upon her head, she was an innocent, my lord. A lamb sacrificed by the Kyn so that they might bathe in her tears. Well, I will give them tears. I will make them drown in them."

"Salva, you are making no sense."

"Do I not make myself clear? I shall have justice," she said. "I shall punish the seven men responsible for murdering my Beatrice."

"Richard and the seigneurs." Robin shook his head. "You know that they did only what had to be done."

"You dare say that to me." She stopped screaming and turned to smile at Chris. "You should know how fond Lord Locksley is of abducting women. He took Lord Nottingham's betrothed, the maiden Marian, on the night before they were to be married. He spirited her all the way to Scotland, where he raped her and left her in a convent. She died bearing his bastard."

Robin hit the bars again, this time with his body.

Chris recoiled, both from the sound of Robin's flesh burning and the smile on the contessa's face. "You're insane."

"Ask him," Salva said. "You should have some time to reminisce before Nottingham awakes."

"My lady, after the *jardin* wars I brought your husband's body home," Robin said, his body still, his voice calm and clear. "I have never asked anything of you in return for that favor. I ask it now. Take Agent Renshaw out of here and put her on a plane for America. She can do nothing to interfere with your plans. No one would believe her."

Chris turned her head. "I'm not leaving you—"

"Shut up, you idiot mortal," he said to her. "You have been nothing but trouble to me." He looked at the contessa. "Bind me and put me in the cage with Nottingham. He will still have his vengeance."

"There is something I never told you, *caro*." Salva walked over to Robin's cell. "I did not send only my husband to fight for Richard during the *jardin* wars. I sent my lover, Caesar, as well." She smiled at the guard holding the manuscript. "Caesar remained steadfast at my husband's side, right up until the moment when the fighting was at its worst. When he had the chance to cut off dear Arno's head, as I had instructed him to."

Robin's strong arm shot through the bars, grabbing for her throat, but the contessa glided out of reach.

"I do owe you a debt for bringing back the absolute proof of Caesar's love and devotion for me," Salva continued. "That is why *you* are not in the cage with Nottingham."

"You can't leave us here like this," Chris said. "Please. What do you want?"

"My legacy." Salva pulled on a pair of latex gloves, taking the manuscript from Caesar and opening it to the middle. Without warning she tore the ancient book in half, splitting it down the center of the spine. As Chris cringed at the wanton destruction, the contessa peeled back the binding cover and revealed a small niche. From it she carefully removed a little stone vial sealed with red wax.

"There you are." She transferred the vial to a crystal box, in which it fit snugly. She held up the box to admire the vial. "Beautiful, is it not? It contains my sister Beatrice's last tears."

"God, no." Robin sounded sick. "Salva, you must destroy that vial."

"My lord, why would I throw away my sister's legacy? She promised them to me. She vowed that if they came for her, she would hide them in the book." The contessa's eyes became unfocused. "Only humans got to the book before I did, and sold it for a handful of gold, never knowing the real treasure she had hidden inside it."

Chris saw Robin's eyes flash copper. "Salva, you cannot do this. You know what can happen if you open that vial. You were there. You know how many died." When she didn't respond, he shouted, "Listen to me."

The contessa stared blindly at him. "I promised her that I would. If they came for her. And they did." She drew a rosary out of her bodice and kissed the dangling cross. "This time it is on their heads." She laughed as she closed her fist over the beads, and tiny shards of broken glass began to fall to the floor. "All of them."

She didn't look at him as she mounted the steps, her men trailing behind her.

"Salva, for God's sake," Robin shouted after her.

Only the light, lilting sound of the contessa's laughter drifted back down to them.

Since arriving at Geoffrey's estate, Nicola Jefferson had spent half of her waking hours on the ward, at first making her own rounds to check on the new arrivals. Once Alex had ascertained that the girl wasn't squeamish, she had drafted her as a nursing assistant and put her to work.

After meeting with Richard, Alex went down to the ward to talk to the Nick about tracking the missing Kyn. She found her changing Blanche's dressings and listening to the Kyn female talk about Gabriel, whom she had known for six hundred years longer than Nick.

Alex helped her finish changing the dressings, and worked on the next several patients with her, chatting casually about the procedures she used on them. After a while she realized the younger woman was barely paying attention to her, and looked as if she wanted to punch out a guard.

"Let's take a break and get some fresh air." Alex pulled off her lab coat and headed for the lift. She glanced over her shoulder when Nick didn't follow. "Come on, kid. We both need it."

Nick scowled. "I'm not a kid, and I don't need a mother."

"That's good, because I don't want an immortal teenager with a chip on her shoulder calling me 'Mom.'" Alex kept going.

Nick reluctantly followed her onto the lift and out of the mansion. Alex walked down the cobblestone path to the apricot orchard, where the delicious fragrance of ripening fruit perfumed the air.

"This guy Geoff has a thing for apricots," Nick observed.

"Michael's the same way about lavender, and I'm betting Gabriel's talked about planting some juniper back at your farm." She nodded when Nick gave her a startled look. "They like to smell us even when we're not around."

A smile tugged at the corner of Nick's mouth. "Glad I didn't end up with a scent like horse manure or burnt plastic."

Alex nodded. "Speaking of the extra crispy, if the patients are starting to get to you, you should take a couple nights off from ward duty."

The younger girl turned away. "I'm fine."

Alex stopped to pick an apricot and brought it to her nose. "God, I miss food, don't you? I mean, I love the super-powers, the autohealing thing, and the great sex, but some-times I just want a pound bag of M&M's so bad I could scream. How about you?"

Nick eyed her. "If you're going to lecture me about my bad attitude, Doc, let's pretend that you did and I'll head back to the ward."

"I didn't want it, either, Nick." Alex rolled the golden fruit between her palms. "And, for the record, my attitude sucks much worse than yours. In fact, I could give you some pointers, if you want."

Nick's mouth twisted. "Give me a few years. I'll catch up."

"Thing is," Alex said, "I'll never kiss your ass or 'my lady' you to death. I'm like you. I never had a choice."

Nick fell silent for a few minutes, and then finally said, "I'm okay. It's mostly the Vampire King. He's been getting on my nerves. Always watching me. I can tell he is, even with the hood covering the goods."

"He's a nosy bastard." Alex squelched a surge of guilt. "Anything else on your mind?"

Nicola kicked a stone across the grass. "Richard wants to

make Gabriel a sig-lord or whatever. Put him in charge of a nest."

"Really." Alex wasn't surprised; Gabriel had been one of Richard's most trusted lieutenants before he'd been abducted and tortured by the Brethren. "Did Gabe talk to you about it?"

"No. The Vampire King came to see Gabriel last night, and they thought I was sleeping. He offered him territory in the north, near my farm. Gabriel said no, but the way he sounded . . ." She hunched her shoulders. "I think he really wants things the way they were. You know, living in the big house, having the servants, wall-to-wall art and swords and warriors and shit."

"But you don't."

Nick stuffed her hands in her pockets. "Doesn't matter what I want. It's his life. He's never going to be satisfied with a life on the road; I've seen that. The guy needs roots. Kyn roots. If making him happy means letting him go, I let him go."

"You can't do it, Nick."

"Watch me." Her eyes glittered.

"When we were in Ireland, and Gabriel thought you'd died in his arms," Alex said, "he asked Michael to kill him. When Michael refused, he asked for a knife so he could do it himself. That's how much he loves you."

She glared at Alex. "You don't get it, do you? I'm not like you and Braxtyn and the other fang-chicks. I can't do this shit. The Kyn took everything away from me. My parents. My home. My whole life. Every time I look at one of you, I remember. So I can't pretend none of that happened just because I got stuck with fangs. Not even for Gabriel."

"First of all, the Kyn never knew you existed. *Elizabeth* killed your parents and forced you to go through the change alone. Believe me, she paid for it." Alex considered telling Nick exactly how Richard had punished his sadistic wife, but decided the girl had enough material for her nightmares. "You really love Gabriel, don't you?"

"Duh." Nick invested the one word with a thousand unspoken ones.

Alex faced her. "Then you have to find a way to deal, Nick, just like I did. Because you love him, because you're bonded to him, and he's Kyn. And no matter how much you deny it, so are you."

The younger girl stared off at the horizon for a time. "I'll have to put up my hair and wear dresses and do all that formal greeting stuff, won't I? I hate that silly shit."

"Or you could wear jeans and a T-shirt and shave your head," Alex said. "You'll be the suzerain's lady; no one would dare give you grief about it. And personally, I avoid the formal-greeting stuff whenever possible. Unless it's another lord I like, most of the time I make Phillipe do it."

Nick looked thoughtful. "Gabriel will need a seneschal if he turns sig-lord." She smiled a little. "I wasn't much into M&M's, but man, there are some nights I'd kill for Reese's."

Alex grinned. "Pieces, or peanut butter cup?"

"Pieces." Nick snorted. "Why ruin perfectly good peanut butter with crappy milk chocolate?"

"Ah, but they have them in dark and white chocolate now." Alex took a deep breath. "Okay, my turn to bitch. We've got a situation."

Nick listened as Alex told her about the reaction of the Kyn pathogen to heat, the missing bodies of the arson attack victims, and the effects of the new ammunition on the survivors.

"What are they doing with the ones they take?" Nick asked.

"We don't know, but you saw firsthand what they did to Gabriel." Alex watched her expression. "Nick, I know it's a lot to ask of you, but no one else has your talent. We need you to find them."

"So that's it. Richard wants to use my fangdar."She studied Alex. "He made you come and ask me. He knew if he did it I'd tell him to go fuck himself with his scepter." She chuckled and shook her head. "Twisted son of a bitch."

"As much as I agree with you, he's right. Gabriel's told us how you work together. He doesn't even have to track them anymore. You always know where they are."

"I'll do it," Nick said abruptly. "On one condition. I want that big blond guy from Ireland to go with us."

"Korvel?" Alex frowned. "Why do you want him?"

"Gabriel told me about him. He said Richard made him his seneschal because he does whatever the Vampire King tells him, no matter how nasty it is," she said. "I want him armed to the teeth and under orders. If it looks like the Brethren are going to grab us, I want Korvel to kill us."

"Nick—"

"No." She looked into Alex's eyes. "You're not there when Gabriel wakes up shaking and has blood on his mouth from biting through his lips, trying not to scream. You don't see how he flinches every time a priest or even a guy dressed in black comes near us. You don't feel the burn scars against your skin while you're making love and remember how he got them. You sure as hell never pulled him off a goddamn cross."

Alex started to say something, and then fell silent.

"I'm never letting those freaks touch Gabriel again," Nick said softly. "And you really don't want them to get hold of both of us. Because they'll use him to make me work as one of their hunters."

Alex felt sick, but slowly nodded. "Okay. I'll tell Richard." Someone coughed, and she looked over to see one of Geoff's guards approaching them.

"Good evening, my ladies." The guard bowed. "Lady Nicola, your lord asks if you will join him in the garage."

"I promised Gabriel I'd show him how to change out a

carburetor on the Triumph," she said, referring to her motorcycle. "I'll be there in a minute."

The guard bowed and left them.

"One more thing." Nick turned to Alex. "Tell Richard
we're even now. He tries anything like this again, and I'll tell
the fucking Brethren myself where they can find him."

Chapter 16

Robin shouted over and over for Salva as the heavy doors to the floor above slammed shut, abruptly cutting off her laughter. He looked over at Chris and Nottingham, locked in the cage together, and went into an abrupt, furious rage. Howling like an animal, he hurled himself against the bars, smashing his shoulder into them over and over until blood began to spread down his sleeve and chest.

Gripping her bleeding arm, Chris limped over to the side of her cell closest to his.

"Robin." She kept her voice low and soft. "Robin, over here." When he did, she saw his lips had curled back from his fangs and his eyes had gone completely copper, never a good sign. "Listen to me. Calm down. We got in. We'll get out."

"We're going to die." He drove his fist into the unyielding bars.

Chris glanced at Nottingham and felt like punching something herself. "No, we're not. Robin, you can't freak out on me like this. I need you. I need to know what to do about him."

"Him." He didn't seem to understand her.

"Nottingham," she said. "They locked him in here with me, remember?"

Evidently Robin didn't, as he looked at the unconscious man and began to swear, furiously and without stopping, in some archaic form of English.

"Will you shut up?" Chris shouted, and felt a surge of dizziness that had her grabbing the bars. By then Robin had stopped swearing. "Thank you. Now, about the unconscious vampire, and what I need to do when he wakes up."

His burning eyes shifted to her arm. "You're bleeding."

"You noticed."

He uttered another archaic, filthy word. "Use one of your scarves to bind that wound. When he wakes, don't talk to him or touch him. Stay as far away as you can from him."

The cage was six feet by ten feet; she could take a step back and kick Nottingham in the head. She removed one of the scarves from around her waist and began clumsily binding her gashed arm. "How long can you two go without blood?"

A muscle in Robin's jaw twitched. "You needn't worry about that now."

"I have to," she told him. "The contessa told the guards not to feed you. I'm guessing she wants you to starve while you watch Nottingham drain me dry."

"We can go without feeding for weeks, months. Years, some say. But he will not wait that long. The smell of your blood will rouse him." Robin curled his fingers around the copper bars, his flesh sizzling until he let them fall away and looked down. "What is in that basket? There, by your feet."

Chris hadn't noticed it, and bent to remove the napkin covering the top. Her head spun, so she was careful to go slowly when she straightened. "Apples, cheese, and bread. Some bottled water. I guess she doesn't want me to starve to death right away." She looked around the cell. "This is my worst nightmare, too. I hate being locked up."

"I know about your childhood," Robin said gently. "I shared your dream on the plane."

"How could you . . ." She stopped, and sighed. "Never mind. Can you eat any of the food?"

He shook his head. "Only blood." He saw her glance at the dead rat. "Animal blood makes us sick. We can endure small amounts, but when the hunger grows too great, we will attack any human near us."

Which would be me. Chris's heart sank. "How long do I have before he loses control?"

"I cannot say. If he has not fed recently . . . a week. Perhaps a little longer. It does not matter. He will attack you anyway." He began pacing around the cell, looking at all of the bars and the stones. "There has to be a weakness in the construction. Old mortar. Something."

Dizziness made Chris's knees finally give out, and she slid down until she sat on the dirty straw.

"Chris."

She looked through the bars at him. "I'm okay. Just a little light-headed. I should have let this thing with Norman go. None of this would have happened if I had." Blood ran down the inside of her arm, and she put her hand over the bandaged gash to apply pressure. "She called you Locksley, and said you stole the maiden Marian from Nottingham."

Robin started to say something, and then hung his head.

"It's okay. I actually have an easier time believing that you're Robin Hood than I do that immortal-who-lives-on-human-blood-and-can't-be-killed thing," she continued, her tone almost conversational. "I am a little confused, though. I've seen just about every movie ever made about Robin Hood. I don't remember him raping and killing Maid Marian in any of them."

"Chris."

She met his gaze.

"What the contessa said was partly true, but not all. I

never forced Marian, and I never meant to get her with child. I loved her. I have never spoken of this to anyone before you." The sincerity of his words echoed in his eyes. "When we get out of here, when we are safe, I shall tell you about her, and what happened between us."

"Robin, I know you wouldn't deliberately hurt a woman. You've had too many chances to do that to me." Pain dulled her voice. "You know, I was so busy blaming you for Norman that I never told you the truth." She forced herself to say out loud what she had been thinking ever since she'd heard the news: "You didn't kill him. I did."

Her claim confused Robin. "You told me that he committed suicide."

"Norman pulled the trigger, but I put the gun in his mouth." She glanced at him. "What I mean is, he did it because I screwed up in Chicago."

"Tell me what happened."

"He never liked working with female agents. He was kind of dinosaur that way. Even on the job he referred to me as 'the bimbo' or 'my secretary.' I put in a dozen transfer requests, trying to get reassigned away from him." Chris's expression darkened. "Sometimes I wonder if that's why I forgot to turn off the camera. I saw too many bruises, and he got too many suspects to confess when I was out of the room. Maybe on a subconscious level I wanted him to get caught and bounced out of the bureau, so I wouldn't have to deal with him anymore."

Robin saw how pale she was and fought back a surge of panic. He had to keep her conscious and talking. "Did you catch him abusing someone?"

"I didn't, but a video camera did. Norman liked to send me to get the coffee when interrogations weren't going anywhere. I was supposed to switch off the video camera when I left the room—it's department policy that two agents have to be present with the suspect during questioning—but that day . . . I don't know. I just forgot." She rested her cheek against her hand. "He punched the suspect in the face and broke his jaw, and it was all recorded on the videotape he thought I'd shut off. When the tape was processed, the tech saw the beating and turned him in to our chief. They had an internal investigation, but it was just a formality. Norman barely avoided criminal charges."

"Chris, you cannot blame yourself for his choices."

"I don't. Not anymore. It's just . . ." She closed her eyes. "Nasty and bad-tempered as he was, and as much as I disliked him, he was still my partner."

Robin saw her head droop. "Talk to me, love."

"I'm so tired."

"I know." Robin saw Nottingham beginning to stir. "Chris, he's waking. Do as I told you."

Chris slid back, curling herself into the corner of the cell, and went still. She was partially concealed by shadows there, Robin saw, although he knew that wouldn't deceive Nottingham for more than a few seconds.

The dark man opened his eyes and pushed himself up from the floor. He looked all around the room until he saw Robin.

"You."

"Are you not delighted to occupy a dungeon again, cousin?" Robin kept his tone mocking, and prayed he could hold Nottingham's attention for as long as it took to find a way out of the cell. "I cannot fathom why you went to such lengths to be played for a fool. Or perhaps it was not such a stretch."

"Where is she?"

"The contessa is on her way to England. She plans to assassinate Richard and the others."

"Not her." Nottingham breathed in, and turned his head toward Chris. "Her."

*   *   *

Chris Renshaw's blood scent filled Nottingham's head; her presence in the cell rolled over his skin. He ignored Locksley's taunting voice and went over to where she huddled. She remained very still and kept her head down. Blood still seeped into the silk she had wound over the slash on her arm.

He crouched down before her and tilted her head back to look at her eyes. There he saw pain, fear, and exhaustion.

Gently he turned her head, but saw only two fresh puncture wounds on her shoulder. "Did she feed from you again?"

Chris didn't answer him. Locksley must have ordered her to remain silent to further bedevil him.

Nottingham lifted her from the stone floor and began searching her skin for other signs of abuse.

"She won't give you any pleasure," Robin sneered. "She belongs to me. She does my bidding."

Nottingham eyed his cousin. "Then you are as responsible as Salva for her death." Chris stiffened under his hands, and he turned her to face Robin. "Look at her, cousin. This time you will have to stay and watch her die."

Robin snarled, seizing the bars and jerking at them.

"Or is it that you fear she will live?" Nottingham deliberately ran his hand down over the front of Chris's body. "I have only to command her, and she will not resist me."

"I'm sorry, Robin." Chris crumpled.

Nottingham caught her and gently lowered her to the floor. "This bandage is too loose. She is losing too much blood." He saw the basket and took the napkin from it, tearing it into strips and binding the wound.

"You cannot feed on her," Robin said.

"I have no wish to." Nottingham finished dressing the wound and put his hand to her forehead.

Chris opened her eyes and groaned. "Are you two

through sniping at each other yet, or do I have to slap you around?"

Nottingham scowled. "I beg your pardon. I do not snipe."

"You do a great imitation. I know you don't want me. You only want to get even with him. So you can stop feeling me up in front of him." She turned her head. "And you are not helping by yelling and insulting him. I'm the one locked in here, not you. Do you really think pissing him off is going to help me?"

Robin muttered something under his breath, while Nottingham sat back on his heels and regarded her for a moment.

"Now that we've established some ground rules," she continued, getting to her feet, "we have to quit feuding and escape from this place. Let's concentrate on that, because as much as you two want to kill each other, I don't want to die here."

"They didn't take your earrings," Robin said, looking at her. "Can you throw one to me?"

Chris removed one of the golden earrings she had borrowed from the signorina, and tossed it to him. Robin straightened the loop of wire and inserted it into the door lock.

Chris watched, anxiety tightening her lips. Robin worked the wire for ten minutes in silence, which sent Nottingham to pace around the cell. The sound of the wire snapping brought his temper to the edge of doing the same.

"You cannot even pick a lock?" he demanded. "What manner of thief are you?"

As he spoke, his talent sent frost inching up the bars of the cage. More ice crystals spread like thin fur over the stones inside the cell.

"The wire was too thin and delicate." Robin tossed the broken earring aside, and only then saw the frost that had raced across the stone to crawl up the bars of his cell. "You bloody idiot, you can't use talent in here. Chris is mortal. She will freeze."

"You did that?" Chris asked, gesturing to the carpet of ice. "Just by thinking it?"

"Usually I must touch it and will it to freeze." Nottingham suppressed another wave of anger. "Sometimes when I am angry, as I am now, it happens on its own."

Chris wrapped her arms around her abdomen, shivering as she examined all of the bars of the cage.

"I know copper hurts you," she said, "but what about ice?"

Nottingham shook his head.

"The bars are solid, but some of these welds look pretty weak. If you can freeze the bars and cover them with enough ice, you should be able to hold them long enough."

He saw what she meant, and pulled off his gloves. "Step back, as far away from me as you can." He pulled off his shirt and handed it to her. "Put this on."

The copper scalded his palms as he took hold of the bars and poured his talent over them. Cold did not affect him, but he saw his breath rise in white puffs as the room temperature plummeted.

Slowly the ice formed and thickened, filling the gaps between the bars and creating a layer of protection between Nottingham's flesh and the poisonous copper. Only when he heard metal groan did he step back and kick at the base of two bars.

Ice shattered, falling to the stone as the bars broke loose. Nottingham grabbed them and pushed, bending the copper to the sides and outward, creating a gap just wide enough for him to squeeze through.

"Chris," Robin said sharply.

Nottingham glanced back at the girl, who sat huddled against the other side of the cell. Frost whitened her hair, eyebrows, and eyelashes. Her lips had blued, and as she tried to speak, they cracked. Her eyes closed and she slumped over, unconscious.

No hatred-riddled Brethren could have tortured Robin as cruelly as Salva had. Watching his cousin handle Chris as if she were nothing more than one of his whores had nearly driven Robin out of his head. Fortunately Chris had brought them both to their senses before things had gone too far.

Nottingham kicked out another bar to create enough space to carry Chris out of the cell. He brought her over to him, placing her on the floor in front of his cell before taking down the keys from the hook beside it.

Robin ignored him and the burning brush of the copper bars as he reached out to rest his hand on her brow. She felt as cold as a Kyn; her body temperature had dropped to a dangerous low.

"She will die if we don't get her warm." He looked up at his cousin, who had not unlocked his cell. "Open the door, Guy."

"I should take her and leave you to rot." He glanced down at Chris. "Perhaps I shall. I can kill the guards and take her safety without your aid."

Robin stood. "Can you hunt down the contessa by yourself? She has a vial of her sister's tears. They were hidden in the spine of that bloody book."

"Beatrice's tears?" Nottingham paled.

"Aye. She means to use them to kill the high lord and his seigneur. You know what will happen when she opens that vial." Robin regarded the man he hated more than any being alive or dead. "We must strike a truce between us, for nothing matters now except stopping Salva. We cannot permit her to unleash her sister's curse upon the world again."

Nottingham opened the cell door. Robin stepped out and hit him in the face, knocking him onto his back.

His cousin grabbed his jaw. "That is your idea of a truce?"

"That was for putting your hands on my woman." Robin bent and lifted Chris into his arms. "There are two guards above."

Nottingham rose to his feet and took down one of the torches. "I shall deal with them." He stopped by Robin and looked at him. "If you attack me again, truce or not, I shall gut you."

Robin grabbed another torch as he carried Chris up out of the dungeon and to the first room with a fireplace he could find. He pulled a rug over by the hearth and placed her on it, and then began breaking up furniture to burn. As he did, he heard screams that stopped almost as soon as they started. Neither of them had the gravelly rasp of his cousin's voice.

He had no love for Nottingham, but it seemed that Guy could hold his own in a fight.

Once Robin had the flames blazing well, he tore down an old brocade curtain, ripped away the rotted half, and wrapped Chris in the rest. He had no body heat of his own to use to warm her, but lay with her and held her close anyway, rubbing his hands over her still, cold body and murmuring to her.

"You will be warmer soon, love, and then you may slap me around as much as you like." He pressed his cheek against the top of her head. "I shall even let you arrest me and put your handcuffs on me again. Think of how much you will enjoy reading me my rights and having a barrister appointed to represent me. Then you may interrogate me as much as you wish."

She did not wake, but he thought the blue color was beginning to fade from her lips. He knew her temperature could not rise too fast, or the swift change might stop her heart, but it seemed to be taking far too long.

How useless his talent was now. He could persuade a fortune out of a skinflint, but he could not do anything to help the woman he loved.

"I do love you," he whispered to her. "I shall tell you again as soon as you wake."

Nottingham came in a few minutes later, his face and hands wet with Kyn blood. "Does she improve?"

"She is not as blue around the mouth, but I cannot get her warm enough."

Nottingham came over and knelt on the other side of Chris. When Robin saw what he was about, he shoved him away.

"You mean to freeze her again?"

"I fed on the second guard before I ripped out his spine. My body is warmer than yours, and I shall not use my talent." His cousin lay behind Chris, pressing her into Robin. When Robin didn't move, he added, "Do you wish her to live or not?"

Robin set his jaw and moved closer to Chris. "Keep your hands where I can see them."

Feeding had made Nottingham's body as warm as a mortal's, and with Robin containing the heat with his body, Chris's body slowly began to warm. He watched her lips and cheeks pinken, and then flush. He only wanted her to open her eyes again, and speak to him, and remove the invisible copper fist that had seized his heart.

"She is young and strong," Nottingham said unexpectedly. "She will recover."

"No thanks to you." Robin regretted the words as soon as they left his tongue, but the answering sneer on his cousin's face kept him from taking them back. "We will have to travel quickly to intercept Salva before she reaches Richard and the others in London. I have a jet at the airport in Rome."

"What plans did you have for Beatrice's tears?" his cousin asked.

Robin frowned. "I plan to toss them into the nearest furnace. If I'd known they were concealed in the manuscript, I'd have not rested until it was in my possession."

"You did not know they were hidden in the book." Nottingham made a contemptuous sound. "Of course you did not."

"No one knew but the contessa." Robin uttered a curt laugh. "My God, Guy, I may be a thief, but I am not a half-witted monster." He narrowed his eyes. "Did you know?"

"No." Nottingham stared past him at the flames. "I only wanted revenge. For Marian. For Sherwood."

Robin felt an ugly surge of fury rise inside him. "Now you may very well get it, you stupid bastard. Perhaps you will live long enough to bury the rest of us. All for your precious betrothal."

Nottingham's lips peeled back from his fangs. "She was mine. As was Sherwood."

"Yet you never pursued us. You gave your name and Sherwood to your bloody half brother, and cowered in hiding."

"As soon as you took Marian, my mother seized control of the keep and my men," Guy snarled back. "I had spent my boyhood fostering in France; no one had laid eyes on me since I was a child. She had intended to kill me on my wedding day and marry her bastard son to Marian. When she discovered Marian gone, she had me thrown in the dungeon and sent my half brother after you. I spent ten years in that hole while he played lord above."

Robin didn't want to believe him, but what he'd claimed had happened at last explained the events that had led to the fall of Sherwood. "Why did she keep you alive?"

"She didn't. She sent a wench sick with plague down to me and locked her in my cell so that my death could never be called a murder. She left us down there for a week, and then came to drag out the bodies." His mouth twisted. "Only

I had come back from the dead. She thought it some form of black magic, and decided to keep me alive. For the next ten years she fed her peasants and her enemies to me while trying to learn the secret of my resurrection."

Robin almost felt sorry for him. "Viviana helped you to escape."

Nottingham nodded. "By the time she came to me, I had learned that I could turn humans to Kyn. I first tried it with that great hulk of a fool, Rainer, but he was too much of a simpleton to carry out my will." He rolled away from Chris and got to his feet. "She is warm now."

Robin would never fully trust him, but the rage he had carried inside him for six hundred years slowly died. "I left a boat docked outside the palazzo. There is a phone on the console. Use it to call London and warn them."

Nottingham nodded and rose.

Robin watched his cousin stalk out of the room before he looked down into Chris's eyes, which were slightly too alert for someone who had just woken from a cold sleep. "How long have you been awake?"

"I came to when he asked you what you had planned for Beatrice's tears." She shivered and nestled closer to him. "I thought it would be better if I didn't jump in the middle of that. Last time I nearly froze to death."

"Very wise of you." Robin bent his head to set his mouth against hers.

He intended the kiss to be a comfort, but the events of the night and the taste of her mouth made him greedy for more. Chris gasped as he tugged aside the silk to get at her breast, and put her hands in his hair as he suckled, working the soft areola into a tight, pointed peak. Beneath him her hips arched into him, her thighs parting to cradle his hips. He reached down to free himself and pull her makeshift skirt out of the way, and felt her melting against his fingers as he fitted the aching head of his cock to the flowering heart of her sex.

"I cannot get enough of you," he said, tightening his buttocks as he squeezed into her. As soon as she enveloped him, he held himself there. Feeling her body grip him made him swell even harder.

"I can't believe I'm saying this, but we have to stop," she said, looking up into his face. "We have to get out of here."

"We do." He stroked into her.

She groaned. "Your cousin is coming back."

"It will take him some time to find the boat." Robin buried himself inside her one more time, and then withdrew from her body to slide down it. "Stay," he said when she tried to sit up. "This will take only a moment."

Under her red curls, Chris had a small, pretty mound, and the strokes of his cock had left her labia wet and rosy. He put his tongue there first, so he could taste her silky heat.

She flowed under him, the muscles of her body as fluid as the moisture seeping from her sweet sheath. The sugary sharpness of her scent intensified as he parted her with his fingers to lick a path up to her small, tight bud.

He rolled her like a pearl over his tongue, and he sucked at her like a thirsty boy. His fingers pushed into her, fucking her slow and hard as his mouth drove her from pleasure to madness.

He felt the brush of her foot against his weeping cock, and shuddered as she rubbed her instep along his shaft. He had only wanted to bring her over, but the heavy fullness in his balls made him work himself against that delicate curve.

Her body changed under him, pulling tight, her thighs taut and her fingers twisting against his scalp. Robin felt the hum of her insides as she fought and then surrendered to it, her limbs shaking, her toes curling. When he moved up to kiss her, his mouth still wet from her climax, her hand found him and gave him two long, tight strokes. He pushed his tongue into her as he pumped his jetting semen over her palm.

Robin could have kept his mouth on hers for the rest of eternity, but there was a promise he had to keep. He lifted his head and looked into the golden brandy of her eyes. "I love you."

Something struck his shoulder, stinging like an angry insect. He reached back and pulled the dart out of his shoulder, and saw Chris's eyes go wide as his vision blurred.

A long shadow stretched across the floor, and Robin reached for Chris before it took him.

Chapter 17

After talking with Nick, and feeling as if she'd whored herself for Richard, Alex decided to take back some control over the situation. Part of that required her to face the one person she had been avoiding since arriving in London, but she thought that would be good for her, too.

The Kyn and their bullshit weren't going to turn her into a spineless bowl of Jell-O. She'd eat a pound of pennies first.

She knew where his room was—she'd asked Braxtyn the first day—and when Michael fell asleep, she slipped out of their chamber and went directly there. She knocked on the door, squaring her shoulders and ignoring the goose bumps racing up and down her arms.

Korvel, Richard's seneschal and captain of his guards, opened the door. He wore only a pair of trousers that he had obviously just pulled on, and his thick fair hair hung over his shoulders like tangled flax.

Alex stared at a point just past one of his broad shoulders. "We need to talk."

He opened the door wider and stepped to one side, and Alex walked in.

Once inside, she began wondering what the hell she was

doing there. She didn't like smelling his scent, which filled the room as if it were packed with larkspur, or the quiet way he closed the door. Looking straight at him was going to be a real problem, too.

"How may I be of service, my lady?"

She gave him an ironic look. "We almost had sex about two dozen times, Korvel. Granted, it was only in shared dreams, but I think at this point you can call me Alex."

"As you wish." He blocked her only exit by leaning back against the door. "How may I be of service, Alexandra?"

He said her name as if it were a synonym for heaven. Either he was still in love with her, or he wanted to get under her skin by acting as if he were. Alex finally looked at his face, but she couldn't tell which it was.

Who cares how he feels? "Nick has agreed to find and rescue the Kyn the Brethren have taken from the burned strongholds. Gabriel will go with her. I assume his high lordness has filled you in about the whole situation." When he inclined his head, she continued. "Nick wants you to go with them."

He frowned, genuinely puzzled. "I hardly know the lady. Why did she ask for me?"

"She knows you'll do whatever Richard orders you to," Alex said. "Such as kill her and Gabriel if it looks like they're about to be captured by the Brethren."

"*Kill* them."

"Yep." Alex took a deep breath, and immediately regretted it. To her nose Korvel smelled exactly like vanilla pound cake: warm and delicious and something she wanted to sink her teeth into. "Gabriel spent years being tortured by the order, and she doesn't want to see him hurt again. She also knows they could use her talent for homing in on Kyn as a weapon against us."

"She is as intelligent as she is brave." Korvel looked thoughtful. "Gabriel is not aware of this request, I take it."

"I seriously doubt it," Alex said. "Just a thought—if you do have to kill them, you'd better take him out first. You do remember what he did to the last guy who attacked Nick."

Korvel nodded, his expression grim. "I shall speak to the high lord. I cannot say whether he will release me from my duties."

"I think someone else can clean out his litter box for a few months," Alex snapped.

"Under the circumstances, I do not think I can refuse Nicola's request," another voice said. "Even if it means dirty litter boxes."

Alex jumped as Richard stepped out of the shadows by the fireplace. "I am getting so tired of you doing that."

"Allow me my personal amusements, Alexandra. I have so few these days." He turned to Korvel. "I believe my captain would like to say something to you about the unfortunate level to which he allowed his infatuation with you to grow."

"It's over," she said. "Forget about it."

"No, Alexandra, he is right," Korvel said. "I took advantage of the temporary bond that formed between us when you were held at Dundellan. When Cyprien took you away, I knew you would bond again with him. Yet I deliberately drew you into the dreamlands so that I could seduce you into returning to me." As he spoke, he moved toward her, stopping a few inches away. He held out his hand. "Please forgive me."

Alex still felt the tug of the bond that had formed between them in Ireland. She hadn't understood it then, and it had come close to wrecking her life after she'd returned to America and Michael. But she also knew that Korvel had fallen in love with her, and the crazy things that she had done because of her own love for Michael made her feel a twinge of sympathy.

She took his hand and let him kiss the back of hers.

"Look, if I could work things out with Michael, I know you can get over this thing for me."

Korvel straightened and looked into her eyes. "Are you certain that is what you wish, Alexandra?"

She felt it then—his talent, the ability to make any woman desire him, was legendary among the Kyn—and tried not to let it affect her. "You're a gorgeous guy, and you can have any woman you want. Literally. You don't need me."

The scent of larkspur turned hot as he touched the dark curls next to her cheek. "We always want what we cannot have, my lady." His hand fell to her throat. "Have you not yet learned that from me?"

The images hit her with slightly less force than a hard slap: Korvel, naked, poised over her. His tongue lapping at her nipple. His fingers between her legs. The plum-size dome of his penis searching against her—

"You conniving son of a bitch." Alex shoved his hand away. "You still think you can mess with my head? Do you have any idea what I can do to you? I'll get a scalpel, come back here, and cut your fucking heart out. You'll be dead before you crack an eyelid."

Korvel glanced at Richard before he shook his head. "I cannot help myself, Alexandra. There is no one else for me."

As Alex tried to regain control of her temper, she noticed how carefully Richard was watching her. It surprised her that Korvel would pull a stunt like this in front of his master. When he wasn't trying to get in her pants, the captain was one of the most reserved, controlled warriors who served Richard.

Something Nick had said about Korvel pounded in Alex's head: *. . . he does whatever the Vampire King tells him, no matter how nasty it is . . .*

"Jesus Christ." She turned to the high lord. "You made

him do this, didn't you? What was the plan? To see if his talent worked on me better than yours does?"

"Evidently it does not." Richard's eyes glinted from the shadows of his hood. "You would do well to remember that you are not immune to everything, Doctor."

"Incredible. You know, just when I think I can do this, that I can be a part of this, you try to slap a leash on me again." Alex turned her head. "And you, you walking hard-on, you're supposed to be in love with me. Hearts and flowers, the whole nine yards. So, what, you go and pimp your power for him? How fucking romantic."

Korvel's face darkened. "I do love—"

Alex whipped up her hand. "Oh, you don't get to talk to me anymore. And you." She turned to Richard. "You tell me what the hell you want from me now, straight out, or I'm out of here, and I'm taking Michael with me."

"Leave us," Richard said to Korvel.

The captain didn't move. "Alexandra, this was not my doing—"

Richard's voice became a lash. "Get out."

"Do what he says." Alex kept her eyes on the high lord. She waited until Korvel left them before she rubbed her hot, damp face on her sleeve. "You're a jerk, but I never thought you were a sadistic jerk. No wonder you fell in love with that psychotic bitch."

Richard turned his back on her. "We will not discuss my wife."

"Fine, let's talk about Korvel. He's the best soldier you've got in your little fang army. The guy would throw himself on a copper sword to protect you. He's probably the only reason I didn't kill you in Ireland. But, Richard, you still use him like he's a disposable razor." She went around him to face him. "Korvel wouldn't have this problem if you hadn't kidnapped me. This is your fault. Trying to use him to manipulate me now is disgusting and pathetic."

"The other seigneurs have petitioned me to remove Michael from rule over the American *jardins*."

"I don't give a flying— What?"

"Michael opposes war with the Brethren," Richard said. "My other six seigneurs do not, and they feel he may become a liability in the days ahead. They have petitioned me to remove him and appoint a new seigneur."

"Really." She planted her hands on her hips. "Who did you have in mind? Phil? He won't do it. Neither will any of the suzerains in America. You already know how loyal they are to Michael. No one will take his place."

"My captain will."

Alex digested this, and then she began to laugh. "I was wrong. You're a cold-blooded, sadistic jerk." She went over and sat on the end of Korvel's bed, still laughing.

"The decision is mine, of course." Richard made a casual gesture. "I can instead send Korvel to protect Nicola and Gabriel, and leave Michael to his rule over America. But war is imminent, Doctor, and time has sorely depleted my armies. If we are to prevail over the Brethren, I shall need something from you."

Alex abruptly sobered. "Like what?"

"You will tell me exactly how you and the other women were able to make the change from human to Kyn."

Alex blanked her expression. "I can't tell you what I don't know."

Richard sighed. "Must I bring out all of the reports sent to me from America? Photographs of the Brethren breeding centers you have visited, copies of the medical files you retrieved from them? Perhaps you wish to review the tests you have conducted on your own blood and the blood of every female changed to Kyn in the last five years."

"I thought *I* was scum for talking Nick into hunting for you." Alex stared down at her white-knuckled hands. "You've got me beat."

"Look at me, Alexandra." When she did, Richard pulled back his hood. "You transformed me from changeling to Kyn. You cannot pretend you do not know how you were changed."

"I don't," she insisted. "Even if I did, I wouldn't tell you. I'm not going to let you do this to anyone else."

"If you wish Michael to remain in power, and Nicola to have her peace of mind," Richard said, "you will." He pulled his hood back over his face. "I shall give you a day to think on it. Tomorrow night you will tell me how it is done, or you and your lover may pledge your loyalty to Korvel when I appoint him as the new American seigneur."

Chris fought Nottingham all the way from the car to the airport in Rome, until he told her he would knock her out and carry her over his shoulder if she didn't cooperate.

"What about Robin?" she said as the dark lord gripped her arm and propelled her toward the gate. "One of the contessa's thugs might come back to the palazzo to check on things. If they find him, they'll kill him."

His mouth curled. "That will save me the trouble."

Nottingham made her sit next to him on the empty plane. He had the same power to control humans as Robin did, apparently, for the crew did everything he said but completely ignored everything she said to them.

The flight from Venice to London took two hours, and for most of it Chris sat in silence and tried not to worry about Robin. She knew Nottingham had taken her from him as payback for Marian, and that when the drug wore off Robin would follow. But would Robin come after them then because he loved her, or because he wanted to even the score?

"You are being very quiet," Nottingham said.

"I'm worried about Robin." She eyed him. "You shouldn't have left him there like that."

"I used but a small amount of the drug," Nottingham told her. "He will have awoken by the time our plane left Rome."

"Why didn't you kill him while you had the chance?" He didn't reply, and she studied his face. "You don't want him dead, do you?"

"My cousin is not afraid of dying," he said. "He courts death. He has been that way since he came back from the Holy Wars."

"When he found out Marian was gone." That explained quite a few things about Robin. "I'm confused. If you don't want to kill him, why go through all this?"

"I want to see him suffer as I suffered," Nottingham said, his voice grating over the words. "Ten years I spent in a dungeon because of him. If the contessa had kept her promises to me, I would have left him to rot in that cage forever."

"After making him watch you rape me," she added helpfully.

He looked away. "He should never have brought you with him."

"I see. It's his fault. Again." She tilted her head. "It's funny how he's always the bad guy, and you're nothing but the victim. But I can see why you wouldn't want to kill him. If he were gone, you wouldn't have anyone left to blame for your problems."

Nottingham gave her a filthy look. "You know nothing. Your mortal life has lasted a handful of years. I have endured centuries alone on this earth."

"Why not kill yourself then?" she asked. "What have you done with your life besides hating Robin, blaming Robin, or planning to get even with Robin? How could you waste all that time on something stupid like revenge over a woman who never wanted either of you?"

Nottingham slapped her hard enough to bring tears to her eyes. "You will not speak of her."

Chris swallowed a sob and turned away from him,

moving as far as she could to the other side of the seat. She sat there for a long time before she felt a brush of leather against her hand, and jerked around.

"I am sorry I hit you," he said, his voice gruff as he pressed a handkerchief into her hands. "You have a talent for provoking me. Stop weeping."

She sniffed and dried her face. "Don't you be nice to me."

"I dislike seeing females in tears."

She took the handkerchief he offered her and wiped her eyes. "At least mine aren't toxic." She took in a deep breath and let it out slowly. "What did the other Kyn say when you told them about the contessa and this vial of her sister's tears?"

"I did not call London."

"You're kidding." She crumpled the handkerchief in her fist. "Oh, my God. You're not."

"There was no need to call ahead," he told her. "Salva is traveling by land. We will reach England before she does."

Chris tried to work that out. "Why wouldn't she fly there?"

"Kyn despise air travel," he said. "She flew to Rome only because she could not spare the time to make the crossing by boat and train."

"You don't seem to have a problem with it," she pointed out. "Neither does Robin."

"My cousin is a reckless fool," Nottingham said. "I fear nothing."

"You seemed pretty terrified of that vial." She saw his hand contract into a fist against the armrest. "How poisonous are her sister's tears?"

"We Kyn each have our own talent," he said slowly. "As you have seen, the contessa can persuade a human to do anything she wishes. Your lover charms them. I command the cold and ice. But there are those with far more powerful talents. One of our kind can shatter flesh and bone with a touch. Our high lord can inflict great suffering on humans and Kyn with his voice."

If he had told her that two days ago, Chris would never have believed him. Now it made her stomach turn.

"Beatrice's talent was the most lethal of all," he continued. "Her blood was poison, and anything it touched—Kyn, mortals, animals, plants, anything alive—died instantly. For a short time her family concealed her talent by hiding her from the rest of us, but she escaped them to run away with a mortal who had fallen in love with her. She did not think about the blood of her virginity. He died in her arms."

Nottingham told her how, weeping with grief, Beatrice had thrown herself into a river.

"She did not drown—we cannot be killed that way—but 'tis said that she wept tears of blood into the water. Every mortal who drank it sickened overnight," he said. "Their bodies swelled with black boils, and they went out of their heads with fever. Anyone who touched them also became ill. So the sickness spread through villages and towns and cities. It traveled on ships from one country to another."

What he was describing sounded like the Black Death. Chris couldn't quite believe that a vampirelike immortal could have caused a plague with her tears, but she'd seen so many strange things already that she was prepared to take it on faith. "How many people died?"

"Too many to be counted." His mouth tightened. "In Florence, where I lived, every mortal who served me died of it. So did half the city. It took us months to collect the bodies of the dead and burn them."

"What happened to Beatrice?"

"She went back to her family and begged them to hide her. They put her into a convent, but she could not overcome her grief. Her tears first killed all of the sisters, and then their livestock and gardens. She poisoned the wells with them, and when the rains came the wells overflowed and plague began to sweep throughout the land again."

"What if it was coincidence?" she asked. "Historians say that rats spread the plague through the fleas they carried."

"I cannot say. Among the Kyn, it was said that Beatrice was the angel of death, sent by God to bring about Armageddon." The corner of Nottingham's mouth curled. "True or not, that belief spread like the sickness, and eventually reached our high lord. He assembled his seigneurs and came to Venice for her."

Chris almost felt sorry for the contessa. "Didn't they test her tears to see if it was true, or give her a chance to defend herself?"

"No," he admitted. "Beatrice's family did beg for her life to be spared, and promised to keep her at the convent, but of course she could have left at any time and they would not have been able to stop her. Richard and the others had seen too much death on their journey to Venice." He gazed at the clouds outside the window. "I think they were right to kill her. After she died, the plague ceased spreading, and mortals began to recover instead of die."

Chris thought about what he had said. "You knew all this, and you didn't call London and warn them?"

"I am an outcast, thanks to your lover." He looked through the window at the clouds. "No one would believe me anyway."

"Oh, give me a phone," she snapped. "I'll *make* them believe it." When he didn't reply, she stared at his profile. "You can't be serious. What do you think you're going to do when we get there? Swoop in and save the day and show them what a hero you are?"

"Be quiet."

Chris saw frost crawl up the inside of the window. "Do you think they're going to pin a medal on you? Assuming the contessa doesn't kick your ass again."

He turned then and grabbed her shoulders, his grip as cold as the air around them. "You know nothing about me, mortal."

"I'm the mortal who got you out of the contessa's cage." She clenched her teeth to keep them from chattering. "I really don't need another dose of hypothermia, if you don't mind."

Nottingham removed his hands and took off his jacket, wrapping it around her shoulders. "Forgive me." He walked up to the front of the cabin and disappeared.

Chris got up and went immediately to the in-flight phone station, grabbing the receiver. It wouldn't budge, and only then did she realize it was frozen solid.

Chapter 18

Michael woke up alone. Alexandra had been rising early every afternoon to attend to the patients in the refugee hospital, and rarely returned before dawn. He knew how important her work was to her, and how it kept her from worrying about John, but if she kept going at this pace she would soon exhaust herself. As he dressed, he decided he would go down there after the latest session of *le conseil supérieur* to talk with her.

"Good evening, master." Phillipe came in with a bottle of bloodwine and prepared a glass for Michael. "Lady Liling called and gave me a message for Alexandra." He glanced around the room. "I will take it down to the hospital."

Michael felt a brief glimmer of hope. "Did Liling have news of John?"

"No, she said she had forgotten to tell Alex something when they spoke this morning. She asked me to write it down." He took a scrap of paper from his pocket. "She said there were forty-seven girls in her group, and only three boys."

"What group?"

"I cannot say, master. Alex asked me to contact Suzerain

Jaus very early this morning. She took the call in Geoffrey's library and remained in there well past dawn."

Michael checked the time. "I think I will call Chicago myself."

Valentin Jaus did not seem surprised to hear from Michael, and dispensed with the usual formalities. "I trust all is going well with *le conseil supérieur*, Seigneur."

"Things could be better, *mon ami*, but they could also be much worse. I understand that our women spoke for a time last night. Did Liling mention to you Alexandra's reason for contacting her?"

"Yes, she spoke to me immediately after the call," Jaus said, his voice turning cool. "Your *sygkenis* stirred up some unpleasant memories for my lady, but Liling assured me that the matter was of great importance to Lady Alexandra."

"Please give Liling my apologies," Michael said. "Alex has been treating a great many Kyn refugees for their injuries, and at such times she often becomes thoughtless of the feelings of others."

"It was not that she was unkind." Jaus sighed. "You know how Alex can be when she wishes to know something. She asked Liling a great many questions about the Brethren breeding centers where she was kept for the first part of her life. Liling was but a child, Michael, and they imprisoned and tortured her and her brother for years. I do not think she will ever speak easily of those days."

"I will have a talk with Alex anyway." He rubbed his jaw. "Has there been any word of her brother?"

"No, nothing, and I can find no trace of him leaving the city. I will continue the search, but if he has been taken by the Brethren again . . ."

"I understand. Thank you, Val." Michael ended the call and looked at Phillipe. "Do you know what Alexandra was doing last night before she placed the call to Chicago?"

Phillipe looked uncomfortable. "I did not see her myself,

but one of the seneschals mentioned that he saw her walking through the south wing, near the high lord's chambers."

Michael nodded. If there was anyone who could infuriate Alexandra, it was their liege lord. "I think it would be sensible for you to visit the hospital while I am meeting with Richard and the others. Perhaps you could help Alexandra with the patients. She may need someone to talk to."

Phillipe nodded, understanding what Cyprien meant. "I think I can assist her until *le conseil supérieur* is over."

Michael went from there to the reception room, which he entered behind Zhang and Tristan. The two seigneurs were discussing the possible locations of Brethren cells in their territories. Both fell silent as they noticed him, but nodded before they took their places.

Michael saw some other, suspiciously furtive glances from the seigneurs already seated, and kept his own expression bland. He knew that opposing war against the Brethren had set him apart from the other Kyn rulers, and he had expected some backlash because of it.

Richard entered last, and took his place at the head of the table. He was about to speak when a servant came and whispered something to him. He nodded and the servant went to the door, admitting Alexandra to the room.

Michael, Richard, and the rest of the seigneurs rose from their seats.

Alexandra had changed out of her lab coat and wore one of the dresses Michael had bought for her. The deep green material complimented the dark honey color of her skin, and the classic design of the garment gave her a decidedly regal air. She had also arranged her curls to fall from a knot atop her crown, and the emeralds he had given her glowed in her ears and around her throat.

"My lady," the high lord said, sounding none too pleased to see her. "I understand this address you wish to make is a matter of urgency, but I think you and I should step out of the room."

"I'm sure you do." Alexandra smiled tightly at Michael before moving to the other end of the table to face Richard. "Please be seated, gentlemen. I want you all to hear this."

Michael looked from his *sygkenis*'s set features to Richard's fisted gloves, and put his hand on his dagger as he sat down with the other men.

"During the nineteen eighties, a group of Brethren in America began conducting experiments on mortal children," she said without preamble. "They isolated orphans, runaways, and abductees in underground breeding centers, where they kept them for years."

"Experiments?" Solange, who had fled the Nazis to prevent them from using the Kyn for their insane schemes of racial purity, looked furious.

"Brethren scientists and doctors subjected the children to treatments designed to alter their bodies, their minds, and possibly their genetic makeup," Alex replied. "I believe the experiments were performed solely for the purpose of turning these children into superhumans capable of hunting, fighting, and killing the Darkyn. I can also provide evidence that at least six of the children who survived these experiments grew up to display extraordinary abilities."

Richard planted his hands on the table and began to rise. "This is all quite riveting, Doctor, but your theories about Brethren breeding practices can wait until—"

"I'm one of the kids who survived the Brethren's genetic experiments." As the men around the table uttered startled sounds, she gave the high lord a smile that glittered with malice. "So sit down, Richard, or I'll show you just how effective they were."

The high lord sank back into his seat.

"You were raised by the Brethren?" Sevarus growled, his one eye ablaze with hatred.

"Seigneur, I was probably bred by them," she said. "As were Samantha Brown, Nicola Jefferson, and Liling Harper, the other orphans who've made the change to Kyn in the last couple of years."

"So the order seeks to infiltrate us with their killers." Cordoba spit out the words.

"We didn't know we were killers," Alex told him. "My guess is that we were created as reserve troops. Most of us were adopted out or raised by foster parents as normal human children. We were never told about the experiments, our abilities, or their purpose. Evidently I was the first to be changed." Her mouth softened as she glanced at Michael.

Solange appeared bewildered. "Were you sent to us by the Brethren?"

"No. I didn't know they existed until after I became Kyn. My change was simply an accident—or a twist of fate. My enhancement, which allowed me to operate faster than any other human surgeon in the world, brought Michael and me together. Samantha Brown's ability to see a murder by touching the blood of the victim, Nick's Darkyn radar, and Liling's ability to remove or inflict pain brought them to the lords who changed them as well."

"Why enhance only women?" Tristan asked.

"The Kyn wouldn't expect female hunters," Michael said slowly. "The members of the order are all male."

"As are the Kyn," Zhang said, looking thoughtful. "Most of us prefer to feed on females. They could get close without arousing our suspicions."

"That was likely the plan," Alex said, "but I should tell you that there were also a few boys involved in the experiments. One who survived is Liling Harper's twin brother, Kyan. However, he has not gone through the change."

"We must put a stop to this," Sevarus said. "Cyprien, America is your territory. You must direct your suzerain to attend to these centers and free these children before they are permanently altered."

"The centers are closed," Alex told him. "The original project was abandoned ten years ago, after one of the major breeding centers was destroyed by a storm created by two of their test subjects. Fifteen of the best geneticists in the U.S. were killed during that disaster, along with most of the Brethren actively involved in the project. The kids are already altered and grown."

Gilanden grunted. "At least they cannot make any more of you."

"I wouldn't be too sure of that. Genetic engineering, as my friend Charlie Haggerty told me in Chicago, has come a long way since the eighties." Alex looked directly at Richard. "I believe the order has found a new and more efficient way to repeat the enhancement process, which is why they've attacked and burned so many *jardins*. Kyn who are badly burned don't die but go into a state like hibernation. Recovering their bodies gives the Brethren plenty of time to harvest their DNA without having to worry about controlling and containing them."

Tristan looked stricken. "Harvest? You mean they are cutting out this . . . DNA . . . from us?"

"Why would they need it?" Zhang put in.

"Without getting into the technical aspects, yes, Seigneur Tristan, they probably are." Alex looked at Zhang. "Using Kyn DNA and modern genetic engineering techniques, they can start altering more humans faster and more efficiently. If they are creating part-Kyn human hybrids again, it has to be so they can build a new army. An army that in fifteen or twenty years can wipe out the Kyn."

"An army of Kyndred," Richard said.

None of the men said anything. Most of them were in shock.

"Now that you know why we survived the change, I think

we need to forget about the war and exposing the Brethren to the world," Alex continued. "There is a secret army of superhuman hunters out there, gentlemen, and they don't even know what they are. The Brethren may be creating more, too. We have to track down these Kyndred, make friends with them, protect them, whatever it takes. They are the real threat to the Darkyn, and they're also the only hope we've got for a future."

"Hope?" Sevarus sputtered with indignation. "They were made by the Brethren to kill us."

"That's true," Alex said. "But their experiments did something else: They made us immune to the lethal effects of the Kyn pathogen. That's why I and the other women survived the change, gentlemen. We really are your Kyndred."

Nottingham rushed Chris from the plane, and barely spared a moment to bespell the customs agent trying to stop them for a search before heading for a row of telephones.

"You call," Chris said. "I'll find a taxi."

"You are staying with me." Nottingham kept his grip on her arm.

"I told him, Jimmy, you wanker, leave off gawping at the hairy bint or I was going home," a bleached-blond woman was saying angrily into the phone Nottingham stopped at. She glanced at him. "Bugger off, mate, I've got another twenty minutes." She scowled into the receiver. "Like I was saying, Sue—"

Nottingham leaned in, spilling his scent all over the girl. "End the call and go home."

Chris watched the girl's face empty as she hung up the phone, smiled dreamily at Nottingham, and wandered toward the exit. "I'll never get used to how you do that."

"Excellent." A long arm spun Nottingham around and seized the front of his shirt. "He'll not be doing it again."

"Robin." Chris almost laughed with relief. "How did you get here so fast?"

Robin didn't seem to hear her. "Did you think you could take her from me?" He dragged Nottingham around the corner and into a men's lavatory.

Chris heard porcelain shatter and saw two human men run out of the bathroom, still frantically tucking in their shirts and zipping up their flies.

She rushed past them and went inside, ducking to avoid part of a sink as it flew at her head.

"She does not belong to you." Nottingham shoved Robin into the side of a stall, denting the aluminum cubicle. "She is a mortal. You cannot have her."

"She is mine," Robin bellowed.

Chris locked the door behind her. "Robin, Guy, you can do this later. We have to get to this council meeting before the contessa does."

Neither man paid any attention to her as they drew daggers and began circling around each other.

"You ruined my life," Nottingham snarled. "Do not do the same to hers."

"I should have cut your throat that night," Robin told him, fangs bared. "She would have been free to have the life she wanted."

"Which you gave her by getting her with your brat?" Nottingham slashed at him.

Chris heard hammering on the door, and strode over to step between them. "This brawl is over."

"It will be shortly," Robin said in a low, lethal voice. "Step out of the way, love."

That did it. "Don't you call me *love*. Not when you're trying to kill him over Marian."

She finally got his attention. "Marian is dead."

"Her death doesn't seem to matter to either of you, does

it?" She gestured at him and Nottingham. "You're still fighting over her. And for what?"

"He killed Marian," Nottingham said. "He had me imprisoned for ten years in my own keep. He stole my life from me."

"Your mother imprisoned you, Guy," Chris said. "You said she had been planning to kill you on your wedding day. She probably would have, too, if Robin hadn't taken Marian. He didn't steal your life. He saved it. And you." She turned and glared at her lover. "How long do you think Guy's mother would have let Marian live after the wedding? She had her land and her money; she didn't need her. Right?"

Both men lowered their daggers as they stared at her, their scowls uncertain.

Chris turned her head toward the voices shouting outside the lavatory. "You two can stay here and pretend that nothing has changed, but the contessa is out there somewhere, and she's not exactly sane, and apparently she has an army of vampires with her. So I'm leaving. Have a good time cutting each other to pieces."

Chris unlocked the door, pushing her way through the crowd that had gathered outside. No one tried to stop her, which was a good thing, because she was angry enough to kill someone herself.

Outside the terminal she went to the first unoccupied black cab she saw and climbed in.

"Where are we off to, love?" the driver asked her.

She didn't know where the contessa could be, or where the Darkyn were meeting for *le conseil supérieur*, and felt like bursting into tears. Then the door opened, and two sullen-looking men climbed in beside her.

"Shoemaker's Heaven," Robin told the driver.

Chapter 19

R ichard contemplated adjourning the meeting after Alexandra stalked out of the reception room. Instead he took Michael to the side as the other seigneurs argued over what the doctor had revealed.

"Did you know any of this?" Richard demanded in a low voice.

"No. Alexandra chose not to confide in me." His smile became ironic. "I assume from your reaction that she was not supposed to reveal this information to anyone but you."

"I thought we had made an agreement. Apparently I was mistaken." Richard felt as weary as if he had spent the last hour in battle. "How much of what she said could be the truth?"

"Most or all of it. Alexandra spoke to Liling Harper for several hours last night. The girl spent sixteen years as one of the Brethren's test subjects; she must know a great deal about them, their methods, and their ambitions." Cyprien gave him a narrow look. "I suggest that you not consider kidnapping Liling. Jaus has never lost a siege or spared an enemy."

"My lord," Sevarus called out, drawing Richard's attention to the fact that the other seigneurs had fallen silent and were watching him and Cyprien. "We have decided on the matter of responding to the Brethren attacks."

Richard nodded to Cyprien, and they returned to their places.

The high lord looked down the table. "Very well. Do we commit ourselves to war?" No one moved. "All who support Cyprien's suggestion to expose the order to the media." He watched Michael, but like the others he didn't put in a vote. Richard sighed. "All who find favor with Dr. Keller's proposals."

Seven hands raised into the air.

"I should save myself a great deal of trouble and simply make her the high lord," Richard observed in a sour tone. "Very well. We will consult with Lady Alexandra and decide what is to be done." He slapped his glove on the table. "*Le conseil supérieur* is adjourned."

Richard didn't feel like celebrating what he considered Alexandra's victory, but accompanied his seigneurs to Geoffrey's gardens, where their seneschals and entourages had been gathering each evening. Word passed quickly through the assembled Kyn, most of whom began fiercely debating the revelations and decisions made.

Michael came to stand beside Richard. "For centuries most of our men have had to settle for the comforts to be had of mortal females," he said as they watched the others. "At least now there is a chance for more of them to find life companions."

"If your damned leech doesn't take it upon herself to cure us first." Richard saw Alexandra working her way toward them. "Ah, here she is. Brace yourself; I expect she brings a liberal amount of salt to apply to our wounds."

Alexandra stumbled just before she reached them, and clutched the side of her head.

Michael stiffened. "She is using her talent." He went to her and helped her to a bench.

Richard, aware that Alex could read the thoughts of human and Kyn killers, joined them.

"*Chérie*," Michael said, putting his arm around her. "Who is it?"

"Kyn." She blinked several times, as if trying to clear her eyes. "Italian. Really pissed off. Somewhere close, maybe in the city. I can't tell if it's a man or a woman. The thoughts are just . . . hideous." She gave Richard an owlish look. "Who is Beatrice, and what did you do to her?"

"Beatrice." Seven hundred years disappeared, and once more Richard looked into the fires of hell. "Beatrice is dead."

"Someone who loved her isn't." Alex groaned and pressed her hands to her ears. "I don't know who it is, but they brought friends. And they're coming for you, Richard. They're coming for all of us."

Salva sent her men to surround the grounds, and went to Geoffrey's gate accompanied only by Caesar.

"You must be careful with the vial," he was telling her. "Do not let anyone take it from you, or cause it to be opened accidentally."

Her dear, sweet Caesar. He still believed she intended to use her sister's tears only as the means of acquiring the high lord's throne. Of course, Salva had never persuaded him to think anything different.

The Darkyn believed themselves to be cursed by God, but Salva knew better. Her innocent sister had been guilty only of loving a mortal, and being made Kyn by their father when he had brought home the sickness that had transformed his daughters and killed their brothers and mother.

Beatrice had never considered her gift a punishment, as she told Salva in the many letters she had written to her from the convent. The Holy Bible spoke of an angel of death that would come to put an end to the world's suffering. Beatrice had been charged with a sacred duty, one she had never been permitted to carry out.

Salva's last promise to her sister had been to assure her that God's purpose would be fulfilled, and the world wiped clean again. After seven hundred years, at last she would.

As Caesar neared the guardhouse at Geoffrey's gate, Salva leaned against him. "Stop for a moment, *caro*. I wish to kiss you one last time."

Caesar smiled as he parked the car and took her into his arms. "It will not be the last time, *bella*," he said against her lips. "You and I shall rule—" He stopped short and looked down at the copper dagger she had thrust into his heart.

"In heaven or hell, I shall find you." She watched the life fade from his eyes, and pressed her hand around the dagger, soaking it in his blood. She smeared it on her face, throat, and the tops of her breasts before she left him in the car and pretended to stagger as she made her way toward the gate.

"Brethren." She gasped as she fell into the wide-eyed guard's arms. "They are just behind me, and they mean to burn the place. You must take me to the high lord at once."

Robin ordered the driver to stop as the cab's headlights revealed the still body of the gatehouse guard on the ground. "She is here. We must hurry."

Nottingham reached the guard, shaking his head as he soon as he saw the gunshot wound to his chest. "Dead."

Chris came back, breathless from running to check the car that had been abandoned on the drive. "She killed her guard, too."

Robin breathed in. "I have her scent. Chris, go to the house and warn the Kyn. Guy and I will track her." He caught her as she turned to run and kissed her hard. "If you see the contessa, do not try to confront her or go near her. She will kill you to silence you."

"Got it." Chris kissed him back and ran.

Lights blazed from all of the mansion's windows, but as Chris reached the front entry she saw two more dead guards, and her heart skipped a beat. *What if she already opened the vial, and they're all dead?*

The house seemed empty, but Chris heard the sound of voices and laughter, and followed it until she saw the open doors leading into the gardens. She saw no sign of Salva, Robin, or Nottingham and hurried out.

"Please, can you help me?" she asked, touching the arm of a beautiful black woman talking with several of the men. "I need to find the high lord."

"You're mortal." The woman frowned. "How do you know Lord Tremayne? How did you get into the house?"

"There's no time to explain," Chris said, feeling desperate as the men surrounded her. "I must speak with Richard right now." She glanced at the Kyn reaching for her. "I'm a friend of Robin's. I mean, Locksley. He sent me to warn you." She felt strong hands take hold of her. "Robin has a scar over his heart, like someone gouged out a piece of his chest." What was the word he'd called her when he told her he loved her? "I'm his *kyara*."

"Wait," the woman said to the men. She held out a hand to Chris. "Come, my dear. I shall take you to the high lord."

The high lord turned out to be a man dressed in a hooded black cloak, standing next to a pretty petite woman and another man with white-streaked black hair.

"It seems Locksley has sent this female to speak with you, my lord," the black woman said. "She is most anxious to deliver a warning."

"She is too late."

Chris turned to see the contessa standing beside the fountain. "She's gone crazy," she murmured to the black woman. "She's going to kill everyone."

"We meet again, Salva," Richard said.

The contessa's gaze shifted to Richard. "Good evening, my lord. How well you look."

Chris glanced at Richard, who had pulled back his hood. His face seemed to be part man, part cat. "She has a vial of her sister's tears," she said quickly. "She's going to use them to kill you."

The Kyn all around them fell silent and began to back away.

"Salvatora," the high lord said with icy politeness. "What are you doing here?"

The contessa gave him a little curtsy. "Keeping my promise to my sister. I swore I would avenge her death on you and your six butchers."

Richard nodded. "Very well. You should know that I and I alone gave the command to kill your sister. I shall give you my life in return. But do not endanger the innocent." He held out a wide, blunt-fingered gloved hand. "Give me the vial."

"What was Beatrice, if not innocent?" Salva asked, taking out the vial and holding it over the fountain. "She starved herself so that she would not kill. Did you know that, my lord? We had to drain mortals and pour the blood down her throat to keep her from starving to death."

"Oh, God." Chris remembered what Guy had told her on the flight from Rome, and realized then what the contessa meant to do. "She's not going to kill you. She's going to dump the tears in the water."

"Contessa," Braxtyn said, her voice tight. "You know that our fountains are fed by springs. If you put that poison into the water, you will release the Black Death upon the mortal world."

"I think it fitting that the Kyn should know the agony my sweet Beatrice suffered." Salva smiled. "There will be no more mortals upon whom you can feed. You will all starve, as she did, or become as the beasts you are inside."

An arrow sliced past Chris's face, burying itself in the

contessa's arm. Salva staggered, but then straightened and fumbled, wrenching the top from the vial.

Chris didn't think; she ran, her hands outstretched to grab the vial. A second arrow came from behind, striking Salva in the back.

The contessa grabbed Chris, locking her arm around her neck and cutting off her air. "Stay away from me."

"Salva." Robin dropped down from the trees and grabbed her free hand, holding the vial upright. "Let it go."

Salva struggled wildly, trying to tip the vial into the fountain. As it spilled, Robin dove under her hand, forcing her hand to his mouth. With one swallow, he drank the contents of the vial.

The contessa screamed, pulling away with a savage jerk. Chris saw a tiny drop of blood fly from the lip of the vial to land on Salva's cheek. The red stain raced across her skin, covering her head and turning her eyes solid scarlet.

The contessa dropped like a stone, taking Chris with her.

Chris shoved the dead woman away and crawled over to the fountain. Robin lay half in, half out of the water, his skin already turning dark pink.

"Robin."

He opened his eyes, the copper irises fading to scarlet-tinged amethyst. "Did any of the tears touch you?"

Unable to speak, Chris shook her head.

He smiled. "I'll be waiting . . . for you . . . love. Take . . . your . . . time."

Robin sagged into the water and didn't move again.

Alex helped the redheaded mortal woman pull Robin's inert body out of the fountain.

"Someone tell me what this stuff he swallowed is," she yelled as she rolled Locksley onto his back.

"Poisoned tears," the redhead told her. "It kills Kyn on contact."

"Not this time." Alex wrenched open Robin's shirt. "He's still breathing. Richard."

The high lord came to kneel beside Robin. "He swallowed the tears." He sounded as if he were dazed.

"What difference does it make?"

He focused on Alex's face. "I cannot say. No one has ever done this."

"All right. Let me think." Alex pressed her hands against her face before letting them fall. "The pathogen is present in our saliva, blood, and body fluids. It must be trying to counteract the poison." She surveyed Robin's skin and the pink flush that was growing deeper and darker by the moment. "What's the antidote for this stuff?"

"There is none," Richard said softly.

"Bullshit. If the pathogen can fight it, so can we." She stood. "We need to get him downstairs so I can draw a blood sample and have a look at it."

No one came near them.

Richard lifted Robin's body into his arms. "I shall take him."

Alex didn't have to clear the way as she, Richard, Michael, and the redhead descended to the hospital; no one followed them but Nottingham.

"Why is everyone acting like pussies?" Alex asked Michael on the way down.

"They are being cautious," he said. "They remember what happened the last time Beatrice's tears were unleashed."

"They're being pussies," the redhead said, giving Alex a fierce look. "I'm Chris Renshaw, and I'll do whatever it takes to save him."

"Alex Keller." She gave her a tight smile. "Ditto."

Alex had Richard place Robin on an exam table and quickly drew a sample of his blood, from which she made a slide smear.

She put the glass slide under the scope and adjusted the power before she took a look. "This chick Beatrice wept this stuff he drank?"

"Her tears were blood," Richard said, "and her blood was lethal."

"Maybe not." She saw the pathogen colliding with a larger, mutated form of itself. The two cells shaped and reshaped themselves, each trying to absorb the other. After a few seconds the mutant pathogen engulfed the other and moved on. "Shit. Maybe so."

Alex moved away from the scope and back to Robin. His skin had turned a dark rose, and his body temperature was dropping rapidly. "Was there anything that stopped it?"

"Killing Beatrice," Richard said.

"We don't have time for jokes," Alex snapped. "This stuff is like leukemia on crack. If I don't do something, right now, he's going to be dead in a few minutes."

"What about a transfusion?" Chris asked suddenly. "Take out all the poisoned blood and replace it."

Alex shook her head. "I can't get every drop out of him, and the pathogen replicates too fast."

"How do you treat this leukemia in humans?" Richard asked.

"Acute cases? Radiation and a bone-marrow transplant." Her brow furrowed for a moment before her expression hardened. "It's not feasible."

"Why not?" Chris demanded.

"Assuming I could find a bone-marrow-donor match, I don't have the equipment to do it here," Alex told her. "Robin won't live long enough to make it to a cancer treatment center. There's just no time."

"Then we stop time." Chris turned to Nottingham. "Use your talent on him."

"Honey, I'm sorry, but his talent will only . . ." Alex's head snapped up. "Guy, get the hell over here."

*   *   *

Nottingham looked at Robin, and then regarded Chris. "Do you love him?"

"What?"

"Excuse me." Alex glared at both of them. "My patient is dying. Can you chitchat about your love life later?"

He bent and put his mouth next to Chris's ear, his cheek brushing hers. "Do you love him?"

"Yes."

He moved back and looked into her wet eyes. "If I do this, will you come away with me? Will you give yourself to me?"

"Guy," Alex snapped.

Here was the perfect revenge on Robin, and all Chris had to do was agree to it. "If that's what it takes to save him, then yes, I will."

"I thought as much." Nottingham lifted his chin and pressed his cool lips to her forehead before he moved over to the table. Arrogance filled his eyes as he regarded the other Kyn. "Give us the room."

Alex put a hand on Chris's shoulder as they went outside. "He'll be okay."

"How would you know?" Chris countered. "Did you perform that many bone-marrow transplants back in the Dark Ages?"

"I'm not actually from the Dark Ages myself," Alex told her. "I was a reconstructive surgeon in Chicago before the Kyn sank their fangs in me. You?"

Chris leaned back against a wall and closed her eyes for a moment. "Federal agent out of Chicago."

"Robin. With a fed." The doctor coughed. "Hokay."

"I'm not here in an official capacity." Chris wasn't sure what she was now, except terrified. All at once she remembered Hutch and Robin's people. "The contessa has hostages back in the States." She filled in Alex on the details, and then added, "She may have already given orders for them to be killed, but if there's any way you can help them, I'd be grateful."

"We'll take care of it." She turned to the man with the white-streaked black hair. "Michael, can you send Jayr and Lucan with the cavalry?"

He nodded and took out his mobile phone.

Whatever Nottingham was doing seemed to take forever. As Chris waited, she saw frost slowly creep over the edge of the door to the exam room, and her breath turned white as the air temperature steadily dropped.

"Here, mademoiselle." Michael removed his jacket and draped it over her shoulders. "You should perhaps go upstairs. You will be warmer there."

Before she could answer, Guy came out of the exam room.

"I have encased his body in ice," he told Alex. "It will last only two or three hours, but it should slow the poison long enough for you to transport him." He started to walk away, but Alex grabbed him.

"You're the only relative he has," she said. "You can't leave."

He gave her a twisted smile. "He will not want me at his side."

"Probably not," Alex replied, "but if this works, he will need a little of your bone marrow." At his blank look, she added, "I'll have to perform a transplant from a blood relative in order to replace the bone marrow that the radiation kills."

"It cannot come from me, my lady," Nottingham said, his expression turning grim. "Locksley and I are not related by blood. Our connection is through marriage only."

"Doesn't Robin have any other relatives?" Chris asked.

"Yeah." Alex suddenly looked miserable. "There's one more."

Nottingham bowed to her and Chris, and continued out of the hospital.

"Guy. Wait." Chris caught up with him just outside the lift. "If you never intended to take me with you, why did you make me promise that I would go?"

"Sometimes knowing what you can have is almost as satisfying as taking it." He gestured toward the lift. "You may still come with me, if you like."

"I think I'll stick around here." Chris smiled. "Thank you."

"If you really wish to show me your gratitude," he said, "be sure to tell my cousin when he wakes that I saved his life." For the first time since they'd met, he produced a genuine smile. "That should bedevil him for the rest of eternity."

He bowed once more to Chris, and then stepped into the lift.

Chapter 20

R obin smelled her scent first, sweet-sharp, like the taste of candied ginger. He had been drifting in and out of shadows for so long that he clung to it, following the trace until it grew stronger, until he knew he was only a hand away from touching her—and then she bridged the gap between them.

Chris's fingers moved over his brow, brushing his hair back. As Robin woke, he turned his face into her palm.

"You're awake."

"I'm dreaming." His voice sounded as weak as he felt. "Or perhaps God has made a tremendous error and let me into heaven. Say nothing to Saint Peter."

"Oh, yeah." Her low, tired laugh caressed his cheek. "You're awake."

Robin opened his eyes to the only face he had ever wished to see again. Chris looked pale and thin, and shadows bruised her eyes. She had slept in the dress she wore, judging by the telltale wrinkles, and had scraped back her tangled hair into a lopsided ponytail.

She was the most beautiful thing he had ever seen, Robin decided.

He finally looked away from her to study the place he

occupied, which he recognized as one of the guest rooms in Geoffrey's stronghold. "In addition to God, I imagine I have Alexandra Keller to thank for this."

"Alex and a few of the others." Some of Chris's smile became forced. "I'd better go get her. She wanted to know if . . . when you woke up."

"Send someone else," he told her. "You, madam, are never leaving my sight again."

"You might want her to step outside the curtain when I perform the ten or fifteen consecutive colonoscopies I have planned for you," Alex said as she came in carrying a chart.

Robin tried to look lofty. "I have no idea what a colonoscopy is, but I am sure the Kyn do not require them." He grinned. "Hello, Alex. You're looking well."

"Hi, yourself, handsome." Alex exchanged a look with Chris, who bent over and kissed the bridge of his nose.

"I should go take a shower before I started attracting flies," his lady told him. "I'll be back."

She left before he could reply.

Robin tried to sit up and go after her, and discovered he was entangled in a mesh of tubes and wires. Bewildered, he lifted his arms. "What the devil is all this?"

"This is your IV," Alex said, pointing to a transparent tube. "The wires are monitoring your heart rate, your blood pressure, and your blood oxygen. I also have you on a catheter, but you can't see that one. Keep moving around, though, and you'll feel it."

"A what?" Robin lifted the edge of the sheet covering him, looked at what she had done to him below the hips, and then dropped it. "Good God. Alex, none of this is necessary, I assure you. I am Darkyn; I do not need—"

"You're not Kyn anymore, Robin. You're human."

He regarded her for ten long seconds in silence before he chuckled. "Oh, very good. Was this Cyprien's idea? I've always suspected a sense of humor lurked under all that dour French sensibility."

"You ingested Beatrice's tears, which contained a mutated form of the Kyn pathogen that feeds not only on human white cells but on other strains of the Kyn pathogen," Alex said, her expression gravely serious. "Your natal pathogen tried to fight it off, but it was coming out of a dormant phase, and it was starving."

Robin eyed the tubes. "Alex, you're going to make me puke."

"That's all the gross part. We put you on ice, transported you to a private cancer center, thawed you, and then irradiated your blood to kill all the pathogens in it." She set aside his chart. "When I transplanted the donor bone marrow, I thought everything would go back to normal. Kyn-normal, anyway. But the bone marrow did not have a trace of the pathogen in it, and your body had other ideas. It began to revert to human almost immediately."

"Alexandra," he said, very kindly, "I cannot be mortal. I have been Kyn for nearly eight hundred years. Once changed, we cannot be changed back."

"I know it's a shock," she said. "I couldn't believe it, either. But after the transplant your digestive and immune systems regenerated and began functioning normally. I've tested your blood about three hundred times, but found no trace of either Kyn pathogen. I can't tell you how or even why it happened, only that it did. You *are* human now, Robin."

"It's an excellent jest, but truly, my lady, you carry it too far." He yanked the intravenous tube out of his arm and went to work on detaching the wires. "I would be greatly obliged if you would remove the blasted tube from . . . my . . ." He stopped and stared at the small hole in his forearm, which was not closing, and the trickle of blood spilling from it, which was not stopping.

Alex applied a swatch of gauze to the small wound and held it there. "You're still on a liquid diet for now, but tomorrow we can start you on some solids."

He stared at the blood staining the gauze. "You aren't jesting."

"No."

He met her troubled gaze. "Will I make the change again?"

"If you were going to, I think you would have by now," she said. "I wouldn't try to force a change, either. I can't say for sure, but I don't think you'd survive it a second time."

"So I am human." He smiled, and then he chuckled, and then he laughed. "A mortal again."

"Robin, I can't tell you how sorry—"

He reached up, grabbed the front of her lab coat, and pulled her down for a long, heartfelt kiss. "I love you, Alexandra Keller."

"That's nice," she said, very carefully. "But I'm taken, and so are you."

"I do want solid food," he said. "As soon as possible. I have a list. Strawberries and champagne to start. Filet mignon, rare, and a baked potato. I want it smothered in butter and sour cream. A side of broiled asparagus will go nicely. Then, for dessert, I want cake."

Her brows rose. "Any particular kind?"

"Just bring cake. I'll tell you when to stop." He laughed again. "Oh, Alex. You didn't just save my life. You gave me cake. And now I can eat it, too." He looked around. "Where is Chris? Does she know?"

Alex bit her lip. "Yeah, she knows."

"We can be together now. I can become an American citizen and vote and file tax returns and complain about the whole lot." He sat up. "My God, Alex—*I can have jury duty*."

"I can see you're all broken up about this," she said, her expression wry, "but try to pull yourself together."

Robin took her hand in his and noticed how much cooler hers was. He looked up at her. "How am I ever to thank you and the others for saving my life? For giving my life back to me? Bring everyone in. I shall try."

Alex patted his cheek. "I'll get the whole gang in here shortly. One other thing: You should know that Nottingham kept you alive by putting you on ice."

Robin blinked. "*Guy* saved me?"

"Without him and the bone-marrow transplant, you'd be dead."

Robin's belly tightened. "He gave bone marrow as well?"

"He couldn't. You guys are cousins only by marriage." She sat down on the edge of the bed. "I needed bone marrow from a blood relation. It's usually a match."

"I have no living . . ." He paused and looked at her, stricken. "No, Alex."

"She was in the middle of a siege, Robin. She wouldn't come until I told her why it had to be her." Alex let out a long breath. "Look, I didn't give her any details. I thought you might want to tell her yourself."

For a moment Robin wished she'd let him die. "What was it you said after the tournament at the Realm? That it would come back to bite me in the ass?" He sat back. "Is she still here?"

"Yeah. She's been waiting with the rest of us."

Robin held out his arm. "Take these tubes out of me, please."

During the crisis with Robin, Braxtyn and the Kyn nurses Alex had trained had taken over caring for the refugees down in the hospital. Geoffrey's lady chased Alex out of the ward after she came down to check on her surgical patients.

"Between treating Locksley and coming here to work on the burn patients, you have barely had an hour to yourself,"

Braxtyn said. "Go to your lord and rest. I know Cyprien pines for you."

"Michael is busy mapping out search grids for Nick and Gabriel." Alex saw the look in the other woman's eye and pretended to yawn. "All right, you talked me into it."

She was becoming a very good liar, Alex decided as she returned to the upstairs room she had appropriated to serve as a lab. Ever since she'd seen the results of Robin's first blood tests after the transplant, she'd been wide-awake.

If Robin could be changed back to human, then it had to be possible to do the same for every other Darkyn.

In the lab, Alex reviewed the scans of Robin's abdomen. His restored digestive system appeared to be functioning perfectly, and the latest CBC still showed no trace of the Kyn pathogen.

Alex glanced at the refrigeration unit where she'd stored the other blood samples she'd taken. She still had two vials of blood she'd drawn from Robin's veins after thawing him but before giving him the radiation treatment, and as they were as lethal as Beatrice's tears, they needed to be destroyed.

She put on three pairs of latex gloves before she removed the tubes from the tray and held one up to the light. The blood looked almost black now.

"It's off to Geoffrey's furnace with you two." She placed them in a holder, and then frowned. Sometime during the short walk from the refrigerator to the lab table, both vials had turned bright red.

"That's weird." She checked the seals on the tubes, which were intact. "You responding to my body heat, or lack thereof?"

She knew the blood was dangerous, but she'd worked with hazardous materials countless times. It wouldn't hurt to draw out a drop of the blood and have a look at it under the scope. No one would ever know she had.

She took all the necessary precautions to protect herself and contain the samples before she made a slide. Geoff had obtained one of the best scopes on the market for her, so she had no trouble seeing the pathogenic cells and what they were doing.

"You look just like Jema Shaw's blood," she murmured, and then went still. Jema, the only female turned by the Kyn who had not been an orphan, had had a very unusual blood profile before and after her change to Kyn. Alex had studied it for months, but as it matched no one else's she had mentally filed it away as an anomaly.

Jema wasn't the odd one out. She was the key.

Alex backed away from the scope and stood staring at it for several minutes. The facts that she had gathered about the Kyn pathogen suddenly began to fall into place, like puzzle pieces that had decided on their own to quit waiting for her to fit them together and make the big picture. And then it was all so simple. The radiation treatment hadn't turned Robin human. Neither had Jayr's bone marrow.

Beatrice's tears, and the fact that he had drank them, had been the reason for his remarkable transformation. His pathogen had attacked, then combined with hers to cause one final mutation.

It was all right there, under the scope.

A laugh escaped Alex, and she slapped a hand over her mouth to smother the sound. "It can't be that simple. No way."

Alex didn't sleep that night. She stayed in the lab and performed a few more tests on the blood samples, but she wrote nothing down about the results.

Every test she ran was positive.

She could run a hundred simulations, but she knew the results would always be the same. The problem was when she made the serum. She had only enough blood to make one treatment, and she wouldn't be able to test it on anyone.

She held up the syringe and stared at it. Here was the answer. All she had to do was roll up her sleeve, shove the needle into her arm, and she could have her life back.

She'd be human again.

"Alexandra." Phillipe burst into the room. "You must come right away."

He startled her so much that she nearly crushed the syringe in her hand. "What is it?" She shoved the syringe into her coat pocket. "Robin?"

The seneschal shook his head. "It is the mortal woman, Chris. She has collapsed."

Alex relaxed a little. "Exhaustion, probably. She hasn't slept for days." She picked up her medical case. "Come on, I'll have a look."

"It is not that," Phillipe said as he accompanied her out into the hall. "She vomited before she fainted. And her scent is changing."

"What?" Alex stopped in her tracks. "Her scent is what?"

"It is changing, Alex," he said, his voice low and tight. "As she is. Changing to Kyn."

Chris felt cool hands on her face and opened her eyes to see the Kyn doctor standing over her. "What happened?"

"Well, for one thing, you puked all over the place. Then you fainted." Alexandra Keller smiled absently as she picked up Chris's wrist and pressed two fingers against it. "Your blood pressure is making me very unhappy, too."

"My mouth is sore." Chris felt the roof of her mouth with her tongue. "What other things?"

For a moment the doctor didn't answer her, and then she sat down on the side of the bed. "You've been through a lot the past couple of days. So has Robin. Maybe too much."

Chris tried to think. She felt as if she were coming down with a bad case of the flu. "Am I sick? Is that it?" She thought of how weak her lover had been. "Robin. Oh, God. Did I infect him with something?"

"It's kind of the other way around." Alex put her hand in her pocket and fiddled with something. "You love him, don't you?"

Chris nodded. "Don't ask me why."

"It never really comes with a full explanation, does it?" Alex sounded tired. "Do you want to be with him, even though he's just a garden-variety human now?"

"I don't think I could handle having a vampire lover," Chris confessed. "At least this way we're the same now. We can be together, and have a normal life."

Alex nodded slowly. "And if you could ever be Kyn, would you want that instead? You'd have the chance to live forever. You could still be with Robin, if you were careful."

"Me, a vampire?" Chris chuckled and shook her head. "No, thanks." She met the doctor's strange gaze. "Why are you asking me all these weird questions?"

"Call it idle curiosity." She stood and took something out of her pocket. "You must be feeling sleepy. Close your eyes and take a nap, sweetie."

The scent of lavender filled her head, making her eyelids droop. As she was drifting off, she felt the sting of a needle in her arm. "What's . . . that . . . ?"

Alex sighed. "Call it a wedding gift."

Robin agreed to rest, stay in bed, and do everything else Alexandra ordered. As soon as she left the room he rolled out of the bed.

For a moment he wondered if he should have listened to her—as he stood there the room upended itself around him—but then he felt steadier, and slowly dressed in the garments he found in the room's closet.

Robin found the gardens with his nose, which, despite all he had been through, still seemed to work. He walked through the pretty flowers to a bower of sweet pea, and sat on the stone bench beneath it.

"Lord Locksley."

She came out of the shadows, bringing with her the scent of tansy blooming in moonlight. She still wore her leathers, but the treatments Alex had given her back at the Realm had changed her body from that of a boyish girl to that of a mature woman.

There came a time to pay for everything, Robin thought. His had just arrived.

"Suzeraina." He didn't move over to make room for her. He could see she did not wish to sit beside him. "You are enjoying your visit to England?"

"Not especially."

"Neither am I."

She studied him for a moment. "You are well enough to be roaming about by yourself?"

"Probably not, but if I had stayed in that bed, Alexandra would have inserted another thousand tubes in me." The words felt like ashes on his tongue, and he abruptly abandoned all the pretense. "I am sorry, Jayr. I never wished you to know."

"You felt it would be better if I assumed that Nottingham was my sire?" She nodded to herself. "Of course. He is a villain. You were a friend. Why would I wish to name you my mother's rapist?" She came to stand over him. "I have been waiting for you to awake. I gave you the marrow from my bones to save your life. Now you will tell me why you raped my mother."

"I loved her." He didn't flinch as she slapped him. "Her mind was addled, and I thought it would bring her back to me." The second slap made his ears ring. "She did not fight me, Jayr." He caught her wrist before she struck him a third time. "I think that is enough."

She yanked free of his touch, breathed in, and went down on her haunches before him. "You're bleeding."

He touched his split lip. "Aye. You have a strong swing. Another slap and I might have lost some teeth."

"You're bleeding and you're not healing." She straightened. "I shall summon Alex."

"There is nothing she can do, other than mop it up." He used his sleeve on his mouth. "Humans bleed."

She turned around to stare at him. "What did you say?"

"Alexandra's poison remedy worked very well. It healed all of me, even that part that was cursed by God." He rubbed his throbbing cheek. "I forgot that pain does not go away in an instant for a mortal. I wonder if I should continue cliff diving and BASE jumping."

"You cannot be human." But she could smell that he was; the shock on her face testified to that. "She has helped others change. I shall have her change you back."

"She cannot, Jayr. Even if she could, I no longer wish to be Kyn." Robin rose and walked as close as he dared to her. How pale and unworldly she was, his girl. "I have good reason to remain human now."

"This federal agent."

He nodded. "When you no longer feel like killing me, I would like you to meet Chris."

"Is she to be my stepmother, then?" Her expression changed. "How will you introduce me? As the bastard daughter you never bothered to claim?"

"When I came back to find you, I had already become Kyn. I had long been branded an outlaw by the king. I could not keep a human infant with me in the forest." He might as well tell her the rest. "Jayr, I wanted to raise you, and love you, and see you grow into a woman. It was all I ever wanted for you. To give you a home and a good life. But I could not. Claiming you would have destroyed any happiness you might have known."

"Why did you save me at Bannockburn?" she demanded.

"I could never call you daughter, but that is what you were. What you are. I could not watch you die." He held out his hand. "Come and sit with me. Let me tell you every-thing."

She came, and she sat with him. She listened as he began with the days of his childhood, when he and Marian were fos-tered together. How much they loved each other as children, and how terrible it had been for him when Marian's father had taken her away to the convent. How it had changed her, and later, how it had made her refuse marriage to Guy.

In his mind's eye Robin saw once more her young, shining face, and heard the eagerness of devotion in her voice. "When her father ignored her wishes and forced the betrothal, she tried to run away. He had her beaten and locked in her room. And that was only the beginning."

He spoke of the abuse Marian suffered as she resisted the betrothal, the strangeness that had come over her as a result of it, and when she had finally lost her mind.

"Her maidservant came to me and said that Marian's fa-ther had taken her to Nottingham so that he might lie with her and consummate the marriage before they took their vows," Robin continued. "The maid said his servants had tied her to the bed and that she screamed and raved. I couldn't bear the thought of her being raped over and over, not in her wretched condition, so I went into Nottingham's manor on the night before the wedding, and I took her."

"If you knew how she felt about men and marriage, if you meant to save her from rape, then why did you force your-self on her?" Jayr asked. "Why didn't you simply take her to the convent in Scotland?"

"I was seventeen. The same age you were when you jumped into that pit and saved Byrne's life," he reminded her. "I loved Marian, and I wanted her to be my wife. But I had accepted that she wanted to give her life to God. It was on the journey to Scotland that I discovered how mad she really was. She waited until we camped and I went to sleep, and then she tried to kill herself. I woke to find her pulling my blade out of my belt. I barely stopped her before she stabbed herself in the chest with it."

Jayr closed her eyes. "My God."

"When I took the blade from her, she attacked me, and we struggled. I kept telling her I loved her, and kissed her, and then she stopped fighting." Robin bowed his head. "I know it is no excuse to say that I was young and selfish, but I was. I loved Marian, and I thought that if I showed her that being with a man didn't have to be rape . . . that if I gave her pleasure . . ." He rubbed his stinging eyes. "I swear to you, she didn't resist. But by the end she had retreated entirely into herself. It was too late to do anything but curse myself for being no better than Nottingham or her father."

"You were young." She looked at him. "You might have married her."

"I intended to do just that. I left her in the convent and went to petition the king." Robin shook his head. "Upon my arrival at his court he had me arrested, and when I refused to tell him where Marian was, he had me tortured and condemned to death. My father arranged my escape and sent me to the Templars before he and the rest of my family were imprisoned and, later, executed. I never knew what happened to them or Marian until I returned."

"Did you know, Aedan was jealous of you," Jayr said unexpectedly. "Before the tournament last year he thought I might be sleeping with you. We fought over it. He is your best friend. Why did you never tell him that you were my father?"

"Before the tournament I thought that he was a better father to you than I could ever be." Robin smiled at the sound she made. "Yes, well, men can be fools when it comes to the women they love, whether they are life companion or daughter. You should have seen my countenance when I discovered the two of you sleeping together in your bed the night after the dance. I almost stabbed him in the heart."

Jayr laughed once, and then fell silent. Robin did not press her to talk; he knew that by telling her about her mother, he had placed as much weight on her slim shoulders as he carried on his own.

Finally she asked, "Do you love this Chris as much as my mother?"

He nodded.

"I am glad to hear it. Since you fell ill she has not left your side. She sleeps in the chair by your bed and ignores Alex's scolding. She followed you out here tonight." Jayr smiled and turned her head. "She is waiting over there, by the fountain. You should go to her."

Robin stood. "Jayr, I know you have no wish to call me father or friend, but I hope in time you will come to forgive me for abandoning you."

"You put me in the care of the sisters in London when I was an infant," Jayr said. "You saved my life at Bannockburn. I suspect now that you even came to America so you could watch over me." She smiled as he averted his gaze. "As you say, it will take time."

She sketched a bow and walked off.

Chris trailed her fingers through the water in the fountain's basin. She felt one hundred percent better since waking up after her faint. Alex had been there, keeping an eye on her, and had insisted on giving her a full exam. While the doctor checked her, she had told Chris that the siege of Robin's stronghold had been successful, and that Hutch and the other hostages had been freed.

"Your partner won't remember any of it," the doctor admitted, "but other than the three-day gap in his memory, he'll be fine."

The high lord, Richard, had also spoken to Chris when he stopped in to check on Robin. He hadn't been as warm and friendly as Alex, but he'd made it clear that he would give Chris anything she wanted as a reward for helping to stop Salva and save the Kyn.

"There's a priceless manuscript lying in pieces on the floor of a dungeon in Venice," she told him. "I'd like to have it returned to the authorities in America. They have experts who can repair it and put it in a museum, where it belongs."

"Consider it done." The high lord put a gloved hand on her shoulder. "Your valor will never be forgotten among the Kyn, my lady."

"You are getting your sleeve wet," a mellow voice said.

"I won't melt." Chris looked up and smiled as she drew her hand back from the water. "Alex is going to yell at you for getting out of bed."

"I put pillows under the sheets." Robin sat down beside her. "I have been told that you have acquired the habit of napping in chairs of late."

She shrugged. "I can't sleep by myself anymore. I have no idea why I fainted. I never faint. Well, not counting that time I tried to slit your throat." She turned, reaching for him and burying her face in his chest.

"What is this?" He set her back and looked down at her. "I stopped the contessa. I saved the world. I did not die. My mouth hurts from Jayr hitting me, but it will mend. We should be calling for wine and food and jugglers."

Chris swiped at her tear-streaked face. "Alex told me that you're stuck with this. You can't change back. What are you going to do now?"

Robin thought for a moment. "Aside from spending a month at the beach sunning myself, eating cake until I retch, and making love to you until I pull every muscle in my body—twice—I would very much like to live out my second mortal life with you."

She shook her head. "I'm still a federal agent, and you're still an international art thief. God, you're Robin Hood."

"I understand that the authorities often consult with reformed criminals in order to crack difficult cases," he said. "Perhaps you could put in a good word for me with the bureau."

"Robin, I'm serious. This changes everything for you. What if you hate being human? What if you're tempted to make the change back to Kyn? Alex told me—"

"I am a man," he said softly, "and you are a woman. We are both human now, and we never have to be alone again. I would not trade that for a thousand immortal lives." He gave her a measuring look. "Unless *you* wish to make the change, and keep me in your harem as your chief mortal love slave. I could speak to Alex—"

Chris kissed him, still laughing, until he set her at arm's length.

"Before anything is decided, there is one more thing I must know."

"What?"

"What is your bloody damn name?"

She let out a long, slow breath. "Christabel, after the poem. My mother loved Samuel Coleridge."

"That's it? That's all?"

She eyed him. "Have you ever read it?" When he shook his head, her smile turned grim. "Good. If you ever tell anyone, I have to kill you. And I can now."

Robin brought her to her feet and took her into his arms, swaying with her as they had the night they met. "Perhaps you could simply torture me. . . ."

Chapter 21

He made the journey to Scotland on foot, walking across England as mortals once had during his human life on their pilgrimages to holy places. The land of Wallace, like much of the British Isles, had become unrecognizable to his eyes. If not for the incomprehensible dialects and suspicious glances, he would have thought himself back in America.

Time and neglect had reduced the old Catholic abbey to a jumble of collapsed walls and fallen timbers. He hated to think of her in this place, cold and damp in a nun's cell, swelling with child, lost in her madness.

He went to the abbey's pitiful graveyard, looking forgotten in a fallow field, and walked through the short rows of old graves. The names chiseled into the stones were almost gone; he could barely make them out. SISTER MARY MICHAEL, 1272. SISTER BERNADETTE FRANCIS, 1244.

The ground before the oldest row of headstones had been disturbed, and he wondered if some inquisitive scientist had been at the graves, wrenching the sisters from their sleep so as to peer at their bones and decide whether they had starved or had been diseased. Modern mortals respected nothing, not even the dead.

"Are ye one of the protestors?" a sharp old voice asked behind him. "I'll not have you chaining yourself to anything."

He turned and looked upon the elderly mortal. "No." He glanced down at the lilies he had gathered from a nearby field. "One of my family is buried here. Her name was Sister Marian Christopher."

"There's one Marian." The old man pointed. "Over there, in the back."

He went to the grave, which occupied a corner beneath the shade of an elm tree, and looked at the stone. Her name, Marian, was all that he could make out. The year of her death had been wiped clean by the wind.

He knelt and placed the bouquet of lilies before the stone. "I loved you from the first moment I saw you," he murmured. "I would have tried to make you happy."

The groundskeeper hobbled over to stand beside him. "The developers began moving the sisters to a Catholic cemetery down the road. They would have taken the stones, too, but the protestors raised bloody blue hell, and now it's in the courts." He nodded toward the grave. "There's nothing there, lad."

"I know." His hell on earth had taken the dream of heaven from him, but he prayed she was there. "She is at peace now."

"No, I mean when they opened that grave and took out the coffin to move it with the others in this row," the old man said. "I remember the fuss they made about hers."

Nottingham stood. "What are you talking about?"

"There wasn't a body, lad." He gestured toward the empty grave. "That box was filled with stones."

"It is good to be home," Phillipe said as he carried Alex's suitcase into her bedchamber at La Fontaine.

"It sure is." Alex sat down on the bed she shared with

Michael and bounced on it a few times. She had to tell him why she'd needed to leave Michael in England and come back to New Orleans a week early, but she still hadn't decided how to explain things. "You don't have to unpack, Phil. I'll take care of it."

He nodded but made no move to leave. "I called Suzerain Jaus downstairs. He tells me that there has been no word of your brother. He claims he never called you or told you that John had been found."

"I know." Alex faced him, and prayed that everything she thought she knew about her lover's seneschal was right. "I lied to you about that. John's still missing."

Disapproval flashed in Phillipe's light eyes. "Why would you lie about such a thing? We are all worried about your brother."

"I had to get away from Richard and Michael, and I needed you with me." Alex took a deep breath. "I'm human."

He frowned. "Yes, you are the most human Kyn who has ever existed, but—"

"No, I'm really human, Phil. I found the answer while we were in England. I found a way to synthesize more of Beatrice's Tears, and to create a serum. I injected myself with it and made the change back to human overnight. That's why I harassed you about leaving before Michael woke up." She approached him and saw him take a step back. "Don't worry; it's not contagious."

He hesitated. "You're ill again. I thought as much as soon as I saw your face; you're gone very pale. Let me call the master and summon him home. The high lord will understand."

"No, Phil, I'm not crazy. I'm just not Kyn anymore."

"My lady." He groped for the right words. "I would not make you angry, but I cannot believe you."

"I could show you my X-rays and my blood tests, but all

you really have to do is smell me or bite me." She pulled up her sleeve and extended her arm. "Be my guest."

Phillipe bent down and inhaled. *"Mon Dieu."* He straightened slowly, as if something had broken inside him. "What have you done, Alexandra?"

"I've found the cure." Tears made it hard for her to see. "I always told you guys that I would. All I had to do was keep looking. I kept looking and looking, and then there it was. I'm a great fucking doctor, don't you think?"

Phillipe pulled her into his arms and let her sob. His big hand stroked over her curls as he murmured in French to her.

Finally Alex regained a grip on her emotions and pulled away. "I have to know some things now. Does Michael's talent give him access to all my memories? Can he look into my mind and find out what I know and what I've done?"

"Non. He must know what it is that you remember before he can make you forget it. But Alex, he will know that you are once more human the very first time he smells or touches you." He hesitated. "He will never force you to become Kyn again."

"Yeah, I'm thinking the same thing." She unbuttoned the collar of her blouse. "That's why you're going to do it."

Phillipe recoiled. "You cannot ask that of me."

"I siphoned out two pints of blood from my veins this morning, so you shouldn't go into thrall when you drain me. You know what else you have to do." When he made no move toward her, she nodded. "Fine, then tell me who else you or Michael turned from human to Kyn. For this to work, I have to be infected with the same pathogen you two carry."

The seneschal sat down and rested his brow against his palms. "I cannot think. Wait." He lifted his head. "What of Lucan's *sygkenis*? Samantha was changed with your blood."

Alex shook her head. "My blood had already mutated before Lucan changed Sam; it would probably be lethal to me now. Also, she's a woman. For this to work I have to get a male Kyn with the same pathogen and re-create exactly what happened the first time, with Michael. Which means I have to be turned by someone who made the change with you and him during the good old days of the Crusades." She saw his expression change. "There is no one else, is there?"

"The master and me," Phillipe admitted. "Everyone else is dead." He squinted at her. "These last five years, all you have ever wished was to be made human again. Why do you want me to force another change on you?"

"Because force won't be involved. I'm choosing to do it this time." Alex knelt in front of him. "Phillipe, I love him, and I know he loves me. But he never wants to be human again. I didn't understand that until Robin was changed back. You saw how horrified Michael was when I told him, and how many times he asked me if I could make Robin Kyn again. That was when I realized it, and accepted it. Michael is Darkyn, and he'll never be happy being anything else."

The seneschal nodded.

"Don't get me wrong; I want to stay human," she continued. "I miss chocolate, and my patients, and getting a nice tan every summer. But there are a million human doctors in the world. The Kyn have only me."

He eyed her. "You could still help us if you are human."

"That's the plan. And can you really see me living out a normal human life, growing old and dying while Michael watches?" She took one of his big hands in hers. "I love him more than I ever loved being human. If you don't change me back, he'll be alone forever."

He met her gaze, his own haunted by fear and doubt. "Alexandra, you know what must be done. What I must do to you. You and I . . ."

"Kind of blows your mind, doesn't it?" She produced a single, dry laugh. "You're my best friend, Phil." She didn't want to press the issue, but she had to make things clear between them. "If you're worried about a repeat of what I went through with Korvel, I don't think it'll happen between us. You have no reason to bond with a woman."

"When did you know?"

"The night I left him the first time, and you came after me, and we danced at that bar." She sighed. "I was pretty clueless until then. I'm just sorry you've had to put up with listening to Michael and me going at it like rabbits."

"I do not always mind." He smiled a little, and then covered his face with his hands and groaned. "What are we doing? This is madness. If you are wrong, I could kill you instead of changing you."

"I wasn't wrong about the cure," she told him, standing up and looking down at him. "I'm not wrong about this."

Phillipe stood and put his hands on her shoulders. The scent of warm honeysuckle surrounded her and made her feel drowsy. "If you found the cure, then you must know what causes the curse as well."

"I was hoping to skip that part." She gave him a sleepy smile. "I had to know what made the change in order to reverse it. Stop making me tell you things that I don't want to."

"Richard would do anything to know how to create more of us." He put his arms around her. "We cannot allow him to discover what you have done, Alex."

"We're not going to tell anyone. If things get bad, I can always have Michael remove the memory. But I don't plan to tell him, either." She yawned and leaned against him. "Can you keep this a secret?"

He pushed her hair out of the way and bent down, his last word whispering against her skin: "Yes."

"Alexandra."

Alexandra Keller jerked awake and saw that she had fallen asleep at her lab table. She looked up and saw Phillipe's face and groaned.

"Nothing happened. It was only a shared dream." He

glanced at the empty syringe sitting next to the scope. "You have injected yourself?"

She remembered the smile on Chris's face when she had spoken of Robin. "No. There isn't any left. I gave it to Chris."

A shadow crossed Phillipe's face. "But why?"

"Because she and Robin love each other, and they were meant to be together. Like me and Michael." She gathered the slides, the syringe, and everything she had used for her tests, and placed tht entire lot inside a cardboard box.

Phillipe followed her through the halls and down to the basement level. He stood beside her as she used a poker to open the door to Geoffrey's furnace. Only then did he speak. "Could you synthesize more of the serum, Alexandra?"

"Maybe." She tossed the box into the flames. "Let's not find out, okay?"

Cyprien's seneschal bowed to her, and then left her alone to watch everything burn until the evidence of her discovery was destroyed.

Alex turned away from the furnace. She put her hand in her pocket, curling her fingers in the emptiness there, and then headed for the stairs.

Epilogue

Luisa Lopez knew when the security guard outside her door dozed off. He took a nap every night just after midnight, when the lights were low and the nursing stations were quiet. At twelve thirty she eased out of the hospital bed, her legs shaking with the unfamiliar strain of bearing her weight, and reached for her wheelchair.

She didn't worry about falling. Her gift of foresight had shown her doing this a hundred times.

The year she had spent at the Lighthouse had also taught Luisa which corridors the nurses used most frequently, and when hospital security made their rounds. It had taken her only a few weeks to work out the best time and route to make it from her room to the gardens. Even so, Luisa could hardly believe it when she wheeled herself through the automatic doors at the back of the building.

The voice inside her, the one that spoke to her whenever her eyes turned white and the visions came, murmured in the back of her mind. *One day he'll come to you. He'll wear a black coat and gloves. He'll watch you from behind the camellias. He won't be afraid.*

Luisa ignored the voice and smiled when she saw that her friend Liling Harper had kept her promise to install lighting around the flower beds and pathways through the gardens she had planted. Liling would be coming tomorrow to read to her again.

She never doubted that the shadow prince would come to her someday. In the dreamlands they had become friends, true friends who could look into each other's souls. It was just hard to wait for him to accept his gifts enough to return to the mortal world. Luisa couldn't tell from her visions how old she would be when she finally met the shadow prince, but she had the sneaking suspicion it wouldn't be for a very long time.

He'll still be young and handsome, and I'll be a scarred, white-haired old lady.

She found a spot under a trellis of moonflowers and sat there in the fragrant shadows to watch them bloom. After a few minutes her head nodded as she slipped into a light doze.

He came out of the night and into her dreams as he always did. *You're here.*

Where else would I be? Luisa held out her scarred hand. When he made no move to touch her, she added, *I was right about the baby deer, wasn't I?*

You were. His big hand made a shadow over hers.

Still so cautious. She bridged the gap between them and stiffly curled her fingers through his. Unlike the others, his flesh was still warm.

I remember when you came to read to me. Even then, I could hear the pain in your voice. She felt her eyes change as he knelt down before her wheelchair. Glowing light covered the hazel of her irises, until her eyes appeared solid white. *Someday we'll find each other, and then we can have a real visit.*

You'd want me to come to you? Doubt still lingered on his face. *You're not afraid of what I can do?*

She shook her head. *You only have to be careful not to*

touch me. She saw his frown and rushed to add, *Only be-cause Liling and Valentin will know. They'll smell you on me*. Her other hand was still bandaged, but she pressed it against his cheek. *I'd be glad for you to visit me any time*.

The shadow prince put his head in her lap, and they sat there like that for a while. She could barely feel his thick, coarse hair against her damaged fingers, but she stroked his head anyway.

The bright eye of the moon watched them as the crickets stopped chirping and the night held its breath.

He lifted his head, tried to speak, and then kissed her mouth. *Close your eyes,* he whispered.

Luisa did. His hands felt so warm, so gentle, and then the light she had seen in her dreams shimmered inside her, spreading and enfolding her in stardust and moonbeams. She had expected pain but there was only life, streaming into her until she thought she would burst.

She felt petals brush her skin as the moonflower began blooming and growing all around them, budding new leaves and flowers and twining around her chair. Luisa felt laugh-ter bubble up inside her, and for the first time since they had hurt her, she set it free, along with every dark thought, every sorrow, every worry.

The shadow price kissed her again. *Be happy, Luisa.*

Luisa opened her eyes, waking from the dream. She still sat in her wheelchair, alone under the moon. She reached for the wheel and then saw her hand. The scars were gone; her twisted fingers were straight.

It was only a dream.

She removed the bandages from her other hand, unrolling them carefully. The stitches from her last surgery fell into her lap, no longer holding her healed, flawless skin together. She felt the brush of them against the back of her hand, where all the nerves had been burned away.

Luisa gripped the arms of the wheelchair and slowly

stood. Her legs held her easily, effortlessly. The constant, nagging pain in her arms and back no longer throbbed. The knee she hadn't been able to bend did so, smoothly and without a twinge, as she took her first step away from the chair.

Carefully Luisa walked over to the reflecting pool. There in the mirror of water and moonlight she saw her face, smooth and dark, and her eyes, bright with tears.

"All their hard work, gone like that." She imagined going back to her room and letting them see her like this. But no, that would be a cruel thing.

Luisa glanced up at the moon. She knew what she had foreseen, the days and months and years and centuries and millennia of change ahead. But this one decision, at least, would not change anything for anyone but her. The path she chose tonight would either end with a peaceful sleep, or take her on a journey into eternity.

Be happy, Luisa.

"I will, John." Luisa looked back at the Lighthouse one last time before she walked away into the night.

Read on for an excerpt from
the first Novel of the Kyndred by Lynn Viehl,

SHADOWLIGHT

Coming in November 2009 from Onyx.

Jessa watched Matthias as he first sorted through and piled the warm strawberries into a crystal bowl, then began adding other things to them. After seeing him work out with his odd stone weights, she expected him to be clumsy. Instead he worked with a chef's confident skill.

"Do you always cook for your prisoners?" She winced as she saw him pour balsamic vinegar over the fruit. "Or is this your way of getting rid of them?"

"You do not eat as you should. That is why you are so quick to anger." He added sugar and cream to the bowl before bringing it to the table. "An empty belly feeds only the temper." He reached for the pepper grinder and twisted it over the fruit.

Jessa muffled a laugh. "Just out of curiosity, have you ever heard of using a cookbook?"

"No." He swirled the bowl a few times before he reached in and plucked out one of the cream-coated strawberries, holding it by its green top as he offered it to her.

"Thanks, but I'm not crazy about—"

"Taste." He rubbed the tip of the strawberry across her bottom lip, smearing some of the cream mixture along its curve when she didn't cooperate. "Are you afraid you will like it?"

She bit the strawberry in half, intending to spit the vile thing back into his face. Then the warm berry's tart juice, made silky and sweet by the sugar and smooth cream, filled her mouth. The vinegar and pepper only amplified the tastes, giving it a very subtle edge and a touch of heat.

"Oh." Jessa didn't realize she had closed her eyes until she opened them. "That's . . . different."

Matthias's faint smile didn't reach the translucent jade of his eyes as he brought the rest of the strawberry to his mouth, his teeth neatly separating the berry from its top. His jaw muscles flexed as he slowly chewed and swallowed, but his eyes never left hers.

"Okay, so I was wrong." Feeling a little self-conscious, she licked the cream from her lips. "It's good." She tried to take another.

One big hand pushed the bowl out of her reach. "Only good?"

He had to rub it in, of course. "It's great."

"Do you want another?" He took a second berry from the bowl, but when she tried to take it from him, he moved his hand away. "Open your mouth."

Jessa didn't like the way he was looking at her—as if *she* were something he wanted to bite. "I can feed myself, you know."

"Not very well." He held the strawberry under her nose. "Open."

With a sigh, she imitated a guppy.

Matthias didn't let her have it this time. Instead he teased her, placing the berry between her lips and then taking it away before she could take a bite, rubbing it here and there until she grabbed his wrist.

Shadowlight.

Jessa stood at the edge of a winter forest. Thick, icy air

wrapped around her, and snow was everywhere—under her feet, weighing down the tree branches, and slowly swirling above her head, spinning and floating as it fell from the sky. The setting sun polished the flakes until they glinted like tiny bits of glass. Ahead of her a clearing funneled its thick white drifts between two enormous, frost-covered stones.

Sunlight.

Her heart beat once, twice, and then she was back in the kitchen, still trying to arm-wrestle a strawberry away from Matthias.

Disoriented as she was by the unexpected touch-sight, she couldn't seem to let go of his wrist. "Is this really necessary?"

"When you want something, it is." He didn't seem to notice anything was wrong with her. With a deliberate show of strength, he brought the strawberry to his mouth, biting it so that streams of juice and cream ran down his palm and onto her fingers.

Jessa released him, but now he took hold of her wrist and guided her hand to his mouth. The shock of returning to herself so quickly faded as he put his tongue to her skin and slowly licked one finger and then another clean. Her breath rasped in her throat as he took the tip of her smallest finger into his mouth and sucked lightly.

"What are you doing?" she heard herself ask, her voice so low and distant it seemed to come from that faraway winter forest.

"Tasting." His free hand spanned the front of her throat before he slid it under her hair and curled it over the back of her neck. "Do you want more?"

He didn't mean the strawberries, which was fine, because she couldn't think about them. As she tried to form the word "no," his tongue found the center of her palm and stroked it before his teeth tested the sensitive mound of flesh beneath her thumb.

That love bite set something loose inside her, a hot, heavy feline ache that climbed over her breasts and inched down to curl in her lap, sinking sharp little claws into the tense muscles of her thighs and drawing a thick, silky tail of sensation between them.

His hand on her nape tugged, urging her forward.

In her mind she saw herself crossing the now unbearable distance between them, pressing his mouth to the tight peak throbbing over her heart. She saw her own hands tearing open her blouse so he could get at it, so he could suck her properly, while she took his gilded hair in small, tight fists. . . .

His face blurred before her eyes as he came closer, and the warmth of his breath touched her lips. "Jezebel . . ."

The name and all its secrets hit her like a slap, and she jerked, finding her feet and almost knocking over the chair as she backed away. A stumble later she had put three feet and a fortress of sanity between them.

If Jessa understood anything, it was the shadowlight. It never lied to her, never showed her anything but cold, hard truth. Matthias had walked through that winter forest; he had left something terrible in it. He might have killed and buried someone there; that might explain what she had seen and felt the first time she'd touched him.

"I think I've had enough." A quick turn allowed her to hide most of the shaking and the stupid look she felt sure was plastered on her face. "Good night."

Jessa didn't hear him following her, but halfway to her room she felt him looming behind her. Confronting him interested her about as much as encouraging him, so she kept moving. She had arrived at her room and was reaching for the pretty porcelain knob when his hand shot past her cheek and grabbed the knob, holding the door in place.

A wall of hard chest muscle brushed her shoulders before he bent his head to murmur in her ear, "You're afraid of me. Why?"

Afraid of him? If he didn't get away from her soon, she was going to climb up him and the wall and dig her way out of here with her bare hands.

Or worse, she wouldn't.

"I'm tired of you." She managed to turn the knob and get the door to open an inch before he pulled it closed again.

Jessa ducked under his arm to get out from under him, but he turned her and had her up against the wall before she could blink. This close she could see that the mark on his throat was a primitive tattoo of some kind—a circle formed from the body of a winged purple snake that was biting its own tail. She forced herself to look up into his face, but light from behind him effectively masked his features.

"You are still empty." His fingers spread over her abdomen, the edges of his fingernails scratching the fabric of her skirt as he pressed them in and out in a kneading motion. "Do you feel it here?" His hand shifted lower, stopping just short of sliding between her legs. "Or here?"

"I said I would stay here until you found the proof I need to take down Genaro and get my life back," Jessa said, keeping her tone reasonable. "You never said that I'd have to sleep with you for it."

"Sleep with me?" He sounded amused. "I don't want that."

"Good." Now she was lying, too. "Just so we're clear."

"Just so we're clear . . ." he repeated, almost thoughtfully. "It means so that we understand each other, yes?"

"That's it." She glanced down meaningfully, but he didn't step back. "Now you say good night and go away."

"But you do not yet understand me. When I have you"—he clamped his hands around her waist—"you will not sleep."

Jessa grabbed his shoulders as he lifted her off her feet and pinned her to the wall. His head bent, but instead of forcing a kiss on her lips he put his mouth to her ear.

"When I have you," he said again, "there will be nothing between us. No clothes. No fear. No words."

The smell of him, like summer rain, clouded her thoughts. "It doesn't work like that."

"You will give yourself to me. I will take you." He pushed up the hem of her skirt with his knee and nudged her thighs apart. "I will put myself inside you here, where you need me. Where I need to be." He bit her earlobe, the side of her jaw, and the spot where her neck curved into her shoulder before he lifted his head. "That is how it will work. Am I clear to you?"

Jessa closed her arms around his neck and held on as the unyielding iron of his thigh rubbed against her. Sweat traced the line of her back as her struggle turned inside out and she fought the wild heat rising inside her. If she didn't put a stop to this now she would do anything he wanted, right here against the wall.

"That's enough." She pushed at his shoulders. "Put me down. I can't do this. Not with you."

"You will," he said, his words as cool and hard as his mouth as he pressed it against her lips.